A Russian Sister

Also by Caroline Adderson

NOVELS
Ellen in Pieces
The Sky Is Falling
Sitting Practice
A History of Forgetting

SHORT STORIES
Pleased to Meet You
Bad Imaginings

A Russian Sister

A Novel

CAROLINE ADDERSON

Patrick Crean Editions
HarperCollins*Publishers*Ltd

Published by Patrick Crean Editions, an imprint of HarperCollins Publishers Ltd

First edition

HarperCollins books may be purchased for educational, business,
or sales promotional use through our Special Markets Department.

HarperCollins Publishers Ltd
Bay Adelaide Centre, East Tower
22 Adelaide Street West, 41st Floor
Toronto, Ontario, Canada
M5H 4E3

www.harpercollins.ca

Library and Archives Canada Cataloguing in Publication
Title: A Russian sister : a novel / Caroline Adderson.
Names: Adderson, Caroline, 1963- author.
Identifiers: Canadiana (print) 2020022218X | Canadiana (ebook) 2020022221X
ISBN 9781443426817 (softcover) | ISBN 9781443426831 (ebook)
Classification: LCC PS8551.D3267 R87 2020 | DDC C813/.54—dc23

Printed and bound in the United States of America

LSC/H 9 8 7 6 5 4 3 2 1

For my sister, Beth,
and my writing sisters—Kathy, Marina and Shaena

To women he always seemed different from who he was, so they loved him not as himself, but the man their imagination conjured and whom they'd eagerly been seeking all their lives; and when they discovered their mistake, they loved him still. And not one of them had ever been happy with him. Time had passed, he'd met women, made love to them, parted from them, but not once had he been in love. There had been everything between them, but no love.

—Anton Chekov, "Lady with the Lapdog"

Characters in the Novel

A Russian Sister

Act One

—

1889–1890

Masha: I'm in mourning for my life. I'm unhappy.

1

LIKA WAS HUDDLED BY THE COAT STAND, THE PALE fur of her collar half concealing her face. A blonde with thick sable brows and silver eyes. Masha was sure Antosha would love her. Love was just the tonic her brother needed, the best cure for his depression.

"You found us," she called down from the landing.

"It was easy from your description," Lika called back up. "Across from the Zoological Gardens. A chest of drawers." This was Antosha's name for the house after the two side-by-side bay windows on each floor. "And I saw the doctor's plaque."

Mariushka, their old cook, had come upstairs to fetch Masha from the parlour. Her banister-clutching descent slowed Masha's now. Something was the matter with the cook's feet. She walked like she was stepping on nettles, and each stair plainted on her behalf.

When Masha reached Lika, she kissed her dimples left and right. Lika smelled of winter crispness mixed with some hopeful scent she'd put on. Sugary snow powdered her shoulders; Masha brushed it off. She was a real beauty, a Swan Princess and, even better, oblivious to it. Though initially shy, she soon threw off a stove's warmth. At school she sang in the hallways and acted out fairy tales. Her pupils adored her.

Mariushka helped her out of her coat. Under it was a jacket the colour of a cantaloupe.

"Oh, how pretty!" Masha said. "Isn't it, Mariushka?"

The old grump had a face like a fist, round and scored with lines. Also a scriptural passage ready for every occasion. "'And why take ye thought for raiment?' Wait. The jam." She limped off to the pantry, then back with the dish filled for Masha. Making the sign of the cross over the door, she announced she was going to bed.

"Come up," Masha told Lika. "Some friends are here. And my brother."

"Anton?"

Masha saw the hope now. "No. Misha."

They were standing just outside Antosha's door, convenient for him to overhear their talk. She pictured him on the other side, stretched out on his bed, smoking and staring at the ceiling like one of his own disillusioned characters, brooding over the failure of his play. *The Wood Demon*, it was called. *There is no play!* said the *Moscow Gazette. Instead, in these clumsily constructed scenes, we see a novel ineffectually squeezed into a dramatic form.* How she hated the play, not for being a rambling mess, but for what it had done to him.

"Misha's our youngest brother. Well, Antosha *is* here, but I can't promise he'll show himself."

Masha started up the stairs, Lika in tow, toward the piano's tinkling.

Lika said, "You didn't tell him I sent that letter, did you?"

"You told me not to, so I didn't. My friend Olga's here too. She's an astronomer at the Moscow Observatory. She's giving me English lessons. We're just about to begin. That's Vermicelli playing."

"Vermicelli?" Lika said.

Masha glanced back. Lika was looking at the paintings on the wall as she climbed. A few of Masha's attempts at landscapes, nothings, and one small window into summer. The latter was by Isaac Levitan, who had given her lessons.

"You'll see why we call her that. So thin! Mother's gone to bed. Maybe Antosha will join us." Masha smiled over her shoulder. "He often does."

With the mention of his name, Lika's face bloomed.

Sometimes when newcomers visited, Masha felt a residual shame. It was irrational, a holdover from their indigent years. In fact, everyone thrilled to get the chance to see where a famous writer lived and wrote. If they were surprised that the rooms were modest, that Antosha was far from rich, why should Masha care? Lika was unlikely to judge them anyway. She lived in the Arbat district, déclassé now, with a querulous great-aunt she called "Granny."

Masha stuck her head into the parlour. The two friends there were old ones from their days in Professor Guerrier's Higher Women's Courses. Vermicelli—auburn-haired and gaunt, cheeks blotched with winter chapping. A piano teacher now, she moved her noodley fingers over the keys. Olga "the amazing astronomer"—Antosha's name for her—sat at the table flipping through the primer, cigarette in her free hand, permanently slouched from her stooped love affair with the telescope. Tonight, inexplicably, she'd pinned a silk flower to her breast; it drooped as though it had the capacity to die.

Back when they were Guerrier students together, a gaggle of friends used to descend on their parlour after lectures because Masha had three dashing, artistic older brothers. Misha, too young during their heyday, was the only one at this shrunken gathering now, perched beside Vermicelli on the piano bench, facing the wrong way, squinting through his pince-nez. The only odd thing about the room was the missing pictures, the darker rectangles on the mustard-coloured wallpaper. They rebuked Masha every time she looked at them. *Why don't you paint something, then?* These shadows marked where her brother Kolia's paintings used to hang, sold after his death to pay his debts.

"Everyone?" Masha announced as they stepped into the room. "This is Lika."

The other three looked up. A paralyzing spell fell over the little brother. Vermicelli's cheeks grew redder, the skeptical slits of Olga's eyes, narrower. The same thing happened when Lika and Masha left school together. On the street outside, men froze on the spot and women burned.

Misha shook himself to life. "Tea?" he asked Lika. With her shy nod, he plunged, an unleashed retriever, toward the samovar.

Everything about the little brother irritated Masha. How he combed his hair back from his forehead. His pince-nez and big ears. He had the same downward-slanted eyes as Antosha, but a broad fleshy nose, like it had been hastily formed from India rubber. Masha's nose, in fact—a gift from Mother. Mainly it was his greed for attention that annoyed her, the consequence of having an older brother he could never hope to emulate, especially not in character. He was studying law, but aspired to be a writer too.

Olga rarely smiled and didn't now. She looked Lika up and down. When she'd fully appraised her, her eyes slid sidelong to meet Masha's, one dark brow raised. Masha felt Olga's searing judgment. To escape it, she crossed the room to where Misha was pouring Lika's tea and set the jam dish down.

"Lika teaches with me at the Dairy School."

Everyone called it by that name, after the farming family that ran it. They'd diversified from cows to girls. Misha mooed, as he did every time the place was mentioned, and checked to see if Lika laughed.

"Infant," Masha told him. To the others she said, "Lika was a Guerrier student too."

Vermicelli said, "Were you? So were we! All three of us. Not Misha obviously."

"They wouldn't have me," Misha quipped.

"What fun we had. Remember Professor K.'s lectures? We thought he was going to eat us with his eyes. Is he still there? Then we'd come to Masha's . . ."

Vermicelli prattled on, revealing in her every gushing word how dull her present life was. Masha still felt Olga's dark eyes on her. If she turned her head, who would she see—the amazing astronomer or that precocious seventeen-year-old Guerrier star who had corrected so many professors? The younger Olga was only proud, not jaded like her present self.

Olga cut Vermicelli off. "Do you speak English?" she asked Lika.

"Me? Goodness, no." Lika nodded to Misha to keep adding sugar.

"Pull up a seat if you want, then," Olga told her. "You can't be more hopeless than Masha."

Lika shrank back from this harsh stranger with absolutely no dress sense. Masha, quick to show that she wasn't offended, exaggerated her smile. Demeaning comments and outright insults were Olga's endearments. If Olga ever complimented her, *then* Masha would be hurt. But as she took her place at the table, she remembered her confusion during the *Wood Demon* catastrophe two weeks before. Olga had squirmed in her seat heaving sighs. Did it mean she liked the play? Masha herself had stopped watching. It was too painful, and she was preoccupied with the conundrum of what to tell Antosha afterward. The truth would not do, but anything less would insult him more.

Olga hadn't liked the play. To put it mildly.

She turned to Masha now and, to prove her "hopeless" verdict, commanded her to say a word in English. "Any word."

Masha opened her mouth. Nothing. Everyone laughed. "Anyway," Masha said, laughing too, "I only want to read and write it."

"I know an English word," Misha announced. Lika had remained standing; he brought her tea. Adjusted his pince-nez and cleared his throat and smiled all around. "*Lawv.*"

Olga erupted in cackles.

"What did he say?" Lika asked.

"It's what I carry here," Misha told her, thumping his chest hard. "*Lawv.*"

Love, he meant.

"I assure you," Olga told him. "There's no such word."

Masha looked curiously at Olga. Was she criticizing Misha's pronunciation, or did the English really not have a word for love? This would explain the dried-up few Masha had met. Or was Olga making a philosophical declaration? As for Masha, she'd seen enough suffering among her friends to wisely sidestep the affliction in any language.

Misha slipped out of the parlour then, just as Masha had hoped. He wouldn't be able to resist telling Antosha about Lika. Masha stood up from the table.

"I forgot something."

Olga sighed.

Masha went after Misha, stopping on the landing to listen without showing herself. He was knocking on Antosha's door.

"Brother? There's a *spectacular* girl here. Blond curls. Grey eyes circled in black. Like five-kopek pieces tarnished at the edges."

No reply that Masha could hear. Smiling, she slipped back in to face Olga, who asked, "Shall we conjugate, or couldn't you find your brain?"

"I'm ready."

Of course, Antosha would want to see what passed for *spectacular* according to the little brother. Lika would lift his mood and therefore Masha's. If not, then his depression was greater than his curiosity. He had twice as many reasons as the rest of them—Kolia's death *and* his demonic failure of a play.

Olga nudged the open primer toward Masha and took a long drag on the cigarette. "I think we may as well review 'to be.' You'll have forgotten."

True. Masha looked down at the page. It was the different alphabet she found so vexing, with its treacherous non-equivalents. B and H, for example. Completely different letters!

"Repeat: *I am, you are, he is, she is . . .*"

"*I am. You are. He is . . .*" She tried a sentence. "*He is man.*"

"A *man*," Olga corrected, snuffing her cigarette in the tray.

Masha glanced back. Antosha! He was framed in the doorway—clothes and bearing elegant, face so kind. Because of his eyes. His eyes were kind even when he wasn't. He wore the enigmatic half-smile he reserved for playing host.

"Brother," she said. "Please join us."

"I've just come to say hello." He nodded first to Vermicelli, who was blushing now as well as chapped.

"Have some tea," Masha tried.

Misha slipped in from behind Antosha. "Olga's teaching Masha English. Apparently she needs a good caning."

Antosha nodded. "When I was in school, the master used to tie the stupidest boy to a stepladder and invite the rest of us to spit on him."

Masha felt herself wince, but Vermicelli bested her by crying out, "But not you! You weren't spat on!"

With this outburst she looked like she'd fallen in the borscht. She spun around on the bench and started pounding out another song.

"The piano's rented," Masha reminded her.

The plunking stopped.

Antosha turned to Olga next. "Amazing astronomer, how are the stars?"

Olga scowled, as was her way. "Quite brilliant. If you squint, you just might see your name written up there."

Then, still in the doorway, not acknowledging the stranger in the room, Antosha detached, the way he often did in a group, sinking into his own thoughts, presumably of imaginary people who hopefully didn't too much resemble living ones they personally knew. Or perhaps he felt stifled by the currents of female admiration swirling in the room. Their banter had stiffened when he appeared. Dialogue should sound natural, should roam like a dog sniffing at non-sequiturs. It never did in plays.

Or maybe it was Lika. Masha hoped so. He was gazing straight ahead, deliberately avoiding her. No, he was staring at the shadow of Kolia's paintings on the wall, rectangular placeholders that they used to remember their poor dead brother. Still, Lika must have been flaring in his peripheral vision. In her pretty jacket, she was the brightest thing in the room, even counting the lamps and the candles on the piano, staring in open-mouthed wonderment at the author in the flesh.

"Antosha?" Masha said. "I'd like to introduce Lika, who teaches with me."

Finally he looked at her, smiling halfway again. "Hello, Lika Who Teaches with Me."

Lika dropped her gaze.

"All the blood's rushed to her face." Olga pointed. "She must have read your stories, Antosha."

"I have." Lika clutched her heart. "The one about Kashtanka is my favourite. The poor little dog. Also, 'The Kiss.'"

"I write too," Misha said.

"Tell them what you really want to do," Masha told her.

They all waited for Lika's revelation, which Masha knew to be utterly commonplace. The longer the poor girl twisted her hands, the more affected it seemed, though both brothers appeared mesmerized.

"Go on," Masha said.

At last she flung out her arms and flapped them. "I'd like to be an actress. It's my one dream. But it will never come true."

By Olga's slitted look, Masha guessed that she'd been waiting to pounce.

"An actress? Antosha, why don't you write a play for her? I'm serious. That *Wood Demon* lacked something. Perhaps you felt uninspired."

"Olechka," Masha hissed.

Antosha betrayed no sign of offence. Unruffled, ever the perfect host, he warmly told them, "I have work. Please, ladies. Enjoy yourselves."

Bowing, he backed out of the room. And though Olga had been the one to drive him off, she called out after him, "But, Antosha. We can't live without you!"

Spoken only half in jest.

No surprise that after Antosha left, the evening dribbled into tedium again, into conjugations, Chopin, and Misha telling Lika all about himself. Law school meant little to him; like Lika, he had a beautiful dream. He bragged about the editors he was friendly with, without mentioning that these contacts came through Antosha.

Skirts rustled disappointedly to the tea table and back. Eventually they rustled home.

Lika and Vermicelli rushed to catch the horse tram, which passed in front of the house every hour. Olga took her time leaving. She punched her arms into the sleeves of her balding coat, drew a glove from one pocket, then the other. Masha, sensing that Olga was choosing her departing words for maximum effect, braced herself.

"Your gloves aren't the same."

"Yes, a mismatched pair. The story of my life. I grabbed whatever was on the table."

Olga stamped her feet into her galoshes, pulled on her cat-fur hat. There was a singed patch at the front from when she'd accidentally set it on fire with her cigarette. Masha handed her the English books.

"I always ask myself why you do it," Olga said.

"I'd like to teach it. I'd earn more from an extra class."

Olga smirked. Briefly, Masha was puzzled. Then she realized Olga meant Masha's matchmaking. She countered with pity. Olga had no family. Where was she going now? To the observatory, or home? She moved rooms so often Masha had no idea where she lived. In a burst of solicitude, she pecked her friend's cheek.

"Get off me," Olga snapped, before stepping into the frigid night.

"*Good evening*," Masha called back in her knock-kneed English.

She shut the door and turned to face Antosha. Should she go in and ask what he thought of her new friend? How frustrating that Lika had been stricken by that stupid-making shyness. And that Olga was so damn prickly and rude. He'd dragged himself away from his desk, depressed as he was, only to be insulted. Better not disturb him a second time.

As Masha started up, the stairs issuing their plaints all the way, Olga's insinuating comment came with her. *I always ask myself why you do it.*

Why shouldn't she invite friends to come by? Olga knew how they'd suffered since Kolia's passing. If she could see Lika at school with her trilling voice and contagious cheer, she'd understand. No, a misanthrope like Olga never would. She seemed to think a sister caring for her brother was unnatural. Caring for her *brothers.*

At the top of the stairs Masha paused and conjured their family portrait in her mind. Two parents—another mismatched pair—flanked by their offspring. On one side, the three eldest—Aleksander, Kolia, Antosha. Then the three youngest—Masha, Ivan, Misha. But now Kolia had been painted out.

Well, there never was such a portrait. And it was not as though they had gathered as a complete family in recent years. At the moment, Father was inflicting himself on their brother Ivan, the other teacher in the family, in his country schoolhouse far from Moscow.

A completely unhappy family.

MASHA DREAMED A FACE THAT NIGHT. EYES GLANCING sidelong in a hairless china head. Then the tattered, sawdust-stuffed body joined it. Her own doll, the one toy she'd brought from Taganrog to Moscow when they'd fled. It seemed a curious choice, both to bring and to dream. A doll who wouldn't look her in the eye.

But then, in that discomforting logic of dreams, the face came to life. The cherry mouth opened to cry. The doll still wouldn't look at Masha. She was angry. Masha woke in the dark, chill room.

She'd had a sister, Evgenia, Mother's last child. Masha was six when she was born. How could she have forgotten her, her own living doll, adored? Pale flossy hair and black currant eyes, plump clapping hands.

She died, leaving Masha with only brothers. Four now.

2

JANUARY CAME. NOTHING HAD CHANGED SINCE the night Masha invited Lika. Winter still blustered around the chest, every drawer filled with grief. If anything, Antosha's mood had worsened.

They'd been close since their childhood in Taganrog, on the Sea of Azov, where they lived in a flat above Father's shop. Father—their undoing. A hypocrite, he made a show of his devotion, kowtowing to the priests, yet at the shop he rigged his scales and dyed old tea leaves to sell as new. And his hand was heavy. He yearned for God's mercy, but had none for his sons. Masha had been exempt as the only girl, but every punch and kick, every blow of the cane that struck Antosha, she felt too.

They took small revenge in a favourite game. When Father was out, they put on his church coat, one sleeve each, and, holding the other by the waist, bumped around the house in tandem, arguing. *We'll sit. No stand! On the sofa. No, the chair!* They kept each other in stitches straining the patriarch's seams. To this day Masha felt they were conjoined. She couldn't be happy if Antosha wasn't.

After work, she gathered the post from the table in the hall and stood riffling through the stack. Another begging letter from Kolia's mistress. Masha recognized her inebriated scrawl and closed the shutters around her heart. The first anniversary of Kolia's passing would come in June. She and Mother planned to go to Ukraine, where he'd died, for the ceremony. Would their sorrow ease then?

She slipped that envelope to the bottom of the pile. At the top now was a letter from Ivan, probably complaining about Father's visit. She dropped it on the table. Then one from Father, no doubt filled with complaints about Ivan. That went on the table too. Most of the rest were for Antosha, publishing business, but some were personal too, such as the next addressed in a familiar hand, though Masha had never met the woman. The frequency of her letters had acquainted Masha with her writing.

Antosha was a celebrity. In restaurants waiters quoted him lines from his own stories, which he hated. His comings and goings were publicly noted. Things he would never reveal to his family came to them as literary gossip, such as his relationship to this exotically named actress living, according to her stationery, in the Hotel Madrid. He'd met her the summer before in Odessa, or so the papers had reported. Kleopatra. The envelope *reeked* of scent.

Masha knocked once on Antosha's door before opening it, giving him no time to arrange his face. The cheerful bowtie contrasted with the expression above it. Dullness. Fatigue. Was he unwell? Her heart lurched at the thought.

"Are you working?" she asked, though the answer was self-evident.

"It's all right. Come in."

He signed the letter he was writing using his whole arm, like he was dashing off a sketch, and dropped it on the postal scale he kept on his desk. She watched him take out the scissors to trim the margins, then weigh it a second time. This was his inner conflict dramatized—the desire for fine things measured against the family's former destitution. Antosha felt compelled to save on postage, yet the paper and ink were of the finest quality.

"You're not throwing those out, are you?" She pointed to the unusable strips. "Why not write a story on them?"

No smile for her quip. He merely took the letters from her and shuffled through them, stopping briefly at the one from Kolia's mistress. Kleopatra's letter he slipped in a drawer.

"That one has a lot to say," Masha chirped.

No reply. He was not in the mood to joke about his affairs.

Some of Misha's law texts were piled on his desk. *You take all the women and then you take my books*, the little brother would howl. These looked like treatises on prison management. She saw the word "Siberia" and shuddered. How could this help Antosha's depression?

She was distracted then by an unfamiliar object next to the grim tomes. A small bronze horse flanked by a pair of empty inkwells.

"From a patient," Antosha told her.

As a doctor, he often took goods in lieu of payment—an embroidered cushion, a freshly caught perch wrapped in the *Moscow Gazette*. He fed them all more on ink than on his meagre doctor's earnings.

"Sad," he said. "She lugged it over in her bag. Lift it."

The base was marble. "Ooof." Masha set it down again. "You'd think the owner of such a thing could pay her doctor."

"She couldn't even pay for the prescription. She just sat there blinking at it. I thought she couldn't read."

"Illiterates don't generally own fancy inkwells."

He squared the stack of letters for later reading. "Exactly my conclusion."

"Did you give her money? Are you sending more to his mistress?" Kolia's, she meant. "She'll only drink it."

"Last time she said she had no coat."

Antosha looked up at Masha now and squinted. This was their usual disagreement; his charity, her common sense. If not for her, he would work himself to death.

But there was something else on his mind, for he stood then. "Sister. Let's take a walk."

"Oh, Antosha. The birds freeze in flight. And it'll be dark soon. How about tea?"

Winter was no excuse. He waved it off.

In the hall the coat stand, with all it held, stood like an upright bear. They bundled up, and it became a stand again. Outside, it was harder for Antosha's weak lungs to draw a cold breath. He rasped. By the time they'd reached the far side of the Garden Ring Road, his beard and eyebrows were beaded with ice.

"Your face is a chandelier," Masha said.

They never went to the Zoological Gardens. It wasn't an outing if you only had to cross the street. Also, Antosha disapproved of the place with its distant howls and cries; an "animal graveyard," he called it, for all the creatures that died of malnutrition or froze. His horror notwithstanding, a running joke had developed between her brothers. Each blamed the elephant when they passed wind.

In late January it was an abandoned place, trees rimed, paths glittering in the dusk. Masha leaned into Antosha as they shuffled along, clinging arm in arm, heads nearly touching. Just like when they shared Father's coat.

"Are you worried about money again?"

He spoke into his fur collar. "The play was a setback. In all ways. But I expected it. Everyone warned me. Unfortunately, knowing in advance you'll be tied up and spat on doesn't make it any easier."

She flinched. "You're so used to praise."

"It's not that. They made such a mess of it. Why should I try, when no one will understand what I'm doing?"

Several times during these broody weeks she'd yearned to point something out: perhaps the theatre wasn't his forte. He wanted it to resemble life, but in life he shrank from anything theatrical. Scenes of any kind repelled him. Arguments, wounded feelings.

She asked, "You won't write another, then?"

"Another play? Never."

She pulled her arm free to shake his hand. "Congratulations. It's decided. Stick to stories." Now he could cheer up.

He didn't. They walked on in silence, until she could no longer stand it. "Brother? I can't feel my feet."

He pointed to one of the pavilions, and they hurried toward it holding hands. Inside, a dim room with a vaulted ceiling, a row of cages on one side. The lanterns probably burned all day. Most prominent, though, was the urinous stench.

"It smells like Father's breath," Antosha said, and Masha laughed.

They stamped and shook themselves to bring their blood back. She knocked the ice off his face with her glove. Then they noticed the matted heap in one of the cages, emaciated and dull-coated, its back leg rubbed hairless by what was surely a redundant shackle.

"Excuse us," Antosha said.

"It's like in your stories," Masha said, drawing closer to the bars. "Whenever anyone's depressed, they lie with their face to the wall."

"Do they?"

The bear was hibernating, no doubt, but eventually it would waken, and that would be worse.

"Her son was a convict," Antosha said.

"Who?"

"The woman who brought me the inkwell. She must have been pawning everything she owned. She complained about a stomachache. Only after my examination did she blurt out the truth. Maybe you don't remember this. In Taganrog we could see them marched off to Siberia from our window."

"I remember spitting sunflower shells out that window."

"Marched off to slavery. We can't get away from it."

Their grandfather had been a serf—Father, too, until he was sixteen and Grandfather bought the family's freedom. But Antosha was speaking about more than their personal history.

"Isn't the theatre slave to its old forms, children to their parents, and women to men? But here's the thing, Masha. When she told me about her son, I didn't feel sorry for her. I actually envied the son getting away."

She heard his tone, saturated with indignation and pain, but was still confused. "I'm not following you, brother, and I badly want to."

"What do you think you're doing?" It was the keeper stumbling in in his navy greatcoat, all brass-buttoned and outraged to see them there. "I just about locked you up. Get out!"

It was dark by then. Despite the moon standing sentry, they had to feel their way down the path toward the lights along the Garden Ring.

"I sense there's something you're not saying," she told Antosha.

In fact, he'd told her everything.

"There's a sort of stagnation in my soul, sister. I'm not disappointed or tired. Not even depressed. Everything's suddenly uninteresting to me. I've got to do something to rouse myself."

At that moment, she slipped on the ice and nearly lost her balance. Somehow, in the darkness, Antosha caught her arm in time.

"A broken leg I don't need," she said when she'd got herself firmly planted again. "You keep me on my feet."

From under his breath, his promise: "I always will."

ONLY MASHA WAS ALLOWED NEAR ANTOSHA'S DESK. The next morning the Queen of the Nile's letter lay there as open as a woman spread across a bed. Masha would read it in due course anyway as part of her organizational duties. Now or later—what difference did it make? Every year after Epiphany, they sat down to this task. Personal letters and literary letters filed according to the author.

> *You hellishly elegant man, you are ordered to show up. Curl your hair and wear a pink tie. Forget the theatre. I have.*

Was this Kleopatra a prostitute? Then Masha thought, If she *interests* him, if she rouses him from his *stagnation* . . .

She'd invited Lika for this purpose, but less cold-bloodedly than Olga had intimated. Despite the fact that Masha was eight years older—or because of it, perhaps—Lika frequently sought Masha out at school, for advice, or to restore order in her classroom, or to stage-snore beside her during assembly. Often she waited for her at the end of the day. All this had started before Lika learned who Masha's brother was, so she obviously liked Masha for herself. For this reason, Masha hadn't at first wanted to bring Lika home, because whatever happened there would affect the currently happy situation at work. *The Wood Demon* forced her. But now she could leave the cheering up to this Kleopatra person and keep Lika for herself.

She folded the scented letter back into its envelope. Under it was a note from Antosha. He'd taken the morning train to St. Petersburg to visit his publisher. Good.

Masha had been a guest of Alexei Suvorin herself a few years before. His ceiling-high aviary came to mind, a live pine tree growing inside it, filled with flitting finches and canaries. Antosha would benefit from Suvorin's luxuries—lavatory, a footman, multi-course inebriating meals. Their eldest brother, Aleksander, lived in Petersburg too, and Antosha enjoyed his company in small doses, or tolerated it, at least. Most importantly, Alexei Suvorin was like Antosha's better second father. Antosha would return pampered and renewed.

She dropped his note in the wastebasket. Nudged the blotter, which already lined up exactly with the edge of the desk. The postal scale was true. Air, it showed, weighed nothing. Why did she feel so restless?

Antosha had begun writing to support the family while he was studying medicine. Comic tales about Police Inspector Moronoff, about Kreepikoff who sneezed on a general at the opera, about Skribblich the clerk. Hundreds and hundreds of sketches, satires and riffs. Masha would copy them out to send to journals, so in a way she wrote them too. At least she was the person second closest to the work, having formed the words with her own hand and picked her way through the crossings-out and blots before anyone judged them perfect. Her script was neat, with no mistakes. Unlike life.

Not restless—useless. Useless to him.

The bronze horse reared between the inkwells. Antosha had filled them. She unscrewed the cap on the pot, dipped his holy nib. A drop clung to the tip, their whole past contained in it.

A black black tear.

3

MISHA FLUNG A NEWSPAPER DOWN IN FRONT OF Masha. It was one of the liberal-leaning papers; they were praising Antosha. *The first writer to visit Sakhalin Island. The first to catalogue the injustices of a penal colony.*

"This can't be true," she said. Then she remembered that grim pile on Antosha's desk, "Siberia" stamped on the spines. She turned her fury on the little brother. "He's been reading your books. Did you encourage him in this?"

Misha's big ears turned an indignant crimson. "He didn't tell me anything. You're the one he talks to. I thought you knew."

She had to leave for school. Somehow she finished dressing, caught the tram and got herself into the classroom. Her mouth opened and closed, words coming out. Antosha had written about this condition in a story. Psychic blindness. *When someone sees without understanding.*

It couldn't be true. Half the things she read about him in the papers were lies.

Meanwhile her girls worked out sums on their slates, the chalk clicking hollowly. They dared not speak. They thought she was in a temper over something, but it was disbelief and horror. The woman who'd brought Antosha the inkwell must have felt just like this. She'd opened the paper and learned that her son was heading off to Siberia. Antosha had gone to St. Petersburg to seek permits to do the same, not, as Masha had thought, to carouse with his publisher.

On the classroom wall hung a portrait of Tsar Aleksander III, his moustaches waxed, thinning peninsula of hair on his pate. Next to him the map of Russia was fixed with pins. Masha went and found the place—shaped like demon pinchers reaching down. She put her finger on Moscow, then moved it northeastwardly across the Urals, to Siberia. She had to take a step to get there. But Antosha's destination was worse than Siberia, and farther. Two more steps. Across the vast amoral emptiness of Siberia too, well beyond where the rail line ended, to the Okhotsk Sea.

Sakhalin Island.

Such a trip would kill him. His health was already comprom-ised, though no one spoke openly of it. Neither did they men-tion what Kolia had died of. A sick man in a penal colony full of murderers. Shackles and gallows and the lash. Despite this carto-graphic proof right in front of her, it was easier to believe in Hell as a physical place than Sakhalin Island. Children were cowed into obedience by the very mention of it.

She turned and saw her girls, their braided, calculating heads lifted, watching her. *Is it Geography now, Miss?* She waved to keep them adding. Later, she anesthetized them with verses to memor-ize. This way she got through the day.

When she finally found herself alone among the empty desks, she went to the window and looked out. Below she saw not the Dairy School courtyard, but the one in Taganrog. The high red-brick wall around it, wooden gates shut. The storehouse made of the same bloodshot brick where Antosha used to hide after the beatings. Aleksander, Kolia, Antosha, punished with relish; when they howled, Father beat them harder. The other two crawled off to secret refuges, but she always knew where to find Antosha.

Inside, the storeroom was crammed higgledy-piggledy with

wooden crates, the air heavy, an olio: tallow, sardines, sulphur, cloves. Mice droppings. The used tea leaves drying on newsprint sheets. She would creep in and find him squeezed behind the crates. To this day, certain combinations of odours made her ill. She couldn't bear cheap tallow candles.

Her head throbbed. Outside the window, the weak light gave way to dusk while the impassive Dairy School cows lined up in the frozen yard, tails flicking as they waited to be milked.

BY THE TIME MASHA LEFT SCHOOL HER SENSES HAD fully returned. The tram stank of wet sheepskin and fur, and the bodies of people terrified of visiting the baths in winter.

The observatory was tucked behind a wooden fence, its tower rising from a complex of white buildings. No one seemed to be around, just the bearded watchman who led her to Olga's office, tsking about the snow she'd tramped in. Masha hadn't seen Olga since their awkward parting the night Lika visited. The English lessons had ceased; apparently, Masha was too stupid. Masha was afraid of Olga at the best of times, which only made her more admiring. Few people inspired fear in Masha. But Olga was also the only one of her friends who'd been involved with Antosha and still remained close to both of them.

She wasn't in her office. "I'll leave a note," Masha told the watchman, who shuffled off, muttering into his beard.

Of the several desks in the room, she knew Olga's by the chaos of books and papers, the nebula stain on the blotter. Masha smelled her cigarettes, could picture her here with her male colleagues, a star herself surrounded by beards.

Loving Olga had been a difficult proposition, Antosha had told her back in their Guerrier days. Yet her difficultness seemed to be the very thing he enjoyed—her exasperated intelligence and her pride. Her shabby clothes. He loved to open the door for her just to hear her snap, "I'm capable of doing it myself. You men are not as essential as you think."

"What are you snooping around for?"

Masha swung around. Olga, unsmiling in the doorway. "You *are* here," Masha said.

"I was in the tower. The watchman found me. What do you want?" She sounded angry, but probably wasn't. She headed straight for her desk, where she retrieved her tobacco pouch from a drawer.

"Did you see the papers today?" Masha asked.

"I try to avoid them. Why?" She lifted out a pinch of brown strands and turned her back. Her pincushion bun sagged at her nape, off-centre.

"There was something about Antosha. Olga, I'm upset. Even Misha's upset."

"Is he getting married?"

"What?" Masha recoiled like she'd been slapped. "He's in Petersburg. Apparently he's planning a trip."

"To Sakhalin Island, you mean? Yes, he wrote me."

This was more of a slap than the marriage joke. He'd confided in Olga but not his sister.

Olga put out her tongue to seal the cigarette. "Don't pout. He said he's written you too. He wants us to look up some things for him. Apparently our library's better."

She searched through the littered desk for a match and, to Masha's amazement, struck it with her thumbnail. The flame burst. Her cheeks hollowed as she sucked.

"They'll never let him go."

The authorities, she meant. This was probably true. In her panic, Masha hadn't thought of this. Except for long-ago explorers and now jailers and the condemned, and any family they dragged into exile with them, no one had seen the place. Yet every word Antosha wrote, every word published in the country, had to be approved by a censor. Anything he had to say would be critical and therefore forbidden, so why would they let him go?

"Since you're here," Olga said, heading for the door, "come see the tower."

"Is it allowed?" Masha asked.

"I'm allowing it."

Masha trailed her down a polished corridor. The place was not as deserted as it had seemed. Some doors at this end were open. Several times a scientific head lifted to watch them pass, spectacled eyes unwelcoming. Masha felt uncomfortable. Olga kept her chin high despite her stooping shoulders. She flicked ash off her cigarette.

In her cryptic, ill-humoured way, Olga had managed to reassure Masha that Antosha wouldn't go. But she still didn't know why he wanted to.

"He said he feels stagnant," she told Olga. "But that's hardly a reason to go to such a place."

They'd reached a set of steps at the end of the corridor. Olga paused. "He's an expert observer of suffering. I think it's a form of homeopathy."

"What do you mean?"

"Like cures like. It's just an idea. Please don't share it with him, or he'll have my head. Doctors don't like to be diagnosed."

She climbed the steps and opened the heavy door at the top. Masha felt as though she were being invited beyond an altar screen, into this circular room lined with dark wood cabinets filled with mysterious devices. In the centre was a large round table on which several charts were spread, weighted at the corners with books. Their embossed titles were in German. The telescope of polished brass stood before one of the windows. The instruments, the books, the arcane charts—all of it filled Masha with awe.

But it wasn't the science that Olga wanted to show her, for she pointed up to the vaulted ceiling. It was painted with gold stars, each in its own piece of sky enclosed in a border of white and gold.

"It's beautiful." Masha turned a circle as she looked up. "I'd like to paint it."

IT WAS NEARLY DARK WHEN SHE STARTED FOR HOME. The actual stars were out, but crossing the Crimean Bridge, she saw the frozen river as an unreflecting void. Her desire to paint had briefly revived in the tower, only to freeze in her veins again. What was the matter with her? Everyone said she was as good a painter as Kolia, that she could have gone to the College of Art if women had been allowed.

Perhaps it was because of Kolia that she felt indifferent. If she began painting again, it would mean he was really gone.

For the first time she considered seeking out her old teacher, Isaac Levitan. He'd been Kolia's friend, and was Antosha's too. A family friend. One year he summered with them, which was when he gave her lessons. Isaac was always tender with his advice to her. With anyone else's shortcomings he'd let rip, for he took bad painting personally. With her, he'd simply circle his long finger over her composition and ask, "Where are you, Masha?" Meaning, what part of herself had she put in the landscape?

But Isaac was a success now, like Antosha. His opinion of himself had always been mighty; why would he have time for a dabbler, even one personally connected to him? Besides, she was always embarrassed in his presence, because that summer, in a manic fit, he'd fallen to his knees and proposed to her. She'd been so taken aback, she'd packed up her things and run.

When she got home from the observatory, there was indeed a letter from Antosha. She tore it open, hoping it would deny the Sakhalin Island story. *Could you please find out the following?* Enclosed was a long list of information required to plan his suicidal trip. Olga would help her, he said.

Olga had been right. When wasn't she?

At dinner, after Mother left the table, Masha mentioned to the soon-to-be lawyer the other thing Olga had said. "Olga thinks they won't allow it."

"Probably not," Misha agreed. "Except he does have the backing of Alexei Suvorin. He's rich enough to pull strings and pay bribes. But still. It's unlikely."

All they could do now was wait for Antosha to return from St. Petersburg and explain himself.

Meanwhile, they hid the news from Mother, who was thankfully not a reader of newspapers. Not a reader at all, not even of Antosha's stories. She would listen to them when they were read aloud, glowing with pride, though Masha suspected that her mind was actually elsewhere during these times, that it was the sound of his quiet voice that lit her from within, not the words themselves, for she often laughed at the wrong times. Worse, she once referred in company to Antosha's "poems," humiliating the family, though Antosha had only laughed.

A few days later, brother Ivan's letter arrived. There was

no train beyond a certain point, he needlessly informed them. Antosha would have to go on by horse and carriage, and boat, perhaps even on foot, as the convicts did. Ivan too was concerned for his health.

Mother got to this letter before Masha did and afterward required nightly propping up.

"Do you remember Taganrog?" she moaned from her bed when Masha came in one night with her compress.

"Of course I do. I was ten when we left." She laid the damp cloth across the corrugations of worry on Mother's forehead.

"I mean when Father went bankrupt and left us on our own." She stared up with small, frightened eyes. "Those men banging on the door, demanding their money. I was alone with four hungry children. Father said not to sell anything, that he would send us what we needed, but he didn't. He didn't!"

"Don't think of those times, Mamasha. They're over."

"Are they? It was Antosha who saved us. A sixteen-year-old boy. What will happen to us if he goes to Sakhalin Island?"

Masha settled beside Mother on the edge of the bed, when she would have preferred to flee the room and those memories. "He won't go. Misha says they won't allow it."

Mother's handkerchief was lost somewhere in the bedclothes. Masha blotted her tears with the hem of the sheet.

In those years, Father had whistled too often inside the house and brought the misfortune of bankruptcy upon them. He'd worked his way out of the peasantry only to destroy his business. Aleksander and Kolia were studying in Moscow by then; like a coward, Father had run off there. He was supposed to find work. Instead he'd had an attack of religiosity and decided to pray in every single one of Moscow's multitude of churches.

Masha went out with Ivan and Misha to catch songbirds. To this day she could conjure the feel of a bird trapped in her skirts, its frenzied wings beating against her thighs. Feel the animal-gnawing of their hunger too. A bird would fetch a few kopeks in the market, enough to buy a *pirozhok*.

Antosha took charge. He sold the furniture, put the rest of them on the train and stayed behind himself to finish high school. He paid his tuition by tutoring, even sent money to them. The following year, when he joined them in Moscow, Father had finally found employment as a live-in watchman in a warehouse across the river. But there still wasn't enough to live on, so Antosha began writing stories.

"I've just lost Kolia," Mother whimpered. "Why can't Antosha stay home and write about things in Moscow, as he always has?"

"It said he was going to collect story ideas," Lika told Masha at school that week. She'd read a different paper. The news was spreading fast.

"That's rubbish," Masha replied. Stories he plucked from the air.

"Well, he's truly heroic."

A dreamy look crossed Lika's already dreamy face; her silver eyes practically filled with clouds. She was eighteen but sometimes seemed like a Dairy School pupil herself, romantic on the one hand, like now, but also adolescent in her complaints. It was terribly dull at home, she'd told Masha. Just her and Granny going at each other.

The word "heroic" made Masha bristle. As soon as Antosha returned from St. Petersburg, he'd be heaped with this sort of adulation. It would encourage him in his folly.

Lika was still lost in thought in the doorway of Masha's classroom, effectively barring her way. Masha was to meet Olga at the Rumiantsev Library. The easiest thing was to invite Lika along.

When they arrived together, Olga was already hunched behind a book-laden table. She scowled at the sight of Lika but soon reassessed her opinion. *When would the ice break up on the Kama River?* Lika found out first.

Obviously she was intelligent; she'd been a Guerrier student too. Not only that—if a slim blonde with silvery eyes asked for the books, the clerks would run for them.

4

NTOSHA RETURNED FROM ST. PETERSBURG ONE night at the end of the month, after Mother and Masha had already gone to bed. Mariushka's frantic shrieks woke them. They rushed to the dining room and found him chasing the fat cook around the table, imitating her distressed-goose gait.

"Look how she hobbles!" he called to Mother and Masha in the doorway. "Just let me see what's ailing you, Mariushka."

"No!" she screeched.

Mother laughed as she hadn't since Kolia died. Masha, in her nightdress, hair undone, leapt into the game, catching Mariushka's arm, solidly muscular from decades of stirring kasha. She got her to sit, whereupon Mariushka threw her apron over her face. Antosha pulled off her dirty slipper, then her oft-darned stocking, long and stained like a bull's entrails. A stream of muttered prayers issued from under the apron.

He sat across from her. "I'm not going to hurt you, Mariushka. I just want to see what's wrong. Look at me. Look." He shook her hideous foot.

Mariushka tore off the apron and glared out of her clenched face.

"Ready?" He pushed back the horned toes, ran his thumb across her sole. Gently. He was a wonderful doctor.

"Ah!" Mariushka screamed. "You're tickling!"

He took her biggest toe between his fingers. "Magpie, magpie . . ." Utter seriousness. ". . . cooked the porridge. Fed it to the children."

Masha felt the grin spread across her own face, a great rush of hilarity, as though he were playing this joke on her.

"She gave some to this one. And this one."

As he pulled each rinded toe, Mariushka howled. The last was so mashed it barely resembled a toe.

"But she didn't give anything to this one, who hasn't done the chores. Nothing for you!" He let go her foot. "They're just warts, Mariushka. I'll mix you an arsenic paste."

Mariushka snatched her stocking and slipper and huffed off, flushed and making spitting sounds, which none of them took seriously. Then Mother came and kissed Antosha's forehead.

"Welcome home, Antonshevu." She blotted her eyes on the sleeve of her nightdress. "You're not going to Siberia, are you?"

"Go back to bed, Mamasha. We'll talk in the morning."

As soon as they were alone, Masha went to the cupboard for the vodka, still smiling like her face might crack. "After that performance, brother? I'll never get to sleep."

"Was it better than *The Wood Demon?*"

She set down the vodka and glasses and the plate of Mother's gingerbread from the sideboard. As she poured, she fixed him with a look of mock astonishment.

"Did I hear right? Was that your long-departed sense of humour?"

She joined him at the table. They raised their glasses, drank, nibbled some gingerbread to soak it up. Antosha made a face over the gingerbread, preferring something salty with this vice. He loosened his tie.

"And Father's still away. I forgot. Could Ivan be persuaded to keep him, do you think?"

"Unlikely. He keeps writing to ask us to take him back."

He smiled at her. How well he looked—a healthy colour to his face again. From chasing Mariushka, yes, but he'd had the breath to chase her. Masha didn't want to say anything that might dampen his mood, but at the same time she was desperate to unburden her worry. She brushed at the gingerbread crumbs on the tablecloth.

"Did you get the permit you were seeking?"

"I was trying to get a pass from the head administrator. The usual Janus-faced bureaucrat."

She looked up, hopeful now. "So you didn't get one?"

"I got a press card. We'll see if that gets me on the island."

"You're really going?"

He heard her anguish, she was sure. His eyes let hers go, and he glanced at his nails, which were, as always, immaculate and trimmed. She'd kill herself if she cried now or made some kind of scene. That was no way to manage him. He'd withdraw, and everything would be spoiled.

He leaned back, hands behind his head. Stretched out one long leg, then the other. "I'm hoping to go. But it's complicated, as is everything. I'm sorry I didn't mention it before I left. I wanted to—but then you would have held me back, wouldn't you?"

There was hope. It was "complicated." Nothing was certain. The main thing was not to show she disapproved or worried. To keep him happy. Then the trip would come to nothing, and they would go on living as before. Before Kolia died and before he decided to write that bewildering play.

Masha tucked her cold feet under herself and raised her hands to fashion a temporary braid. For once, her hair obeyed; wavy brown hanks clung to each other like vines. She smiled—a facsimile, but never mind. Antosha smiled back, possibly as falsely. Or perhaps he was relieved that she'd controlled herself.

"Did you see Aleksander? How are his little boys?"

"I saw them once." The smile vanished. "Kolia was so sweet when he was drunk. And look at us. Shall we?" He filled their glasses again. "It cheers us up, but the elder brother turns nasty. Thank God for sisters."

Rare for her to take a man's drink, rarer two. Already she felt the vodka working on her, lightening her. The gingerbread melted on her tongue.

He remembered something. "Oh, and thank you for your help with the research. Olga said you conscripted your prettiest friends."

Olga had mentioned Lika to him? Likely something sarcastic. In no way had Lika been "conscripted." She'd jumped at the chance.

"Just Lika," Masha told Antosha. "You remember her. She visited about a month ago."

He pulled a face, comical with exasperation. "I'm sated with women. They all smell like ice cream."

"The one who teaches with me."

His mouth twitched—he did remember!—and he ran a hand over his moustache and beard to conceal it.

"With the dimples?" she added.

"Medically speaking, dimples are a deformity. The poor thing."

"She wrote you, you know."

Antosha brightened. "She did? When?"

"Oh, ages ago. Before we met. She told me all about it. I thought you didn't remember her."

He filled his own glass a third time. "I must look for her letter."

Yes, even two on a midnight stomach made Masha feel quite untroubled herself. Giddy. How fun it had been playing matchmaker back in her Guerrier days. And now the idea returned. If bureaucratic complications failed to keep him home, mightn't Lika help?

Masha leaned onto her elbows, the end of the braid in her fist. A different feeling flickered behind the giddiness then, like a tallow candle guttering in her centre. She let it go out.

"She signed it 'Anonymous,'" she said.

"Hmm. How will I know which Anonymous is her?"

"She'll be the one who sounds like a besotted young lady."

"They all do."

"You're terrible." She reached out to pat his cheek, and the braid, released, unravelled. For a moment he took her in. Was this how he looked at his women the moment before they tore out their hearts for him?

"What?" she asked.

"Come." He swung sideways in his chair, pulled another closer.

She changed seats, sitting as he indicated, her back to him. His fingers combed through her hair.

"How does one do this? You weren't even looking."

"Plait? Make three sections." She showed him, hands in the air. "Like this. Over then over then over. Is this for a story?"

"Tell me more about your spectacular friend. Where did she come from? Heaven?"

"Her mother's a pianist in Petersburg. She's been living with her great-aunt. Maybe they moved for Guerrier."

"Ah. She's a Guerrier girl? Damnation, are you born knowing this plaiting, or does that Guerrier teach it too?"

"Certainly. Literature, mathematics, and plaiting— Ouch!"

She was teasing. With each section he wove, she silently named her truest feelings for him—love, admiration, gratitude. A single strong rope.

5

A WEEK LATER, ANTOSHA HIMSELF ANSWERED Lika's knock, just as Masha was descending the stairs.

"Ah! Lika Who Teaches with Me. Come in. Where's Mariushka? Never mind, I'll take your coat. There's Masha. Go on up. I'll join you later. Wait! Don't walk past this."

Lika was wearing her good jacket again. Antosha took her melon shoulders and turned her toward Isaac's painting at the bottom of the stairs, the one that seemed more like a window than a picture, as though summer were just beyond that wall, and in the distance flowed a river, a sky mirror, its reedy banks giving way to the different greens of grass and shrub, then the fields of yellow flax beyond.

Much taller, he bent dotingly toward her. "Our friend Isaac Levitan painted this. Not a single extraneous detail. Each stroke either called for or beautiful. I'd like to write like that."

"But you do!" Then, flustered by his attention and his touch, Lika ran up to join Masha.

"Our stairs are singing to you," Antosha called after her.

She blushed but didn't turn around to show him.

"Perhaps Isaac will drop by," Masha told her. "He was my painting teacher." She offered a belated "Hello."

Lika replied, "I can hardly believe I talked to him. He was in the paper again this morning. How thrilling it must be to see your own name in print. What a wonderful world you live in, Masha."

With Lika's arrival, the house opened for the night. This past week, friends and acquaintances had been dropping by every evening. Magazine editors, theatre and university friends, admirers and hangers-on—they all wanted their news straight from the source. Was he really going? When and why? If he was seeking adventure, why not go abroad like everyone else, to Italy or France?

Masha had listened to his answers.

"From the books I've been reading it's evident that we've destroyed millions with the most casual barbarity. Driven them in fetters ten thousand miles, their families trailing after them, only to deprave them further."

"Well, they're convicts, aren't they? Guilty as charged."

"*We're* guilty. And what's more, a convict serves his sentence, yet he can never return home. Is that justice? If exile is permanent, punishment is perpetual. My only regret is that it's me going and not someone who could rouse more public indignation. Nothing will come of the trip."

He would smile then and change the subject to the grisly weather, or ask where his guest had found such a novel tiepin.

But Masha knew the longer one talked on a subject, the less interest it held. Antosha's trip to Sakhalin Island was this season's gossip, and surely he would tire of it too. So she played the enthusiastic hostess, the way she used to after Guerrier lectures.

Unlike for her, these gatherings were a trial for Antosha; he hated to be the centre of attention. His preferred situation was off to the side, observing, the writer's situation. To stand alone among others. The night Lika came again, he got a reprieve.

There were always fewer women than men. Hopeful Vermicelli lingered for an hour, at least making herself useful by playing a few songs. Olga was a no-show. The male gaze settled naturally on Lika.

She attracted admiration the way amber, when rubbed, attracted airborne threads and motes. When she showed up, Antosha was free to retreat to the icon corner and watch the magnetized circle round her, the little brother among them.

Eventually, they found each other. Masha spotted them later, talking by the samovar, Lika's hands moving like she was trying to wash the nervousness off them. Masha came over.

"There's no exaltation. No," Antosha was telling her. "I enjoy it when I'm at it, that's true. And I like reading proofs. But as soon as something comes out in print, I can't stand it. It's never what I intended."

"I can't believe that," Lika said.

"Enough about me. Let's get back to your stage fright." He turned to Masha. "We were discussing Lika's stage fright."

"Is it stage fright?" Lika asked him.

"That's my diagnosis."

Lika had lamented these fears at school. Sometimes she'd sit down for dinner with Granny and speak the roles she'd memorized. "*He took me by the wrist and held me hard . . .*" she'd said as Ophelia. Granny had burst into tears. So she knew she had talent. She just lacked nerve.

"When I was little, Mama used to take me to her concerts," she explained to Antosha now. "She made Granny drag me out on stage after she took her bow. The hot lights on my face. Everyone staring. It was terrifying."

Antosha nodded. "A theatre must be huge to a child. The blackness so deep. As it is for the playwright."

Lika looked into his handsome face, reading sympathy where Masha saw a tongue in his smooth cheek. "I have nightmares about it."

"So do I. One is painfully recurring. All the dark-haired people in the audience are hostile, and all the fair-haired ones are asleep."

Masha laughed, somewhat disloyally. Everyone had been hostile to *The Wood Demon*, regardless of hair colour.

"Yet I love the theatre," Lika said. "If only I could say my lines behind the curtain. What do you advise? Should I give up my dream?"

"Be careful what you tell her, brother," Masha said. "Her fate's in your hands."

It was a tossed-off remark. A joke. Antosha didn't get the chance to reply, for they were interrupted then by a newly arrived guest, a short man of small importance—apparently a writer too.

"Are you ready to go, good man? My God, I don't believe you're doing this. Sakhalin Island!"

He wore his moustache long enough to suck. Despite this ragged brown curtain, Masha saw his lip curl in revulsion when he named the place. Then he noticed Lika, and his mouth fell open.

"I present my sister, Maria, and Lidia Mizanova, who wants to be an actress," Antosha told him. To Lika he said, "Last summer I spent ten days in Odessa as physician in residence to the Maly Theatre's travelling troupe. I could probably get you an audition. I don't recommend the Abramova Theatre, which staged my last play."

"I could never audition," Lika moaned.

"Never? Oh, little hands." He leaned in to address Lika's hands directly. On one she wore a ring with a small green stone. "Why do you twist so?"

Lika gave an honest answer. "It's because I'm talking to you."

Smiling, Antosha held out both of his. She offered hers. "It's like cradling a pair of sparrows," he said.

The unstatured writer barked a laugh. "There's a line I might have to borrow."

"I know what to do." Antosha slid the hand with the ring into his jacket pocket, just as Mariushka blundered past to check the samovar.

"'Do not let her capture you with her eyelashes,'" the cook muttered.

Everyone burst out laughing then, except Lika, who plucked back her hand. "She probably thinks I'm picking your pocket."

"Have you ever?" Antosha asked.

"Picked a pocket? Never!"

He smiled again. "*Never*. That's all you say."

"I'll stop if you don't like it. I'll say . . . I don't know. *Jamais?*"

Masha turned from their little group, satisfied. Lika and Antosha were getting on well despite the moustachioed hanger-on. The room was crowded by then, filled with smoke and happy noise. It lacked only music.

Then Isaac Levitan came through the door, wild black curls grazing the frame, eyes dark wells of emotion. A string plucked inside Masha—her embarrassment again. By the time Isaac reached their side of the room, she was fine.

"My spiritual brother!" Isaac embraced Antosha. "When I paint a blue road? Or the sadness in a shaft of light? That's me. My spirit. Only you understand this. Oh, Antonshevu, how can you leave us?"

In a way Isaac was Antosha's opposite, an egoist who squeezed drama out of every moment. But he truly was an exceptional painter, and a kind and generous friend. He used to lend Kolia money when he had none to give.

"Ladies and gentlemen, look!" This from a raven of a woman dressed in bright gypsy clothes coming up behind Isaac. She pointed with her long amber cigarette holder. "These two in each other's arms? Double greatness!"

"Friend, you're wrinkling me," Antosha said.

Isaac released him. He turned to Masha and greeted her as "my pupil," giving no sign, as usual, that he remembered proposing. He introduced the gypsy with the masculine handshake as Sophia K., a painter too, and host of a popular artists' salon. Their affair was common knowledge, last year's gossip. She looked a decade older than Isaac.

With Sophia still pumping Masha's arm, Isaac's eyes fixed on something across the room. Masha followed his gaze to its beautiful end—Lika in her bright jacket. His roaring must have scared her away.

"Who's *that?*" Isaac asked.

"A friend of mine. Do we need more vodka, brother?"

"We can never have too much." He offered to get it, probably for a chance to escape. He gave Isaac's shoulder a brotherly pat as he stepped away.

Antosha stopped where Isaac's eyes had, at Lika; the short writer had her trapped next to the piano. He asked to borrow her sparrow hands, or so Masha guessed, because Lika nodded and followed. Everyone watched them weave through the smoky parlour, Isaac too, rumours forming behind their eyes. They were gone a noticeably long time.

At last they returned carrying the bottles by the neck, Lika a few steps behind, both looking like they'd swallowed the pits along with the cherries. Both flustered. As soon as Lika set the bottles on the table, she fled.

Masha went to Antosha and immediately saw what was wrong. Blood trickled down the side of his nose. Her shock must have showed—she couldn't bear anyone to hurt him—for he plucked out his handkerchief and dabbed the place.

Crimson drops on the cloth. Every spring, when his cough was at its worst, they dreaded this. Last summer, they'd torn old bedsheets into squares for Kolia to bleed through.

Antosha seemed amused by the sight of his own blood. "I deserved it," he said, smiling. "Why don't you fetch her back?"

Lika was already downstairs putting on her coat. "Where are you going?" Masha asked from the top of the staircase.

She shrank as Masha descended. "Home."

"What happened?"

Masha sounded sharp even to herself. Why? Because of the grim image of Kolia.

Lika lifted her hand with the ring. "He asked me to take down some glasses. The room was dark. He— I'm so embarrassed."

"He what?" Masha asked, softening her voice.

"Bowed." Lika reddened even more. "He was trying to kiss my hand. My ring . . ." She resumed her struggle with her buttons.

She really was a child! "Antosha kissed your hand in the dark and got scratched for it? Why do you have to leave? He's upstairs grinning about it."

Lika stopped buttoning. "Really?"

"Yes. Why don't you stay?"

"Granny will be waiting up. It's late." Then she said, "You frightened me coming down the stairs like that, Masha. Now I know why my pupils listen to you."

Masha drew back. Was she that bad? As though taking a challenge, she put her hand on Lika's shoulder, which, even under the fur of the coat, felt small. "He won't hold your ring against you. You play the piano, don't you?"

"Yes. But I haven't for ages."

Lika's coat went back on the stand. Obediently she followed Masha up their musical stairs to the parlour, where she sat down at the piano.

At first she seemed reluctant to settle her fingers on the keys. Stage fright? But it was more than nervousness. Her nose crinkled, lips pinched into a bud. Once she began to sing, though, she seemed to master her feelings, or at least play through them. "*Un petit verre de Clicquot.*"

Afterward, the room fell silent. Why had she never said she played so well? Masha supposed she should have guessed. After all, Lika's mother was a pianist.

When the applause broke out, Lika smoothed her dress and gazed into her lap, as though instead of basking in this appreciation, she were alone in the room with some privately unhappy memory.

6

AND SO IT BEGAN AGAIN. MASHA NO LONGER HAD to read between the lines in the gossip pages. She got her news directly from Lika, the way she'd learned everything from her Guerrier friends when they used to gather for tea and whist after lectures, gossiping about their professors while they waited for her brothers to turn up. Waited for Antosha. Aleksander and Kolia served only to up the stakes, to fill their glasses and the room with their smoke and competitive flirting. Olga, Dunia, Ekaterina, Vermicelli.

Dunia, hot-tempered and olive-skinned. A Jewess. She confided all, even swore that she and Antosha were secretly engaged. Bespectacled Ekaterina was studying, of all things, entomology. Antosha sent her a beetle through the post. Olga was tight-lipped with the details. Vermicelli wished for a chance.

And now Masha had lured Lika back up their serenading stairs to the piano and her brother.

As for Dunia's claim all those years ago, it had been nonsense. Antosha declared himself to be "constitutionally unfit for matrimony." He revelled in his "bachelor habits"—grinding his own coffee, folding the newspaper with Japanese intricacy. He was "married to his work."

Why had Masha invited her friends? Because she'd enjoyed their gatherings and the status they brought her; all the Guerrier girls had hoped for an invitation.

With Lika there was another reason for Masha to be encouraging—her ardent wish that Antosha's interest in her friend would surpass his humanitarian yearnings. So that he would *stay*.

But the talk around the Sakhalin Island trip had changed. No longer were they saying "if," but "when." The end of April. And "how." First by train, then steamer. Maps went up in his study and in the parlour too, over Kolia's rectangles, the emptiness he'd left behind. And would her other brother, the one most precious to her, be taken from them too?

Now Lika came most nights. She was a great success, especially at the piano, and increasingly less shy for it, though still unaware of the sensation she created just by being herself.

Who is that girl in the corner, Masha? Where did you find her?

Congratulatory nods for Masha.

When Antosha finished his work and joined their guests, Lika would fly to him. His delight, what he showed of it, was obvious. He bowed and whispered something to tease the deformity of her dimples out. While playing host, his eyes would continually stray to Lika, until at some point the two of them contrived to disappear. By then their guests seemed more interested in what was happening between the writer and the Young Woman Who Taught with His Sister than in his heroic journey.

One day at school Lika confided to Masha that Granny didn't like her going out so often, or coming in at two a.m. The previous night she'd forbade her to leave, so Lika had claimed she was off to sit vigil at the convent. Granny made enquiries.

"Now she has me under lock and key. Mama wrote such an infuriating letter from Petersburg. 'A young lady's reputation is the only security she has, particularly one in your circumstances.'"

"What circumstances does she mean?" Masha asked.

Lika's expression contracted momentarily. "That she even mentions my reputation is ridiculous considering how many lovers she's had." She hugged herself, shuddering over that crowd of remembered men.

Masha attached no importance to the gesture. Instead another came to mind: the first night Lika visited, how she'd instinctively sidled up to the coat stand as though it were her chaperone. Lika's father had abandoned the family when she was three. She had no brother in her life, not even some sad whiskered uncle. She really was defenceless—unlike Masha, surrounded by brothers.

"And she accuses me of being unkind to Granny," Lika went on. "Granny who, two days ago, took me by the hair and dragged me all around the parlour. Anyway, I won't be at any more parties." The end of her nose pinkened. "Please explain why to Antosha. I wouldn't want him to think it was anything he did."

"I'll pass the message on." Masha laid a comforting hand on her shoulder again.

She relayed the message, and the next day Antosha dropped in at the Arbat flat Lika shared with Granny. Later Lika told Masha all about it.

He'd brought along a signed copy of the *Northern Herald*. "It's 'A Dreary Story,'" he told Granny over tea. "Page three. Don't bother reading it."

"You're a doctor as well as a writer, I understand," Granny said, gazing at the journal in her lap.

Antosha shrugged off these accomplishments as he always did. Somehow the conversation came around to the behaviour of today's young ladies, too free-spirited by half. "But should Lidia be allowed to visit us, I assure you my sister is always present, as is my mother, a righteous woman."

This way Lika continued as a nightly fixture in their house—at least until Easter.

THE EGGS WERE DYED. THE CHEESE WEPT IN ITS MUSLIN sling, filling the basin with milky tears. The bread waited for the oven, carved deep with Christ's initials.

Brother Ivan, the schoolteacher, came home, bringing Father with him. He seemed to have grown up since he'd ventured out in the world and stopped relying on Antosha. Grown his hair long too. He kept tossing it back, an affectation the other two brothers began imitating. When Ivan finally noticed, play-slaps and scalp-knucklings broke out, negating Masha's impression of his newfound maturity.

"And who's this girl everyone's talking about?" he asked Antosha. "They say you're going to Sakhalin Island to escape her."

Antosha played dumb, so Misha answered with his fairy-tale nickname for her, Lika the Beautiful.

"She's a friend of yours, Masha?" Ivan asked.

"Yes, but why would he want to escape her? She's perfectly delightful."

Ivan wanted Antosha's opinion.

"Height: average. Skin and mucous membranes: normal. Chest: satisfactory. She respires normally, I mean."

They roared with laughter. Then Father shuffled in wearing felt slippers. No reaction from Antosha. He didn't flinch or alter his handsome face, the same way he concealed his opinion of their numerous boring or parasitical recent guests. Even in his own family, he was the perfect host.

As usual, their dread of Father's return proved worse than the man himself, tyrant of their memories, fool at their table. Masha poured tea into a saucer for him so it would cool faster. As though she respected him. Was it better that he'd spent all those years at the warehouse, coming home only for holidays? It meant that no intervening good years might have erased the bad ones. Antosha, Aleksander and Kolia had lived through the worst of him in Taganrog. Once they moved to Moscow, Father had had to learn to control himself because one night while he was laying into Ivan with his fists, the landlady came running and threatened to evict them.

He held his long beard in one hand and bent to sip his tea. Masha remembered when the whiskers were black, not white. Remembered his satisfied grunts that accompanied each blow. Now it was his peasant slurps that made her gorge rise. He spent his retirement in prayer and harebrained theorizing, such as his latest. "I have figured out the reason more people get sick in winter than summer. There aren't any flies to clean the air."

"Flies *spread* germs, Father," the doctor told him.

Misha wiped his pince-nez on his sleeve, and after replacing them, peered across the table at Ivan. "No, Father's right. I can hardly see my brother's beautiful locks for all this dirty air between us."

They left for church. Father, a familiar of so many, had chosen the Exultation of the Holy Cross, pale green and white, its cupola holding a single black onion to the sky. It stood on the edge of town. Antosha hired cabs to take them, one for the men, another for Mother and Masha—and Olga, who had nowhere else to go.

Despite Masha's feeble faith, Easter service always moved her. The scent of juniper, the candles dabbing at the darkness. When the altar gates swung open, a cloud of incense rolled into the room, and she felt, as she often did, that her life was twice-lived. This exact moment she'd copied in one of Antosha's stories. Easter on the page and the actual mass, the fictional bells and the real ones—all blurred together.

In Taganrog, where Father had been cantor, he'd conscripted Aleksander, Kolia and Antosha into the choir. Three little boys kneeling on the icy floor, convicts to early matins and interminable rehearsals. Brutal clouts for wrong notes sung. It had driven the love of God right out of them. She looked over at Antosha. Was he thinking about his harsh upbringing, or about his journey? He might still stay. Masha prayed for it. *Please, God, keep him here. He is the only person I truly love. I'm terribly afraid for him.*

If only she believed, but she too had been disillusioned in childhood, soon after they'd got to Moscow. They had no money for school fees, so Mother took her to the bishop and made her beg for a free place. Masha kissed the floor at his feet. Dirt and hairs stuck to her puckered lips while he glowered down like God Himself. His reason for refusing? "I'm not a millionaire."

Midnight. The voices of her complicated family cried out in unison, "Christ is risen!" Father planned to stay until dawn. He rarely missed an opportunity to demonstrate his zeal. Best of all, he loved to walk in the procession around the church, singing louder than anyone else.

The rest of them went home to break their fast. Afterward, bells still pealing, the young ones set out into the streets, arms linked. That multitude of jubilating churches—forty times forty—the sky streaked with green, the earth thawing and breaking into bud along the wooded Tverskoy Boulevard. They were giddy with sleeplessness, hatless, and being silly. Masha linked arms with Olga, who tolerated it. Big-eared Misha and long-haired Ivan splashed slush at each other, but not at Antosha, walking behind the rest of them. He took his trousers seriously.

"One of your galoshes is missing a buckle," he told Olga.

"That's just what you're best at," she snapped. "Pointing out to people what they don't even know they lack."

"Olechka, you've made me happy on this Easter morning." He dashed forward and tried to kiss her.

"You've misunderstood me, then, as usual. Get off me."

"But that's all I want," Antosha said. "To show people their own dull, impoverished lives."

"Cruel man."

"Not at all. Perhaps then they might choose a better life."

"Or kill themselves."

In the middle of this banter, Masha remembered a line from his Easter story: *Why in this season of great rejoicing can't a man forget his woe?*

A heaviness settled in her chest. She heard the birds competing with the bells, breathed in the green of spring. But what would any of it matter if Antosha left? She would bump around in her half-life, one sleeve empty.

THEN A MIRACLE HAPPENED, MORE ASTONISHING THAN the resurrection they had just celebrated.

The following afternoon Father heard Lika singing. It was a romantic song, yet still he climbed the stairs to the parlour and listened, hovering in the doorway; he didn't dare step inside because Olga was there, and women smoking was sinful, as was drinking spirits. Christ didn't drink vodka.

"Only because rye doesn't grow in the Holy Land," Masha told him. "He certainly drank wine."

After Father left for prayers, Misha and Antosha teased Lika that Beauty had tamed the Beast.

Lika's voice, not her eyelashes, had captured Father.

The last of Lika's shyness seemed to moult under Father's unexpected admiration. She asked Masha to draw her so that Antosha could take her likeness with him to Sakhalin Island.

By then Masha understood he really was going. The floor of his study had disappeared under books and supplies. A massive trunk. A leather coat to shed the weather. The whole room stank of it. He slashed the air with a savage-looking knife.

"For cutting up sausages and tigers."

Her meticulously dressed, weak-lunged brother was heading off to an unimaginable place, a place that existed solely to inflict suffering. To get there would entail months of gruelling travel. Would he ever come back?

Lika posed on the edge of Masha's bed, hands folded in her lap. Masha took her in. Despite Lika's ebullience, her trilling voice, her five-kopek eyes, her slender figure, despite even her alluring deformity, Antosha was leaving. What was the point of her, then? As Masha put pencil to paper, the silly girl made everything worse by flinging herself down and moaning the sort of stage moan that Antosha parodied when he was reviling the theatre.

"Masha, I'm dying. Dying of love."

How stiff Masha's fingers felt. She hadn't picked up a drawing pencil in so long.

"Have you ever been in love?" Lika asked.

Masha traced a long line. "Never."

"But I see you playing hostess. Everyone admires you. You must have had suitors." She propped herself on one elbow, suddenly curious. "Who? You're smiling."

"Lie still," Masha commanded, and Lika fell back.

She found herself wanting to tell Lika, especially about Isaac. Why? She hardly needed to impress her. What did proposals even prove? Masha winced over that last thought. She sounded like Olga, who was admirably brilliant but also pathetic in her shabby dresses and mismatched gloves. Masha did not want to be pathetic.

"The first was a nonentity. One summer he hung around the dacha we were renting. Lieutenant Egorov. Bald, with an annoying sense of humour. The same joke over and over. Antosha sent him packing."

She added shading to the drawing, aware that she had removed it from Lieutenant Egorov. Not that she had thought much of him over the years—just that when she did, it was not harshly like this.

"Who else?"

"Isaac Levitan."

Lika lifted her head again to gape. "Isaac Levitan proposed to you?"

"Don't move. And don't sound so surprised. I told you he was my painting teacher."

"Tell me more."

"It was a few years after Egorov. Isaac came to the dacha we were renting and gave me lessons. I didn't see the proposal coming at all."

She remembered how he'd bent close to her easel, a hesitant look on his face. She'd assumed he was trying to think of a kind way to criticize her, that he was about to circle his finger, his usual prelude to "Where are you, Masha?"

"What happened?" Lika asked.

"He suddenly dropped to his knees and began babbling, 'Masha, my little queen! I paint only for you. The trees, the fields, the mist, the sunset. Marry me and we'll paint it together.' Something like that. You know how he talks."

"I only met him once. What did you answer?"

"Nothing." She was drawing Lika's arm now as it dangled over the side of the bed. "I ran away as fast as I could. Cried the rest of the day. When I didn't turn up for dinner, Antosha came and asked what I was blubbering about. I told him. He said I could marry Isaac if I wanted but that he, Isaac, greatly preferred women of a certain age."

"Does he?" Lika asked.

"Sophia must be forty. Isaac's mother died when he was young. That's what attracts him. Antosha's theory."

"So you refused him?"

"I didn't have to, thankfully. When I went down to dinner, Isaac acted like nothing had happened. He's never mentioned it since."

"I think he's handsome," Lika said. "I could swim in those dark Jew eyes."

"You and everyone else. What a little ninny I was to cry like that— Stop wriggling."

It wasn't just that she'd been taken by surprise. Masha remembered now. Isaac had come to them that summer because he'd been depressed. Suicidal. Antosha had invited him to bring him back to the world. She'd been afraid he'd relapse if she had to reject him.

"Don't you want to get married?" Lika asked.

"No. I'd rather be sister to a great man than wife of a nobody. I'm *honoured* to be Antosha's sister."

To manage his household. To interpret his needs and moods. "What is the matter with Antosha?" Mother would ask because Masha alone could figure it out. His cough. His "downstairs complaint." His finances. That he was not able to write, or not writing well. An uncured patient, a bitter memory, a bad review. Other people's stupidity, or their suffering. The general state of the world. Masha alone could diagnose the doctor.

Lika's brow crimped while the rest of her lay still. After a moment she said, "That doesn't make sense, Masha. Isaac Levitan is a great painter. And you'd still be Antosha's sister no matter who you married."

How had they got onto proposals? Then Masha guessed. Lika expected Antosha to propose before he left. Who was the ninny now?

The next thing Lika said really was too much. "When your brother kisses me, Masha? He puts his tongue in."

Masha thought of a gudgeon swimming in her mouth. Dunia had been too free with the private details as well. Masha had severed their friendship.

"I simply melt," Lika said.

"Extraordinary. A transmutation of matter." She pressed so hard with the pencil that the lead snapped.

"Don't," Lika told her when Masha crumpled the page.

She rose and stuffed the picture in the wastebasket.

THE MORNING ANTOSHA LEFT, HE SHOWED MASHA THE letter he'd written Alexei Suvorin, who had given him an advance to fund his voyage.

> *If anything untoward does happen, please bear in mind that every-*
> *thing I possess and may possess in the future belongs to my sister.*
> *She'll pay off my debts, including this one.*

Masha sank down on the divan and sobbed into her hands. He, who hated all damp scenes, said, "I need you to take over while I'm gone. You will, won't you?"

"I can't," she cried.

"Nonsense," he told her. "You already hold the place together. The old ones are useless, as you know. Well, Mother's a wonderful cook. Keep her happy. Make the little brother study hard for his exams so all that I've invested in him isn't wasted. Try not to mind the crackpot patriarch. Sister?"

"Antosha, I'm afraid for your health."

"I'll take good care. It will make the trip more difficult if I know you're worrying. But if I know you're happy and enjoying life, I'll feel lonely and come home."

She dried her face with her sleeve. What choice did she have? She stood and kissed his cheek, which made him smile.

Shortly afterward Lika came bursting into the house, stamping her little boots, flinging off her hat. She wasn't the tidiest person. With her tear-stained face and melodramatic gestures, she forced her way in. How dare she. She barely knew him! Even as Masha bristled, she recognized what was behind her irritation. Easier to take offence at a silly lovesick girl than be angry at her risk-taking, too-kind brother.

Their landlord lived next door. An amateur photographer, he gathered them together for a farewell picture. Masha, Misha, Ivan, Mother and Father arranged around Antosha, their sun, dressed in a bright yellow jacket. Then Antosha called out, "Jamais!" and beckoned to her. As soon as Lika squeezed in beside Antosha, the landlord waved in his own children too.

"The famous adventurer and all his admirers! Say 'raisins'!"

Just as he ducked under the black cloth, a hen strutted past like a wooden toy pulled along on a string. Misha, cross-legged on the ground, nabbed it. What next? Masha thought. The kitchen basin? She only just managed to erase her scowl before the disappointing moment was fixed on glass.

According to custom, the whole family gathered in the parlour and seated themselves for a moment of silence so that Antosha would journey safely. Then Mother started off the crying and kept it up as they made their way out the door to the waiting cab.

A larger farewell party was expected at the station. A group of them planned to travel along for a time with Antosha to see him off properly drunk. Ivan and Misha had gone ahead with the trunk. Antosha went with Mother, Masha and Lika—Lika sniffling too now as she gazed besottedly at Antosha.

Masha stared sullenly out the window. It was her own fault. She'd invited Lika— not to the station, Antosha had done that— but to fall in love with him. As usual, Masha the instigator suffered more than he did.

When they arrived, the advance guard was there waving and hallooing. Antosha called out to Ivan to get everyone on the train. Then he turned to Mother. It was really happening. He bowed to accept her blessing. She gave it through sobs.

Next he faced Masha, lifting her chin and forcing her to meet his steady gaze. Their secrets lived in that look, their treasured closeness too.

"By September, I'll be home."

Words spoken as solemnly as a vow. Even if he did survive, five months without him may as well have been five years. Her legs trembled. He wrapped his arms around her and held her until the shaking stopped.

Meanwhile, Lika stood flapping her hands and acting as though she were in a crying competition with them.

"It will hurt less if you make it quick!" Ivan shouted out the window of the train.

Antosha let Masha go. From his pocket he pulled a package wrapped in coloured paper. For Lika. Greedily, she tore it open.

His photograph. "Allow me to read you the inscription, Jamais," he said, which gave him an excuse to wrap an arm around her shoulder and bend close. *To the dear creature who scratched me and sent me running to Sakhalin Island. I advise all suitors to wear thimbles on their noses.* He turned it over. *P.S. This gift obliges me to nothing.*

He kissed Lika's forehead. Until the third bell rang and broke their mutual trance, he spent his last moments with her. Then, without a backwards glance, he boarded. The last Masha saw of him was the joyful streak of his yellow jacket through the window as the train slid by and tore her in half.

7

SCHOOL ENDED. THEY GAVE UP THE CHEST OF drawers house; they couldn't afford it with Antosha gone. Misha and Father went to relatives, and Mother and Masha, with Mariushka, left for Ukraine.

Such a paintable countryside—green meadows, willow stands and farmsteads, quaint towns strung together with telegraph wires. It all flashed past Masha, barely remarked upon, for Antosha was presently travelling in the opposite direction, to that unpaintable place. Masha and Mother were bringing their fears for his life to Luka, where Kolia had died the year before.

As well as sorrow, the dacha at Luka held pleasant memories, mainly from their first summer there, when an enduring friendship had developed with the owners of Luka, the Lintvariovs. The fishing was excellent too, the walks poetical. Almost every day Masha had found a subject to paint—the nightingale nest on her windowsill, the orchard, the charmingly down-at-the-heel manor house. There were two Borzois, long-haired as Bohemians, one black, one grey.

The plan this summer was to stay until Kolia's memorial ceremony at the end of June. Unfortunately, Natalia, the exuberant, big-boned youngest of the Lintvariova sisters, was away helping with her newborn niece in Moscow. Her eldest brother was under house arrest there for advocating for representational government. Once Natalia was back, she and Masha would travel on to Yalta for a seaside holiday.

Driving up the long avenue now, Masha reinterpreted the dusk. Not night falling, but the deep shadow of last year's tragedy still hanging over everything—the peeling shutters, the perpetual puddle in the courtyard, the half-feral pigs rooting in the grounds. It no longer seemed charming, but depressing. Gloomy.

The whitewashed dacha was just visible on the other side of the orchard. They followed the path and mounted the steps to the broad veranda where Kolia had lain coughing in his hammock. Once inside, the first thing Masha did was check for the nightingale nest. Gone! The odour of fresh paint hung in the room. Worse, propped up on the dresser was a letter Antosha had written Natalia. She'd left it for Masha, probably thinking she'd find it funny.

Dear Little N,

I regret to inform you that this summer I won't be visiting because in April I'm departing for Sakhalin Island, returning in December. Bears and fugitives abound there. In the event I fall prey to Messieurs les Wild Animals, or some vagabond carves me up, remember me as fondly as I do you . . .

"December!" Mother cried the next morning. "I thought he said September!"

Masha had held off showing her the letter. There was no point in both of them fretting all night. Now they were heading out the door with Mariushka, who carried on the broad shelf of her hip the copper basin containing the sponge, soap and towels. At the sight of the hammock, Mother stopped. She'd walked right past it yesterday.

"Everywhere I look, I see Kolenka. My poor Kolenka."

Masha saw him too, his scarecrow body—sticks stuffed inside his clothes—his flat suffering face. With each cough, the hammock had swayed.

"Mariushka, is he in heaven?" Mother asked.

Mariushka, stumping down the steps, grunted that it was for God to decide, not her. She sounded dubious.

"They knocked down the nightingale nest," Masha said bitterly.

"And now Antonshevu's gone too. He told us he'd be back in September, not December. He never mentioned bears or Frenchmen with knives."

"Mamasha. Stop," Masha begged. "You're making it worse. Let's visit the grave when we're done bathing. You'll feel better then."

"I doubt that!"

The orchard was racketing with bees. As they walked through it, Masha remembered one of the few funny moments from the summer before. "The Artist," as Antosha had called Kolia, dozed on a rug; Mother, exhausted from nursing him, leaned back against a tree, chin wilting on her chest. While Masha sketched this pitiful scene, Georgi's playing filtered down from the house. Georgi was the youngest Lintvariov, Misha's age, a concert pianist then labouring over the dolorous second movement of Tchaikovsky's Piano Concerto No. 1. Along came Antosha with his fishing rod. At the sight of them he shouted, "Why hold back, Georgi? Let's have something *really* sad!"

In the bathhouse now, Mother stepped out of her drawers, then sat on the bench and picked them up with her toes. "You might have babies one day, Masha. Then you'll understand my loss."

"Might I?" Masha snapped. It enraged her when Mother said things like this. Did she think she was mooning around waiting for a man? And if one did come along, who would do the accounts, hire the servants and look after her and Father?

Mariushka slammed down the heavy basin and went to work on Mother's buttons. Masha took out her combs. She glanced at Mother's doughy body as, garment by garment shed, it was revealed. Fully dressed she looked thin, but her clothes hid flesh that had loosened with each child she'd borne. Seven, including their brief sister Evgenia.

Mother glanced down at herself just as Mariushka pulled out her hairpins. Braids tumbled down veined breasts. Mariushka dipped the sponge and squeezed it over her head. Mother looked so abject then, grey-haired, grey-skinned, naked and dripping, that Masha had to ask herself why anyone would want to be a mother.

What an ordeal to be bathed by Mariushka! Then, thoroughly soaped, blinded by the sting of it, savagely scrubbed, they felt their way out of the bathhouse and stepped into the wide green river to rinse.

KOLIA'S GRAVE WAS ON A HILL. THEY CLIMBED TO IT and, breathing hard, arranged their offerings before the wooden cross: sweets Mother had brought from Moscow, wildflowers Masha had gathered into a bouquet as ragged as her dead brother. They settled on their knees in the grass. *Lord, give rest to the souls of Thy departed servants in a place of brightness, a place of refreshment, a place of repose, where all sickness* frayed sheet torn into strips, then into squares *sighing, and sorrow have* bled into, burned. *Pardon every transgression which they have committed,* awful things he said at the end, *whether by word or deed or thought* lies. Took commissions, never finished. Drank the money. Shamed them. Antosha waking every pile of rags he found lying in the street searching for him. *For Thou art a good God and lovest mankind; because there is no man who lives yet does not sin.*

The tears came and they choked on them. Mother collapsed onto her side and howled. In the face of this animalistic display, Masha stopped weeping to comfort her. She remembered Mother bent over the cradle in Taganrog when Evgenia died, Masha eight years old, flinging herself across her back, wrapping her arms around her waist, rocking with the force of each howl. A lurching pony ride of grief.

Eventually, Mother quieted. They sat in silence, Masha wrung out too.

A range of timbered hills stretched to the right. To the left, beyond an expanse of fields, stood the village with its bulbed white church. Below, the Psiol flowed past a tumble-down mill, past the pits dug by potters, the red clay piled up on the banks like strange geological formations. Just the sort of view Antosha loved to get right on the page. The previous year, or the one before, Masha would have come back and tried to paint it.

Overhead, a circling hawk touched them with its shadow. Mother gasped and crossed herself. Even Masha shivered, though she didn't believe in omens. She helped Mother to her feet.

As they neared the dacha on their way back, they heard Georgi practising, the same minor phrase over and over. He was incapable of playing anything happy!

Masha said, "I'll go up and say hello."

Elena Lintvariova answered her knock. Both elder sisters were doctors, Elena the plainest one. They'd all inherited their philosophical mother's dark eyebrows, but Elena's face was long and earnest, pinched with worry for her patients, her sister Zinaida in particular. Zinaida was their household saint, blind from a brain tumour and in constant, unmentioned pain, yet carrying on—not just valiantly, but gaily, treating the peasants in their free clinic in the morning, then laughing on the terrace when they read out Antosha's stories in the evenings. By contrast, Elena seemed to have taken a vow never to smile.

She embraced Masha, then held her at arm's length to ask, "How are you?"

"Fine."

Elena saw through her. "And so will Antosha be."

Masha shook herself free. "How do you know?"

"The weather's an unknown, true. But he's a medical man."

Masha burst out with the bears and vagabonds, though she'd thought Mother hysterical for doing the same thing. "They're an unknown too. And how will being a doctor help against a bear? They don't ask your profession before they eat you."

In a soothing tone, Elena said, "You are so close. I understand. Mother and Zinaida are resting, but why don't you say hello to Georgi? You know where to find him."

Embarrassed now, Masha followed the music to the drawing room.

The Borzois were dozing under the piano as Georgi played, their wavy coats spread out like silken mats. Georgi had been cast in the family mould too, but he also resembled the dogs. Long nose, long waves of hair falling in his eyes, prettier than handsome, despite his attempts at a beard. The prettiest of the Lintvariovs, in fact—almost delicate compared to sturdy Natalia.

Georgi looked up then and saw her in the doorway. In the second that his eyes held hers, Masha noted ambivalence. Here was something she hadn't considered: If coming back revived for her and Mother the terrible memory of Kolia's death, wouldn't it do the same for the Lintvariovs? Perhaps they hadn't even wanted them here, but felt it would be a sin to refuse them.

She waited for Georgi to finish so she could say hello and leave. Lika came to mind then, playing *"Un petit verre de Clicquot"* that night and having no awareness of her effect. Masha noticed one in herself now, a decided lightening, as though there were homeo-pathic properties in a minor key. Or perhaps she simply wanted to get away from Mother. When Georgi reached the end of his piece, she asked if she could stay.

"That depends," he said.

"I'll be quiet."

One Lintvariov eyebrow rose. "Hang that. I want applause."

Thank God, someone with a sense of humour! She entered and collapsed on the divan.

So those sanity-preserving visits began on the first day.

MOTHER'S MEMORIES OF KOLIA WERE MATERNALLY DIS-torted. *He'd had the sweetest disposition.* (A happy drunk, in other words.) *He would have been a great artist.* (Had he bothered finishing his commissions.) At breakfast, Masha listened to her deluded prattle, waiting for the right moment to set down her coffee cup.

"Well, Mother. I think I'll go up to the house and see if the post has arrived."

"I hope Antonshevu has written us."

Masha wasn't only annoyed by Mother, she realized after a few days. She was angry. Angry at Kolia for how he'd wasted his life. And if she was angry at him, then her grief must be nearing its end, or one stage of it, at least. There was no room in her heart to grieve for him while she worried about Antosha. Where was he now? Was he keeping warm and dry? Were the people that he met honest, or the thieves and murderers that they feared?

If Georgi wasn't at the piano, Masha would usually find him wandering dreamily through the big, dusty house, playing the air, his untucked shirt billowing and a Borzoi or two stepping elegantly behind him.

"Oh, Masha," he'd say. "Thank you. Let's get to work, shall we?"

While Georgi played, Masha would look at the pictures. The landscapes were uninteresting, places without feeling, too dull to visit, or worse, idealistic scenes of peasant life. The portraits were better. There was a pleasant one of their father, his expression tinged with regret, as though he were apologizing for dying prematurely and dooming his family to the numberless ranks of half-broke gentry forced to rent to holidaymakers.

Georgi paused in his playing. "That's Papa."

"Yes." From what Natalia had told Masha, he was of a completely different species from theirs. The Lintvariovs were radicals; they, nothing. This was something for which Antosha was frequently criticized in the papers. He rejected all labels, was neither radical nor reactionary, but a writer and a doctor who happened to be in possession of a conscience.

Masha said, "He bests the priests."

"You mean the beard?" Georgi stroked his own wispy chin. "What do you think of mine?"

"The moustache is a success."

The eyebrow rose again, he with it. He went to the mirror, turned this way and that. After a minute of this, Masha clapped her hands.

"Back to work."

Georgi loved to be managed like this, differently than she managed Antosha. These were classroom methods. Beaming at her, he said, "You're saving me from myself, Masha."

An hour later—sometimes she lost track and it became two—
Masha returned to the dacha.

"It takes you long enough to check the post," Mother would tell
her. Then, noticing Masha's empty hands, she'd begin to wail. "Why
hasn't Antosha written?"

"I'm sure he has. We're just farther away."

"I'm worried about his health!"

Finally they did get a letter, written from the Volga steamer
he had boarded after the train. The best thing about the boat, he
reported, was the toilet raised like a throne. Too bad he was constipated and couldn't use it. But he'd slept "artistically" all night, and
his money was intact. The countryside would be pretty if the sun
would come out.

Constipated? This was so like him to focus on the trivial. His
life was in danger!

No word about when he was coming back.

SINCE THEY'D STARTED VISITING UKRAINE THREE YEARS
before, Antosha dreamed of buying an estate there. Last year a
landowning friend of the Lintvariovs, Aleksander Smagin, offered
to show him his. Antosha ended up visiting Smagin several times,
usually with Misha or Ivan. Though the trip took a full day, Smagin
would drive them back to Luka himself. Soon Natalia was teasing
Masha that she was the reason he kept coming.

"Just think, Masha. If you marry Smagin, your children will
turn out like this." She stuck her face into Masha's, crossed her
eyes and sang a rendition of Alabiev's "The Nightingale." "*Oh, my
nightingale, my cross-eyed nightingale!*"

She exaggerated. Smagin's eyes were only close-set. His moustache drew more ridicule. Behind his back, everyone called him the King of Persia.

The same day Georgi astonished Masha by shaving off his failed beard, the King of Persia showed up. Mrs. Lintvariova ushered him in wearing a wide, well-meaning smile. There it was, the coarse boot-brush fringe even more comical compared to the delicate feathering above Georgi's lip. Mrs. Lintvariova, buxom in her striped dress, gave Smagin an encouraging nod.

He smoothed the moustache and strode over, extending the same hand to Masha. His grip was moist. Mrs. Lintvariova invited him to sit—beside Masha! Thankfully he declined.

"After that long drive, I prefer to stand."

For several minutes Mrs. Lintvariova managed the small talk ineffectively. She was a great reader of Schopenhauer and liked to lead the conversation toward a ready quote.

"Well, Aleksander. We forfeit three-quarters of ourselves in order to be like other people, don't we?" She opened the French doors. "Where are the pigs?" she called, and the Borzois heaved themselves up in unison and tore outside. She stepped out after them, closing the doors behind her.

"She says such wonderful things," Smagin told Masha. "Yet I have no idea what they mean. I guess I'm simple. I'm just a farmer. How are you? It's been a year!"

Masha shot an entreating look at Georgi, who played on, seemingly oblivious to the visitor.

"You look so well," Smagin told her.

"Do I? I'm not, actually. You know Antosha's on his way to Siberia? The post is excruciatingly slow in bringing news. Mother and I are quite ill with worry."

Was the moustache false? A theatre prop? It had that look. He

kept patting at it as though it might come unglued. In her mind
Masha spun a scenario to write to Natalia. She'd say that it got
stuck on the bottom of his boot and that despite the whole house
pitching in to search, they couldn't find it.

"Your brother's a brave man, I'll give him that. Foolish perhaps.
I prefer to stay close to home. Yes, I'm a homebody. It's too bad you
never came visiting with Anton last year. It would have been my
great pleasure to show you around my estate."

Hands clasped behind his back, he began to pace. His breathing matched his heavy steps, air bristling through the moustache
as he waxed on—what he grew, the horses he owned. "All of them
named in honour of the royal family. Aleksander, after our beloved
Tsar, not me! He's an Arabian. Fifteen hands tall. Do you ride?"

"No." She sat up straight on the divan. Georgi, she realized, had
segued into "Nightingale."

"I have a Mikhail as well, an Olga, a Xenia . . ."

Georgi had been matching Smagin's pace, but now he sped up.
And Smagin did too, without realizing it.

"Anton is still interested in property, isn't he? Because an estate
has come up for sale. Quite close by. It would be convenient."

"Convenient?" After more than a week in a musician's company,
she heard the distressed tremolo in her own voice.

"For visiting." Back and forth, wiping the perspiration off the
boot brush, spurts of air quite voluble now. "Miss C.—?"

Masha would probably have screamed when that great body
landed beside her on the divan, but just then Georgi brought his fist
down on the keyboard. Smagin started. Masha jumped up.

"You scared her," she heard him tell Georgi as she fled the room.

Half the day passed before she dared creep around the house to
see if Aleksander III was still tethered in the waterlogged courtyard

developing hoof rot. She found Georgi writing a letter on the terrace in the cooling shadow of the linden tree. The heat, the scented
air, the linden's shimmering yellow starbursts. The hypnotic drone
of the bees. No wonder she sounded tipsy calling out, "Thank you
for Smagin!"

Georgi looked up. His smile had nothing on that morning's,
when she'd come into the drawing room to find he'd done away
with the ridiculous patches of beard she'd not-so-secretly detested.
"Surprise!" he'd called out before playing a merry little flourish on
the piano.

"I'm almost done," he said now, waving her over.

She took the chair across from him, watching as he blotted and
folded the letter and tucked it inside the envelope. All his movements were rhythmical, even the way he recoiled when he noticed
her arms.

"We went nettle picking," she said.

"It looks awful! Painful, I mean. I can't bear things that aren't
beautiful."

"Excuse me for offending your sensitive soul."

She yanked her sleeves over the blotches. Though a few days
ago she might have been offended, she was pretending now. They'd
assumed the same teasing rapport she had with Natalia. He'd
become his sister's substitute.

Just like his sister, he asked, "What are we going to do about
the King of Persia? He has it bad for you."

Masha groaned. "How did he know I was here?"

"Mother wrote to him. I told her not to."

"Oh Lord." Masha covered her face. "What if he comes back?"

"He will. Did Anton tell you? Last summer he mentioned
marriage."

She stared. "Smagin? When?"

"When we went to see him. He was dropping hints like mad. Anton was so funny about it. Ivan and I nearly split our trousers. Didn't he tell you?"

Some old bitterness reinsinuated itself. The bad taste of something previously swallowed filling her mouth. Isaac Levitan. Lieutenant Egorov.

"What did he say?"

"That there were a few things Smagin should know before he proposed."

"Such as?"

"You crack your knuckles at dinner, and you're addicted to whist."

She had to laugh. "The whist part is true."

"All this was discussed over vodka and Smagin's cucumbers. You'll *want* to marry him if you taste those cucumbers. Should I ask Mother to tell him to bring some?"

She slapped his hand. "What did Smagin say?"

"Nothing." Georgi's face clouded. "The telegram came. The one saying that Kolia had passed away."

It was the first time any of the Lintvariovs had spoken Kolia's name. The angel of silence swooped down. Masha heard the bees again, insistent in their pleasure, filling the void. Tears mustered.

"I'm sorry," Georgi said. "I shouldn't have brought him up."

"No. I'm glad you did. I wish I had my handkerchief."

He offered his with such a sympathetic expression that she almost heard Tchaikovsky playing out of his eyes. She buried her face. The cloth smelled of scorch from the iron.

"Why didn't we become friends before, Masha?"

She looked up. He wasn't teasing. Under the waves of hair, sincerity. "I guess you were either at the piano or running off with my brothers. And I had Natalia."

"I'm glad they're not—" A bee flew by. He jerked back. "—here now. I didn't want to go with him last year. I still feel bad about it. He practically made me."

Masha was still puzzling over his first statement. That he was glad it was only the two of them. "Who? Go where?"

"To Smagin's. Anton made me. Elena and Zinaida said Kolia was about to die. Anton had looked after him all those weeks. He must have known it too. But he took us off to Smagin's."

Now she stiffened defensively. She remembered the day. "Our brother Aleksander arrived. They often rub each other the wrong way."

"I'm not criticizing Anton. He's above reproach. I'm explaining myself."

"But you are criticizing him."

"I wish I hadn't mentioned it." Georgi ran a hand through his hair. "Will I make it worse if I tell you what else they said?"

How had the conversation soured so suddenly? They'd been enjoying themselves, and then the suitors Antosha had rejected came up, then Kolia. And now he was insulting her brother, who certainly *was* above reproach, except, perhaps, in the matter of suitors, if she was to be honest. But that was a bygone and pointless to brood about.

She balled up Georgi's handkerchief and tossed it on the table. "It's too late now, isn't it? Tell me."

"They said no doctor would want to see his brother die, particularly if they shared a disease."

Something broke inside her in that moment, a dam holding back their worst fear. Not bears and vagabonds, which lived in fairy tales, but that he would die the way Kolia had here at Luka. Bursting. A scarlet fountain. Blood everywhere. The handkerchief on the table slowly changed shape, unballing itself. She snatched it up as a sob escaped.

After a torrenting minute, she heard Georgi's chair scrape the stones. Then he was holding her, and she felt his softness through the linen of his shirt.

THAT NIGHT SHE TOSSED IN THE HEAT, UNABLE TO sleep. She kept thinking about her conversation with Georgi, the painful places he'd touched and the comfort he'd given.

Lieutenant Egorov. Georgi hadn't named him, of course. He didn't know about him.

That summer, when Masha was twenty, three officers used to visit, men who got on well with her brothers. Egorov was the only one she could still picture. He talked endlessly about resigning from the army and doing something useful instead. He came from the gentry and felt guilty for it. Every time he quaffed a drink, he'd say, "I'm not a good soldier. I'm not even good-looking."

About his soldiering abilities she was ignorant, but the latter was true. He shone with baldness, though his eyes were striking. He had a habit of looking straight at her, then blinking rapidly, as though he'd seen something astonishing. She was young enough then to find myopia flattering.

Once, in front of everyone, Egorov said, "Anton, your sister's so stern. Let's see if I can make her laugh. Come here, Maria. I want to show you something."

An arm around her shoulder, he brought his finger to her face, closer and closer until her eyes crossed. She thought there must have been some tiny speck on it that he wanted her to see. A freckle?

"What is it?" she asked.

"What is it? It's a finger!"

She did laugh then, along with everyone else. After that, every time she saw him, he'd hold up his finger and crook it, which quickly grew tiresome.

One day there was a party at one of the estates. They all went. Masha was depressed about something, so when the dancing began, she slipped into the library to read. Egorov came and found her.

"Here you are."

She refused to lift her face in case he showed her that finger of his and she had to throw the book at him. He started on again about giving up the army.

"What kind of work do you think would most suit a man like me?"

"I've no idea." She was pretending to be absorbed by the story. A window must have been open. She remembered the scent of lilacs in the room.

"If you do come up with something, would you let me know? And would you by any chance marry me?"

She looked up then. He was blinking fast. Taken aback, she could think of nothing to say but "Father's in Moscow working at the warehouse. You'll have to speak to my brother."

A smile spread over his face, reminding her of a baby playing Magpie. "Kolia?" he asked, Kolia being the eldest present.

"Anton." Kolia would marry her to a peddler if one happened by.

Egorov thanked her with a bow and hurried off, presumably to find Antosha. Once the surprise wore off, flattery took over. By the time she left the library, her blindsided heart was aflutter.

What happened after that, she never found out. Ever since, a

bad feeling attached itself to his name. She should have cleared
the matter up with Antosha years ago, but was too embarrassed.
Besides, if she did, there would be no feeling whatsoever.

She got up and went out to the veranda to cool off, pulling the
sheet off the bed as she went. What time was it? The moon told her
nothing. Georgi was still awake. She could hear him playing. What
had he meant when he said he was glad that the others weren't
there?

She settled in the hammock, shrouded in the linen sheet, listening to Georgi start and stop, rocking herself with one foot. Back
and forth. Her skin felt tacky, like the piano's notes were sticking to
it. Back and forth.

Eventually Georgi gave up and came out on the terrace and for a
long time stood in the moonlight, just like in one of Antosha's stories. So many moons to be gazed at. So many lonely, stifled people.
Was she seeing him or reading this? The orchard was laden now
with fruit. Yesterday Elena had asked Georgi to play a mazurka
that might scare off the birds.

Footsteps sounded on the path, or was she imagining it?

Back and forth. Did he know she was here?

She stopped rocking. Yes, he was beside her now. She sensed
his heat, smelled the dogs on his hands. Bending over her, close
enough that the loose fabric of his shirt brushed her face, he whispered, *You're dreaming, Masha.*

BY THEN LUKA SEEMED ITSELF AGAIN, LIKE THE FIRST
summer they came. A family of ducks moved into the courtyard
puddle, making it a pond. Masha preferred a neglected garden, she
realized, and dragged a chair out to sketch it.

The thorn had been extracted, the poison drained. They had not loved Kolia enough. He'd been too hard to love. She put her guilt away and seated herself on the chair, her sketchbook in her lap. With her penknife, she sharpened the pencil. Then left it all—pencil, knife, book and shavings—on the chair and went to find Georgi.

Lately he'd begun confiding in her, telling her about life with the perfect Lintvariovs. How they were all so passionately *good*. Except him.

Today when he brought this up, Masha turned her book face down on the divan to keep the place. "You're a good person, Georgi."

He gestured out the window. "Masha, I can't go down there."

To the dacha, he meant. The day Kolia died, after the servants had scrubbed it out, Georgi had met one of them coming up from the river. Bad luck if a woman approaches carrying an empty bucket.

"I almost turned and ran. Then I saw it was full of water. They were washing Kolia away, and I'd never even gone to sit with him. So you see, I'm a terrible selfish person, as well as a superstitious one."

Just then Mother called from outside, more than annoyed that Masha had left her alone again. Masha said goodbye.

The next day Georgi interrupted his playing to resume the conversation. He seemed to want reassurance, or absolution. He often felt trapped in the house, he told her. If he tried to leave by one door, he'd meet a line of scrofular peasants waiting to see the free doctors, Elena and Zinaida.

"But if I go out the back? I walk right into the Ukrainiac's schoolroom."

Natalia's nickname. She not only spoke Ukrainian, but ran an illegal school teaching local girls to read and write it.

"A dozen little girls with lousy braids staring in bewilderment at their slates. The truth is . . . Do you want the truth, Masha?"

"Yes!"

"All I care about is Art. That's it. The rest of it? Humanity, I mean. The sick and the illiterate? Even the do-gooders some-times—they rather turn my stomach."

She was sitting beside him at the piano so they could whisper, because who knew when Mrs. Lintvariova or his sisters would walk in? Masha would have done what she did next if Antosha or Misha had offered her such a pained confession—consoled them with a peck on the cheek. Except when she did, Georgi turned his head, and the kiss landed on the feathery corner of his mouth.

"Did you just try to kiss me, Masha?"

Masha felt like Mother in the bathhouse, doused not with water, but with a scalding embarrassment. But then he laughed and played his merry little flourish and put things right again.

"What was I saying?" And they drifted on to another subject.

Later that evening, sitting on the veranda steps waiting for Georgi to play, she thought of "The Kiss." The story of Antosha's that Lika had gushed over. The twerpish army officer kissed by a strange woman in the dark. How madly and tragically in love with her he falls, despite the fact he never finds out who she is.

Georgi was probably still dining. What were they talking about? Did he ever mention her?

A persevering nightingale kept insinuating itself into her thoughts, the homeless one perhaps, putting voice to its justified grievance. Mother was inside squinting under the lamp, sewing Masha a new summer dress. The feathery feel of his moustache against her lips . . .

Such a call that bird made! Patternless trills and cheeps and whistles. It seemed utterly confused.

MASHA KEPT EXPECTING SMAGIN TO RETURN. MRS. LINT-variova had probably written him an encouraging letter with a luring, enigmatic closing. *As you know, Aleksander, the two enemies of human happiness are pain and boredom. Come and visit!*

But he didn't. Instead Mrs. Lintvariova began to greet Masha with a new warmth and a lift of her significant brows. Good to see you're cheering up now, Masha, she seemed to be saying. You didn't need that old Smagin after all! Once she popped her head in the door of the drawing room and declared, "Oh! I'll leave you two alone." Meaning, Masha assumed, *Georgi's taking care of you.* She even invited Mother to tea.

"Have you heard of Schopenhauer?" Masha asked Mother before she went.

"That German who worked with Father at the warehouse?"

She was gone an hour. Afterward, Masha asked what they'd talked about.

"Georgi."

"What about Georgi?"

"Oh, I don't know. I was hardly listening." She hardly seemed to be now as she peered at her sewing.

"I suppose he's not contributing enough to society, in her opinion. But you know, Mother, he's a brilliant pianist. Everything he has, he gives to his music. Not every artist—few, in fact—are like Antosha."

"What do you mean?" Mother asked.

"Antosha's a doctor as well as an artist. Medicine is socially useful. And now with this trip—well, he's practically the saviour of humanity, isn't he?"

"I'm so worried about Antonshevu," Mother said, dropping her work in her lap.

"I am too. But Mrs. Lintvariova should let Georgi be himself. They all should."

ELENA NEVER STOPPED WORKING, BUT ZINAIDA HAD TO because of her headaches. She would dose herself with morphine and lie down with Mrs. Lintvariova. Afterward, too groggy to see patients, she would come and listen to Georgi.

They all doted on their blind sister. If there was something amiss in her appearance, a crumb on her face or a button missed, one of them would hurry to fix it, signalling to another to distract Zinaida, so she wouldn't realize a correction was being made. Whenever she appeared in the drawing room, Georgi immediately softened his playing. He'd instructed Masha not to help her, but to say her name or make a sound so that she could orient herself and cross the room independently. This Zinaida did like a sleep-walker, tentatively, with arms outstretched. Settling beside Masha, she would turn her head and smile. It was easy to forget she was blind because the problem was in her brain, not her eyes. But her gaze didn't quite line up with Masha's; she always seemed to be looking *into* instead of *at* her, looking all the way into Masha's jumbled heart.

One day, discussing the motives for Antosha's trip, Zinaida said, "When I hear his stories, I sense such compassion. That kind of compassion comes only with a deep knowledge of human suffering. I don't know how he possesses this knowledge, but it seems to be drawing him now to the place where suffering is the greatest."

"Yes," Masha said. Olga had said something similar.

Because of the morphine, Zinaida often leapfrogged in conversations. Next she said, "We heard he got engaged."

"Antosha engaged? No."

Georgi looked over. "We got a letter from Natalia yesterday. It's the rumour all over Moscow."

Masha snorted. "I think I know the source of those rumours."

Lika. Masha pictured her on the platform, Antosha reading out the joke inscription on the back of his photograph. *P.S. This gift obliges me to nothing.* He couldn't have made it plainer, yet Lika still hadn't understood his meaning, the way Ekaterina hadn't when she received her beetle by post. Or Dunia.

How angry Masha had been that day at the station. Why? Lika was just another young woman infatuated with her brother. She should pity, not resent her. Masha had introduced the two of them. She'd have to make up to Lika when they met again in September. Make up for Lika's disappointment and Masha's bad mood that day.

Zinaida rubbed her temple. Again *apropos* of nothing, she remarked, "Masha, you seem so pretty and gay these days."

Pretty? An odd thing for a blind woman to say.

FINALLY, ANOTHER LETTER. IT DESCRIBED ANTOSHA'S trip down the Kama River and how, though the ice had broken up, the countryside was still in the thrall of winter, trees bare, the ground brown and barren. Too rainy and cold to stay up on deck. *I plead for you not to worry about me and not to imagine dangers that do not exist.*

Yet he used two dangerous words: *cold* and *wet*. He was only a month into a two-month voyage. And when he finally arrived on Sakhalin Island, what crude conditions would he find? What horrors? And still no mention of when he was coming home. In all of

his few-and-far-between missives, Masha and Mother had waited
for the September-or-December confusion to be cleared up. Now
Masha realized there was no confusion. He'd simply lied to them.

All that day and the next, she was furious, as much over
Antosha's risk-taking as his patronizing falsehood. Did he think
this would make his absence easier? The heart does not consult the
calendar! And come September, what then? They would be hysterical with worry over him and *les Messieurs*, human and animal.

Georgi invited her rowing. She was still suffering the after-
effects of her mood, yet she accepted. His company was her only
respite from worry.

They piled shoes and stockings in the bottom of the boat and
pushed it through the reedy shallows. The boat nearly tipped as
they climbed in; Masha fell forward, causing Georgi to whoop.

Infant, she thought. Tucking up her skirt had been an ineffect-
ive precaution, for it was half-drenched now. As soon as she was
safely seated, she wrung it and spread it out to dry.

Georgi took up the oars. "You've got legs like your brothers."

It took her a moment to realize what he meant. He had three
sisters, yet her legs, far from hairless, weren't like theirs. Unlike when
he commented on her arms, she was insulted. Worse, she had to
stew in the offence while she waited for a discreet moment to tuck
her legs back under her wet skirt.

She stared down at the water, at the turquoise of a different
sky, the one below them with its own clouds and birds. A man with
a fishing rod came along in a dugout. They passed the place on
the bank where two years before she'd sat at her easel stippling the
grey-green of the far bank, the willows leaning down to drink. A
view with which she and Georgi were now one.

He tossed back his hair, yawned. "Excuse me. We had a medical emergency at first light. Then that's all they talked about at break-fast. How they make me suffer."

She seized this opportunity to yank down her skirt. "Do you ever consider that your sisters suffer living with you?"

Perhaps she'd spoken sharply, for now *he* took offence, or his eyebrows did, dropping halfway down his face.

"Because you're an artist," she added.

The glower melted. He was flattered now. "What do you mean?"

"Antosha the writer hurts me more than Antosha the doctor."

"How?"

"A doctor keeps hours. A patient rings at the door. We know not to disturb him. But the writer's hours are a mystery even to him. He'll be sitting with us, enjoying himself, or so we think, until he stands up and walks out without a word. He wasn't really there. Psychic blindness, it's called. Off he goes to jot something down."

A mosquito came to listen. She grabbed it in her fist.

"Then there are the fawning visitors whose fawning conversa-tions we all have to endure." Not their parties, which she enjoyed. She meant the drop-ins. "Antosha can't stand to be fawned over, yet these people call any time and eat and drink at his expense and then won't leave. Antosha can't write and is irritable the next day. Irritable with us."

A smear of blood in her palm. It brought out the deceased's relatives.

"And he explains nothing. Nothing! He can't say, 'Sister, I'm thinking. I'm on the brink of something here.' No, he just winces, meaning literature will be forever impoverished because I knocked on his door to tell him dinner was served."

She already regretted her outburst, yet kept rolling downhill with it. But wasn't this what Georgi had been doing, complaining about his family? It didn't mean she was disloyal, or didn't love them.

"Why Sakhalin Island? He gave us such insincere excuses. Why did he leave? The mosquitoes are eating me alive."

"Isn't he writing some kind of treatise?"

She slapped the one feasting on her neck. When she faced Georgi again, she saw he was looking at her with a peculiar, disarming intensity. Her temper evaporated. He tucked the oars under his arms and beckoned to her.

Something happened then. Despite the fact that Georgi had stopped rowing, that they were now floating along on the current's sluggish whim, the boat rocked. She clutched its sides. No, it was her heart, that caged thing his blind sister had peered into, lurching to life inside her, desperate to satisfy its deferred necessities. Georgi leaned in with puckered lips, and she felt herself falling forward to meet him. Falling with closed eyes.

He blew into her face. One sharp puff. His breath stank of tea.

Her eyes flew open as though he'd slapped her.

"You had an eyelash on your cheek. And don't dare ask me what I wished for. It won't come true then."

Apparently he took up the oars again and resumed rowing, for soon they reached the romantic old mill. Masha just sat there, an arm's length away, heart unstilled, actually raging now, her idiotic lips still parted, unnoticed by Georgi, who was looking over his shoulder, leaning forward and back as he rowed.

Was he mocking her? Forward and back. *Were you trying to kiss me, Masha?*

"Take me home," she told him.

"Why? We just set out."

"Take me now." She gripped the sides of the boat and made to stand.

"Don't!" he shrieked. "We'll tip. I have my watch."

Georgi turned the boat around. After three strokes, Masha saw she wouldn't drown if she took a chance. She lifted one leg over, then the other, and plunged in nearly to her waist while Georgi screeched and scrambled to stabilize the boat.

What a mistake. The mucky bottom suctioned her in place, her skirt blooming on the surface like a grotesque water lily. Georgi watched her struggle.

"Masha, what's this about? Oh Lord!" He heaved a sigh. "So Elena was right?"

She grabbed handfuls of reeds, trying to haul herself up the bank. Half of them uprooted, and she stumbled backwards. Mosquitoes needled into her. She had no idea what he meant about Elena.

"I do love you, Masha. Like a sister."

Finally she got enough purchase to stagger up the bank, flushing a pair of jeering blackbirds. She swung around to face Georgi, who was working the oars to keep the boat stationary.

"What are you talking about?"

"The look on your face when I made that wish. Even Zinaida noticed how you hang around. And Mama's been encouraging you. She's such a matchmaker. It's that damn Schopenhauer perfect-complement-of-the-other nonsense. Natalia was reading Marx before she went to Moscow. I begged her to leave Marx and get Schopenhauer out of the house. What, Masha? I enjoy your company. I told you that I do. I just don't want a misunderstanding. I wish Natalia was here."

"I'm hanging around because I'm bored! I have nothing to do! My mother is irritating, and I'm worried about Antosha! I don't love you!"

"That's wonderful, Masha!" Georgi said. "We don't love each other!"

She started walking away, hobbled by her wet skirt pasted to her hairy legs. Georgi followed in the rowboat, moving against the current now, slower than before.

"Let's not spoil anything with broken hearts," he said, falling behind.

She did not turn back.

The last thing he called out was "Do you want your shoes?"

Masha made it back to Luka before him. She knew he wouldn't come down to see her in the dacha. He was afraid to.

Her crying jags resumed.

It really was odd what Antosha did in "The Kiss." He inserted, in parentheses, a doctor's aside: (*physicians call this condition, when someone sees without understanding, 'psychic blindness.'*)

Mrs. Lintvariova popping her head in the door. Dark brows lifting, her encouraging smile. *I'll leave you two alone.*

Stop going up there all the time, Mother had said. *You're making a fool of yourself.*

8

W HAT A DISASTER—HOW SHE'D HUMILIATED
herself in the rowboat, then her awful mood when
she and Natalia went to Yalta. Antosha had given
her the money for the holiday, so added to everything else, Masha
felt guilty for misspending it.

Yet if she'd gone alone instead of with Natalia, Masha probably
would have recovered. Instead, no amount of bathing and prom-
enading could cure her when every morning she saw Georgi's likeness across the breakfast table. Georgi, Georgi, Georgi. The magic
lantern show of tormenting images began again: Georgi waiting to
surprise her with his beardless face, Georgi parading in his poetical
shirt, Georgi in the rowboat.

"Masha?" Natalia had said. "How nice it would be to see a smile
one of these mornings instead of *this*." And she put on her cross-
eyed Smagin face, but with an ugly down-twisted mouth.

The entire trip Natalia kept waxing on about her new baby
niece. Such a good sleeper! She could already hold up her head!
Hardly traits to brag about, thought Masha, who daily expected a
fond description of the contents of the infant's nappy.

"I didn't think I even liked babies," Natalia said one afternoon
while they waded in their bathing costumes. "Do you want babies,
Masha?"

Mother had annoyed her on the same subject in the bathhouse
at Luka. Masha pictured Mother's pendant breasts, like a pair of

Easter cheeses draining into a basin. Something else to look forward to.

"Babies with whom?" she snapped at Natalia. Then she stomped off, or tried to. Stomping is impossible in water. She flung herself under the waves and prayed she'd drown.

Had she wanted to marry Georgi and have his babies? She burst back up for air, humiliated, hair like seaweed.

By the end of the vacation, Natalia was showing up at breakfast with *The Communist Manifesto*. Instead of greeting Masha, she'd slap down the book, flip it open and begin furiously to read.

ON MASHA'S RETURN TO MOSCOW, SHE DISCOVERED that Mother and Father, in their ineptitude, had rented a horrible, buggy flat. Every night, they spread themselves out in their beds, fare for the feast. It fell to Masha to find somewhere more habitable to live. Antosha should have reached Sakhalin Island by then, but how could they know? Until his homeward journey, there would be no more letters.

Now she missed him more than ever. So desperate was she that even old news would console her.

She thought of Olga first. Antosha had written in an early letter that after the rest of the farewell party had disembarked, Olga had stayed on the train like those wretched women who follow their husbands into exile. Easy to picture the two of them—stubborn, unkempt Olga puffing away, filling the compartment with smoke, arguing with Antosha, who would enjoy her company for three stations, then begin coughing out of desperation. She could go see Olga and find out how he'd seemed. Except that Olga would question her about her summer and, sniffing out her humiliation, mock her. Why wouldn't she? Masha had spared her no sympathy over Antosha.

Was Georgi mocking Masha to his sisters now? Natalia must have complained about her. She imagined Georgi countering, *But did you have to fend off her repulsive kisses the way I did?*

In the end Masha didn't seek out Olga, not out of fear that she would dig, but because she realized she couldn't trust *herself* not to bring up Georgi. *Natalia's brother? Fancies himself Tchaikovsky's ultimate interpreter . . .*

"Georgi, Georgi, Georgi," Mariushka had grumbled one night as she cleared away the plates.

The other friend Antosha had mentioned was Lika. *I must be in love with Jamais since I dreamt of her again last night.* Perhaps he'd been writing to her. But Masha had been rude to Lika and couldn't face her, not while she felt so miserable. She'd wait until school started. She longed for school—the distraction of work and the relief of seeing those rows of girls like sunflowers open to the world.

Sunflowers before they go to seed, heads dried up and bowed in submission.

The house Masha eventually rented was on Little Dmitrovka Street. Little street, little yellow house. If they'd previously inhabited a chest of drawers, this one was a jewellery box, a half hour's walk along the Garden Ring Road. No separate parlour, but if they called the room a "dining parlour," they might get used to it. When they first moved to Moscow all those years ago, they'd squeezed five unhappy bodies into two damp-walled basement rooms. Until Antosha returned, if he ever did, they were only three. Misha had found his own accommodation and a job as a tax inspector.

They let go the piano, stored some furniture, crammed in the rest. Soon after the move, the big-eared, big-mouthed little brother dropped by to inspect the new nest and regale Masha with all the gossip.

"Guess who's been escorting Lika the Beautiful all summer?"

He had!

"Well, not just me. She's in thick with Sophia's crowd now."

Sophia K., Isaac Levitan's lover? Masha pictured Sophia in the chest of drawers before Antosha went away, a raven in gypsy costume gushing over the men. The long cigarette holder she used as a pointer.

"Lika goes to all the salons," Misha said.

On the first day of school, Lika wasn't at assembly. Masha went to the office to find out what had happened to her. The headmistress must have thought that Masha had come to demand the previous term's unpaid wages, for she backed away like a cornered mouse. She was happy to give out Lika's address.

Masha went around after school. The flat was on the third floor of a building that smelled of cat. Granny answered her knock, bewhiskered and pale with powder, peering suspiciously at Masha until she identified herself. Then she blossomed with friendliness.

"The writer's sister?"

"Yes."

Whenever Lika had talked about Granny, or acted out their arguments, she put on comical voices. Granny came across as dotty. But Masha saw now that Lika's impersonations were unfair. The old woman was clear-eyed and well-spoken, her posture as erect as a ballerina's.

"Lika is out with Sophia," she told Masha. "Do you know this Sophia person?"

"I've met her."

"Will you come in?"

"I can't, thank you. I work with Lika at the Dairy School."

"She quit." Granny's lips tightened briefly in her floury face. "Your brother's still away, yes? When do you expect him back?"

"We're not sure. December, we hope."

"He's a first-class person."

Masha got a strong whiff of matchmaking and stepped away.

Granny said, "Please. May I ask you something? What do you think of Lika? You're her friend."

"She's very pretty."

Wrong answer. Granny threw up her hands. "If only she wasn't. It's the least of her merits, but the one that gets the most attention. Lika has a kind and generous heart. She wouldn't refuse anyone. Wouldn't hurt a soul. May I beg a favour? Since I can't seem to stop her from flitting off, would you watch out for her? Her type is so easily taken advantage of."

"Of course," Masha said. "May I leave a note?"

COME TOMORROW! LIKA WROTE BACK, AND THIS TIME, Sophia answered the door in another florid dress, the long amber holder in her teeth. She recognized Masha and lunged to shake her hand.

"Masha! What news have you of your brave, brave brother, that genius?"

Lika came up behind Sophia. There was something different about her, Masha noticed at once. Something unfluttery, despite her dove-coloured dress. Lika had gained confidence running with the arty set all summer, while Masha had lost heart.

Masha answered Sophia. "We haven't heard anything. There's no post."

"But he arrived safely?" Sophia took a long drag. "I read that piece of his in *New Times*." She flicked her wrist and released a smoky ejaculation. "My God! Levitan says he just can't see it, Russia's greatest writer wearing the same trousers day after day. Anyway, I'm leaving. Come to the salon on Wednesday. Levitan praises your painting. Please bring one."

"She has a pet crane," Lika said. "Grus-grus."

Sophia flung her shawl around Lika's shoulder, taking her under her embroidered wing. "Isn't Mizanova gorgeous? And she sings like a bird. We're all mad for her, simply mad. Hopefully Lensky will turn up. You know him? From the Maly Theatre. We must get her on the stage. It's criminal that she's not there."

They kissed goodbye, and Sophia departed, trailing smoke. Lika beckoned Masha to the parlour.

"I'm so happy to see you."

A grand piano took up most of the room. Scattered around its feet was sheet music, and on the lid, strewn petals from a half-dead bouquet. Ash-and-crumb–covered plates were piled around the samovar. All this sloppiness, yet her person was perfect and neat.

"I've begun playing the piano again, thanks to you. Remember you made me play that night?"

The night her ring scratched Antosha's nose. Masha did remember. Lika had hesitated, yet everyone in the room who wasn't already in love with her was after "*Un petit verre de Clicquot.*"

"Sit, please." Lika went over to the samovar to pour the tea. "I hadn't touched the keys since Granny and I came to Moscow."

Masha sat stiffly on the divan. Piano talk reminded her of Georgi. Georgi, Georgi, Georgi. Would he never be ousted from her thoughts?

"Mother used to have parties and get me to play for her friends. I hated it. Sugar?" She used the tongs for Masha, then scooped a handful of nuggets, popping one in her mouth and the rest in her glass. She settled beside Masha, crunching the sugar in her teeth.

"How was your summer? I guess you know I quit the Dairy School. I'm applying for a job at the town council instead."

"What about your acting?"

Her shoulders sank with the sigh. "I think I'd do better singing. With the stage fright, I mean. For some reason my mind goes blank if I have to speak, but not when I sing. Will you come to Sophia's? You should see their flat. One room's draped all over like a harem. The sofas are crates covered in rugs, but you'd swear they were Turkish. She's so clever."

Masha sipped the too-sweet tea. "I need a new coat. Maybe I'll just wrap myself up in an old curtain like she does."

Lika shifted very slightly away from Masha's rudeness. Mother always complained that Masha never apologized, only excused herself, which wasn't the same. Antosha never apologized either, but he was immune from maternal disapproval. Now Masha turned her glass around in her hand and, instead of taking back her words, thought of Georgi. Really, it was a form of madness. She'd never forgive herself if she ended up snivelling among Lika's ashes and petals and crumbs. Meanwhile, she could feel those questioning five-kopek eyes on her.

"Are you still angry with me?" Lika asked.

"Why would I be angry?"

"You seemed so the day Antosha left. I wasn't sure what I'd done. Whatever it was, I'm sorry. I suppose Misha told you I've been running around with him. We're just friends."

"I wasn't angry with you," Masha told her. "I didn't want Antosha to go, that's all. And I don't care what you get up to with

Misha." But saying it, she did sound angry, even to herself. What was she doing here?

"After Antosha left, I cried for a week. I only let Misha drag me out because I wanted to hear about Antosha. He never shuts up about him. He hates that Antosha won't praise his stories."

"It's just brotherly rivalry. They'd do anything for each other."

Lika sighed again, precipitating an awkward silence, while Masha thought of Georgi. Maybe she should kill herself.

"How's your funny father?" Lika asked.

Masha looked at her. "Funny?"

"I think he is." She set her glass on the table. "Masha, what's wrong? You seem crushed."

This was why she'd come. She lowered her gaze to say it. "An awful thing happened." When Masha looked up, Lika had paled.

"To Antosha?"

"No," Masha said. "Me."

Emotion swamped her. When Lika pulled the glass out of her hand and hugged her, Masha imagined Georgi's arms, the rise and fall of his chest. He'd blown his tea breath in her face and made a wish on her eyelash. For what? How wonderful that they didn't love each other! What a fool she was.

"Did he make promises?" Lika asked.

Of course, she guessed it was a man. Masha must have looked boiled when she untangled herself from Lika's embrace. "No."

Lika only made everything worse then, shifting and bobbing her head, trying to insinuate her sympathy into Masha's sights.

"I can't speak about it," Masha told her. "I wish I hadn't mentioned it. Let's drop it."

"So it was bad." Lika stopped trying to force eye contact and hugged herself instead. "It only hurts that much the first time."

Falling in love, Masha thought she meant.

Lika rose and went over to the piano. No, no, no, Masha thought, but predictably, she began to play something horribly sad. *Why hold back, Lika?* She played with feeling, swaying and dipping her blond head. If not for Georgi, who also spoke through music, Masha would have found Lika's performance overblown, especially when she abruptly closed the fallboard. Petals from the vase rained onto the lid. Elbows propping her up, she hid her face. "And yet we run after them," she said.

"I didn't."

Lika turned a contorted face to Masha. "Worse, then. Did you even know him?"

Confusion descended on Masha, confusion as to what they were actually talking about. They stared at each other, Lika twisted on the piano stool. Gradually her expression changed. She folded it up and put it away.

"You must miss Antosha terribly," she said.

DID YOU EVEN KNOW HIM?

There were times, despite growing up with five brothers, that Masha felt terribly naive. She used to overhear their sniggering and, not understanding, bristle with indignation. They meant to keep her ignorant.

Lika thought Masha had slept with Georgi, that was clear. Later that evening, she recalled the moment and let out a sour laugh, causing Mother to look up from the letter she was writing. They were both sitting at the dining table, Masha correcting her girls' first compositions.

She was sensibly chaste. Why take a risk? They'd suffered

enough ignominy with Father's bankruptcy and Kolia's drunkenness. Aleksander was alcoholic too, but a functioning one. He could hold a job, though not his temper. What would the papers say about Antosha if his sister disgraced herself?

She certainly would have kissed Georgi, had he taken the initiative. Thinking about it (continuously) was uncomfortably pleasurable. Throbbing beads of sensation she yearned to press and rub even now. But that was madness, or would lead to it.

"What are you sighing about?" Mother asked.

Masha smacked the pile of papers before her. "My pupils. They're hopeless. Isn't it cold in here? Did Mariushka light the fire? What a drafty place we've moved to."

She rose and went off rubbing her arms, a ruse to get away. But it reminded her of how Lika had hugged herself earlier that day, and at other times too. When she talked about her mother having lovers, for instance.

Things happened to girls. In Taganrog, convict gangs were sent out as dogcatchers. They grabbed the curs with hooks, then beat them to death.

"That would be preferable," Mother had warned her, "to what would happen should some man catch you on your own."

MASHA DID GO TO SOPHIA'S SALON, WITH MISHA. SOPHIA and her husband, a police doctor, lived in a precinct watchtower on the edge of a slum where the flophouses and brothels serviced the open-air labour exchange. The sort of neighbourhood they'd lived in when they first arrived in Moscow. Dr. K. tended to the district's unending stream of crime victims.

They took a cab. On the way, Misha recounted a long, boring story about once having his coat stolen in a local den of iniquity.

Masha only half listened between thoughts of Georgi. It was dusk, and the bells were ringing for evening service. They passed the square where the jobless were still milling, smoking and talking in listless groups.

"Careful," the driver told them as they climbed out of the cab. "You're right in front of the police station, and still they'll rob you blind."

Sure enough, a man staggered over to accost them. But he was only begging. He could have been Kolia, Masha thought. They turned their backs.

Sophia answered the door in a black dress brightened by a wide crimson sash and ropes of coloured wooden beads. "How exquisite that you came!" She shook Misha's hand, then Masha's. "Did you bring something to show, Masha? Yes?"

Masha had not.

"You're like your brother. Anton, I mean. Not this one." She poked Misha's arm, which he took as encouragement to reach into his coat and pull out a roll of pages.

He waved them. "A new story. Finished today. I'm ready to read."

"See?" Sophia told Masha. "Anton we have to beg and beg."

She stepped aside to let them in. Masha started, for just behind stood the crane. As tall as Sophia's hip, it was grey with black and white flourishes. The featherless patch on its head matched her sash. Its amber eyes scrutinized them as Sophia had. Then the crimson patch began to bob.

"Look, Masha. Grus-grus likes you. Of course, she generally likes who I like."

They followed Sophia up the stairs, her velvet skirt swaying, Grus-grus stepping woodenly behind her, jerkily lifting stick legs and hopping.

The room they entered first was as Lika had described, tented with tacked-up fabric and hung with Sophia's paintings and sketches—quite good. She would have to be to consort with Isaac. A folksy miscellany hung on the walls: Oriental parasols, bast shoes, even a rusted sickle.

A spiralling iron staircase took them to the next level in the tower. This room was larger and even smokier, crowded with guests. A table covered with a rug stood in the centre with an album lying open on it.

"Masha, please. Bring your spirit and artistry to this altar of the muses. Draw something. Or write. And we'll want to hear your brother's news."

"There is no news," Masha said.

"Oh, look! Lensky's arrived. Where's our Lika?" Sophia rushed off to greet the Maly director.

Misha had fallen behind, probably waylaid by someone he knew, despite promising to stay with her. Masha turned a few pages of the album. Sketches, poems. A pastel caricature of Sophia in evening dress, hair a black meringue of curls. Pressed flowers fell out. Sophia and Isaac went on painting excursions along the Volga River every summer. Did the husband know about their affair? Masha glanced around, trying to spot him. The fat, pouch-eyed man Sophia was fawning over was Aleksander Lensky. And there was Isaac, pontificating. He hadn't seen her yet. No Misha. She gave up and took a seat on one of the clever sofas and wished she were dead.

Sophia lauded each arrival, then moved through the room, cigarette first, offering unctuous seconds of praise. Now and then Grus-grus pecked and had to be reprimanded. A man with pheasant tiepin and dandruff came over and asked if she was Antosha's sister. He was standing, Masha sitting. The view up his nostrils was to a void. He'd been to the house; Masha remembered the pin. It struck her that ninety-nine out of a hundred men had no brains.

"Any news?" he asked before calling to someone. "Anton's sister is here!"

Anton's sister. Her great claim to fame, the only reason she'd been invited, and presumably why Georgi had even tolerated her presence. There was something she could write in Sophia's album: *The great writer's sister came tonight. Felt like a dolt. Left.*

Masha didn't notice Lika until her admirers thinned enough for them to spot each other. She waved and came right over, holding a cigarette. Masha pointed out Lensky.

"There's your future director."

Lika shrugged. "I got on at council. I just found out this morning." She took a drag on the cigarette, which made her look worldly. Masha remembered the shy flapping girl in their parlour, flying across the room to greet Antosha. A woman now. And look at the admired hostess from that night, cowering on a tea crate covered with a tattered Turkish rug. A furnishing fit to spark another Crusade.

"When did you start smoking?" Masha asked.

"It seemed a prerequisite. And Antosha? Still no news?"

If only everyone would stop asking! Thankfully the party reached the saturation point for arty argument, and the entertainment began.

First to play was a flautist. Grus-grus began to dance, and everyone pressed the walls to make room. She stretched out her wings, flapped, hopped, croaked. Her feathery bustle shook. There seemed something obscene about a wild creature dancing uncoerced in a smoke-choked room. She simply danced. Her true nature had been destroyed, and they watched it as entertainment, like they might watch dancers in a brothel.

"Brava, Grus-grus!" Sophia cried, leading the applause.

A melancholy cellist played next; the crane ignored him. Lensky recited a passage from *Richard II*, bare cheeks jiggling as he intoned. Then Lika sat at the piano. Masha really couldn't stand it a moment longer. Was she to go through life avoiding pianos? Almost everyone had one. She spotted Misha, sprang up and went to him.

"We can't go now," he told her. "It would be rude."

Lika played and unintentionally made herself a dozen more admirers. After that, the artists were supposed to place their work on one of the easels set up around the room and lecture on its significance. Or they could draw something on the spot. Isaac stepped forward; he would do the impossible and draw a portrait *by feel*.

Laughter and scoffing while Sophia produced one of her bright kerchiefs, blindfolded him and set him fumbling among the guests. Unsurprisingly, his hand fell on Lika. He could probably see through the weave of the fabric.

A circle formed around them, Lika stiff with embarrassment while Isaac's hands explored her face. Eventually Sophia gave an uncomfortable laugh and, pulling him off her protégée, put a stick of charcoal in his hand.

"The book is here, Levitan." She led him to it. "Ladies and gentlemen! Gather round!"

Before they could, the doors to the dining room swung open on a burly man with a goatee like grey moss hanging from his chin. He held a knife and fork. "Ladies and gentlemen? Refreshments are served."

Sophia rushed over, took his face in her hands. "Friends, just look at this man's face. So kind and expressive. Oh, my darling!" She kissed him, then they all stampeded into the dining room.

Masha grabbed the little brother by the arm.

"Why did you come if you didn't want to stay?" Misha grumbled as they started down the iron spiral. "I'm starving. They put on an amazing spread. Oysters and caviar. I don't know how. What does a police doctor earn? It can't be much."

They stepped into the gloom and set off in search of a cab, passing clusters of indigents on the way, menacing in the half-light. One ruffian turned and boldly stared; Misha gripped her arm and picked up his pace.

"Do cabs even come down here?" he asked. Ahead, light from a pub divided into six panes. It stretched across the pavement. Carousing inside. "Shit. I just stepped in some."

Then a drunk fell out the door, stiff as a plank, and landed in front of them, feet still inside. An eddy of dirt and fallen leaves swirled around his head. Misha steered her roughly around him.

"I wanted to read my story. It's as good as anything *he's* ever written."

Masha's feet turned to stone and stopped her. "Maybe you don't remember what happened in Taganrog."

"What are you talking about?"

"Fine. You were only six. But surely you remember who paid your school fees and your university fees at the cost of his own health. If you're so talented, go back and read out your precious story. Then repay your brother for all he's done for you."

The pince-nez lifted. It took him a moment to think of a retort. "Do you think you'd arrive home intact?"

They stared at each other, both breathing hard. Then Misha said, "Let's go."

"Infant," she muttered.

——

FINALLY, A LETTER.

Dated early October, it only reached them as November shut her doors. For three months, Antosha had travelled to every prison and settlement on Sakhalin Island, had spoken only to convicts and jailors, thought of nothing but penal servitude. *But I'm well other than headaches, flashes of light in one eye and a heaviness all over.* He was sailing back via the China Sea, the Indian Ocean, the Red Sea, then the Black. He would disembark in Odessa and take the train from there. *And then, oh my beloveds, this lonely, hemorroidal personage will be home . . .*

Masha planned what she would do when he stepped off the train. Throw one arm around his neck and, as fast as she could, snake the other down his sleeve. *There! Try leaving again with your sister attached to you like this.* No doubt, she'd follow this with an explosion of relieved tears.

Nine months without him!

On the day of his arrival, several trains failed to deliver their loved one. Mother and Masha stood close enough on the platform to allow for bickering. Misha paced within earshot, but far enough not to be drawn in.

"Why hasn't he arrived yet?" Mother asked for the thousandth time. "Didn't he say twenty past one? It's ten-to-two now. See?" She pointed at the station clock.

"The clock hangs in view of us all, Mother. No need to keep telling me the time."

"Well, where is his train?"

"Do I control the railways?"

"I know you don't, Masha. A good thing too, when you can't even control your tongue."

Masha heaved a sigh. If Antosha didn't show up soon, she'd throw herself on the tracks like Anna Karenina. Where was he?

Mother belched into her glove. "My nerves are giving me gas. Misha!"

The little brother came over, looking agitated himself. Just then a sooty wind blew through, announcing another incoming train. They watched the travellers disembark. After the gentry trickled out, they moved farther down the platform in case Antosha was in another class. A kerchiefed peasant woman with a basket stepped down last. A duck popped its head out from under the cloth and looked around. It was too much for Mother, who let out a wail and sank into Misha's arms.

"I'll go ask," Misha told Masha, handing Mother over. He put on a lawyer's strut all the way to the stationmaster's office.

Five minutes later, he returned with a perplexed expression, the pince-nez hiking up his nose.

"His train was *early*."

Masha let go of Mother's arm and raced off to the refreshment room.

That a crowd had gathered was to be expected. She forced her way through. There he was, sitting at a table with two sailors, as long-haired as Ivan last Easter, bronzed from the homeward journey. Calmly he sliced into the cutlet on his plate; the fork delivered it. He ate so beautifully! Then his companions laughed at something he said. That meant he was happy, or at least able to make a joke. Or maybe he was just glad to be home. Masha was paralyzed with joy.

Around her people were hubbubbing. "But what are they? Monkeys?" Gradually, it registered that the crowd's astonishment was unrelated to hers. In fact, no one seemed the least bit interested in the famous author, which might have been the true reason for his contentment.

Only then did she notice the pair. About the size of half-grown kittens, with small rounded ears placed low on tawny heads, they were catlike but not cats—not standing erect as they were, paws tucked neatly against their chests. One elongated himself enough to peer over the edge of the table. He snatched a scrap off a plate. The crowd applauded.

Misha pushed up beside Masha with Mother on his arm. "Antosha!"

Her brother leapt up, and Masha forgot the strange creatures. Forgot to force her way into his coat. Then the four of them were laughing and crying, kissing and patting each other all over to be sure they weren't dreaming. How thin Antosha felt. How exhaustedly he turned his back to cough.

"I thought you'd forgotten me. Let's get out of here."

Mother and Masha rushed off to hail a cab while Antosha and Misha collected his bags. A few minutes later the two brothers walked out of the station with the porter. Nestled in the crook of Antosha's arm was one of the cat-monkeys, which, to Masha's astonishment, he deposited in her lap.

"This is Svoloch. Don't look at me like that, Mamasha. I didn't name him. One of those foul-mouthed sailors did. Now he answers to it. What can we do?"

Mother blinked at the creature, as unable as Masha to believe him.

Antosha took his place beside Masha. "He's a mongoose. He's tame, though I can't say the same for his spouse."

Svoloch. *Bastard.* It perfectly described this mingled species. Antosha had bought him during a stopover on his long homeward journey, in a dusty roadside market in Ceylon. Later he went back for the wife so he wouldn't be lonely. She was presently hissing in the basket Misha was loading in the cab.

"What possessed me? I'm terrified of matrimony. These two? Well, you'll see. They've reinforced my fears. But how are you all? What's the news? Talk to me, but don't mind if I close my eyes. I have a headache. Stop crying, Mamasha. I'm home."

In her lap, the mongoose busily fingered Masha's coat buttons, then leapt across to investigate Misha. Masha won him back by pulling off her hat, every inch of which, fur and lining, Svoloch inspected before climbing inside to test its purpose. Spotting her comb, he stood and reached for it. They were face to face then, the mongoose's ochre eyes bright with curiosity, the pupils horizontal slits. His musky smell filled her nose.

Off they drove, Antosha sagging exhaustedly against Masha. Yet she barely noticed his weight. She was entranced by Svoloch entranced by her comb, turning it over and over in his clever paws, as though it were the most precious thing he'd yet seen in this strange cold world.

Act Two

—

1891–1892

Masha: You must help me. Help me, or I'll do something
stupid, something that'll make a mockery of my life
and mess it up. . . . I can't go on like this . . .

1

BROTHER?"

His eyes flew open.

"What are you thinking about?"

"Wheelbarrows," he told her dully. "But now that my eyes are open, I have to wonder about these sparks. They're beautiful, but also excruciating. Much like life."

"Should I make a compress?"

"No. Don't leave me."

Most of January he spent in this wincing recline, exhausted, coughing, too ill to leave the house. At Epiphany they had to put off sorting his correspondence. Correcting lessons in the evening, Masha would glance over to where he lay and be gripped by an irrational fear that he'd expired, with her mere steps away.

What had he seen that sickened him like this? She dared not ask. He would speak about it when he was well again, or ready. Or perhaps he never would. He never spoke of Father. Perhaps she would have to wait to read about it. Meanwhile, Svoloch merrily went about his mongoose business: digging up the plants, uncorking bottles, disembowelling cushions. He kept Masha so busy it was impossible to feel low herself.

At first Svoloch was the only one to coax Antosha into smiling. Then one evening the little brother came, and during the course of the visit brought over a photograph from the sideboard, the one their landlord had taken the morning Antosha left for Sakhalin

Island. All of them arranged on the stairs, including the hen in Misha's lap that had strutted past as they were posing. Masha's determined scowl.

Misha put on his lawyer's voice. "Now tell me the truth, Anton Pavlovich. Rumours are circulating. Please clear them up. Were, or are you, the betrothed of anyone in this photograph?"

"Yes." Antosha put his finger on the hen.

Then he smiled, but not because of his joke. Because Lika was in the picture too. The smile lingered on his face even after Misha put the picture away.

Since Masha's visit to the Arbat flat last autumn, an awkwardness had attached itself to her thoughts of Lika, separate from these tedious marriage rumours. That day Masha had felt pitied, and pity was something she couldn't abide. She'd learned this from Antosha—hold your head high, outreach your class. No one would guess then that they were of serf stock. Meeting Lika at Sophia's salon a few weeks later had only deepened the awkwardness. Lika had seemed so different. She'd crossed the room and spoken to Masha with friendliness, but also as a society habituée would speak to a—what? A wallflower?

But then Masha remembered that strange cross-purposed conversation in Lika's parlour. The way she'd hugged herself. The tight fingers of Masha's pride loosened.

Lika has a kind and generous heart. She'd been kind to Masha that day.

That evening Masha wrote her. *He's home. Ill, though I think he'd like to see you.*

ONCE LIKA BEGAN VISITING, THE AWKWARDNESS MASHA had felt—or imagined—was replaced by gratitude, for every time she arrived, Antosha would call out, "Jamais!" and finally summon the strength to push himself out of his apathetic recline. Such a relief to see him upright.

One day, after Antosha's headaches had been diagnosed as myopia and cured with a pince-nez, Lika brought a packet of cords he'd asked for. With both he and Misha wearing a pince-nez now, Svoloch had taken a hungry liking to these cords.

Lika placed the packet on the floor and lightly stepped away. A moment later, Svoloch appeared out of nowhere, sleek in his glossy furs. "I knew it!" she cried. "Look at his little hands. He's actually pulling the string."

Masha laughed too, as Svoloch dragged the paper packet around the room. He pounced, shredded it, then tossed about the contents.

"Just what I need," Antosha said. "Thank you. It's all right when I'm lying down, but see what happens when I'm not?" He shook his head. The pince-nez fell into his lap.

Lika sat beside him, drew one of the cords out of the bundle and handed him the rest. Svoloch, standing on hind legs, one paw on Antosha's knee, reached for them.

"What is the attraction of pince-nez cords?" he asked Svoloch, who had eaten the original one. "Shoe strings would be more economical. Masha?"

"He thinks they're snakes."

She took the spare cords and, with Svoloch scampering after her, went to look for a safe hiding place. Not a cupboard—that he could open. There was Antosha's strongbox, but no doubt Svoloch would soon learn to use the key. A drawer in the pantry would do.

When Masha returned, mongoose in tow, Lika was fixing the pince-nez cord to Antosha's buttonhole while he looked tenderly down at her, his hovering arms an arrested embrace. Then he did something that Masha was coming to recognize as a pattern. Though he was obviously glad to see Lika—he'd roused himself for her—as soon as she sat beside him, he used his precious energy to tease.

He told her, "With a pince-nez, I look as intelligent as my younger brother. Maybe you'll want to be seen with me too now. When I'm well, of course." He gave her a nudge, and reluctantly, Lika stood to give him room to stretch out again.

Masha came and plumped the cushion behind his head.

"It shouldn't be too long," he assured Lika, who looked confused. "I've embarked on a new treatment. Mongooseopathy."

Father stuck his head in the door. "Is she there?"

"Jamais?" Antosha asked.

"The wife."

Father meant Mrs. Svoloch, whom they rarely saw. Her habits were nocturnal and arboreal, her preferred hiding spot curtain rods.

"Lika and I aren't married yet," Antosha told Father. "She has so many other suitors, she can't make up her mind."

At Antosha's quip, Lika's shoulders slumped. Meanwhile, Father went from window to window checking for Mrs. Svoloch, who, a few nights earlier, had hunted him down in his bed and bit his large toe. Assured she wasn't crouching in wait, he greeted Lika. Masha filled a saucer with tea for him.

"Anyway, she won't come out with *him* around." Antosha gestured to the mongoose perched now on his chest. The only time the unloving couple had crossed paths, fire tongs had to be used to separate them.

Father did a double take. "Antosha! I thought you were Misha." To Lika he said, "I can't get used to his pince-nez. He came home with sparks in his eyes. We thought he had a tumour like Zinaida

Lintvariova, God have mercy on her." He leaned in. "The things Antosha saw on Sakhalin Island affected his sight."

"Father?" Antosha said. "If looking at unpleasant things affected our eyesight, we'd be a country of blind men."

Father slurped his tea. "They shackle them to wheelbarrows." Spoken with approval, it seemed. He smacked his lips.

How had he found that out? Masha wondered. Pressed Antosha for details? She glanced over at Antosha just as a wave of revulsion crossed his face.

"Will he object if I smoke?" Lika asked Masha.

"Father?" How Masha hated him at that moment. Actually, she hated him most of the time but usually managed to keep her feelings below a boil. "You can do no wrong," she told Lika.

Lika went to the hall for her bag and came back with her cigarette lit. She looked pleadingly down on Antosha, who, feigning reluctance, made room for her to sit. Svoloch had fallen into a doze on his chest, but when Antosha shifted, he woke and became interested in Lika's cigarette, then her ring.

"Put your little hand on my forehead," Antosha told Lika. "Not the one holding the cigarette."

Laughing, she changed hands and waved the smoke away. Wriggled the ring off her finger and tossed it on the carpet for Svoloch. No matter if the mongoose ate it; it would turn up later in Mariushka's dustpan.

"I liked you better before, Jamais. You remind me now of Sophia's salonists."

"Shh. I won't go any more."

"Now there's a picture worth the canvas." Father nudged Masha and pointed at the two of them. "Go get your paints."

Lika the Beautiful bent over the suffering hero. If Masha had painted them—would she ever feel the urge again?—she might have titled it "He Recovers." Except he didn't. Soon Lika left, and Antosha rolled to his side and lay with his face to the wall for hours.

EVENTUALLY HE DECLARED HIMSELF PHYSICALLY WELL enough to travel and went to stay with Alexei Suvorin. After Sakhalin Island, the thirty hours by train to St. Petersburg seemed close. Nobody begrudged him going. He had publishing matters to deal with, though to Masha he gave a different, disturbing reason. His soul was seething.

Olga hadn't seen the new house, or Svoloch, so Masha invited her one night after Antosha left. The house didn't interest Olga. That a dwelling had a roof, walls and a door deemed it sufficient, just as any clothes she put on were satisfactory whether or not they matched. The wallpaper Masha had chosen, her arrangement of the pictures—irrelevant.

Olga wanted to know what Antosha had said about Sakhalin Island.

"Not much."

Svoloch bounded into the room then, made straight for the stranger and tried to climb her skirt. Olga shrieked and jumped to her feet. He scampered off, Olga glaring after him.

"Where's the other one? The wife, as you call her?"

They went searching. Meanwhile, Svoloch found Olga's hat on the chair in the vestibule and shat in it.

Mrs. Svoloch was crouching behind some tins on top of the pantry cupboard, eyes glowing in the dark. Masha held the lamp while Olga stood on a chair to get a better look.

"I don't think they're the same creature at all." She stepped down.

"They're male and female," Masha said as they returned to the parlour.

"That's your explanation?" Olga said. "She's shy, but underneath simmers with savagery. He owns the place, beats her and annoys everyone. And this is because she's female and he's male?"

Masha poured Olga a glass of tea. "Isn't it? Olechka, tell me how I've erred."

"First, by not noticing that these creatures are physically and behaviourally dissimilar. Second, by swallowing false assumptions about your sex. Women are fearful because they have much to be afraid of. Also, since men like them that way, they oblige. And men are brutes because they get away with it. None of them are *inherently* so." She gulped the scalding tea as though it weren't even hot and held the glass out for more. "You surprise me, Masha. I thought you had brains."

"I had no idea you thought that. Thank you."

Olga was just reaching for her tobacco pouch when Father came in, red and annoyed behind his beard. Olga must have disturbed his prayers, or he'd heard and didn't like what she was saying. Those two burned each other's cheeks with their thoughts.

Olga waved away the proffered tea, said, "Good night!" and huffed out. A moment later, a stream of invective issued from the vestibule, over Svoloch's misuse of her hat.

Yet just a few days later, she returned—in triumph—while Father was at church. She must have timed her visit with the ringing of the bells. She'd come directly from the library. Masha could hardly believe she was still wearing her singed and mongoose-soiled hat.

"Olga? I have numerous hats. May I give you one?"

"It's fine. The stain's inside. That's not why I came. Mrs. Svoloch is *not* a mongoose. She's a *civet cat.*"

Olga explained the differences. Being right and proving Masha wrong put her in such a jolly mood that when Masha offered her a meal, leftovers from their lunch, she accepted, as long as Svoloch stayed locked up.

Mariushka served. Mother came in to say hello then left again while Masha fondly watched Olga chomp through her pork and fried mushrooms like a horse eating oats, the appalling hat beside her plate now. Did she even taste anything? Her views on food were the same as her views on clothes and shelter; they were necessities, not enjoyments. What did she enjoy besides arguing and calculating the movements of the stars?

Olga dispatched the meal in less time than it had taken Mariushka to carry it from the kitchen. She tossed the napkin down.

"I wrote Antosha in Petersburg. He didn't answer."

Masha was trying to ignore the complaining mongoose in the other room.

"Why did he go away again?" Olga asked.

Masha looked at her unkempt friend. Months ago she'd considered seeking Olga out to confide her fears about Antosha. Now Olga had come to her for the same reason.

"Olechka, he went to Sakhalin because he said he needed rousing. It had the opposite effect."

"Naturally it did. I tried to tell him that on the train." When she'd journeyed on with him, she meant.

"What did he say?"

Olga shrugged. "Joking is his default when things get personal. I switched to silence. He prefers it to sympathy."

As in the storehouse in Taganrog. He never wanted Masha's

comfort, just her presence. She would sit on the floor listening to him breathe. But Olga was speaking of a different time, much later, when she was enrolled in Guerrier courses and Antosha in medical school. Before she proved herself to be such a difficult proposition. Had he told her about their childhood?

"We watched the countryside out the window," Olga went on. "He loves the country. I hate it. I love the city, where intelligent people aren't so vastly outnumbered by idiots."

Masha laughed. Maybe she loved Olga because she thought worse things than Masha did. Meanwhile, Svoloch was scratching at the door now as well as crying.

"I'm going to have to let him out," Masha said.

"He has a scar here, just under his hairline. I never noticed." Olga pointed to the place on her own head.

Masha winced, for she remembered how Antosha got it. A memory as unbearable as Svoloch's complaints, which resembled a baby's crying. She opened the pantry door. Olga stood and defensively snatched up her hat.

After she left, Mother came back as though she'd been waiting for Olga to go. "Masha, can't you take Olga to the baths? She looks a fright."

"She likes to frighten people," Masha told her.

MASHA HATED TO THINK OF TAGANROG, THOUGH IT was pretty with its shallow harbour and cascade of stairs leading down to the tree-lined promenade. The Greek merchants' houses were as grand as in any town. Beyond, fields of sunflowers, then the beautiful steppe.

Better to keep her thoughts on the present. Antosha had

insisted that Svoloch's havoc wasn't vandalism, but scientific enquiry, so she made her own.

HYPOTHESIS: *Unattended articles will be put to alternative use where a mongoose resides.*
METHOD: *Offer no warning to guests who leave their hats in the vestibule.*
OBSERVATIONS: *Mongoose knocks hat to floor. Mongoose inspects hat. Mongoose uses hat as chamber pot. (Guests speechless. Mother mortified. Father enraged. Cook appealing to God for protection.) Hypothesis proved.*

She laid a trail of interesting objects—a coin, a spinning top, a dented cigarette case, a spoon—then raced barefoot and night-dressed up the stairs. From her bed, she pictured his elastic bounds from gift to gift. Heard the *tap, tap, tap* of each one tested.

Waiting at the end was the egg she'd managed to sneak past Mariushka. He must have smelled it, for the moment the door pushed open, he darted over, chirring his song. Rolled it to the wall, about-faced, then in one smooth motion flicked it between his legs with the precise force to crack just the shell. Now his tongue had a point of entry. He sucked out the viscous contents, warbling with pleasure.

Masha drummed her fingers on the floor. Svoloch left the empty shell and came and climbed her arm. He burrowed in and let her cradle him.

"Ladies and gentlemen, look at this intelligent face. Oh, my darling Svoloch."

2

MASHA GOT TO THE SKATING POND FIRST. In the crackling cold, she watched a pair of young girls skating, their mittened hands reaching for each other, then their friendly woollen clasp. They made her think of her pupils, but somehow not herself. She had friends, of course, many from her Guerrier days, yet few from before, not even from their early years in Moscow. Childhood was a story. Once upon a time. There had been some joy. Sitting on a barrel in Father's shop playing with the guillotine that cut the sugarloaf.

Along came Lika, hat pulled low and chin tucked in, most of her face obscured by fur. Those curved shoulders and dragging steps hardly seemed to belong to the same woman who in a motion as graceful as a curtsy had set down a package of pince-nez cords in their parlour.

"I've been ill." Lika coughed to prove it. "Granny was worried it might be consumption. Really."

What a bore they were, these lovelorn friends. The sun was glinting off the ice-coated trees, sparrows carousing in the naked bushes. Their plan had been to skate.

"Let's have coffee, then." Masha struck off toward the refreshment pavilion, the supposedly ailing Lika trotting obediently after her.

Inside, they scanned the crowded room in search of a free table. By the window, a harried mother had risen from her seat and was entreating her two daughters to wipe the chocolate off their mouths. As Masha and Lika approached, the mother noticed the mess on the window—they'd painted it with chocolate—and the shouting began.

Lika swept over, placing a hand on each girl's head, and in a stage-whisper said, "Don't worry. I'll *lick* it off."

"Wasn't that lady nice, Mama?" one of them warbled as they left.

No wonder Lika had been so popular at the Dairy School. She was a half-child herself, settling across from Masha and emerging from her coat as from a fur cocoon.

"My throat *is* sore." She extended and stroked it, just as the waiter approached. His eyes bulged.

"Honey cake," Masha told the exophthalmic youth. "And coffee."

"Two." Lika turned to Masha. "You look well. You look happy."

"Mongooseopathy," Masha said.

"Sugar, Miss?" He set down their cups, lifted the tongs.

Lika nodded for a second lump and a third, and then, head propped up with one hand, stirred as though she had no hope of dissolving them.

"Why does Antosha keep running away?"

Masha shifted on the chair. She could see why Lika was frustrated. Before he left for Sakhalin Island, he'd been putting his tongue in her mouth. Then he came back with a seething soul. His pull–push behaviour during her visits hurt her. Masha knew it did. She'd been on the receiving end of Lika's bewildered glances.

"It's not your throat?"

"It is. Look." Lika opened wide.

Masha saw nothing of note except that even her tonsils were pretty.

The cake arrived like a slice of a book on a plate. When they ate honey cake as children, she and Antosha had made up a story for every layer. This was before their troubles. After Father's bankruptcy, there was no cake at all.

Masha took a bite and pronounced it stale. Lika agreed, yet consumed it in three gulps. The coffee she sipped while both of them watched the scene outside, Masha waiting for whatever Lika was working up to tell her. The pond was scribbled over by skate blades. Children and novices tentatively pushed chairs or sledges along the ice while the experienced raced laps. Even the elderly were out, clinging to each other for dear life. Bruegel, seen through a chocolatey smear. At the next table a man complained that his corns had hampered his skating.

"Do you still think badly of me because I had fun while Antosha was in Siberia?" Lika finally asked.

"Actually, I forgot all about it until now," Masha told her.

"Honestly, Masha? I swear Misha and I are just friends. Isaac too."

"Isaac?"

This was a surprise. Then Masha remembered Sophia's salon—blindfolded Isaac caressing Lika's face while everyone ogled them. The forlorn dance of the ruined crane. Her own feeling of revulsion. She felt a twinge of possessiveness. Isaac was their dear friend. He'd spent that summer with them recovering from his depression. He'd *proposed* to her.

"You said he prefers older women," Lika said. "And Sophia was always around. Masha?" She took a breath deep enough to swell her chest. "I love Antosha." Her exhalation carried away the declaration. "I love him."

Masha believed her. As for Misha and Isaac, she accepted Lika's excuse. If you're miserable over someone, replace him. Hadn't the same thing happened to her on that frigid December cab ride? Svoloch plucked out her comb, and Georgi went *poof.*

After months of her obsessing over him, he had become an embarrassing memory.

It hadn't worked for Lika. Perplexed, she said, "He left again without even saying goodbye. Why?" Her welling tears looked like mercury.

"Don't cry here, Lika. Everyone's staring at us."

"I'm trying not to." She used her cuff to blot her eyes. "I just feel muddled."

Antosha did too, it seemed. There had been such need in his voice when he called out, "Jamais!" Then he'd send her on some errand, when it was obvious that he was desperate for her to stay. Or he'd tease her to the point of exasperation.

Everyone noticed. Mother had whispered one night, "Do you think he'll marry her?"

"Not likely," Masha had retorted.

"Maybe you don't want me to talk about him," Lika said. "It puts you in an awkward position."

"It's nice of you to recognize that. No one else does."

"Who?"

"Vermicelli, for one. Antosha is her sole topic of conversation."

Lika winced. "Poor her. Poor me. I don't want to jeopardize our friendship."

Masha softened. "Go ahead. Tell me what's the matter."

"I asked Misha for his address. The letter he wrote back? I don't know what to think." Lika's coat was hanging over the back of her chair. Out of the pocket she drew an envelope addressed in that familiar, elegant hand, and slid it across the table to Masha. "I told him I'd been coughing blood, and what Granny thought."

"What?" Masha exclaimed.

"We really thought it was consumption. But then I remembered we'd had beetroot at dinner. Anyway, I invited him to view my remains on his return. So perhaps I'm guilty of starting the teasing off."

Masha unfolded the letter. There was some silliness about Granny. *As for your coughing, stop smoking and gossiping in the streets. If you die, Trofimov will shoot himself. I'll rejoice. Farewell, villainess of my heart.*

"Who is Trofimov?" Masha asked.

"I've never heard of him. I think I deserve more than irony, Masha."

Lika didn't know she'd written a jokey letter about consumption to a man who had it, whose brother had died of it. In Masha's opinion, Antosha had shown restraint. It was generous of him to reply at all considering his despairing mood.

"Masha? People are still asking if Antosha and I are engaged."

Masha folded the letter and slid it back. Now was the time to spell things out. That would be a true kindness. These affairs, if that was where Antosha and Lika were headed—it certainly seemed so—always ended the same way.

"Lika, I know a dog Antosha was supposedly engaged to. 'Artists are married to their art.' Those are his words."

Lika sniffed, then turned toward the window. A burst of sparrows passed, but from Lika's pensive expression, Masha surmised an inward gaze.

"When's he coming back?" she asked.

Soon, Masha hoped. It distressed her to think of him lying with his face to the wall in Alexei Suvorin's mansion, being cared for by a footman.

Another reason presented itself shortly. Masha had noticed a growing sluggishness in Svoloch's movements. The manic leaping lessened. Then, for the first time, she saw him walk instead of bound. If she'd thought to question Mariushka, the person who ran around the house with the brush and dustpan, she would have learned that his normally voluminous output had ceased. She didn't; whenever the cook saw Svoloch, she spat three times over her left shoulder.

By the time Masha sent her telegram, Svoloch had retreated to the bottom drawer of her dresser, a listless ball. Food didn't tempt him, not even an egg delivered on a china saucer.

Svoloch dying. Return.

Antosha took the next train and arrived looking as pale and drawn as when he'd left for St. Petersburg.

"He can't die. He really can't," Masha said, hovering behind the doctor, who had swaddled the struggling patient in a towel. "He's the only thing I've ever had that's mine alone."

How strange to hear herself say this. She'd been unconscious of this impulse, had thought she loved Svoloch for his charms, not her needs.

Antosha managed to dose the mongoose with Hunyadi Janos Water and Stool Softener. Released, Svoloch humped back to his hiding place while Antosha tended to the bites on his hands.

"I've done my best, sister."

As he always had. He'd rescued them, fed, housed and educated them, lifted them above their station.

Masha crouched beside the drawer where Svoloch panted, waiting to see what would happen. Before long, he was tearing the wood with his teeth, splintering it.

"It's like he's giving birth," Antosha marvelled.

He watched like a curious author while Masha knelt in helplessness. Eventually the mongoose's labour issued forth the blockage. A half-dozen pince-nez cords in an agonizing gnarl inside him. They both had to laugh over this foul offspring. That was the moment—while Masha was stroking the exhausted creature in her arms, overjoyed he'd survived—that Antosha chose to tell her Alexei Suvorin had proposed a tour of Europe.

"Soon?"

"In a few weeks."

"Are you going back to Petersburg now?"

"No. I may as well stay till then." An odd expression settled on his face, and his hand pressed his waistcoat.

"What is it?" Masha asked.

"My heart's been doing the strangest thing." He looked at her, puzzled as much as worried. "Just now it stopped."

"Stopped?" Masha asked in alarm.

"Yes. For a second or two, it simply doesn't beat."

No wonder, with the burden that heart carried. He'd gone to St. Petersburg not to recuperate, but to petition the authorities on behalf of the child beggars and prostitutes of Sakhalin Island.

"*Child* prostitutes?" Masha said.

"They exist."

These horrors came out over the next few nights, after Mother and Father had gone to bed and Masha sat quietly reading, waiting for him to speak. Antosha stretched out on the divan, smoking a cigarette.

"I've brought back with me a horrid feeling. While I was there, I worked so hard I didn't have a moment to myself to think. But now it seems like I've been to hell."

As she waited, noises usually unremarked came to the fore—the pages she turned without reading, the watchman banging his stick in the courtyard, sibilance inside the stove. The scratching in the pantry was the civet cat trying to open the sealed crock in which Mariushka had stored the coffee beans. Svoloch heard and went after her. Animal scrambling.

Silence.

In one of the northern settlements, the worst part of the island, Antosha had met a girl who'd worked the trade since age nine. In the same place, a man sold his own daughters, even haggled over the price.

Her brother was holding back, Masha could tell. But as he talked, she pictured it as clearly as if he wrote it and she were copying it out. A road in a desolate place. Was "road" the right word for furrows of mud? He was driving with the warden at dusk when it was hard to see, particularly with the rain constantly borne off the sea. His eyes had been giving him trouble too, even before he got there. A fecal odour from an open latrine. A few shivering trees here and there, leafless, like skeletal hands.

Out of the gloom, a collection of squat wooden huts appeared. As their carriage neared, a figure detached from the bleak background, recognizably human, wrapped in a shapeless grey cloak. Driving past, they saw inside the hood. A young face, not an old one, not more than twelve, he guessed.

"Two kopeks, sirs?" She hugged herself to stay warm.

Starvation. Blind children, filthy and covered in eruptions. A toddler holding onto her father's fetters. The children weren't the only ones who suffered—far from it—but what happened to the children was the hardest to comprehend.

He'd conducted a census, interviewed every soul on the island—settlers, prisoners and exiles. Put his head inside rooms where cockroaches coated the walls and ceiling like living black crepe. Wardens put him up. Until two in the morning, he would copy his data to the despairing groans from the prison barracks.

He blew out smoke. Svoloch came back and leapt onto his chest. Antosha stroked him.

"They serve two years in the prison, unless they try to escape. If they do try, they're caught. There's nowhere to run. Then they're flogged. They're flogged for misdemeanours too. For *vulgarity*. Ragged men soaked with rain, covered with mud, beaten, starved.

"I watched a flogging. I forced myself. Four nights passed before I could sleep again."

Masha listened, saying nothing.

"After two years, they become convicts in exile, living in the settlements, serving the rest of their sentence either in hard labour, as before, or as servants to the warden. Convicts were everywhere. You never knew if the man setting down your knife and fork at dinner wasn't there for slitting someone's throat.

"But then a strange thing happened. Once I got over my fear and interacted without prejudice, the difference between prisoner and non-prisoner blurred. The whole island was a prison, after all. Our whole country is. We're just trying to survive it."

"Brother?" she finally said.

To her relief, Antosha held up his hand to stop her speaking. She could not find adequate words to express her revulsion, or her sympathy. No such words existed.

He asked her not to tell anyone he was back. Did he mean Lika? Olga maybe. But you can't sew buttons on your neighbour's mouth, or your little brother's.

THE KNOCK CAME QUITE LATE, MADE BY FORCEFUL FISTS. Masha heard it from her bed.

Father roused himself to answer, muttering all the way to the door on scuffling slippered feet. He'd probably armed himself with a newsprint cudgel in case he met Mrs. Svoloch.

The baritone of a joyful greeting came next, followed by Father's cry of recognition. Isaac? Masha blushed, as was her habit. Isaac was not exactly welcome, but better than some third-rate scribbler wanting to rub up against Antosha at eleven at night. She threw her legs over the side of the bed.

More than one set of footsteps came stumbling up the stairs. A second voice, a woman's, pleading. Too feminine for Sophia. Lika?

Instantly Masha was furious. What was she doing running around with Isaac at this time of night? Antosha's room was next to Masha's. His door, flung open, struck the other side of her wall.

"Ho!" Isaac roared. "We were just at the Maly. Misha too. So you snuck home from Petersburg. Are you hiding?"

Masha pulled a dress over her head, not bothering with the corset. She straightened herself in the mirror. Antosha was inviting them to sit now, Isaac praising the play they'd just seen. She heard Antosha say, "The theatre doesn't interest me anymore. Not in its present form."

Masha went downstairs for refreshments. Where was Svoloch? With their guests, she guessed. She passed through the dining parlour, gritting her teeth on Antosha's behalf.

Something on the table caught her eye then. She brought the candle close. The gore of half a mouse on its own spreading stain. Cringing, she rolled the cloth with one hand, mouse bits and all. She was still deciding where to stash it when she noticed two greenish orbs fixed on her from the pantry door. An icy shiver worked through her. Now Masha understood Father's fear. In Mrs. Svoloch's presence she felt, if not evil, then a focused viciousness. How could Olga claim this wasn't inherent?

Masha climbed right onto the table. After a minute, it occurred to her that Antosha himself would soon venture down for vodka and snacks and find her in this ridiculous position. She peeked over the edge, then had to laugh. Mrs. Svoloch had retreated under a plant stand in the corner, obviously as terrified as Masha.

Bravely Masha climbed down and went to prepare a tray. On her way back upstairs, she crouched before Mrs. Svoloch's hideout to test Olga's hypothesis. Extending her hand, she made the friendly clicking sound that her spouse answered to.

Mrs. Svoloch lunged. Masha drew back just in time. "Oh! You wicked, wicked thing!"

The tray shook as she carried it up.

When she entered Antosha's room, Isaac called, "Masha, my pupil!" from his odalisque recline on the bed. He looked so handsome, she was glad she'd got her blushing over with. Svoloch was beside him, conducting an inventory of his pockets. Pencil stub, a ticket torn in half—each examined and tossed aside.

Lika was perched on Antosha's chair, elbows on knees, wearing a champagney look as she gazed at his back. She gave Masha a timid smile, just a crimp in her prettiness. The one Masha returned was brittle—her shock over what had just happened with Mrs. Svoloch mixed with disapproval. Chastened, Lika dropped her eyes. Silver coins tossed to the floor.

Antosha, with his morbid fear of being seen in just his waistcoat, had hurried into his jacket. He was dealing with the papers on his desk. Until he could overcome his irritation, he would prolong the task, pretending to order his pages but actually creating meaningless stacks. Then, as with countless other unwelcome visitors, he'd turn to face them with a smile.

As Masha came up beside him, he noticed her expression. "What happened?"

"I just met a civet cat."

He probably would have laughed if he wasn't annoyed. She set down the tray in the space he'd cleared among his dirt-spattered notebooks. His Sakhalin Island notes, the ink on one page half washed away, like those mud-soaked, degraded men. The work these two had so frivolously interrupted. How awful that they came.

Now Antosha was ready. He fixed the smile and turned.

Isaac straightened to make room on the bed. Side by side, their backs against the rug on the wall, the two of them sat, long legs stretched out. Isaac's tie was loose. Masha caught a whiff of turpentine and vodka. Quite drunk. Lika too, drunk and embarrassed.

Isaac circled his long finger at Masha. "How's the painting?"

"She's been bad," Antosha said. "She has talent, but no discipline."

After her aborted skating outing with Lika, Masha had thought about going back to the pond with her pencils and sketchbook and reclaiming the window table. Sometimes she thought about drawing Svoloch too, but he never stayed still long enough.

Isaac didn't believe in discipline. "Where's your passion, Masha?"

"It seems I've misplaced it."

"Then look for it. Get out of this miserable city. Go find yourself a field. Lie down in it. Do not get up." The long finger came out. "*Do not get up.*"

"Last time I looked, it was winter." Yet even delivering this rejoinder, she wondered, where *was* her passion?

Antosha had yet to acknowledge Lika, just like the first night they'd met. Was he annoyed about what she'd written in her letter? Annoyed she was out with a womanizer like Isaac so soon after writing it? If Masha couldn't tell, Lika certainly couldn't.

Finally Antosha addressed her. "Miss Mizanova. You're quieter in person than in your letters. Have you recovered your health now?"

Lika pulled herself out of her dreamy slump, coughed and nodded. Then she glanced at Masha, who began passing around the glasses and plates of bread and butter. Why should Masha rescue her?

"Should you be out in the cold like this?" Antosha asked her.

His tone, though teasing, was cool. He was speaking from his dark mood. It brought the heat to Lika's face, which made Isaac steal Antosha's pince-nez and pretend to inspect Lika through it. He held it out at different lengths, the way he would measure a view with his brush. Svoloch grabbed at the string.

"And where's Trofimov," Antosha went on, "that you had to find yourself this low sort of escort?"

Isaac laughed. Lika pulled herself up in the chair.

"Who is this Trofimov you keep talking about?"

Antosha whispered in Isaac's ear, loud enough for them all to hear. "She denies her other lovers."

"She must have hundreds. Just look at her." Isaac handed back the pince-nez.

"Watch out for Trofimov."

Masha grew uncomfortable then with their tone, which bordered on unkind. She set the bottle of vodka on the floor for Svoloch to uncork. He leapt down from the bed and started on it.

"He's like a waiter!" Isaac marvelled. "Hire him out at the Hermitage."

The feeling in the room lightened with the mongoose's antics. Svoloch succeeded in opening the bottle, then cavorted with the cork while Masha filled the glasses.

"To what shall we drink? Friendship at inconvenient hours?"

Lika had refused her glass, but Isaac and Antosha drank.

"What does this Trofimov look like?" Isaac asked. "Just so I can be on my guard."

Lika had had enough. She rose, teetered over to the window and drew aside the curtain. Frost feathers covered the pane. She pretended to look out, her back to the rest of them.

Antosha bit into his bread and brushed the crumbs off his beard. "Trofimov's an Adonis." Then, "Pretty skimpy with the butter, sister."

The waiter leapt back onto the bed, forcing Antosha to hold his slice out of reach. He told Isaac, "We don't stand a chance."

"The greatest painter and the greatest writer in the country don't stand a chance? The only ones who understand the landscape?"

"Do tell us more about the landscape," Masha said, refilling the men's drinks.

Isaac took the bait. Even if he hadn't been drunk, he would have begun shouting. Vodka splashed out of his waving glass, and he nearly clobbered Antosha beside him.

"It's more than a pretty view. More than setting. It's metaphor!"

"No talk of metaphor," Antosha said. "There are ladies present."

"The ladies can go to hell!" Isaac roared. "We're on the true path. No cheap external effects. Paint and write simply—show *that which is there*. It's the hardest thing to do. Are you laughing at me, Masha?"

She curtsied. "No, dear master."

He turned back to Antosha. "I've told you this before."

"Now and then," Antosha said. But with these words, he bumped his shoulder against his spiritual brother. The vodka taking effect. "Hang it, Svoloch. Take the crust."

Svoloch snatched it, leapt down and disappeared under the bed. Antosha brushed the crumbs off his lap.

"What are you working on?" Isaac asked him. "What are we rudely interrupting? We are, I know. I saw that pinched look you get."

"Nothing at all." His eyes strayed to Lika at the window, her back still to them.

Masha had assumed she was sulking. She went over now. "Where's your chaperone?"

Lika was scratching something on the feathered window with her fingernail. "Sophia, you mean? Ill. Or so he said." She glanced at Masha, then away. "Coming here wasn't my idea. I tried to stop him. But, as I'm sure you know, that's impossible once he gets an idea in his head."

"Why were you with him in the first place?"

"He dropped by with the ticket. I just wanted to go out. Is that wrong?"

Her eyes fully met Masha's then. The expression in them took Masha aback—she was more hurt by Masha than the men. You could expect this sort of ganging up from men. It was what you endured to keep company with them. But Masha was acting like a civet cat.

"What are you two whispering about?" Isaac called.

Masha turned and said, "The boorishness of men."

Then, as though the two of them had orchestrated this revenge, Lika held aside the curtain for them to see the words she'd scratched into the frost.

Trofimov! Help! I'm trapped here with two egoists!

Both men burst out laughing. When was the last time Masha had heard Antosha laugh like that? Probably the night he chased Mariushka around the dining table. Already sorry for her harshness, Masha was suddenly glad they'd dropped in. More so because of what happened next.

"I'll get her out of here before the cad shows up." Isaac struggled to stand. "But first . . ." He poured out another round, telling

Antosha, "You'd better come, friend. Two against one makes better odds."

Masha saw the three of them to the door, clutching the squirming mongoose to her chest. Isaac wanted to take Svoloch with them, and Svoloch wanted to go. Her brother accepted her peck on his cheek. One of his hands was pressed to his chest, feeling for a beat.

"Lika!" Masha called after them. "Thank you!"

With one over-the-shoulder smile, Masha was absolved.

Off they went, laughing again, Lika a wisp between them, no longer embarrassed but giddy now that Antosha had been convinced to come along. Lika was in love with him, and it made her reckless. She didn't know that in little more than a week he would be gone again and not back for months.

Perhaps it was then, more than at that first meeting Masha had contrived for them, that everything was set in motion. With her cold hand waving in the midnight air, giving away her blessing.

3

THAT SUMMER, NO ONE WANTED TO GO BACK TO Luka. Instead they were on their way by train to the dacha Misha had rented through an advertisement, six hours from Moscow on the Oka River. Antosha had only been home from Europe for three days when they left, just long enough to unpack and pack again.

Train travel with a mongoose might have been the subject of one of Antosha's early tales, the silly ones he used to write to support them while he was in medical school. The mongoose's vocal resentment at being contained drives the ineffectual patriarch out of the compartment to pace. The aged cook takes a seat in third class. Passersby, seeing the shrieking basket move on its own (its hidden means of locomotion the mongoose's violent self-hurling), assume the Devil is riding the train and disembark en masse.

Antosha kept them all in stitches with this narration. Svoloch had grown so wild during those months Antosha spent in Europe that if they didn't laugh about him, their only recourse would be tears.

Yet with the grateful burden of Mother's head resting on his shoulder and the half-smile on his face, Antosha seemed truly himself again for the first time since Kolia died—no longer the grieving brother, the humiliated playwright, the exhausted post-Sakhalin traveller clutching his inconsistent heart. Masha couldn't stop smiling at him.

"Look at this countryside." He waved at the window just as the train slowed. "Isaac is right. Russia is our soul. Italy and France had nothing to say to me."

"Russia is saying it's going to rain," Masha replied. The clouds were darkest in the direction they were heading.

"Let it," Antosha said. "I'll love it just as much."

They eased into a station. The squealing basket jerked forward another inch. "Bravo, Svoloch!" Antosha said. Then, giving Mother's knee a tender pat, he informed them he was getting off to rest his ears. Misha went with him.

Once they were gone, Mother shot a look of loathing at the wobbling carrier. "That animal is making the journey unbearable, Masha."

"He'll be fine once he's free, Mamasha. I thank you for your patience." She turned away, closing the subject.

Out the window, Antosha was charming a tea-seller. How easily he laughed now. Why had he even gone to Sakhalin Island? Everyone had told him to go to Europe instead, and they'd been right. Since his return, she hadn't dared ask about his work on behalf of Sakhalin's children. The young girl standing in the rain, the one he'd told her about, insinuated herself in Masha's thoughts. Two kopeks, sirs.

Masha shuddered.

The basket convulsed.

Mother grimaced and crossed herself.

THUNDER IS ONLY AN OMEN AS IT PERTAINS TO WEATHER. But charged air can change the mood. The rain Antosha had welcomed soon joined forces with the wind. To set foot outside the dacha was to invite a dousing.

It was an incommodious place, snugger even than their jewellery box in town. Nearby, an arthritic railway bridge groaned in anticipation of its own collapse every time a train crossed. No outhouse—just a gully for their convenience, in full view of the trains, reached through a terrifying nettle thicket.

Antosha, fresh from the splendours of Paris and desperate to work, was the most put out. The first morning, he told the little brother off.

"Apologies, Your Excellency," Misha replied. "The advertisement for the dacha mentioned no bridge, so how could I know about the trains keeping us awake? And am I responsible for the weather?"

Masha was preoccupied with Svoloch. He seemed to consider these smaller quarters as confining as the basket. Or maybe it was his new widower status. Several weeks before, Mrs. Svoloch had met her end when the floor polishers came. She bit one, and he struck back. Masha came home to gleaming floors and the civet cat's corpse in the pantry, lying on a sheet of newspaper.

She kept the wild widower in her room. Every time she entered, a fresh atrocity awaited. Ignoring his newspaper latrine, Svoloch shat on her bed. Shat in the drawer she'd left open for him. Ate her corset string. Once, when she carelessly opened the door, he escaped and made straight for the kitchen, where he broke the crockery with celebratory glee.

Mother and Mariushka screamed. Father raged. "How much longer are we to suffer this demon?"

"Call the floor polisher," Misha quipped.

Masha turned on him. "That is a vile thing to say! Vile!"

This happened at the close of their miserable first week in the cramped dacha. Misha went off to the nearby town in a huff. While there, he took it upon himself to improve their general discontent by, of all things, inviting a guest. But since that guest was shapely and ebullient, not to mention musical, everyone did cheer up at the thought of Lika coming, even Masha.

The previous month while Antosha was still travelling in Europe, Masha had met Lika at Filipov's Restaurant. Lika had entertained her with leering imitations of the council clerks she copied for, her face a landed perch's gasping for life. Masha had laughed.

"Actually, it's horrible, fending them off. They remind me of mother's beaux. I miss my Dairy girls."

Lika had invited Masha, so Masha kept expecting Antosha's name to come up. Finally, she mentioned him herself. "Has my brother been sending his impressions of Europe?"

Lika's stilted answer surprised her. "I haven't heard from him."

"He hasn't written to you?"

"That's not why I asked you, Masha. You and I haven't seen each other in months. Not since that night Isaac dragged me over." The night she'd scratched her message to Trofimov in the frost on his window, and the three of them had gone off to the restaurant at the Hermitage Hotel.

"Are there poppy seeds in my teeth?" Lika bared them.

Still puzzled, Masha said, "Antosha mentioned you to us."

It was Lika's turn to be surprised. "Really? What did he say?"

I took a moonlit ride on horseback. There was a glorious fragrance in the air. I breathed it in and gazed at the moon and thought of her—that is, of Lika M.

Romantic nonsense, which Masha now paraphrased. "'Moonlight. A horse. Et cetera. I thought of her—'"

"Oh, *her*." Lika gestured dismissively.

"'Of Lika M.' Mother read it out and is now completely convinced he's a poet."

"Well, he was joking. As you said, it was nonsense."

But jokes and nonsense often conveyed deeper feelings. What had Olga said that time? It was Antosha's default when things got personal. It also made some feelings bearable. Masha didn't say this. She relayed his message to her.

"He asked me to give you his respects."

This completely befuddled Lika. Masha realized then why Lika had invited her. Antosha had left for a third time and, again, had probably not told Lika. She'd decided it was pointless to pursue him and was now testing her mettle by meeting his sister. This was not so different from when Masha, lovesick over Georgi, had sat across the table from Natalia in Yalta. Except that Masha had had no choice.

She conveyed the rest of the message. "He also said to tell you not to eat starchy food and to avoid Isaac."

"He mentioned Isaac?" Lika's dimples showed.

Masha got the feeling that she'd come with one resolution, but would leave with another.

"Masha? You should have seen Antosha that night at the Hermitage. It was like a doting contest between the two of them."

"Isaac and Antosha?"

"Yes. Remember the night at your house when he put my hand in his pocket? At the Hermitage, he did the same, and held it too. And played with my ring, as though to remind me of the time I scratched him. All under the table, while Isaac wooed me above it. If only Isaac had left. He has a camel's bladder."

Masha laughed. Lika poured out more tea and sat pressing the black seeds on her plate with her finger. She grew pensive, then sad.

"What are you thinking about?" Masha asked.

"That if I'd dropped by that night without Isaac, Antosha

would probably never have taken me to the Hermitage. Or held my hand and played with my ring. Why is another man's regard more stirring than a woman's sincere feelings?"

IN ANSWERING MISHA'S TELEGRAM, LIKA HAD BEEN vague about which train she'd take. When the knock came a few days later, they all started. Misha hurried to answer it, stopping first to check his reflection in the samovar. He licked his palm, smoothed his hair. Adjusted the pince-nez. Antosha stepped out of the bedroom he shared with Misha, smiling and tugging on his waistcoat, seemingly as eager as the little brother to see Lika again.

Masha wondered something then. Had Antosha too been testing his resolve when he dropped Lika's name in his letters, just like Lika that day at Filipov's? Trying to forget his feelings for Lika, as Lika had been trying to forget hers for him?

Then, in the vestibule, two voices crowed, "Surprise!"

Hearing Isaac, Antosha's shoulders fell. His hacking started, and Masha watched in alarm as he retreated to his room. It took several minutes before the coughing fit passed and he could rejoin them with his congenial mask in place.

Masha couldn't believe Lika had brought Isaac. What a farce! The rest of the family gathered around their guests, feigning joy, even Mother, who was surely panicking over where Isaac would sleep. He was too tall to curl up on one of the trunks. Masha could barely look at them; this felt too much like their last unexpected visit. For the first time, Isaac had failed to induce in her a blush.

Lika was nervous, Masha could tell by her twisting hands and her unprompted laugh. When Antosha finally appeared, her metallic eyes slid sideways to him. She smiled and he smiled.

"We came partway by boat," she told them. "Isaac couldn't stop swooning."

Isaac concurred. "You don't get those slow views from a train."

Yet he couldn't tear his soulful gaze off Lika now, so how had he taken in the views? Something had happened between them, or to Isaac, since the last time they'd all met. Also, his hair was receding. Masha noticed it when he ran a hand through his curls. He was the same age as Antosha, thirty-one, yet now he seemed older.

They crowded into the parlour, with Father comically insisting there was plenty of room, though the walls could barely contain Isaac's oversized gestures, let alone him. Misha sat on the floor. Masha stood. Svoloch's entreaties were more audible here.

"Antosha, we dropped your name, I confess," Lika said. "Presto! We made so many friends. You really get to know people on a boat."

When Lika said Antosha's name, Isaac spared him a glance. In place of his brotherly greeting, he said, "Nice tie."

Antosha looked down at it. "Yes. I bought it in Italy. Neckties are marvellously cheap there. I almost took to eating them."

"What was that boring man's name?" Lika asked. "We called him B.-K. Bylim-Kylim? Isaac?"

The way she was gushing, she seemed fully Sophia's type now. Or— Masha jolted with the thought. Was she acting? Maybe she really could.

Lika turned to Antosha again. "He adores your stories."

Mother groaned. "Oh Lord. I hope you didn't tell all these people where we're staying."

Lika turned in the direction of the mongoose's plainting. "What's that sound?"

"Svoloch," Masha said. "He's been naughty."

Isaac laughed. "I thought it was a tree creaking in the wind. What a miserable spot. Will we get some *plein air*, Masha? The river's close by, isn't it?"

Antosha and Misha volunteered to take the painter for a walk. Isaac pouted when Lika wouldn't come along.

"I want to pay my respects to my mongoose friend," she told him.

Shortly after the three men left, the sun broke out. Mother clapped and Father crossed himself. It wasn't just the sun that lifted their spirits, but Lika's sunny laugh.

In Masha's room, Lika played peek-a-boo with Svoloch, crouching on the floor eye to eye with him. She concealed herself behind the bed skirt. Svoloch tore it from her hand. Even he seemed glad to see her.

"But where's Mrs. Svoloch?" Lika asked.

"Dead."

"What?" She sat back on her heels.

Masha told her the story of the floor polisher. "And now this one's twice as wild. I didn't think they had anything to do with one another, but it seems her presence had been felt."

Lika gave a little huff. "Is that our lot? To be *felt*?"

A rhetorical question. Even if Masha had had an answer, she would have been drowned out by the moans of the railway bridge. Lika turned alarmed eyes on Masha.

"It's a train, not the end of the world. Are you running around with Isaac now?"

The train chattered past, shaking the walls. Lika resumed her game with Svoloch. "We're just friends."

"It doesn't look that way," Masha said.

Svoloch tore away the bedskirt again, and Lika smiled—at Masha, not Svoloch. "Doesn't it?"

"Does Sophia know he's here?"

Lika settled fully on the floor, clasping her hands around her knees. "I apologize for inviting him. I can see why you're annoyed." She waved at the smallness of the room, its chairlessness—just a bureau and a bed—without seeming sorry. She actually looked pleased with herself.

"I'm glad you like the floor," Masha told her. "That's where you'll be sleeping."

"Oh, Masha. Come and sit beside me. Or on the bed if you want. Sit above me."

Above her. Lika saw right through Masha, who got down on the floor and was rewarded when Svoloch popped out from under the bed and curled up in her lap. He rarely snuggled anymore.

"It's the Hermitage all over again?" Masha asked. "That's what you're playing at?"

"It's obvious?" She seemed to expect an answer.

Instead Masha gave a warning. "You know about Isaac's moods, don't you?"

MASHA DID LET LIKA SLEEP WITH HER. PRESSED RIGHT up against Masha's back in the narrow bed, she smelled like a love letter. Masha could almost feel her heart beating.

The men were still up, talking about Antosha's trip to Europe and Isaac's some years earlier, at ease now that Lika had retired. Their steps sounded in the hall, back and forth, as they got ready for bed. They made no effort to be quiet. They too wanted to be felt, particularly Isaac, who, like a devoted dog, made himself a bed on the floor in the hall, close to Masha's door, heaving sighs and exaggerated yawns. Whenever a train passed, Lika tensed in the bed and Isaac cursed in the hall, waking Masha, who was by now deaf to the straining piles and girders.

In the morning she loaded the thrashing mongoose into his basket and coaxed Isaac and Lika into playing whist, with Misha as their fourth. Antosha, who hated whist, was writing in his room, or trying to. Because no one wanted to waste the sun, they dragged the table and chairs outside, despite the flies attracted by the spoils in the gully.

Masha worried about Isaac. Should she have been explicit with Lika about his suicidal tendencies? Antosha was still projecting his porcelain calm, but Isaac seemed agitated, so different from that night he and Lika had dropped in. Then, he and Antosha had teased Lika together. They'd all walked into the night, arm in arm. But that was months ago. Antosha had been out of the picture since then while Isaac had been painting it all along. Now he was as possessive about Lika as he was with his work, even with the little brother.

"Lika, Lika. My hand is full of hearts," Misha said, causing Isaac to straighten on his chair and, with an attention-seeking flourish, throw down his hand prematurely. Pouting ensued.

They were into their second game when a pair of troikas stopped on the road in front. These were a rich man's horses, groomed until they glowed.

"Is this where the writer is staying?" one of the drivers called out over the snorting and harness jangling.

"Who wants to know?" Misha called back.

"Master Bylim-Kolosovsky sends for you."

Isaac recognized the name. "That's B.-K. from the boat. He'll bore us all to death." He called out to the driver, "What does he want?"

"They're saying in town that you're unhappy with these quarters. The master's got nicer ones to let."

At these words, Antosha appeared in the doorway of the dacha. "What kind of quarters? Bigger than these?"

"I should say, sir. It's his estate, Bogimovo."

Masha didn't want to leave Svoloch with the old ones who might let him out, accidentally or not. Or they'd be furious at Masha for subjecting them to his unrelenting din while she was gone. But if Antosha wanted her opinion, she couldn't beg off.

"IT'S NORMALLY TWO HUNDRED ROUBLES," SAID B.-K. "But I'm a great admirer of yours. I thought one-sixty for the whole summer. To thank you for your good work."

His mistress, a redhead lacking a critical number of teeth, beamed at his side. "We followed your trip to Sakhalin in the papers. The suffering must end."

"I hear this same sentiment daily at the tax office," Misha quipped.

Blank looks from their earnest hosts. B.-K., like the Lintvariovs, was rich in land but empty of pocket, the pockets in his case in a long peasant coat worn in sympathy with a class of people who probably laughed behind his back. He and his gap-toothed mistress rented out the manor while living in intentional simplicity in one of the dachas beyond.

The house was enormous even with another family on the upper floor. In the drawing room, the still-surprising sun poured through the ceiling-high windows. Isaac beckoned Masha over to take in the view. Was that all she needed to begin painting again? To *look*? Instead she was worrying about what Svoloch was doing back in her room.

At the next window Antosha ran his hand along the capacious

sill. "I could write here. I wouldn't even need a desk." He took a few steps. Stopped. Reapplied the toe of his shoe to the squeaking parquet. "A floor that talks to you."

"So we'll take it?" Masha asked.

A huge leather divan stood in the centre of the room. Other than that, there was more dust than furniture. Antosha liberated a whole cloud of it by sitting on one end and letting himself fall back. Lika came and looked down on him.

"Happiness at last," he told her.

Isaac was still investigating pictorial possibilities. The linden avenue they'd driven up, the clotted sky. He missed what Masha saw. Perhaps Lika and Antosha had been doing this all along without Masha noticing either. Passing something shivery and invisible back and forth with their eyes.

"It's going to rain again," Isaac announced, finally turning.

B.-K. was waiting in the doorway. "Please, come see the dairy. I think you'll be impressed."

They got out of meeting his cows because Antosha asked for a tour of the grounds.

"Brother," Masha whispered. "I need to get back."

"Are there mushrooms?" he asked B.-K.

The picking was capital, and Antosha wanted to see for himself. Off they traipsed, back down the avenue and into the woods, where B.-K. pointed out his secret troves. He'd inserted sticks in the ground to mark where they grew.

"There and there and there. Normally I don't tell people this, but for a man of your stature, I'll make an exception."

"*I'm* actually taller," Misha said.

Isaac had really let his guard down. If not for Masha shepherding him along, he would have fallen completely behind. No slower companion on a walk than a landscape painter. He stopped every few paces to look around. Just as they emerged back onto the avenue, the skies opened.

"As I expected," the cloud-master said.

At last an excuse to hurry. Lika and Masha ran back to the house, where they took breathless shelter under the eaves, waiting for the men to catch up. The men barely picked up their pace, just turned up their collars. Isaac was asking B.-K. something, moving his arms in a flagless semaphore, Antosha and Misha listening. Were they trying to prove who was most waterproof? Was everything a competition?

As they neared the house, Antosha was first to lift his gaze—to Lika with her wet curls sticking to her cheeks and her wet dress a second skin. That shivery thing Masha had seen in the drawing room, she saw again and recognized now. It was how they'd looked at each other every time Lika had stepped into their parlour when he was recovering from Sakhalin Island.

Do you think he'll marry her? Mother had asked.

No, Masha had said. But whatever had been stopping him then—stopping his heart—it was gone.

Under her feet, the ground seemed to shift. One of her ankles wobbled and she nearly lost her balance. Antosha was right there, but still gazing at Lika. The wall of the house kept Masha upright.

THEY COULDN'T MOVE UNTIL BOGIMOVO HAD BEEN cleaned, which left them squeezed together for the next two days, the remainder of Lika and Isaac's visit. Antosha gave up trying to write, saying he'd catch up later on the windowsill. Instead they dedicated themselves to amusements. Sketching and croquet. And long lingering meals when, over Mariushka's thrice-daily nettle soup, Isaac lifted his soulful eyes to Lika and intoned, "In this tureen, in this very shade of green, I see our melancholia and spiritual loneliness." And Misha, screwing up his face behind his pince-nez, told her, "In this tureen, I see what stung my backside this morning."

Lika bestowed tolerant smiles. But when Antosha teased her for taking too much food, though she ate like a bird, her smile seemed part of nature. A flowering on her face.

What Masha saw in her bowl was bile. Antosha often wrote about love. Yet she'd never seen him in love with anyone, never seen him look at any of her friends as he'd looked at Lika under the eaves at Bogimovo. Not one! He'd looked *through* Lika, through her wet dress to her wet skin, and deeper still, peeling away her layers. It hadn't mattered that Masha was standing right there, so private and exclusive was their mutual stare. And Masha was the one who'd introduced them!

This was not her intention. Not actual *love*. Someone to cheer him up, then to stop him from taking that terrible journey. Someone temporarily purposeful, like the wind. Let it flap dry the washing, then go away.

Masha excused herself from the table and returned to Svoloch. Soon Lika came to find her, flushed with a distressing happiness.

"We're going for a walk. Come."

Masha smiled, or at least stretched her mouth, and shook her head. She gestured to Svoloch, who was not actually misbehaving, but lunching on his tray of scraps in the corner of the room.

"I have to keep an eye on him."

"I'll stay with you, then," Lika said.

"Don't. I may nap."

Lika hesitated before leaving. "Do you think you could take Isaac off painting tomorrow? This morning he was waiting for me at the top of the gully. I hadn't even washed my hands."

She was oblivious to Masha's distress, or Masha hid it too well.

That night, Lika turned over in the bed, jostling Masha. She hummed herself to sleep while Masha lay stiff as a corpse. Would Antosha marry her? All that talk of being terrified of matrimony, of being married to his work, was that just to keep his sister happy?

Under the bed, the mongoose scraped at something with his teeth. Masha heard, too, the determined mechanical huffs of an approaching train.

If he married, what would happen to her, she who had not even wanted to sit on the floor with Lika? *Ahhhh!* screamed the trestles. *Ahhhh!* the piles and abutments. She would become an unmarried sister-*in-law*—*Ahhhh!*—which no sane person wanted to be.

Lika didn't know what they'd been through. She thought Father was *funny*! No one but Masha had put on the same coat as Antosha or sat for hours in that dark storeroom, so still that not even the mice knew they were there. Lika would resent their closeness and drive herself between them. Then the babies would come, Lika growing fatter and more tyrannical with each one. Antosha didn't earn enough. He could barely pay for the jewellery box. He would work himself to death. Lika would kill him.

Ahhhh!

Svoloch came out from under the bed. There was just enough moonlight for her to see the object he was tossing around. A white bone gnawed clean.

———

As they walked, Lika asked if anything was the matter.

"I didn't exactly drown in sleep," Masha told her, adding, "Not with those trains."

In a few hours Lika and Isaac would be gone on one, thank God. Isaac and Antosha had set off early to fish. Masha and Lika were searching for wild strawberries where the meadow met the woods. Father walked ahead, sweeping his stick through the undergrowth. The heat was such that they'd put on their white summer dresses for the first time.

Wild strawberries are secretive. They had to push aside the leaves to get to the fruited jewels. Their sugary fragrance exacerbated Masha's vertigo, as did the stale smell of her dress just out of the trunk, and the sun's hot fingers on her nape. Her nerve endings outside her skin.

Father looked over to where Masha and Lika crouched. "During serfdom the girls had to sing while berry-picking. Otherwise the master would accuse them of eating his berries and beat them."

Masha translated for Lika. "He's asking for a song."

Lika indulged him with one that Masha had never heard, a conversation in alternating verses between a mother and her child. The child hears voices, a fancy her mother refutes.

Thou'rt dreaming, darling daughter. It's just the night wind sighing.

Angels, the fevered child insists.

I follow on, she says, dying.

When Lika finished, Masha saw that Father had been moved to tears, as Masha herself nearly was. How could Antosha not love her?

Father asked the name of the song.

"'Angel Serenade.'"

"I just heard one," he said.

Masha braced herself for an attack of religiosity, but Antosha came into view then, crossing the meadow dressed in his sailcloth fishing jacket and broad-brimmed hat. Lika turned, then waved, prompting Antosha to clutch his chest and stagger; she threw back her head and laughed to shame the birds.

As he approached, Lika held out her bowl. There was nothing coy in the gesture. She did it out of natural generosity. Antosha popped a berry in his mouth. The first wild strawberry of summer. On his face, the same look that had shoved Masha aside.

"I thought you were fishing," Masha said.

"They weren't biting. Mother told me where you were." He picked a handful of strawberry leaves and put them in his pocket.

"What good are the leaves?" Father asked.

"They're medicinal." To Lika he said, "They steady the heart."

"Where's Isaac?" she asked.

"Ah," he said to Masha. "She thinks of him every minute. Only him." He put a leaf in his mouth and began to chew it. "He's gone after Trofimov."

"What?" Lika smiled now. "Is Trofimov here?"

"He just showed up. And you won't believe how he got here."

"How?"

"He swam!" Antosha held out his arm for her to take. "Did I hear right? Were you singing?"

"Yes, she was." Father sighed.

They set off together, deeper into the woods, where fewer, if any, strawberries grew. Lika began to sing again. Father and Masha resumed picking, not speaking, instead listening to Lika's serenade grow fainter. On second hearing, a cloying song.

Lika had succeeded in getting him alone without Masha's help.

The singing stopped, and Father said, "They must be eating the berries."

The last thing Masha wanted was to be standing there when they emerged hand in hand. She straightened from her crouch, shook her bowl to level the berries.

"I'm done," she told Father. "I'm going back." Her skirt, she noticed with irritation, was speckled with bright red droplets, like she'd been stabbed all over with a pin.

Before she'd taken a step, she heard a halloo. Isaac waving his hat, half striding, half running toward them. He reached them, breathless and looking panicked.

"Where's your brother?"

Masha was guilty only of a reflex. Of their own accord, her eyes veered in the direction the two had gone. Isaac charged past her and Father, bellowing again.

Moments later—Masha had only just begun to walk away herself—Lika came up from behind. Hands shielding her face, she hurried past, along the green twice-trampled path. Masha glanced back to see Father watching Lika too, his white brows united in consternation.

Next came the strained, comradely banter of Russia's greatest writer and painter—*the landscape, the landscape*—then the great men themselves. Seeing Masha and Father still there, Antosha put on a surprised face. Lika's empty bowl was in his hand, but he acted as though nothing out of the ordinary had happened to its tearful owner.

He stopped to pick; Isaac too. When Antosha straightened, Isaac did as well, a pair of convicts shackled together. Neither would meet Masha's questioning eye.

Back at the dacha, Masha found Lika at the washstand, splashing like a sparrow so no one would know she'd been crying.

"I guess Isaac interrupted something," Masha said.

No reply from the sparrow, which made Masha feel quite terrible.

Isaac came in a few minutes later. They packed then and left to catch the train as planned, Lika scrubbed pink and flashing lying smiles all around. But for Antosha, a mere nod.

WHILE ANTOSHA WOULD SOMETIMES LEAVE A LETTER on his desk for Masha to chance upon, he'd never before put one in her hand. When she copied out his stories, he'd expressed no interest in what she thought of them.

She should have just asked him. "Are you planning on getting married?" She opened her mouth to do it.

No words. She was afraid of what he'd say. The floor would open and swallow her. She'd faint, and he'd let her fall to the floor. Or he'd lie.

He watched her closely as she accepted the page. Masha sensed something like agitation. It made hers worse. Was it a proposal? Why seek her opinion? Did he expect her to approve? Lika had rushed out of the trees in tears. Why?

It was Masha's fault. She'd given them away to Isaac with a flick of her eyes. She hadn't wanted them to be alone. But neither had she wanted to make Lika miserable. How had she sounded when she questioned her at the washstand? Not sharp, she hoped. She could be so sharp—frightening, Lika had once said. Masha hated that part of herself. She truly wanted to be kind, the way Lika had been kind to her when she'd cried over Georgi. Lika had consoled her like a sister. A *sister*, not a *sister-in-law*.

Masha could be one, but not the other.

She looked into Antosha's eyes, impatient now, then began to read.

Golden Lika! Come back and smell the flowers, walk, fish, blubber. Ah, lovely Lika! When you bedewed my right shoulder with your tears (I have taken out the spots with benzene) . . .

She began reading from the top again, puzzled. She'd assumed that Isaac had been implicated in Lika's distress as much as she was. That he'd burst in on her and Antosha because of Masha's signal. But that wasn't what happened.

. . . and when you sat at our table and ate (if truth be told, far more than your share), we greedily devoured your face, your hair, your perfect form, with our hungry eyes. There being nothing else left to eat. Ah, Lika, Lika, diabolical beauty! Come back!

    Yours, Mr. Hunyadi Janos

P.S. When you're at the Hermitage with Trofimov, I hope you accidentally jab out his eyes with your fork.

She handed him the letter. "You made Lika cry, brother."

This was not the reaction he wanted. The corners of his eyes had started to crinkle in expectation of her laugh, but now he drew back.

"Did she tell you that?"

"No. You wrote it yourself. 'You bedewed my right shoulder with your tears.' Antosha, Lika is my friend. I ask you to be careful with her feelings."

4

T HEY'D BEEN AT BOGIMOVO FOR TWO DAYS WHEN
Masha returned from a walk to find Svoloch gone.
Everyone helped with the search, including the family
staying on the upper floor of the manor, the Kiseliovs, and the
German zoologist, Dr. Wagner, in the dacha next to where B.-K.
and his flame-haired mistress lived. They swarmed the park, beating the bushes, calling Svoloch's name. The Kiseliov children, a boy
and a girl, eight and ten, seemed to treat it as an amusing game,
calling out in falsetto, or mimicking Dr. Wagner's accent. The mistress, who could not understand what manner of creature they
were searching for, made inappropriate honking sounds.

Dr. Wagner was short with wiry hair, a dandy as well as a
zoologist, always dressed in colourful paisley shirts. Though his
field was arachnids, he was eager to meet a live mongoose. He was
the last of the search party to give up, other than Masha.

"If I recall correctly, they emit a high-pitched noise commonly
called 'giggling' when they mate. Can you corroborate?"

"No," Masha told him. "Svoloch didn't get on with his wife."

"That doesn't preclude mating."

"I wouldn't know."

By then it was dusk, nearly dark among the trees, the paths
fading before their eyes. Masha found herself having to take the
arm of this man whose scientific curiosity so outweighed his sense
of decorum.

"In nature, the sexual instinct is unconnected to affection. That's a human complication."

Did he expect her to comment? Now she was flustered as well as panic-stricken.

At last they emerged onto the linden avenue leading to the house. The lamps were already lit, and Masha saw figures moving across the windows. When Dr. Wagner began to titter suggestively, she wrested free her arm.

"I was merely conjecturing about the giggle," he said as she picked up her skirts and ran.

A lamp waited for her in the vestibule. The barely furnished rooms, bereft of rugs, were echo chambers. She followed the meal-time clamour to the dining room, where Mariushka had set out cold fare. The whole search party was noisily digging in. Mother noticed her first.

"Masha! Did you find him?"

Mariushka looked almost jubilant as she served. Masha marched over to her.

"You let him out."

By her expression, Masha knew she hadn't. Mariushka was a terrible liar, would sputter and shift from warty foot to warty foot, denying she'd broken a plate or let the samovar boil dry. She was firmly planted now.

"My tongue is not deceitful!"

Mother came and put an arm around Masha. Masha threw it off.

Had anyone even searched the house? She called Svoloch's name down the hall and into the high-ceilinged gloom of every room, half-heartedly, because if he was in the house, he would have joined them at the table, jumped brazenly on it and snatched whatever took his fancy. Unless he'd got himself trapped. She stopped calling and listened instead. They were talking about her in the dining room, deciding who should go after her.

In the drawing room that Antosha had claimed as his, she threw herself on the divan. Blew out the lamp and abandoned herself. Like Svoloch in his basket, her weeping was an animal inside her clawing to get out.

"Why are you crying?"

Antosha, silhouetted in the doorway. She heard a squeak and sat up, expecting to see his smile and Svoloch squirming in his arms. Another joke. But it was only the floor giving its opinion as he crossed the room.

He looked down on her, a shadow with the ghost of a handkerchief held out.

She took it, and he sat beside her, shifting in discomfort, while she wept it to saturation.

When she'd calmed enough to hear him, Antosha said, "He's wild, sister. It's been hell living with him, you have to admit it."

Meaning he was prepared to let Svoloch go? That he'd be glad if the animal died? Everyone had rejoiced over Mrs. Svoloch beaten to death by the floor polisher, her beautiful corpse tossed onto the ash heap. Still weeping, she could feel how uncomfortable Antosha was with her emoting. She thought of Lika crying in the woods, *bedewing* his shoulder. Antosha had probably recoiled. Or perhaps he'd changed the subject, as he did now.

"I meant to ask what you think of these Kiseliovs. Not as fun as *our* Kiseliovs. The adults, I mean. The children are a delight. Remember that summer?"

Kiseliov was also the name of the family from whom they'd rented a dacha five years before.

Antosha went on. "Spectacular fishing. Spectacular dairymaids. Isaac was giving you painting lessons." He laughed. "Wasn't that when he proposed? I bet you're glad now that you refused."

She blew her nose in his sopping handkerchief and handed it to him. "I didn't refuse. He dropped the matter."

"Thank God. Let's hope he doesn't break Lika down."

How hard did he hope this? Here was another chance to ask what his intentions were with Lika, but his mention of Isaac's proposal brought the memory back. Just now she'd overheard them deciding who would come to her. Antosha had come that time too, when she'd been crying in confusion in her room.

The moon made plated rectangles of the windows. Masha saw Antosha's profile clearly, handsome even as he frowned over the thought of Lika and Isaac.

"Did you speak to him? After he proposed to me, I mean," Masha asked. "Did you say something to him?"

Antosha looked at her. "Isaac? I can't remember. It's ancient history." A flickering thought caused his brows to lift. "You're not in love with him, are you?"

"No."

"Isaac is, as you know, polyamorous. It would not be pleasant to be married to him. Where did you put the lamp? And can I find a match? Damn that mongoose. Are you ready? We'll find our way if we hold hands."

He extended his. It looked silvered, a steel gauntlet. Cold. Her mind darted around. How funny that she noticed its movement, as though it wasn't her mind but a bird hopping between related memories. Related, but only after the fact. For there was that other proposal, which had also evaporated. And was he going to marry Lika?

"Do you remember your conversation with Lieutenant Egorov?"

"Who?" Antosha asked, not following her logic. But then he did, and his tone cooled. "Ah! Egorov. Yes. I do remember." Now he was irritated, either by the unpleasant recollection, or because he'd spent hours searching the estate and wanted his dinner. "What do you want to know?"

She remembered Egorov with fondness. His deep stare and crooking finger. His slightly stooped back in his grey uniform, the clean skin on the dome of his head as he ducked out of the library after he'd proposed, rushing off to find Antosha.

"What did you say to Egorov?"

Antosha sat for a moment with his head bowed. How delicate a man he was, how different from, say, Dr. Wagner, the zoologist. When he finally spoke, she smelled his breath. Georgi's had a tea smell, but Antosha's was always tinged with sweetness.

"Do you know where we met Lieutenant Egorov and the others?" he asked.

"No."

He shifted farther away, angling his gaze so the moonlight seemed to shine out of the lenses of the pince-nez. The sound of laughter reached them. Masha heard a stomach grumble but couldn't tell if it was hers or his.

"We met them one evening at a house in town."

He coughed, little huffs into his fist, out of embarrassment or to stop her from asking more. The sound deepened, and soon his whole body began pitching forward and back like he was riding a slow-moving horse. He felt around for the handkerchief, which had fallen beside his feet. Alarmed, she picked it up and pressed it into his hand, this cold scrap of material that she'd vindictively soaked, waiting to see if when he lifted it off his mouth, he would have anything to show for this racking labour.

"Oh, brother. Are you all right?"

He held up a hand to silence her.

It was only a few minutes, but it felt like an hour before the coughing stopped. He wiped his lips with the handkerchief—unstained, thank God—and returned it to his pocket.

The thing about Egorov was that Masha hadn't even considered him a suitor. But after his proposal, she'd ached over his bald head and blinking eyes for many months. He never came back. And neither would Svoloch. Some creature would murder him, or some hunter shoot him. She knew that these two disappearances, eight years apart, had nothing to do with each other, but the way they were talking now, in near-whispers in the dark, complicated her feelings after the fact.

"I wish I wasn't human," she said.

"'A chicken is not a bird, a woman is not a human being.'" When she stiffened, Antosha hastened to add, "I'm joking, sister! I didn't coin the expression. Come here. Come."

He held her to his chest, kissed the top of her head. "Tomorrow we'll look again. We'll visit every estate in the district, every peasant hovel. We'll find that little devil. I promise. And still you cry!"

"I'm twenty-eight," she told him.

"I know your age," he said.

IN PARIS, THERE WERE NIGHTCLUBS THAT DEFIED imagination. Men wrestled boa constrictors, and chorus girls kicked their legs as high as their heads. Masha had overheard her brothers discussing these wonders the day after Antosha returned from Europe. She heard Misha's eager queries about the brothels.

A brothel was what Antosha had meant by "a house in town."

Antosha had answered Misha that the ones in Paris were no better than anywhere else, that his favourite experience had been in Siberia with a Japanese whore who'd made intercourse seem like advanced equitation.

Then he offered an older brother's advice. "Listen, Misha. You must be careful when you go to brothels."

"Yes, Doctor," Misha said.

"I'm not speaking about diseases. Well, not only. In every establishment, you'll find a particular girl, happy-seeming and preternaturally kind. She's always young. It's an act. The happiness, I mean. You destroy them when you touch them. Understand?"

"Snore. Any other advice?"

"Yes. Don't use so many adverbs when you write."

Masha thought back on this unpleasant conversation—unpleasant to *her*—as she unpacked her trunk in Bogimovo. She knew Moscow's brothels were mainly clustered along Sobolev Lane, though she'd never seen them. She did remember the wretched establishment in Taganrog, though, and how she and Mother had accidentally found themselves passing it one day. A woman's glove was nailed to the door right through the palm, the empty fingers curled.

Men went out of exigency. Masha had learned this years back when Anosha was studying medicine. Kolia and Aleksander stopped by one evening. Neither was sober, and they were less so by the time they left. Masha moved in and out of the room, unnoticed. They were laughing over a case study Antosha was writing for his course, about a young railway clerk so afflicted with "spermatorrhoea" that he was continually soaking his own trousers, the unmistakable legacy of "onanism." She was unfamiliar with these words.

"And what did you prescribe?" Kolia had asked.

"Nux vomica, potassium bromide and a month of daily baths each a degree colder than the previous."

"Hasn't he ever heard of a whore?" said Aleksander. "What does he think they're for?"

Which was when Mother, normally docile, came flying into the room, raging at them for their vile talk, in front of their sixteen-year-old sister no less. Chastened, her crazy lumbering brothers surrounded Mother, fell to their knees and kissed her hands. Kissed up her arms all the way to her elbows, begging for her blessing, which of course she gave.

Then they thundered out, probably to Sobolev Lane, so they could relieve themselves in the medically recommended manner, unlike that dolt of a railway clerk.

THE NEXT DAY, ANTOSHA BORROWED ONE OF B.-K.'s troikas and three of his model horses. Pulled by these satisfied beasts, they set out to search the neighbouring estates. Antosha brought along a photograph taken during his homeward journey—he and a sailor also mad enough to buy a mongoose, posing with their folly in their laps.

"What are they?" asked the first landowner, a short man with a purplish, capillaried face.

"They're like minks, but tamer," Antosha told him.

"The eyes are different. The pupils." Masha made a sideways motion with her finger.

"What an evil-looking snout. Do they bite?"

Antosha and Masha exchanged sheepish glances.

"God in heaven! I hope I don't run into it."

Yet they secured permission to speak to his labourers. The first hut they knocked at, a woman answered who could have been twenty or fifty. Fear sprang onto her face, and she bowed and stepped aside to let them in the black hole where they lived—one room, most of it taken up by a chimney-less stove. Soot had painted the ceiling, and Masha could see a dark band around the walls level with where the smoke hung when the stove was lit. On the stove's shelf lay an old woman who had apparently soiled herself. Or the stench came from the scarlet-faced baby screaming in the wooden cradle hanging from one of the beams. The snoring heap on the sleeping bench contributed his alcoholic fumes. Through this thickened air, a corps of flies wheeled.

Masha stayed by the open door where she could steal breathable gulps of air. What made the room seem more pathetic than squalid was that someone had actually tried to better it. Pasted sadly around the icons were paper wrappings from sweets and labels off vodka bottles. And most of the country lived like this.

The woman and two others began scurrying around with a cockroach-like alacrity. Antosha, who showed no sign that he shared Masha's repulsion, asked them not to bother with the samovar. He took out the photograph and explained why they were there. After much back and forth, they at last understood that he wanted the animal returned alive.

"No tea. No, thank you. But may I?" He gestured to the unheeded baby.

One of the women—the mother was working in the manor, they explained—lifted the baby out of the crib. Antosha wiped the streaming mucous off its nose with his handkerchief. The screams grew louder. He peeped under the dress, then gently removed the ragged garment, revealing a bulbous stomach blotched with red.

Did they have water? Someone shuffled out on bowed legs and came back with a basin of what looked like weak tea. Antosha unwound the sodden napkin, revealing the fat worm of the infant's sex. Then he seated himself on the bench by the drunkard's blackened feet and laid the screaming, naked child along his legs. He dipped his handkerchief in the basin and squeezed it out over the distressed brow, letting the water run onto the dirt floor. The baby stopped crying at once and stared up at Antosha. Sleep hurriedly replaced the child's astonishment.

Antosha asked for a fresh napkin, put it on the baby himself, dressed him again, and laid him in his cradle. So deeply did the baby slumber, his arms and legs hung limp. Antosha might have been placing him in a coffin. Would someone soon be doing this very thing?

The women crowded around making the sign of the cross as they left.

Out of earshot, Masha asked what was wrong with the child.

"What's wrong with all of them? That was a scene out of Ryurik's time, or Ivan the Terrible's. Three decades since Emancipation, and they live worse than cattle. A cow tends to a feverish calf. What a country."

"Your trousers are soiled."

He looked at them in feigned horror. "My trousers are soiled."

"Let's go home. I feel sick."

He stopped and pressed his lips to her forehead. "Yes, you're hot. It's contagious, you know."

She pictured the distended stomach patterned with rash. "But what's the matter with him?"

"The child? He has Sixth Disease. You're suffering from Moral Indignation. Don't worry. Neither lasts." And he strode toward the next hut, vowing to find the blasted mongoose.

After the long day of searching—three estates, including barns and outbuildings, and two score huts, each worse than the last—they returned to Bogimovo, and Masha fell into bed. Svoloch finally appeared, but in the form of a man. Long narrow face, pointed nose, tawny hair. He lifted the covers and, still wearing his fur coat, slid in beside her. As they snuggled, he asked which suited him more—to be human or animal, man or child. She told him that she loved him as an animal, but this was nice too.

"Choose," he said.

How tenderly Svoloch chewed her fingers as a man.

THE NEXT MORNING, SHE STRUGGLED TO RISE. ANTOSHA came to find out what was keeping her.

"I think I'm ill."

"Ill?" He made her name her symptoms, then fetched his bag and listened to her heart. "And now we have a use for those strawberry leaves."

Mariushka brewed the tea according to the doctor's instructions. Masha drank it and slept again, alone this time, only to wake hours later feeling worse—headachy and dizzy.

Not until the next day did her delirium fully manifest, but it must have started then. Or had she caught a chill the week before, standing under the eaves in the rainstorm? What else could account for what she did next?

Antosha had so much work, yet he'd put it aside to fulfill his promise to find Svoloch. And here was Masha, lying lazily abed. With a feverish determination to do her part, she threw off the covers. She made it as far as the door, then had to lean against the jamb and wait for the vertigo to pass. Like blind Zinaida, she kept one hand on the wall.

She left by the back entrance, but immediately sank down on the steps and folded herself over her drawn-up knees. An oriole screeched, then sang. She heard Mother and Mariushka in the kitchen querulously discussing dinner. "Cover the sour cream. The flies!"

On her feet again, she set off weak-leggedly, past the kitchen and along the path to the dachas. The Kiseliov children were trying to launch a kite. When they saw her, they shouted for her to help; she pretended not to hear. Past the vegetable garden with its tidy rows of cabbages. The wattle fence, the rows of bee skeps smeared with mud. The bees were making a ferocious sound. Even after she'd passed them, her ears buzzed.

Then she saw B.-K.'s mistress and stopped. The woman was trudging along the path toward her, a pail in each hand.

Masha shouted, "Empty or full?"

"Full!" The black spaces in her mouth showed when she laughed, crenellations on a parapet.

As she neared, Masha saw that the pails brimmed with milk.

"Going for a walk?" the woman asked, innocently enough, though her mocking expression belied it.

For the first time, Masha noticed her eyes—greenish with yellow streaks. Why the mockery? She looked down at herself. She'd forgotten to dress, was barefoot too. She could guess the state of her hair, but still she lifted her chin and answered as though nothing was amiss.

"I'm looking for the mongoose. Could he be in the barn?"

"I looked yesterday. I'll check again, if it will put you at ease. But if you don't mind me saying, you're going to an awful lot of trouble over that creature, when there are so many people in need."

"I don't like people as much as that creature."

How hard-hearted she sounded. She thought of the sick baby, and a fresh wave of vertigo hit. And now the do-gooding mistress would launch into the tedious sort of lecture they kept hearing from B.-K. No one was more of a humanitarian than Antosha, who never speechified.

Indeed, the mistress set the pails down on the dusty track and straightened the kerchief that hid her red hair. A dark apron of wet showed under the arm of her dress.

"I hope you'll forgive my frankness."

"That depends."

"You should get married."

Masha gaped, but the mistress carried on.

"I see the same thing in my girls. They're restless and despondent until they calf."

Had she just compared Masha to a cow? The buzzing in Masha's ears grew louder. And here was further proof that she wasn't thinking straight. She gave the woman such a feeble retort.

"Why don't you have children, then?"

"I do. They're with their father. Happiness is over for me. I may as well look for the wind in a field."

She stared at Masha with her cat eyes. Until then Masha had thought her scrawny and dim. What B.-K. saw in her, she couldn't fathom. But now the halo of self-sacrifice shone all around her. Her pride in her sacrifice too. She'd been there all Masha's life, staring out of the icon corner.

Had she spoken these blasphemous thoughts out loud? The mistress seemed to hear them, for a look of horror crossed her face.

"What?" Masha asked. "What are you gawking at?"

She dropped her eyes again. Spattered down the front of her

nightdress were bright droplets of strawberry juice. A second later came the gush.

Nosebleed, fever and malaise could be typhoid, Antosha said, but nervous prostration was more likely. In either case, for the rest of the week he monitored her condition in between all the other things he did.

From her sickbed, Masha stared out the window at the trees and the swathe of sky above them, its endless parade of clouds. Everything falling under the spell of light. Why couldn't she paint? How had she lost her passion? If she found it again, she would never have to leave this bed. Viridian treetops, an ultramarine sky.

Next time she woke, it was to charcoal trees with a thin sap-green line behind them.

Olga came for a visit. Antosha collected her at the station and bought her lunch in town before bringing her to Bogimovo.

"I gathered you weren't going to die, or we would have come directly," she told Masha. "I'll make you a cigarette. That will revive you." She unloaded her requirements onto the windowsill—tobacco pouch, papers, matchbox. "Your brother's lost his head over that Lika. He's actually exerting himself. When has he ever had to do that?"

"What do you mean?"

"He saw a photograph in a shop. Rushed in and bought it, then wrote a phony inscription on the back. 'To Lika from Petya—a thousand kisses.' Something like that. A postscript about how he'd been reading his own delightful stories and that she should buy them too. We stopped to post it on the way."

She lit the cigarette and held it out to Masha, who waved it off.

"Yes. It will invigorate you." When Masha refused a second time, Olga said, "You're boring."

She settled on the sill and proceeded to smoke it herself. "What a view! I feel like a tsarevna sitting here. Tsarevna of my own life, unlike you. You're a serf to your misery."

"I can't help it."

"Yes, you can. Take yourself in your hands. As for your brother's infatuation, I'm forever disgusted that a woman's character and intellect aren't enough. Like every other man, he wants Lika's body. But here's what he fails to see, Masha." The cigarette jabbed in emphasis. "Miss Mizanova will grow old and ugly, but I'll never grow stupid."

The reason Olga was so merry instead of her usual misanthropic self was that Antosha had taken her to lunch. She didn't even care that he'd talked the whole time about someone else. Olga was a pretend tsarevna. And what she'd said about Lika wasn't true. Lika wasn't stupid. If all Antosha had wanted was her body, he could have seduced her long ago, as he had so many of her other friends, including Olga.

What did he want from Lika? Why dash off joking letters and make your sister read them? Why do it in front of Olga, a former lover? If jokes and nonsense really were the means by which he conveyed deeper feelings, he must be head over heels. Why not propose and let Masha know where she stood?

Smoke leaked out as Olga frowned. "Women should stop living for men. And mongooses."

"Is he going to marry her?" Masha asked.

"Lika?" Olga snorted. "Only if she corners him. Then she'll be an unhappy woman."

There was such bitterness in her words that Masha had to probe. "Why do you say that?"

"Love isn't easy for him." Olga averted her eyes as though she'd betrayed an intimacy.

Had she? Masha knew the other side of the story. Olga was "a difficult proposition." Wasn't she generalizing outward from herself?

"Anyway, why would he marry when he has you?" Olga noticed something out the window then, slid off the sill and pitched down the cigarette.

"Hey!" came Antosha's cry.

"Where are you going?" Olga called.

"Mushroom picking! How's Masha?"

"Fine! Wait for me! I'm coming!" She turned to Masha. "Another thing I'm brilliant at."

Out she went, sashaying and singing, "Tsarevna, Tsarevna!"— the hem of her skirt, down at the back, dragging along the floor. In the doorway, she passed Mother entering with the post and nodded to her.

Did Olga mean that Antosha loved Masha more than his other women? Or that Masha running his house freed him from having to marry? A sister, after all, could be fed on scraps.

"She smells better than the last time," Mother said, handing Masha a letter. She made her sit up, plumped the pillows, then settled at the foot of the bed.

The letter was from Natalia. Zinaida was bedridden. Elena cared for her day and night. Her sister-in-law had just visited with the baby, the dote! Georgi was away playing concerts in St. Petersburg. And the nightingales were singing a new song. *When's that Masha coming to visit us, tra-la, tra-la!*

Masha dropped the letter on the floor and waited for Svoloch to dart out from under the bed and pounce on it.

"What's wrong?" Mother cooed.

She would get no sympathy if she spoke of Svoloch. "Do you still think about Evgenia?"

"Who?" Mother said, her expression blank.

"Baby Evgenia. My sister."

Mother's features collapsed. It seemed to Masha a mirror held up to what she felt.

HOW COULD SHE GRIEVE AN ANIMAL AS MUCH AS A human child? Masha wondered this on her way to Ukraine. Because humans are animals too. Even chickens are. What a stupid expression. She missed him so. His bright eyes with their sideways pupils. His scientific ways. Even his wildness and destruction. It gave her something to wonder about when she went out. What chaos would she find when she returned?

She grieved because she had no one now. Antosha would lure Lika back. They were in love. Masha would be displaced. She had not understood her position to be insecure. She couldn't live with insecurity on top of grief. To that end, she was taking herself in her hands, as Olga had suggested. Her travelling case on the rack above her bulged with as many clothes as she'd dare bring to Luka without rousing Mother's suspicions. Pinned inside her bodice, a tightly rolled wad of rubles in a linen pouch, all she had, including some borrowed from Olga, who could hardly afford to lend yet gave without question. When Masha returned to Moscow, she'd go round to the Dairy School and raise hell about her unpaid wages.

Except she wouldn't return for a long time. She couldn't be in the same city as them. She'd stay with Natalia while she made her plan. (Thank God Georgi was away, or there would be nowhere for Masha to go.) Maybe she'd settle in St. Petersburg. Her brother Aleksander would surely keep her until she got on her feet.

She lifted the hand that pressed her money through her layers of clothing. A lightness flooded in then, and she found she could name it, this feeling that was genuinely strange to her. Freedom. Beyond the window, the paintable countryside flew past, green smears of fields, the blurred houses. This was only what Svoloch wanted—to be free. And now they both were, he leaping through the forest, she riding this train into uncertainty. It suddenly seemed thrilling.

At Kursk she disembarked again to stretch her legs, still strong in her resolve. Except then it began to rain, which was depressing. A peasant with a bound stump leaned on a crutch. Masha climbed back on board and got stuck in the passage behind a group of black-robed monks. When the bells rang and the train began to move, the holy blockage finally dispersed.

In Masha's compartment, a beak-nosed woman in the facing seat was snacking from a basket in her lap. The compartment smelled like a delicatessen. Spatters on the window. Masha denied the beggar a second time by averting her eyes as he slid from view. If she paid every beggar she felt sorry for, she would soon be one herself. Olga's generosity came to mind, but Masha didn't want to think of Olga. She was afraid of becoming her—unkempt, over-worked, bitter, always on the search for cheaper lodgings. Masha couldn't afford second thoughts. Yet they came.

How wretched she'd been when Antosha went to Sakhalin Island. Could she really part from him?

Svoloch was probably dead.

She covered her eyes with her hands. She wanted to see her life, or its palette at least. At first there was only blackness, but eventually her eyes adjusted, and she saw it—not black, but grey. The grey of dawn before the birds awaken. Before anything happens. The grey of diluted ink.

The woman seated across asked if she was ill. Masha took her hands away. "No." She refused the offer of a boiled egg.

She reached Sumy station in a state of exhaustion. Evening, but it was still hot. As the hired carriage drove the rutted road to Luka, she struggled to fashion her mouth into a smile. She'd been invited as relief from the desperate situation there—Zinaida's suffering and imminent death. Masha forbade herself from repeating last summer's debacle at Yalta.

The door flew open, and there was Natalia, the only woman who made Masha feel delicate. The brows that proved her lineage lifted. She held a finger to her lips.

"Zinaida's sleeping. You must be weary too. Come in. Are you hungry? Leave your bag. A telegram came for you."

It was lying on her waiting plate. Masha sank onto the chair, struggling not to burst into tears now.

"Open it," Natalia said.

Creature found. Come back.

MASHA RETURNED THE NEXT DAY TO BOGIMOVO, BRINGING Natalia, who was grateful for a holiday from sickness. On the train, Natalia kept shaking her head over Masha's miraculous transformation. She'd opened the door on a limp specimen of misery.

"But now you're like Zinaida on morphine. Are you going to marry this mongoose, Masha?"

5

SUMMER ENDED. FALL CAME, THEN WINTER AGAIN. Five months of Russian weather.

At Epiphany, Masha and Antosha sat down to file his correspondence, as they usually did, except for the previous January when Antosha had been ill from his voyage.

Towers of envelopes on the dining table, a castle built of paper and ink. They bowed heads, passed letters back and forth. Their murmured reminiscences of the year usually felt like Masha's reward for living through it. This year, though, there was less pleasure—even dread. Eventually one particular letter would surface. She did not want to see it.

She glanced across at Antosha—his kindly downward-tilted eyes, the polished pince-nez balanced on his handsome nose. With the tight bud of an Italian tie at his throat, he appeared so proper and contained, in contrast to last summer. Last summer he'd been consumed by Lika fever. Masha had been ill too, bedridden, and Antosha had worried there might be something the matter with her heart. Mother had laid her grey head on her Masha's chest, the weight of it a surprise, considering the triviality of most of her thoughts.

"I hear nothing," she'd finally said.

Of course not. A cleaved stone had lodged in Masha's breast. In its cleft, no living thing hid. And now, without the little dis-

turbances of a mongoose—he was gone, really gone!—the jewellery box was unnervingly quiet. No squeaking. No outraged fits
from the eavesdropping Mariushka, who kept bringing *pirozhki* as
a ruse.

But Antosha had been right to do what he'd done. He always
had her best interests in mind. A mongoose was a wild creature from a land so far away and strange that it could have been
make-believe. What did she really understand about his ways?
She'd seen Svoloch abuse his wife and wreak havoc all over the
house—behaviours she'd chosen to laugh off. Bloodlust had been
more difficult to excuse.

That gory, needled smile.

Creature found. Come back. A hunter had located him in a quarry
squeezed into a crevice, hiding from the dogs. "Amazing he could
get in for how fat he's grown," Antosha had remarked.

Fatter, indeed! Masha had rushed to him upon her return,
had cooed and strummed the mesh of his cage. Svoloch had been
imprisoned since his capture, so when she opened the door, he
set off at once to reacquaint himself with the room. She followed,
clicking her tongue. When this failed to bring him to her, she sat
on the floor and drummed her fingers.

"Come, Svoloch."

He remembered his name, for he cast her an over-the-shoulder
glance. But he did not come. Worse, when Natalia entered, Svoloch
ran to her instead. His natural curiosity impelled him to a stranger.
His curiosity was stronger than his love.

This cooling of his interest in her perplexed, then hurt, Masha.
When she managed to seize hold of him, he battled his way out of
her arms. After a day, she began to take offence and punished him

by leaving him in the cage. An hour later, when she returned, he chirred happily at the sight of her. But as soon as he was free, he ran off again.

One afternoon they were playing at croquet, happily swinging mallets—the Kiseliov children, who'd grown wild by then too, and given up wearing shoes, Misha, Antosha, Ivan, and strapping, laughing Natalia.

The Kiseliov girl dropped her mallet and screamed, "Snake!"

They cleared the area. Nearby, Dr. Wagner was hunting for spiders. All summer they'd joked that he was merely counting their legs. "Eight again, Dr. Wagner?" they asked when they met him on the grounds. Now he raced over to where Antosha was scanning their makeshift court.

"There. *Vipera berus*. Female."

Diamonds lined the snake's back. She was frozen on the spot, the full length of her stretched out in the grass, a necklace on a jeweller's tray.

Misha went and fetched the mongoose. Once released from his cage, Svoloch immediately sensed his natural enemy nearby. His eyes lit up, and he inflated himself into a threatening ball. The snake gathered up her coils. For a full minute they faced each other, mutually hypnotized, until deep in Svoloch's throat, a burble sounded. He began circling. The snake lunged; Svoloch retreated. Each time she came close to striking, the balletic mongoose took a gravity-defying leap. Then, faster than the eye could perceive, he clamped his teeth into her head and lashed her against the ground until she fell limp. Dragging this lifeless whip, Svoloch disappeared into the trees.

The scientifically curious—Dr. Wagner and Antosha—followed, and Masha, so she could take the conquering hero home.

When Dr. Wagner drew aside the foliage, Svoloch looked up at them and hissed. More than the battle, that was the moment that stayed with Masha. Svoloch curling back his lips to show them his merciless needles stained pink.

After he had killed, he was completely uncontrollable. They endured him for the rest of the holidays, took him back to Moscow, but his behaviour only worsened there.

And now there was this emptiness inside Masha and a ravenous urge to fill it, obscene under the circumstances, for the summer heat they'd enjoyed at Bogimovo had given way first to a crop-withering autumn, then record-breaking cold. The papers were reporting widespread starvation, which Antosha confirmed. He headed one of the famine relief committees.

Mariushka brought another plate of snacks. Masha picked up the next letter—from Ivan, not the one she dreaded from the animal graveyard—and guiltily popped another *pirozhok* in.

Why did she keep eating them? *Pirozhki* reminded her of the Taganrog market. Selling the birds, then rushing off with the coins to buy something to eat. *Pirozhki* because, stuffed with humiliation as well as meat, it sat in their stomachs the longest.

She dipped her fingers in a saucer of lemon water and wiped them, so as not to stain the paper. Across from her, Antosha chewed with a clear conscience, thanks to his good works. He was so good. She respected him more than she was angry with him.

"For the Levitan file." He coughed and tossed a page across to her. "Read it if you want."

Meaning he wanted her to.

Isaac's letters were as immaculately formed as Antosha's, but they slanted on the page.

Everything on earth, from the air I breathe to the most insignifi-
cant bug I accidentally squash, is imbued with the divine Lika! She
doesn't love you, pale cerebral author. She loves me, *the volcanic,*
swarthy painter. It hurts you to read this, I know, but my devotion
to the truth prevents me from hiding this fact. She's joining Sophia
and me.

There was a postscript in a different hand. Sophia's, accusing
Antosha of jealousy.

"How ridiculous," Masha said.

"Am I pale?" Antosha asked.

Mariushka was pretending to dust the photographs, but now
she drew closer, as though she could actually read the letter over
Masha's shoulder.

"What's it say?"

"Gossip needs no carriage when there's an old woman in the
house."

Mariushka's glower multiplied her wrinkles. She stumped off.

Antosha's pride was hurt too, the way it had been when *The*
Wood Demon failed. He was accustomed to success; he expected it.
He'd probably never been passed over by a woman either. Lika had
not returned to Bogimovo; instead another triangle had formed
without him: Sophia, Isaac, Lika. Pale cerebrals unwelcome.

Masha still remembered Lika's tears while strawberry picking
and her adamant claim that Isaac was just a friend. She couldn't help
wondering aloud how Lika had ended up with the two painters.

Antosha clearly wanted her to know the details. Lika, he said,
had gone to the country to stay with her aunt. Isaac and Sophia,
instead of taking their usual Volga River excursion, had found a
dacha nearby and settled in.

"Which was when he sent me that letter. Then I found out from the little brother that Sophia went back to Moscow a few weeks later. On her own."

So not a triangle. Isaac had won over Lika.

Antosha looked across at her, waiting for her outrage. More than anything, Masha felt disappointed in Lika. How she blew with the wind. Granny's entreaty came to mind. *Watch out for her.* Masha had failed. As for Isaac, it was a sad situation. He was like family, their closest living connection to Kolia. How many times had Isaac, just like Antosha, picked their drunken brother off the street? Isaac and Antosha had enjoyed vying for Lika, but now that she'd made a choice, surprising as it was, things were different.

"It's too bad," Masha said. "You're such old friends."

"Isaac's a friend? What sort of friend sends such a letter?"

She remembered then the complicating factor. The one thing that could explain Lika's behaviour.

"You took Lika into the woods and made her cry, brother. Did that have anything to do with her ending up with Isaac?"

He drew back, either offended or pretending to be, she couldn't tell. "If so, she's a child. I certainly made it up to her with my begging letters." He reached for the last *pirozhki* on the plate, so he wouldn't have to meet Masha's eye when he asked, "What did she tell you?"

"Nothing," Masha said.

"I thought you women told all."

"You're mistaken."

He hadn't been pretending offence. His tone cut the air now. "You assume I'm in the wrong. Why? I wasn't the one hurling accusations that day."

"What accusations?" Masha asked.

He put the gentle in "gentleman," but his words were barbed. "That I play with her feelings. That I'm not serious. That I talk nonsense. Me?" He pressed his hand to his chest in mock affront. "I suppose she would have preferred that I lie. That I ask her to marry me. Does she want me to marry her?"

Now they were openly discussing this thing she'd so dreaded last summer. All the remaining threat went out of it. She'd been silly to worry. Yet his outburst perplexed Masha.

"I'm sure she does want to marry you."

"Then why doesn't she propose? I've been waiting long enough. And what does she tell Isaac, who is undoubtedly flinging these same accusations at *her*? Mariushka? Are there any more *pirozhki*? I just ate the last one."

The crone had been listening behind the door. Now she popped her head in. "Better to marry than to burn!"

He laughed, but Masha didn't. She felt vaguely sick from the greasy dough and his ungentle tone.

"Anyway," Antosha said, "they've given me the plot for a story. I can thank them for that. I have more important things to occupy me at the moment. Peasants starve while they frolic."

It wasn't like him to mention his charity work. Masha took note of how he was sitting in his chair. If he was shifting from side to side, it would mean his downstairs complaint was back. She glanced under the table. He appeared solidly seated.

He picked an envelope off the pile and flapped it in disgust. "The King of Persia, yet he writes like a fishmonger."

Sighing, Masha took up another letter too. One glance at the return address sent a current through her. *The Garden Ring Road. The Zoological Gardens.* The reply to Antosha's offer of the mongoose. A spasm of resentment seized her. They came in waves like this, like cramping when she bled. She shut her eyes and forced a picture of the croquet incident, the revelation of Svoloch's teeth.

"You'll have to go," Antosha said.

She opened her eyes. "Pardon? Go where?"

"To Ukraine. Sister, I have to write continually. I can't afford to stop. Not with the rent I pay here." He glanced irritably around the dining parlour. "And it's too small."

Too small for him. For her too, brimming with memories. Antosha supine on the divan, soul-seething. Svoloch capering. Yes, they should move.

"This excess scribbling is playing villain with my health."

Masha said, "Your health is the most important thing."

"Agreed. I asked Smagin to help find an estate. He's come through for me, but I have to go to Nizhni Novgorod to meet the governor and see if they're actually supplying relief with this money we're sending."

It sank in what he was asking. "You want me to drive around with Mr. Smagin?"

"He's an excellent driver with excellent horses. Every one named after a member of the royal family."

A WINTER TRAIN JOURNEY TO UKRAINE WAS LESS PIC-turesque than a summer one, the countryside doubly lost under snow and behind a rimed window. She placed the flat of her palm against the frost and melted it with her angry heat. A peephole to look out. Snow was the hardest thing to paint.

She dreaded most seeing Georgi, who had been away during Masha's brief visit to Luka in the summer. But he was there now and would be shooting her pitying looks, lugubriously accompanied, until her rescuer showed up. The buffoonish King of Persia. Antosha knew that Smagin was interested in her. Why had he put her in this awkward position? Did he want Smagin to propose? Why? So he could say no again?

Natalia was waiting on the platform, waving her arm. At first Masha failed to recognize Georgi standing beside her, staring off at nothing. Despite his furs and Cossack hat, he seemed slighter, hands in his pockets instead of playing the air.

"You're growing your beard again," Masha said.

Georgi touched his face, still not meeting her eye. "I forgot to shave." Then he went ahead to tell the driver to unbutton the sledge cover.

If Masha had been worried that her feelings for Georgi would inconveniently reignite, she needn't have. He clearly despised her. Her impulse was to return the sentiment.

The Ukrainian cold lashed out as she and Natalia left the station. Frost sugared the horses' muzzles and clung to their tails. Natalia tucked the furs around them. Masha was in the middle, trying to put a space between her and Georgi. They'd given her the warmest place, yet already her eyelashes were freezing together.

Finally Natalia stopped fussing. "I have to warn you, Masha. We're living strangely these days."

Zinaida had died more than three months ago, in October. Their mother still couldn't be comforted, Natalia said, not even by Schopenhauer. Elena seemed to be trying to join her sister by working herself to death.

"At night she wanders about muttering. At first I thought she was reciting a poem. But when I asked, she said it was the names of all the patients she's lost. She's kept a list, and Zinaida's on it now. And Georgi? Tell her what you've gone and done."

"I cancelled my concerts."

"He practised so hard!"

How stupid Masha felt then. Georgi's behaviour had nothing to do with her. Couldn't she distinguish grief from animosity? For the rest of the ride, she shivered with cold and inward blame.

When the sledge drove up to Luka, evidence of the promised strangeness came into view. The fir branches that signified their bereavement still hung above the door. They should have been burned ages ago.

Entering the house, they tracked the desiccated needles inside with them. Elena and Mrs. Lintvariova came to greet Masha. Behind them stood the Borzois, their lovely heads hanging, as though they too were heartbroken. Georgi disappeared.

Elena asked Masha to thank Antosha for the obituary. "'In her presence everyone was reminded not of her approaching death, but of our foolish unawareness of our own.' So true."

She wished Masha and Natalia a safe journey the next day, and taking her mother's arm, led her away. Mrs. Lintvariova hadn't said a word. The corners of her mouth looked crusty, and her dress gaped at the bosom where a button was missing.

Later, after Masha had washed up, she joined Natalia in the drawing room. It was dark by then, the lamps lit. She'd expected Georgi to be playing, had steeled herself for it, but he wasn't there.

"Do you see how it is?" Natalia asked, handing Masha tea.

"Yes. I'm sorry Antosha made me come." The angry spasm again. "The last thing you need is a guest."

"Honestly, Masha? Your presence is irrelevant. Don't take offence. An army could descend on us and they'd take no notice."

"Still. I'm annoyed with Antosha."

Natalia dipped two fingers into her glass, fished out the sugar nugget and dropped it on the tray for later. Still no Georgi. Finally a sad event, but no musical accompaniment.

"Masha? I wish I'd been a better friend to you when Kolia died. I had no idea what you were going through."

Masha's memories seemed so anguished, but now she remembered the numbness too. Going through the rites, she'd felt like a china figurine being moved about on a shelf.

The piano stared at her. Georgi really wasn't coming.

Natalia said, "I'm going to show you something. I wasn't going to, but now I think I will." She exchanged her glass for the lamp and gestured for Masha to follow.

They went down the hall, stopping at Zinaida's room. Lit from below, Natalia's brow became a shadow. She seemed to be bracing herself before she opened the door. Trepidation seized Masha, as though she feared that Zinaida's body was still laid out. It was a horrible thought, but it gave way to something worse: Kolia. She saw herself kissing the icon on his chest. Antosha had run away the day before, gone to Smagin, where Masha would go tomorrow. What had Antosha written in the obituary? That they were all foolishly unaware of their own deaths. It was a lie. Antosha *did* realize it. Kolia's blood-soaked end was his too.

Her anger over Svoloch she'd directed at her sick brother all these months. Her *dying* brother. How long did Antosha have left?

Natalia opened the door on a narrow room. No decorations. Even if Zinaida hadn't been blind, Masha doubted there would have been anything on the walls but icons and strings of medicinal plants.

Natalia turned up the wick. "Be careful where you step."

Masha saw the glasses then. Starting the day Zinaida died and continuing for forty nights while her soul still roamed the earth, they'd laid a place at the table for her, poured her a glass of water, and covered it with a piece of bread. Now forty glasses with bread lids lined the windowsill and crowded the bureau and the floor. In some the water was green; in others, a strange tangle of white threads hung down, a beard of mould reaching for the clouded water. Alive, though Zinaida no longer was.

Natalia said, "I only discovered it yesterday because we were short of glasses. Every night Mother brought Zinaida's here after we'd left the table. I think she must be mad."

Masha had never seen Natalia cry before. She was so strong. She identified with the peasants, liked to slap her big arms and say, "I *am* a peasant!" Desperate as Masha was to escape the room and its implications, she hugged Natalia.

"You don't have to come with me tomorrow," she said.

"Of course I do." Natalia pulled back to say. "If I don't, Smagin will propose for sure."

THAT NIGHT MASHA LAY AWAKE LISTENING FOR ELENA'S wandering recitation, the way she used to lie awake listening for Svoloch as he followed her trail of delights. Svoloch. How was he handling his imprisonment? She couldn't bear to go and see him. Couldn't they have put him in his cage and kept him?

She forced him from her mind by picturing those glasses and their swampy contents. Svoloch was just a creature, not a sister or a brother. It was wrong to mourn him. She forgave Antosha, would forgive him anything if only he wouldn't die.

In the morning there was kasha on the table and the sound of weeping coming from another room. Smagin was due any moment.

He'd spent the night on a neighbouring estate and was going to take Masha, with Natalia as her chaperone, to see the properties that interested Antosha. After her tormenting night, instead of dreading Smagin, Masha found she couldn't wait for him to take her away from this stifling grief.

As though summoned by her thoughts, his looming bulk appeared in the doorway. He'd forgotten to give his hat to the maid and now clutched it to his chest. The boot brush still bristled on his face. His odd eyes darted all around, avoiding Masha's.

"Please sit, Mr. Smagin," she said. "Natalia's not ready yet. Tea?"

He set down the hat and noisily pulled out a chair, jarring the table when he sat, so that Masha's tea slopped into her saucer.

"It must be very cold out," she said.

He stared at the mound of fur before him. "The birds freeze in flight. But don't worry. I have extra sheepskins. I'll keep you warm. It's a promise."

In came Natalia. Seeing her glittery eyes and swollen face, Masha realized she'd been the one crying. Natalia feigned cheer and clasped Smagin's hands in welcome. Natalia he looked at, but then his emotions overwhelmed him. He tore free his hands, thumped his elbows on the table. The tea already in Masha's saucer sloshed out, reminding her of something Antosha once said. The sign of good character isn't *not* spilling on the tablecloth, but not noticing when someone else does.

"Aleksander, please," Natalia begged.

He couldn't stop. His shoulders heaved. "I can't bear that she's not here. That she suffered so, and you're all suffering still."

"Thank you," Natalia said. "But it will upset Mother if she hears you. She'll feel she has to comfort you, when she needs comforting herself."

He lifted his face then and thrust a shaking hand into his breast pocket for a handkerchief. Honked and wiped the moustache. "I apologize," he told the hat. Breathing noisily in and out, he mastered himself.

What Natalia did next surprised Masha. She took Smagin's hands again and shook them until he met her eye.

"It's all right, Aleksander. You are a good friend to us. Will you warm yourself with tea before we set off?"

He nodded. Natalia reached toward the samovar, but he wouldn't let go of her other hand. She stretched for a glass, wriggled her fingers for it. Smagin held on.

Natalia's teasing had been a game. Smagin, so big and awkward, was made for jest. If he'd been an actor, he would be cast in comic roles. Natalia had never mentioned how dear a friend he was.

Unlike her brother, Masha could be moved by an emotional scene. Blinking back her own tears, she filled Smagin's glass.

THEY WERE SUPPOSED TO VISIT THREE ESTATES, BUT only managed two that day. Both landowners knew that Smagin was coming with a prospective buyer, a famous writer, yet when they saw his proxy, they didn't bother disguising what they felt. Natalia was bid to warm up in the parlour. Best if Masha stayed there too.

"But, Peter," Smagin reasoned. "She's here to see the estate. You must let her look around."

The affronted landowner then switched to Ukrainian. After much gesticulation, a smile appeared under Smagin's moustache.

"After you, Miss C." He swept his arm gallantly.

Now when he failed to meet Masha's eye, she assumed that

he was embarrassed, which he ought to have been. Every question she asked—How old was the roof? Which crops grew the best?—was answered to Smagin, as though she were an imbecile. They inspected the house, then tramped along the waist-deep paths to the barn, bathhouse and privy. Hard to imagine what things looked like when not blanketed by snow. Back to the house before they froze. As soon as Masha mentioned money, the sensitive land-owner would take Smagin's arm and pull him into another room for a round of fierce whispering.

Fuming, Masha joined Natalia in the parlour. By then she'd drunk the samovar dry. Eventually, Smagin came to fetch them.

"He was damnably rude," he said the first time. And the second.

Then the wind came up, strong and biting, driving sheets of snow across the road. Smagin's moustache, completely frozen, turned from black to white.

"Miss C., Natalia? Perhaps we should put off the last stop. I'm having difficulty seeing." They nodded. Smagin flicked the reins. "Aleksander! Xenia! Olga! Go!"

When they arrived, Smagin apologized for the modesty of his home. The lacy trim on the eaves vied prettily with the icicles, but the house was clearly in poor shape, crooked inside the way a building gets when it wearies of its foundation. The door wouldn't properly close; after they entered, the maid pushed a table against it. She was dressed in a traditional blouse, which Natalia compli-mented her on.

"The samovar?" Smagin asked.

"Boiled to a sparkle, sir, with joy that you've safely arrived, thanks be to God. We were worried you'd be caught in the storm."

"I'll tell Kalina to bring it and see how long till supper. Please. Ladies. The parlour's the warmest room this time of year."

Natalia knew the way. More crookedness—in the stove tiles squeezing each other out like bad teeth, the stacks of teetering catalogues and correspondence that confirmed Smagin's bachelor status. Like Antosha, he probably gave orders that nothing be touched, though Antosha was fanatically neat. He didn't want the inkwell moved from its logical place. Smagin had no logic, or it was hidden in his personal chaos.

The door flew open. Smagin led in the cook, also in native dress, grinning widely and carrying the samovar on a tray. He hastened to clear space on the table by transferring some ledgers to a chair. The cook returned with glasses and a plate of fried and sugared delicacies.

"Oh, *khrustyky!*" Natalia said, rushing for them. "Try one, Masha. You'll die."

"To tide you over till supper," the cook said, curtsying.

Smagin, the lingering cook, Natalia—they all watched as Masha bit into a cookie. The part in her mouth melted while the rest crumbled down her front.

"Good," she told the cook.

"Ah," Smagin said with relief. "We *didn't* kill you."

THE NEXT DAY, A FULL BLIZZARD DESCENDED, AND THEY were stuck. While Smagin went about his farm business, Masha made notes on the two estates they'd visited. She'd looked at Smagin's pictures the day before, photographs of his rigidly posed family and paintings of horses, all askew on the wall. Natalia snooped in the bookcases, took out a small balalaika painted with flowers, and strummed.

"Shall we ask him to play? He's quite terrible." She put it back and read the spines of the books. "Finally! Something not about animal husbandry." She held out Antosha's *Motley Tales*.

Smagin joined them for lunch, smelling of manure and leather. The meal was as generous as the night before. Soup, dumplings, cutlets, more sweets.

Masha ate just as much again, and afterward asked, "Mr. Smagin? Do you play whist?"

"I don't. But that doesn't mean I can't learn. Is it difficult?"

"Not at all. We'll need a fourth, though."

He enlisted the excited maid. Smagin easily picked up the rules and seemed to enjoy the game. Every time he fanned out his cards and held them to his face, the ends of his moustache showed on either side, and Natalia kicked Masha under the table.

The first night, Natalia had crawled into bed with Masha and cried herself to sleep. Masha hadn't minded; the stove was no match for the cold in the room. As soon as Natalia began to snore, though, Masha sent her staggering across the chilly gap to her own bed.

The second night, with the wind hurling handfuls of sleet at the windows, the Ukrainiac made her move again.

"Stay where you are," Masha told her. "You snore, and there's no room."

"Even less for Mr. Smagin, after you marry him. Are you going to marry him, Masha?"

She'd been expecting this conversation. "Certainly not."

Natalia propped herself up on one elbow, her braid hanging almost to the floor. Masha waited for her to hum "The Nightingale."

Instead she asked, "Why not?"

"For one, he hasn't asked."

"He will. Don't think his servants normally look this pretty. He's got them gussied up for you. They know what's going on too.

It's like a livestock market the way they keep showing you their teeth. I do get the sense you're starting to like him."

This was true. "I don't love him."

"Hard to love that moustache. You could dissuade him from it and anything else that isn't to your taste. The same way you've got him imagining he likes whist."

"He breathes like his horses. Could I dissuade him from breathing?"

She heard herself—so petty! Smagin was decent and kind. For some women that would be enough. Every day ursine men with too-close eyes and ridiculous moustaches lay down with wives who found them physically repellent. Wives they had to tear into. What did the wives do? Clench the pillow in their teeth?

"I gather love is a thing that grows," Natalia offered.

"If you're so fond of him, you should marry him yourself."

"He doesn't want to marry me. He wants to marry you."

"But why?" An open invitation for a ribbing, but Masha was genuinely curious what Smagin saw in her.

She received an unflatteringly honest answer. "Who knows? Why do people fall in love? I've friends who've lost their heads over utter nincompoops. When the delirium passes, they're as baffled as I was. Sometimes it's too late, they've already tied the knot. Georgi doesn't have anything to do with how you feel, does he?"

Masha looked across. "What's *that* supposed to mean?"

"Mother told me, Masha. I'd already guessed it from your foul mood in Yalta."

"Told you *what?*"

"So he's not the reason you're cold on Smagin?"

"I'm not cold on Smagin! I just don't want to marry him. Or Georgi, for that matter. Why should I get married at all? I'm perfectly happy. Antosha depends on me." She paused to steady her voice. "As your family depends on you."

Natalia studied her for a moment before replying. "Forgive me for saying this, Masha, but you don't seem happy."

Masha rolled over, showing her back. "Good night!"

Natalia sighed and snuffed the lamp. Within minutes Masha heard her breathing deepen.

So she didn't seem happy. She should grin her head off dealing with these imbecile farmers? Laugh when she was worried about Antosha's health again? And marrying Smagin would make her happy? She imagined the mattress sinking next to her. Louder breaths than Natalia's. A heavy fumbling hand. *That?*

She shivered. The wind was still howling, but it was either diminishing or the snow had entirely encased the house.

AT FIRST LIGHT SHE WOKE IN SUCH A TEMPER THAT SHE couldn't wait for Natalia to stir.

"Did you talk to Georgi about me?"

Natalia groaned but didn't seem to wake.

Masha stepped down onto the icy floor and used the pot. Urine streamed angrily against the copper. Smagin had kindly provided slippers, which she put on before going to the window and drawing back the curtain. Some Ukrainian frost fairy had embroidered the pane too thickly to see out.

"When you're really asleep, you breathe like Smagin. So I know you talked about me to Georgi."

Natalia laughed under the covers, then threw them off. "I wanted to make sure that he didn't lead you on. Though I knew he wouldn't. Georgi's indifferent to women."

"What did he say about me?"

"Nothing. Just that he was innocent."

Nothing. There was nothing to say about her. Masha sat before the mirror and looked at this nothing. Mother's nose and curls and broad face. Except for that anomaly Kolia, her brothers looked like Father, who was actually handsome, though it was hard to see it beyond his personality.

"I think you're pretty, Masha," Natalia said. "And so does Aleksander."

What could they do about the weather? Smagin decided it had calmed enough for them to carry on with the viewing in spite of the continuing wind. Natalia bowed out, so Masha and Smagin set out alone, heading for the estate they'd previously missed. When he invited her to sit up front with him, she agreed. She'd freeze to death if she refused.

The same sort of boor greeted them each time, and Masha found herself wishing that she'd come with Olga instead. Olga would have put these farmers in their place the way Smagin couldn't, not if he wanted to maintain good relations. And what would Olga say about Smagin laying his big arm along Masha's shoulders to shield her from an icy blast? *Get off her, you bear!* She thought of Lika too, beating off those awful clerks. Masha made herself rigid and wondered if Smagin had arranged the weather for just this purpose.

After dinner that night, Natalia excused herself again. She wanted Kalina to show her how she made those delicious fried cookies that, no doubt, the Lintvariovs' own Ukrainian cook knew how to make. Smagin smoked and paced the parlour in his loud boots. Not only was his tread heavy, but the leather spoke.

Masha could taste her dread. She didn't want to hurt him—for both their sakes. As soon as she refused him, she'd feel guilty. Things would become even more awkward. And wouldn't he resent her? As well as all this, there was the honest fact that Masha enjoyed being admired, even by Smagin. She thought of Lika again, how admiration showered down on her every time she left the house, yet she was blind to it. Perhaps it was like being blind to the air.

Heavy boots, heavy nervous breath. Masha looked up.

"Should I read to you, Mr. Smagin? I found one of my brother's books on your shelf." She had it in her lap.

He seemed not to hear, was looking across the jumbled room to the icon corner, possibly praying for courage.

"*Motley Stories* is so funny. Now he's such a *serious* writer. Did you like it?"

Smagin turned, squinting through his own smoke. "Where did you find that?"

"On your shelf."

He looked as if she'd discovered something entirely incongruous, a ladies' shoe or a human skull. Then he remembered.

"Yes, your brother gave it to me. I don't actually read." Some tic gave her away, for he quickly sensed her disapproval. "I can! Quite obviously." He gestured around at the chimneys of ledgers and catalogues. "But stories? No time, I'm afraid. Here's my poetry. He picked up a random volume, *The Book of the Farm, Volume 3*, and waved it at her. "I've been meaning to ask you something."

It still worked, her cracked heart. She felt it quiver.

Smagin inhaled noisily again, and dropped the book in a new place. "How did you find the Lintvariovs? I haven't visited since Zinaida's fortieth day ceremony. I'd hoped they were faring better by now."

"They're shattered. Natalia puts on a brave face, but she's crying a lot."

"And Georgi?"

"He cancelled his concerts."

Nodding, Smagin drew on his cigarette. "Did you have enough tea?"

"My tears are brown. I wonder where Natalia is."

He checked that the moustache still hung on his face, patting both sides. "So Georgi cancelled."

With this second mention of Georgi, Masha wondered if he was hinting at something. Red blotches appeared on his face, and likely hers. He glanced at the icons again.

"The last time I saw you, Mrs. Lintvariova discouraged me from visiting again."

"Because of Georgi?" She threw up her hands. "That's ridiculous."

"Really? I should have returned?"

She wanted the record set straight regarding her infatuation with Georgi. "You should do what you want. Not listen to people like Mrs. Lintvariova who actually know nothing."

The red blotches joined together on Smagin's face in a joyful blush. "I will, then." He strode over to the table to snuff his cigarette. The whole room trembled. "I'll do what I want."

Masha shrank in her chair.

"What I want, Miss C. What I really want? Why do you look at me like that?"

He was torturing her, dragging it out like this.

"Like what?" she whispered.

"You're cowering. I'm not going to hit you. I just want permission to call you by your first name."

Masha released the armrests she'd been gripping. "Please do, Mr. Smagin!"

"And I want you to call me Aleksander."

"I will!"

He took several more unquiet breaths, then backed toward the door, keeping his eyes on her. "Well—Maria. That's enough happiness for today. I wouldn't want to get too used to it. I'm going to check the horses." He bowed. "Good night."

"Good night. Aleksander."

After he left, Masha sat a moment staring at Antosha's book in her lap. Then she smacked herself on the head with it.

Natalia she found in the kitchen watching over a pot of hot oil. She and aproned Kalina gave her a questioning look, which Masha ignored. She sampled one of the cookies cooling on a plate and promptly burnt her tongue. Kalina rushed outside for a handful of snow.

"Did he propose?" Natalia hurried to ask.

"No!"

Kalina returned and tied the snow up in a napkin for Masha. Natalia gave her a not-too-subtle head shake, which caused the cook's shoulders to slump.

"Would you please just keep out of my business, Natalia?" Masha said, before showing the two of them her back.

In the parlour, she irritably laid out a game of patience with one hand. She'd barely started playing when the door opened. Assuming it was Natalia, she refused to look up.

"Maria?"

Smagin again, snow dropping off his boots, his furred bulk filling the whole frame. "Would you consider marrying me?"

This was the third proposal of her life. The other two had caught her equally off guard. She was holding a snowball. Her tongue burnt, then frozen. He just stood there. She couldn't refuse outright. It would be too cruel.

"I have my family to think of, Mr.— *Aleksander*. I couldn't make a decision without consulting them."

"I see. But your family will be close by when Anton buys his estate. And I would welcome your parents here. I've met them and esteem them."

"But what about Antosha? He'd be alone."

"He'll get married himself."

"He's married to his work."

"That's only what he says, Miss— Maria, while he looks for a wife."

"Really? I think you don't know my brother well."

"Perhaps not. In any case, he'd be close by. With his work."

She could pass this burden off to Antosha. She'd discuss with him how to word the rejection, but he would send it.

"Would you write to him, Aleksander? Write my brother, not my father. I wouldn't go against Antosha's advice."

Like a bear that swallowed a woodsman—that was how happy Smagin looked.

"I will! I have great hopes, now, Maria. Thank you. Anton asked me to help him secure an estate. He obviously trusts and respects me."

"Obviously," Masha said.

"I'm going back out. Thank you for considering me. Good night, again."

He closed the door behind him. Masha stared at it, a brief moment of blankness before the ambush of guilt.

THE NEXT DAY, THE FOUL WEATHER CLEARED. NATURE, embarrassed by her recent tantrum, put on all her charms, casting sequins on the new snow, welcoming the birds. Ice tasselled all the telegraph lines.

Smagin drove them to the station shielding his eyes. His horses flicked their happy tails. He insisted on waiting with them. When the train pulled in, Masha thrust her hand out to bid him goodbye first, in case he tried to kiss her.

"I'll write to your brother," he said. "And to you, farewell!"

"It's so strange," Natalia kept saying on the train. "I was sure he was going to ask you."

They parted at Sumy, which left Masha with her thoughts to keep her company. Away now from Smagin and his moustache, she fell into a fugue of irrational fondness for this man who could weep with such tea-spilling force. She shrunk him down to an acceptable size, dealt with the moustache as Natalia had suggested. Replaced the horsey smell with scent. Dressed him in a proper waistcoat instead of the homespun blouse. It was like playing with a doll. Could she then rouse some ardency for this doll? Did she want to?

She scraped her nails against the window and made a peephole. They were passing a cluster of huts, abandoned, she could tell by the dormant chimneys. Then a dead horse lying on a hill. No, a hill of dead horses half buried in snow, limbs tangled, lips drawn back, teeth enormous. No eyes—they'd been pecked out by the birds, who, without the left-behinds from the threshing, were starving too. The worst thing was that the horses had been flayed, their flesh peeled back, arches of bare ribs spanning snow-filled cavities. About this desolate place not a single human track showed in the snow.

The peasants were eating raw flour, Antosha had said. Or they made "famine loaves," flour mixed with bark and moss. He predicted cholera in the spring. While she'd been struggling with her resentment of him, he'd been delivering aid.

———

ANTOSHA WAS STILL AWAY WHEN SHE GOT BACK. As promised, two letters came addressed in Smagin's crabbed, unmistakable hand, one for her, and one for her brother.

My desire to be your husband is so strong that neither your love for Georgi nor your negligible affection for me would stop me from fulfilling this desire, should you agree to it. I've written Anton, as you asked, and been clear about my feelings for you. I'll send you his answer. I'm not afraid of his judgment—I want it!

She cringed at his reference to Georgi. Antosha's letter she left on top of his growing pile, mostly famine donations. She could tell by the clink inside the envelopes. Every time she brought his post, she added it to the bottom. That way Smagin's letter would remain on top. This way Antosha would read it first, and they could discuss what to do.

When he did return, though, he was unwell. Fever, chills, and—most alarmingly—a stabbing pain in his side. The anxiety she'd felt for him at Luka renewed, overwhelming her personal preoccupations again.

"Medically? It's pleurisy," he assured Masha and Mother as they fussed. "Morally, it's shame."

He'd expected corruption, but not to this extent. Relief funds embezzled, peasants without a crumb forced to beg, then steal, only to see their villages under Cossack guard, so they couldn't leave. Nothing to eat and no plans to prepare for sowing. They had no seed, so how could they sow?

"We discussed the crisis over dinner. 'What, oh, what shall we do for these unfortunates, and could you please pass the caviar? More wine? I say, this *is* damned fine caviar.'" He broke off coughing, a futile hack that lifted him off the bed.

"As soon as I'm well," he said between bouts, "I'm taking Suvorin out there. Let him see for himself. Make him open his big fat wallet."

Masha told him what she'd seen from the train. "Don't tell me they all died."

"They and five hundred thousand others. Do you remember being hungry?"

"Yes." The memory twisted inside her. "Yes, I do."

SEVERAL DAYS PASSED BEFORE HE ASKED ABOUT THE estates. "It wasn't the best time of year to do this, sister. I'm sorry. It's just that I'm desperate. We can't stay here. I can't afford it."

He turned on his side and, coughing again, closed his eyes.

"You have a lot of post piled up here," Masha said, before he fell back to sleep. "Do you want me to read it out?"

"I'll get to it, if I don't die first."

He was joking. She didn't laugh.

The next day he was up and about, but in a shuffling way, wearing slippers and a dressing gown and giving strict instructions not to let anyone in, as he was too weak to put on clothes. He let Mariushka prepare his coffee, and she rejoiced. He was well enough to want it, thanks to the power of her icons and her prayers.

After school Masha found him sitting at his desk. He'd opened most of his correspondence and had begun his replies. An envelope waited on his scale, beside it a pile of slivered margins. Scraps from a taciturn man. All the things he left unsaid.

This was her fault. She should have refused Smagin herself.

"So you got something done."

"Yes," he told her. "With a lot of reposing in between."

She lingered in the doorway. "Can I get you anything, brother?"

He dipped his pen. "No, thank you."

Eventually she understood he wasn't going to speak about Smagin's letter, either because the matter was unpleasant, or because it was too trivial. Masha couldn't argue with the latter. What were her small affairs compared to half a million starved to death? She didn't even want to marry Smagin. Then why not speak?

That night she sat up in the dark. She wanted *him* to speak— out loud, to her—about *her life* and its value to his. Then it wouldn't be just a grey thing overshadowed by him.

They met in the kitchen the next morning. He was grinding his own coffee now, moving his arm in that meticulous circle. The emboldening smell of it. She would force him.

"Did you receive a letter from Smagin?"

A glance and a cough. "I did."

"Did you write back?"

"Not yet. I've still got a damnable pile to get through. Oh, I forgot to tell you something. You'll never guess who I met." He spooned the bitter grounds into the pot. "Lieutenant Egorov."

Masha started at the mention of his name; her determination dissolved with her surprise. "Egorov? I can't believe it. Where? Where did you meet him?"

He stooped to light the brazier, successfully avoiding her eye. "He's been organizing relief in Nizhni, one of the few to do it honestly and intelligently. Not only has he started a soup kitchen on his estate, he's set up an actual workable scheme to get the planting going."

"Does he look the same?"

"Minimal hair. But he greeted me quite warmly and said he had no hard feelings. He left the army years ago."

"No hard feelings?"

"No. It's too bad, though. He turned to be a fine fellow after all."

He looked right at her as he said this, and it seemed that his eyes were apologizing, even if he wasn't.

Masha dropped her gaze too, shaken. Was he married? Did he have children? Had he mentioned her? If she'd asked these things, wouldn't his answers be too painful to bear?

Of course, of course. No.

What was she doing in the kitchen? She'd come to ask him something. It took a moment to remember.

"And Smagin? What do you plan to say?"

His back was turned now, and he kept it that way. "I'll say he has the most hideous, heathenish, desperately tragic handwriting. He'd have more success with women if he'd learn to write."

Masha made herself taller. "And if I feel differently?"

He glanced back, the surprise his now. "Do you?"

"No," Masha said, and walked out.

ANTOSHA'S STORIES WERE FILLED WITH UNHAPPY MAR-riages. With promising marriages that drifted into boredom and indifference. Into misery. He didn't want that for himself, or for her either. And she didn't want Smagin. Yet for several weeks she felt quite low.

After church on Sunday, she took the tram to the Zoological Gardens. In exchange for donating Svoloch, they'd given Antosha a free ticket. She drew it out of her muff and handed it to the gate-keeper.

She knew where the bear was housed. Now she began her search from reeking pavilion to reeking pavilion. Across the grounds, a wolf howled, and a band of half-drunk students howled back. A creature's plea met with human mockery.

Eventually she found him imprisoned with none of his species. Weasels, marmots, lemmings overcrowded each other, but Svoloch was alone in his cage. He kept up his air of busy curiosity, circling the mesh walls, rushing over to peer at every visitor, turning in ever-smaller circles. After a few minutes this behaviour seemed more insane than antic.

When the room cleared, and they were alone, she spoke his name at last. He reared right up. Two leaps and he thrust his narrow snout between the wires.

She offered her finger, which he nibbled. She pressed herself right against the cage until the wires scored her forehead. How she loved him. His small hands touching her wet face, exploring her hair while she wept.

Tenderly, one at a time, he removed her combs.

Act Three

——

1892

*Masha: All this is just nonsense. Love without hope—
it only happens in novels. It's really nothing. You've only got
to keep a firm hold on yourself, to stop yourself hoping for . . .
hoping for the tide to turn. . . . If love sneaks into your
heart, the best thing to do is to chuck it out.*

1

IN THE GAZETTE, MISHA NOTICED AN ADVERTISE-
ment for a country estate seventy-five miles from Moscow, six
from the nearest railway station in Lopasnia. Antosha, away
again on famine relief work, sent Masha with him to look at it. All
they saw of Melikhovo was a collection of brightly painted buildings perched like iced cakes in the snow. Winter kept the pond and
fields a secret. The house, though a single storey, was organized in
a spacious L.

Buy it, Antosha wrote by return post.

The side door, the one they mainly used, led to a vestibule
cheered by a stained-glass window. Two other doors opened off
it, one to Antosha's study, the biggest and brightest room in the
house, the other to the Pushkin Room, named for the portrait
they hung there. Antosha liked to confuse first-time visitors by
leading them in a circle: vestibule, Pushkin Room, main parlour,
his study, back through the vestibule, then into the Pushkin Room
again. Not realizing they'd seen Pushkin twice, they invariably
exclaimed that the house was much bigger than it looked from
the outside.

Masha's bedroom was off the main parlour, with space for an
easel, a settee and chairs. Over her bed she hung Kolia's portrait of
Antosha, the one with the unfinished ear, which Antosha refused
to have in the parlour because portraits of himself were as embarrassing as waiters reciting his stories by heart.

Those were the rooms in the small leg of the L. The ones leading off the longer leg were Antosha's bedroom, Father's (crammed
with icons), the dining room, Mother's room with her sewing
machine, and Misha's while he was on leave from the tax department. Mariushka cooked and slept in the cramped kitchen next
to Misha's room, until they built the new kitchen out back. No
conveniences yet, just an outhouse. The men used Antosha's washstand, the women Masha's.

They still needed Masha's income, irregular as it was. She
would not have wanted to give up teaching anyway. She found an
inexpensive room for the week and took the train to Melikhovo
every weekend to help out. Scrubbing, papering, waging war with
the cockroaches. For this alone she would have loved the place, for
giving her a purpose again.

WHEN THE WINTER TERM AT SCHOOL STARTED, MASHA
glanced across the assembly hall. Over all the plaited heads she
caught sight of a blond one. A double take and she recognized the
dazzling smile. Lika. Masha waved back, startled by the happiness
she felt.

After school Lika came to Masha's classroom. She looked thin-
ner, face drawn, but her girlish gestures and ready laugh cancelled
out these signs of worry. She'd had enough of the council clerks, she
told Masha from the doorway, miming a smack she'd no doubt had
to give numerous hands. Faces too, perhaps.

"I earn half as much here, but I love it twice as much."

Her main news was that her long-lost father had unexpectedly
reappeared and was paying for singing lessons.

"How did he find you?" Masha asked.

"Through Mama. She gave him our address. She didn't ask me if I cared to meet him, just sent him along and left me to deal with him. As usual."

"What's he like?" Masha half expected a Swan Princess to have a cob for a father.

Lika shrugged. "Handsome, I suppose. Anyway, he has a guilty conscience, and offered an allowance for clothes, which I refused. But it was hard not to accept the lessons when I so want to improve."

Then Lika said that she had run into Misha by chance. "He's met someone. Klara. Do you know her?"

Masha didn't. "I guess he's keeping her a secret." From Antosha, no doubt.

Lika's expression softened. "He told me about poor Svoloch. I felt so bad for you, Masha. He was like your child."

Two months had passed since Svoloch's banishment. Masha's visit to the Zoological Gardens haunted her. No one had expressed sympathy, let alone recognized her particular loss, except Lika now. Masha was supposed to be annoyed with Lika over last summer's nonsense with Isaac and Sophia. She *was* annoyed, but at the same time grateful to have her feelings understood.

"I can't see such a lively creature locked forever in a cage," Lika said.

She was still standing in the doorway. Masha replaced the pen in its holder and invited her in with a nod.

The summer must have been on Lika's mind too, since she brought it up herself next.

"I'd planned to write you from my aunt's. But things happened." She leaned forward on her elbows, so a shard of light from the window cut her cheek. "You warned me about Isaac. I should have listened."

"Yes. He has a tendency to want to shoot himself."

The summer he'd proposed to Masha, Antosha and Kolia had found him in a nearby cottage, sleeping with his gun.

Lika shuttered her face with her hands. "I wish you'd spelled it out."

Her dress was light blue, her hair yellow. When she dropped her hands, she was a study in primary colours—cheeks and lips red. Masha remembered drawing her and then crumpling the page. The insufficiency of black and white.

"I'll tell you everything," Lika said. "But you mustn't tell Antosha."

She began with that troubling incident, the day they picked strawberries, when she and Antosha had finally evaded Isaac and found themselves alone in the woods.

"Except we weren't."

Masha, who had heard Antosha's version of their argument, couldn't think what she meant. "You ran into a woodsman?"

"No. Remember how Antosha said that Trofimov had come?"

"That's who you met? Trofimov?" Masha laughed.

"In a way."

Masha leaned back, fully attentive.

"Don't you sometimes wonder where all these people come from? The people he writes about, I mean. They're so real. So heartfelt. They hardly seem imaginary."

Some weren't. Recently Antosha had published a story featuring a barely disguised Dr. Wagner, right down to the paisley shirt. Thankfully, a man of pure science was unlikely to read "The Duel" and see the nasty sort of person Antosha had turned him into. There were plenty of other examples in his work, explicit lampooning even. Borrowing from life was a life-like writer's prerogative.

Lika said, "I think Trofimov is real. He's the part of your brother that can actually love, not just joke and tease." She held up her hand to stop Masha from contradicting. "Please don't bring up his charity. That's not what I'm talking about. I'm talking about *feeling* something." She pressed her chest. "He either can't—or won't—let himself. It was Trofimov who kissed me that day, I'm sure of it. And then Antosha—how would he put it? He drove a fork into his eye."

Masha recognized the words from Antosha's letter. *I hope you accidentally jab out his eyes . . .*

"There's a look he gets," Lika went on. "Like he's on a commode and straining, but no emotion will come out."

Despite herself, Masha burst out laughing, because Lika had no idea how often Antosha was in just this position. But what childish logic. Because Antosha wouldn't babble love talk, he was *incapable* of loving? Even as she thought this, an uneasy feeling settled on her. Olga had hinted at something similar. Yet Antosha certainly loved *her*, his sister, in his wordless way.

But there was this fact to support Lika's assertion: Their summer at Bogimovo had been a happy and productive one for Antosha. His only frustration had been that Lika wouldn't answer his teasing letters. That she wouldn't return. Could it be that her absence was the reason he'd been so happy? He could be in love with her if she wasn't there crying all over him.

"I'm glad you think it's funny," Lika said. "I think it's sad. For me, of course, but for him as well."

Heavy footsteps sounded in the hall. A door creaked, then the steps resumed, coming nearer.

"And so you took Isaac as your consolation prize?" Masha asked.

Until that comment, Lika seemed to have softened to the point of bonelessness in the desk. Now she pulled herself up straight.

"Is that what Antosha thinks?"

Her grey eyes flicked toward the door, causing Masha to look over her shoulder to their walrus-like custodian leering in.

"You may close the door," Masha told him in a tone he hastened to obey.

"Wait," Lika said. "How's your daughter, Mr. Abramtsev?"

The walrus turned back, not leering after all. "The same. Pray for her."

"I will. And for you I'll sing." She produced a few lines of some folksong that obviously meant something to him, for he beamed. Then, bowing, he continued on his rounds, opening doors along the corridor in search of someone with a heart.

Masha remembered something else Olga had said about Antosha. That he only wanted Lika for her body. But didn't he want her kindness too, just as Masha did?

After the interruption, the rest of the story came spilling out. What was going on while Antosha was sending Lika letters and photographs of imaginary suitors. Lika had to walk around to tell it, pacing from desk to desk, flapping as she spoke.

After she and Isaac had left Bogimovo, she decided to give Antosha up. Give up everything to do with him. She'd cried on the train and stupidly mentioned that she would be going to stay for the summer with her aunt in Tver province. Her plan had been to get completely away from the Moscow crowd. But to her horror, Isaac and Sophia showed up a few days after she arrived at her aunt's. Isaac had convinced Sophia that they'd painted out the Volga, and it was time for some fresher landscapes.

So there had been no running off together.

"My aunt helped them find a place nearby to rent. It was awful, Masha. They came over every night. Isaac charmed Auntie, of course, but she couldn't disguise how she felt about Sophia once she learned she was married to someone else. So I thought it would be better if I went to them in the evenings. Mistake! One day Sophia would be at my throat for turning Isaac's head, next she'd be sobbing on my shoulder, confiding everything. She feels wretched about her husband, but her soul has attached itself to Isaac's."

"I suspected she had claws," Masha said.

Lika paused before the window, ignoring Masha's comment, looking out, shoulders child-sized.

"One day they had an awful row. She demanded that he swear his love to her in front of me. He stormed out. Sophia chased after him. After that I refused to go and watch them torture each other. So what happens?"

"What?" Masha asked.

"Sophia went back to Moscow. We had to take Isaac in."

"Why?"

She faced Masha then. "You know why. The yardman found him lying in the garden, drunk, with his gun across his chest. What were we to do?"

Masha didn't have to imagine this scene. She had her memories. Antosha and Kolia had found out where Isaac was staying from the gossip in town. He'd been shacking up with a potter, who was now scared of him and wanted him gone. As they entered the cottage, Isaac had sat up in bed waving the gun. It was a miracle her brothers had managed to wrest it away without bloodshed.

"And now?" Masha asked Lika.

"I've extricated myself, I hope. At any rate, Sophia's taken him back." Something out the window caught her eye and she smiled, breaking the tension. "Here they come."

Masha rose and came to the window too. Below, the bovine

parade. They clattered into the yard, heads low, their mapped sides bulgingly pregnant. Another weary convict line.

Lika laid her head on Masha's shoulder. "Don't tell any of this to Antosha. Don't mention me at all. I just want to forget about him and get on with my life."

So that was that. Lika had escaped with her heart more or less intact, unlike Masha's other friends. Masha's matchmaking had come to nothing.

No. Masha had gained a friend instead of lost one. It was the best possible outcome. Not only that, at school the halls rang again with Lika's innocent songs. Too bad that outside of school, Masha had no time for friendly pursuits, commuting as she was back and forth to Melikhovo.

Later in the spring, Lika complained in passing about her dull life. "Granny's making me stitch. The way I keep pricking myself, my cushion will be embroidered in blood."

Masha loathed womanly make-work just as much and laughed. "You'd be welcome for Easter," she said.

She expected a refusal, not only because Lika had sworn off Antosha. Lika had her own family, Granny and her mother who would surely come for Easter, not to mention her aunt in Tver. And now her magically reappearing father.

Instead, Lika accepted on the spot without bothering to conceal her happiness. Either her resolution not to see Antosha had weakened, or it had been feeble from the start, like Kolia's when he swore abstinence in the morning but succumbed by lunch.

Masha always hesitated to ask Lika about her family situation, in particular why she and her mother lived apart. She sensed a story, for every mention of her mother brought out in Lika a grimace or a self-embrace. Masha assumed, or preferred to assume, the usual daughterly complaints, which she herself knew well. Except that Lika had mentioned her mother's "lovers" and compared these men to the groping clerks at town council. This only made Masha take a mental step back, the way she did from subjects too personal to broach. Menses and the facts of life. Whether or not every woman's breasts were lopsided the way hers looked in the mirror. Intimate subjects to discuss with female relatives, though Masha didn't talk about them with Mother, who was too stuffed with superstition and peasant lore to offer any useful advice.

Regarding the Easter invitation, she was mainly worried about how Antosha would react when she told him Lika was coming. The last time he'd mentioned her was while they were sorting letters at Epiphany. He'd used harsh, uncharitable words then.

But she needn't have worried. Since buying Melikhovo, Antosha had been in fine spirits. "No rent! We have no rent!" he daily sang. When he learned Lika would be visiting, his glow resembled hers.

"I knew something was missing from our paradise, besides a water closet. I'll write her too."

The next week, Lika came to Masha again. She'd changed her mind.

"The things he writes! Wouldn't I rather spend Easter where my heart is, in the police watchtower? When is he going to let up about Isaac and Sophia? He won't stop rubbing it in my face. Then he complains that he's nothing to me, that you're all last year's starlings whose song I've forgotten. It's the other way around! 'Don't consign us to oblivion as you did before.'" She laid the back of her hand against her forehead. "'Pretend that you remember us.

Deception is better than indifference.' Honestly? I wanted to tear that letter up."

Masha herself was bewildered that he'd written these things when he'd expressed such pleasure at her coming.

Her conversation with Lika about Trofimov had happened months ago. Since then, Masha had often thought about Lika's assertion. Though at the time she'd scoffed, she'd also realized that Lika had sensed something true. Something from when Masha and Antosha were children. That game they used to play with Father's coat. Or when she would seek him out in his hiding place in the storeroom after a beating. The reek of tallow and mice. Sometimes Father used to put them to work picking weevils out of the flour. Feelings were not so easily separable. Love and shame. Love and anger. Didn't Father love them? Sometimes it was better not to open the sack.

"Did you tell him what really happened last summer?" Masha asked.

"Yes. It seems he doesn't believe me."

Was Antosha just clinging too hard to his wounded pride? Masha wondered. Or did he make these jokes about Isaac and Sophia to show how inconsequential the matter was now? Either way, it proved Lika was still very much on his mind.

Just before Easter, Antosha sent Masha his list of things to bring from Moscow.

Tobacco. Seed. Lika.

Masha tried again.

"Actually, there's something I need to discuss with your brother." Lika threw back her shoulders and elongated her neck as though to demonstrate a bounteous pride. "So I will come, though Granny will be furious."

——

ON THE TRAIN LIKA ACTED AS THOUGH SHE WAS STILL
cross, hinting to Masha that Antosha had done "a bad, bad thing,"
but keeping mum as to what it was. Once they arrived at Melikhovo,
and she and Masha stepped into the vestibule, everything changed.

Antosha's study door flew open as though he'd been standing
right behind it waiting for them. Lika and Antosha faced each
other for the first time since the previous summer.

"Don't move," he said.

He came and tilted up her chin, as though he was about to
kiss her lips. The light falling through the coloured windowpanes
washed her face. Lika in blue, red and gold. *He loves her*, Masha
thought. A simple fact.

Lika let out a funny squawk and threw her arms around his
neck. He crooked his arm for her to link. Smiling fully, he led her
around the house and twice through the Pushkin Room. When
she burst out with "It's bigger than it looks!" he kissed her forehead.

"Dearest Lika. Hold your arms out like you used to. At your
sides, yes. Now fly."

She flapped.

He roared with laughter. "And what a pretty jacket. All the
women I know dress like widows. But you? You dress like a cantaloupe."

Shortly they sat down for dinner. Antosha warned her then
that they'd become country people since Lika saw them last.

"We rise at four, bed down at ten."

"Her usual routine reversed," quipped the little brother. "In bed
at four. Up by ten."

"Hardly!" Lika protested with a laugh.

Misha was Melikhovo's overseer for now. Antosha's praise of
his competence had put an end to the rivalry between the brothers,

even in love, for Misha had his own blonde now. Unfortunately, Klara was the type Masha had assumed Lika would be when they first met—stunted by her looks. Or so she'd seemed when Misha brought her around for tea in Moscow.

"We won't have time for you," Antosha told Lika. "Misha and Masha are working all day. Me too, until eleven, at which point I hurry to the dining room and stare meaningfully at the clock, until Mother notices and gets lunch. Afterward I lie on my bed and think."

"Noisy thoughts," Masha said, passing around the platter of Lenten perch.

"Then we're all back to work. Work, work, work. What can we do? We must go on living. Do you see? Our days are difficult, our evenings tedious, but we patiently suffer the trials that fate imposes on us landowners. How will you stand it, dear Cantaloupe?"

Her grey eyes welled up. "I'm so happy to be here."

"How long are you staying?" Father asked.

Antosha said, "Look how much she's heaping on her plate. The real question, is how long can we *afford* her?"

That night, while Masha and Lika bent over the washstand together, Masha asked, "Did you speak to him about this terrible thing he did?"

Lika pressed her face with the towel, then slowly dried her hands. "I don't think I will after all." The smile was tugging at the corners of her mouth, but only the dimples showed.

IVAN WAS EXPECTED FOR EASTER TOO, BUT THE NEXT day someone else turned up while Masha was cutting pussy willows and Antosha showing off to Lika their first success as farmers—the dozen yellow chicks Mother Hen had produced, scuttling around the lingering dollops of snow.

"Just think," Antosha said. "One day you'll have as many children. And be just as fat."

How flattering. Masha looked up to see Lika's reaction and so was the second to notice Isaac, overnight case swinging in one hand, gun strap across his chest, overcoat open, its tails filling with air. A whirl of manic agitation. They hadn't heard a carriage. He must have asked to be dropped off on the road.

"Why do you look so crushed?" Antosha asked Lika, who had seen Isaac over his shoulder. "Doesn't every woman long to be a mother?"

A hand came down hard on his back. Antosha swung around. Such sangfroid, Masha thought. He didn't hesitate to open his arms in welcome.

"Isaac! What a surprise. How did you find us?"

Isaac stared at Lika. "They gave me directions at the station."

Masha came forward to greet her teacher, glancing at Lika, who had turned away with her hands in fists. Isaac accepted Masha's embrace as passively as he had Antosha's, eyes still fixed on Lika's angry back.

Antosha guided him toward the house, gesturing all around them. "This is it. Melikhovo. What do you think? See any respectable views?"

What Antosha was thinking, Masha had no idea. Perhaps he'd expected Isaac, the way you know a character will step on stage in a play you've seen before. This had become, after all, a farce on an extended run.

But Lika hadn't expected him. She held Masha back. "I didn't breathe a word that I was coming here. He must have gone to the flat and got it out of Granny. Tell Antosha. He won't believe me."

Isaac, looking anxiously back for her, almost tripped on the threshold. Mother and Father came to the door and offered their joyful greeting, surprised to see the painter instead of Ivan.

They kept their coats on, so they could take tea on the veranda. The sun was out, and Antosha said they should encourage it. Masha guessed he was worried about some sort of outburst, for Isaac was twitching all over. Thank God he'd left his gun with his bag in the vestibule.

The two men stepped out first.

Antosha said, "You look well, Isaac. Swarthy. What's your news?"

"The Petersburg show was a success."

Isaac craned to see inside, where Lika was still trying to calm herself, taking deep gulps of air. Finally she stepped out onto the veranda and dropped sullenly into a chair. Masha took the one beside her and waited for something horrible to happen.

"What's that bird, Masha?" Antosha asked. "It sounds like someone blowing across the neck of a bottle."

"I hear starlings." She pointed to the birch copse in front. The birds were hopping from branch to branch, setting the trees in motion, so that they seemed to be waving their arms. *Help, the egoists are back!*

"Go on," Antosha told Isaac, who was gazing rapturously at Lika's profile. "You were saying?"

"My *Deep Waters* sold for three thousand. Do you remember it, Lika? The log bridge."

"Painted last summer?" Antosha asked mildly.

Lika reddened. Mariushka came out with the tea tray and began to unload it.

"Anyway, Isaac," Antosha said. "Tell us how Sophia is."

Isaac sniffed. "I haven't seen her."

Masha fixed a questioning look on Antosha, who seemed to be trying to provoke an outburst now. Just then a volley of snipe passed overhead, expert embroiderers, stitching the sky with their long needley bills. At the sight of them, Isaac propelled himself right out of his chair and down the steps to see which direction they were heading. They all started, even the starlings, who lifted off the trees en masse.

As soon as he was off the veranda, Lika covered her face and groaned.

"What's wrong?" Antosha asked with just the trace of a smirk.

"I didn't invite him, if that's what you're thinking," Lika snapped.

"I'm not thinking anything. But tell me, do you find me *pale*?"

Masha had overheard his "swarthy" comment. Now here was "pale." Did he think Lika had read Isaac's taunting letter of last summer? He appeared so gracious. What he was actually doing, with malicious or comic intent—she often couldn't tell which—was leading the conversation to that excruciating place, to their competition last summer, the volcanic swarthy painter pitted against the pale cerebral author, when Antosha believed that Isaac, whom he otherwise loved, had defeated him. But he was wrong. He'd routed the painter.

Isaac was still standing on the softening path, shielding his eyes as he watched the sky, no doubt waiting for Antosha's question to evaporate. All there was to see now were tufts of clouds, like Father's ear hair. Finally he clumped back, spring mud on his shoes. He scraped them on the steps.

Antosha carried on from where he'd left off. "I thought you were a salon fixture, Isaac."

"At Sophia's? I haven't been for ages. You were there recently, weren't you, Lika?"

"Look at her," Antosha said. "She's turned crimson."

Lika had. She was burning up.

"She must have met someone there," Antosha said.

"Trofimov?" Isaac barked a laugh.

And Lika said, "Stop it!"

Never, not even in the classroom, had Masha heard her speak so sharply. And they did stop! This new tone threw them off. Antosha began fussing with his cuffs, pulling one sleeve, then the other, as though his coat were suddenly too small. Isaac cleared his throat. The samovar arrived, and Masha busied herself with the tea.

Antosha finally broke the tension. "So, Isaac. I noticed you brought your gun. Tomorrow we'll hunt."

"What about the ladies?"

"Miss Mizanova, you mean? You'll have to tear yourself away from her for a few hours."

Masha fixed on Antosha another look, which he also ignored.

When she handed him his tea, she whispered, "Is hunting wise?"

"I HATE THEM . . ." LIKA SAID LATER, CLARIFYING, "WHEN they're together like this."

They were in Masha's room, Lika lying on the bed, Masha across from her on the settee. Lika glanced at Masha and seemed to intuit an accusation.

"You're thinking about the Hermitage. It's different now. Isaac is crazy. I wish I hadn't come. I only did so I could tell Antosha off. As soon as I get the chance to, I'm leaving."

"I wasn't thinking about the Hermitage. I was wondering if you really did tell Antosha what happened last summer."

"I did! He's being unspeakably cruel. Those things he wrote, and now this."

"What things he wrote? His letter, you mean?"

Masha only wanted to understand what was going on. But Lika was so very angry. Everything about her seemed clenched—jaw, hands. Her shoulders lifted to her ears, as though someone were squeezing the back of her neck.

"Lika? What did he write?" Masha asked, but a knock came on her door then. Mariushka. Dinner was ready.

They got through it thanks to Misha and Ivan, who hadn't stopped ribbing each other and Antosha since Ivan's arrival. Lika, who had waited for Isaac to take his place so she might seat herself as far away as possible, was left with the corner seat—meaning, according to superstition, that she wouldn't marry for seven years.

"Don't sit there!" the men cried out. "Lika, move!"

"Masha, make her!"

"Four hearts are breaking here!"

They played musical chairs and brought in two empty ones. Then, after thoroughly embarrassing Lika, the four men whose hearts had been imperilled proceeded to ignore her, talking amongst themselves while Lika quietly poked at her food.

After the meal, they needed her again. Lika obviously didn't feel like playing, but agreed out of politeness. Because it was Holy Week, Father, supposedly abstaining from all pleasures, hid himself in the Pushkin Room and listened from there.

Isaac asked for Chopin. Lika played beautifully, swaying on the stool. Isaac's dark eyes closed, the music seeming to soak right into his turbulent soul.

After they applauded, Antosha said, "You sang something for us last summer. What was it?"

Masha saw the frustration pass in a wave across Lika's face.

"'Angel Serenade,'" Father called from the next room.

Lika riffled through her music. Now Isaac pitched himself forward in his chair like a conservatory examiner, his high brow wrinkling, his gaze shuttling between Lika and Antosha.

When she played, when she lifted up her clear voice, Father stood in the doorway, tears running into his beard, weeping for the dying child in the song. This man who had once lived by the motto that a beaten child is worth two unbeaten ones.

ASSES, MASHA THOUGHT THE NEXT DAY, WATCHING Antosha and Isaac set out from the house at dawn. They were dressed in tunics, trousers stuffed into boots, breath hanging in the air, both carrying their guns. Their stamping and Isaac's booming voice had woken her, though they'd clearly hoped to waken someone else.

Let them shoot each other, she thought, as they splashed away. Above, the clouds were stained like Easter eggs boiled in beetroot, wisps and streaks pouring out of the horizon, two figures in silhouette sloshing toward it.

It came back then, unexpectedly and unforced—the thing she'd been waiting for for years. She was not particularly moved by the scene, more irritated than anything. But before she knew it, she was creeping to her room for her sketchbook and charcoal, trying not to disturb the sleeping Lika.

Back at the window, she saw that they'd only got as far as the road before stopping to smoke. Then Isaac got the same idea as Masha, as though he'd seen her from the window, which was impossible. As though it were infectious. He pulled his own book from his pouch and dashed off some lines that no doubt perfectly depicted the soul of spring.

Something in their gestures told her they were talking. Isaac removed his hat and scratched down the back of his collar with the pencil. Antosha lifted his fist to cough, threw down his cigarette, sloshed on. Making haste to follow, Isaac stuffed away his book. She kept watching and drawing until they disappeared, and the sun had risen and burnt away the red, leaving only the transparent blue of day.

Easter preparations kept her busy all morning, but she still snuck back to her room to look at her drawing, expecting it to be awful. It wasn't. Not until she opened her paint box and added colour. The trick was knowing when to stop.

"When are they coming back?" Lika asked from the doorway.

Masha folded the picture and dropped it in the wastebasket. "I thought you wanted to get away from them."

"I do. But I don't want Isaac to kill himself. Or Antosha." She was twisting her hands. So she didn't hate them very much.

Just before lunch, Masha heard the crash of the door. She hurried to the vestibule and found Isaac struggling to take off one of his dirty boots. The other lay on its side on the floor.

"Where's Antosha?"

He responded with a groan. Giving up on the boot, he limped to the Pushkin Room, tracking in mud, throwing himself face down on the divan and smearing the upholstery.

Lika appeared then. "Isaac? What happened?"

He began shaking with sobs, and Lika turned her horrified face to Masha, who had until that moment been frozen on the spot.

The same way her body had moved to get her sketchbook before she'd been conscious of the urge, she was already exchanging slippers for shoes and throwing open the door—

To Antosha coming along the path toward them.

"Thank God!" Lika cried out behind Masha, speaking for them both.

Antosha lifted the single lifeless snipe he carried by its feet. "One fewer lovelorn creature in the world. Two fools come home for lunch."

ISAAC WOULDN'T EAT, WOULDN'T EVEN RISE. NEITHER would Antosha explain his enigmatic comment, or tell them what had upset Isaac. Not until he'd finished his meal.

He cut and chewed with his usual unhurried precision, thanking Mariushka for every course she brought.

"Observe how the writer creates suspense," Ivan said. "Brother?"

"Should I check on Isaac?" Misha asked.

At last Antosha brushed the crumbs off his beard and lit a cigarette. "Isaac shot it." He didn't lower his voice. Perhaps he hoped the swarthy painter would overhear and come running to defend himself. "But it turned out he'd only winged it. When we went to retrieve it, it was thrashing about in a puddle. He begged me to bash it."

"Did you?" Lika asked. "Bash it?"

He squinted across the table at her. "I told him the person who shot should put it out of its misery."

He'd called the bird "lovelorn." A writer's embellishment. Masha could picture the scene, not so different from that morning, when she'd watched them standing together on the road.

"So who did it?" Lika asked.

"Who else? He was trembling all over, suffering as much as the bird. Ah, I see you blame me."

Lika looked down at the tablecloth, one hand at the base of her white throat.

After lunch, Mother asked Masha to check on Isaac.

"Shouldn't the doctor see him?" Masha said.

The doctor was napping.

Masha peeked in the door of the Pushkin Room. Isaac was still wearing the boot, though the floor had been swabbed clean. His back to the room, he burbled snores. In this position he remained into the evening.

"What are we going to do?" Lika asked Masha when they were getting ready for church. "We can't leave him by himself."

"Go and wake him, then," Masha said.

Her eyes widened. "Masha? This is what happened last summer. Better you go."

Masha went and sat at the foot of the divan, causing Isaac to stir and reach blindly for her.

"Likusha," he moaned, face still pressed into the upholstery.

"It's me. Your student."

He took her hand anyway. Dried mud became powder in their clasp. "Masha. Something terrible happened." He turned his head, eyes glittering, hair thin and disorganized. "We're nothing in the face of Nature. She wants revenge."

"What are you saying, Isaac?"

"Your brother killed it, not me. I only wounded it. But then this terrible noise. A chittering and clicking. It rose up and swept across the field toward us." He let go of her hand to trace an arc with his arm. "Snipe. Thousands of them darkening the sky. Where's Lika?"

"We're all ready for church. Lika too."

He sat up, rubbing his eyes, dirtying one socket. Shook himself. "Where's my boot?"

"In the vestibule. You wash and change. We'll wait for you." She made to stand, but he held her back.

"Nature's angry. Lika's angry. So's your brother. They didn't want me here, but I'm glad I came. He's no good for her. He killed it with the butt of his gun." He acted it out. "Bam, bam, bam. Like that."

"But, Isaac? You asked him to."

This left him chastened and confused, a child stumped by logic. When she said, "Hurry. We're all waiting," the child obeyed.

They'd hired a priest from the nearby monastery to conduct the service in the little wooden chapel on Melikhovo's grounds. Isaac stood with the rest of them, but did not sing. It had nothing to do with his Jewishness, but rather his state of mind. He seemed to be processing the scene he'd witnessed that morning. The darkened sky, the thousand grieving snipe bearing witness to mercy's complications.

The explosion came the following morning, when Isaac had to return to Moscow. He could have gone before breakfast with Ivan, which would have saved his hosts a trip to the station on a muddy, rutted road. Instead he waited until Lika woke. Then he cornered her in the parlour. Masha was next door, in her room trying to draw again, able to hear everything.

"Aren't you leaving with me?"

"I'm going back with Masha," she told him.

"We can all go together."

"All right," Lika said.

"But I must leave now. I have an appointment."

"I guess you'll be travelling alone, then, Isaac."

"Likusha. Why are you so cold? I love you. I adore you. What more do you want?"

Discordant notes. One of them had backed into the piano.

"Isaac, stop. Please." Her firm steps walked out.

Masha poked her head out of her room and saw him on his knees. Without a trace of embarrassment, he rose and staggered toward her.

"Masha? Can't you help me?"

He followed her right into her bedroom, where she dropped onto the bed. Isaac went down on his knees again and came crawling toward her with beseeching eyes.

"Talk to Anton. Tell him to leave her be. He can't love her as I do."

Masha looked down on him. A fresh scab showed through his thinning hair. He must have hit his head ducking into the outhouse that morning. This made her doubly embarrassed for him.

"Isaac, I can't tell Antosha what to do."

"Why not? You're the only one he listens to."

Misha appeared in the doorway looking for him. Masha expected him to laugh, but Misha saw her desperate expression. How he'd matured, their little brother. After just a few months caring for livestock and dealing with the peasants, he'd become an adroit tactician, one able to take the manic painter in hand.

"Isaac, what a sky we have for driving."

Isaac immediately looked toward the windows. He planted one unsteady foot, then the other, and lurched to the window, where he yanked the curtain back.

"If we leave now," Misha said, "there'll be time to stop and sketch."

Nodding, Isaac silently went, Masha trailing worriedly behind them.

Everyone had gathered in the yard to see him off. Isaac shook hands distractedly all around. When he got to Lika, he kissed her hand so profusely that she was forced to tear it away and hide it behind her back. Misha and Antosha steered him to the carriage.

As Misha drove off with their unpredicted and unpredictable guest, the rest of them slackened with exhaustion and relief. Father announced he was going inside to pray. Mother asked, "He won't shoot himself in Moscow, will he?"

"Shooting oneself is a country pastime." Antosha kissed the top of her head.

Reassured, Mother went inside to lie down.

And now Antosha turned to Lika with an amused expression, for they were standing in almost the same place as they had been when Isaac surprised them.

"Wasn't I showing you around?"

"Yes," Lika said, smiling in return. She gestured to Masha. "Come with us."

Masha had been about to take Mother's cue and lie down herself, but she remembered now that Lika had an unrevealed purpose for coming. After all the emotional upheaval over Isaac, she had no desire to witness Lika's promised telling-off.

"Yes, come, sister. Let's show her our garden," Antosha said.

For weeks, they'd been passing the seed catalogue back and forth. His enthusiasm conquered her apprehension. Also, it would be easier to deal with Lika's accusations later if she heard them for herself.

Antosha took Lika's arm. "We have grand plans. Eggplants here." He stooped for a stick to point with. "Next to them. You'll never guess."

"Artichokes," said Masha, who had doubts.

"By mid-summer Melikhovo will look like the south of France."

They passed the post with the bell that Father rang daily at noon. Antosha commented on the thawing earth, so fragrant and fecund. He'd prefer a woman to daub mud behind her ears than scent.

Masha laughed. Lika didn't.

"Her brow furrows," Antosha said to Masha. "Some profound thought, or is it corns?"

He was enjoying himself now that they'd survived the melodrama of Isaac. He had no idea that Lika was angry, possibly doubly angry now. As Masha listened to him, something else occurred to her. He felt free to flirt because he knew what train they were taking, that Lika's departure was imminent.

"Not corns," Lika answered calmly. "I was thinking about your story."

"Which one? Never mind. None are worth a thought once you reach 'The End.'"

"To the contrary. I've been thinking about it ever since I read it."

Antosha looked as confused as Masha felt.

"Yesterday you said I must have met someone at Sophia's." Lika slowed her speech, as though her words might explode if she didn't pronounce them with the utmost care. Her colour was rising. "I did. A poetess. Quite pretty and smart. A polyglot. She's only eighteen. Sophia's completely in raptures over her."

Antosha let go of Lika's arm.

"Tatiana Shchepkina-Kupernik. Such a mouthful. Everyone calls her Topsy-Turvy Tania. Have you met her?"

"Never heard of her," Antosha said.

"You'll love her. She downed a few too many and ended up sitting on the floor. 'I simply don't understand,' she kept moaning.

'He's been here, hasn't he? He's enjoyed your hospitality? Isn't he your friend? I've had such a wonderful time tonight. I simply can't understand why he wrote such things.'"

"What things?" Masha asked.

"She'd brought the journal with her. Of course, Sophia rushed off to read it. Not aloud, thank God."

"Which story is this?" Masha asked, turning to Antosha. Such colour on his face! It was redder than when he coughed.

"She wouldn't come back to the party, she was so upset. We were all dying of curiosity then. The next day I went out and found a copy. I didn't show it to Isaac, but someone will. You should know that Sophia considers herself libelled."

"Libelled?" Antosha's brief laugh sounded like a stone rattled in a box. "She's what? Forty-two? Dark as a Chechen. And she sees herself in a twenty-two-year-old blonde? That's delusion, not libel."

He stuffed his hands in his pockets. The pince-nez tilted, clung to his nose for a second, then fell. As he squinted into the distance, it swung back and forth across his chest like a man on the gallows.

In the same measured voice, Lika said, "A twenty-two-year-old blonde? Antosha, I've long wanted to tell you this. When you say or do hurtful things, I understand it's not deliberate. You're not *trying* to cause pain. It's just that you don't give a damn about anyone. And, by the way, I'm twenty."

She turned and walked back to the house, leaving brother and sister standing there. On Antosha's face, an expression rarer even than his previous blush. The last time Masha had seen it was at Kolia's graveside when the priest tipped the censer and the grey snow of ash fell. She'd struggled to name it at the time. Regret?

He replaced the pince-nez and gave her a faint smile.

———

LIKA HAD BROUGHT THE OFFENDING JOURNAL, SO Masha read "The Grasshopper" on the train. How did he do it? The story was tongue-in-cheek, "Olga's" salon a lampoon of Sophia's, Olga herself superficial, stupid and cruel. She marries the doctor who saved her father's life but, yearning to associate herself with artistic genius, begins an affair with her painting teacher, with whom she goes on summer excursions to the Volga River. Almost everyone in the story was recognizable as an actual person, or a simple composite, from the real-life salon. All of them Antosha mocked except the long-suffering doctor, called Dymov in the story.

But when Dymov dies—commits suicide, really, for he's intentionally careless and infects himself with diphtheria—Masha actually cried. How did Antosha go from parody to tragedy without her noticing?

She blew her nose.

Lika said, "You're crying for me, I hope."

"Dymov, actually."

"Yes, the doctor. The only one he spares." She glared prettily out the window. A porter walked through and stopped to look at her.

"But, Lika, much of it is complimentary. He describes Ryabovsky—"

"You mean Isaac."

"—as a genius. Isaac will concur. Also, he made him fair-haired and blue-eyed."

"A brilliant disguise." Lika snatched the journal back and read out a passage. "'I'm madly in love with you. Say the word and I'll stop living, I'll give up art. Love me, love me . . .'"

Her angry eyes were on Masha, who bit her tongue until she nearly tasted blood. Then she burst out laughing.

"You're as bad as him, Masha! It's not funny!"

"But it is, Lika. Isaac sounds just like that. And you should be flattered, you with your flaxen hair and your slender cherry tree of a figure."

"She's horrid." She meant Olga in the story.

"You're fine about being written about? You just don't like what he says."

"I don't." She turned to glare out at the countryside.

"He's mocking Sophia, not you."

Now she turned back, lowering her voice, though they were alone in the compartment. "And Dr. K.? How do you think he feels seeing their affair laid out for the whole country to read?"

"Are you telling me he doesn't know?"

"Of course he does, but it's unseemly, Masha. The man's a saint."

"Antosha has portrayed him as a saint."

Lika threw up her hands. "All you do is defend him. He can do no wrong."

Masha bristled. "Of course he can do wrong. But to say he doesn't care about people? Do you really believe that?"

Lika nodded several times, taking this in. "You're right. He loves humanity, just not people."

She slumped against the window and closed her eyes, leaving Masha alone with her confused thoughts for most of the trip. Masha's loyalty to Antosha would never waver, but it did chafe now against her affection for Lika, who rightly took umbrage. Added to this was her female sense of hurt.

As the train neared Moscow, Lika said one more thing. "If he did write about me? With a heart, I mean. The way he wrote about that little dog Kashtanka, or even Dr. Dymov? Then I would be happy. I could read it over and over and at least imagine that he had some feeling for me."

2

THE NEXT WEEKEND AT MELIKHOVO, WHILE THE three siblings lingered at the breakfast table, Masha learned of the repercussions of "The Grasshopper." Along with the general furor, Isaac was threatening to challenge Antosha to a duel.

"So he's not actually challenged you?" Masha hastened to clarify. "He's just threatening to?"

Mother, who happened to be passing in the hall, stopped in the doorway, ashen-faced from what she'd overheard. "Antosha! I thought you said Isaac would put his gun away. Why is he challenging you?"

"It's nothing, Mamasha," Antosha told her. Indeed, he was taking it all lightly, smiling his demi-smile, while Masha listened to Misha's report. "I wrote something Isaac didn't like. He'll get over it."

"What did you write?" Mother's voice quavered, as though she too feared his pen.

"Life can imitate art just as art imitates life. Do you remember I put Dr. Wagner in that story?"

"Which story?"

"It was called 'The Duel.'"

"That's what gave Isaac the idea?" Mother said.

"It must be. You saw the state he was in."

Appeased, Mother carried on her way. Misha stood up from the table and tapped Antosha on the head.

"Quick thinking. Let me just say I'm glad I'm your brother, not your friend. Family's off limits, isn't it?" He smiled unpleasantly.

After Misha left, Masha said, "Antosha, just apologize."

"To whom?"

"Isaac."

There was no trace of defensiveness in his reply, unlike at Epiphany, when he'd been so angry over Isaac's letter.

"Apologize for what? For depicting life as it is? He can't go bellowing that that's the sole purpose of art, then object when others do it."

"Brother, he's ill."

A peculiar expression settled on his face. In it she read, *So am I*, and dropped her gaze.

"When Isaac was visiting," Antosha went on, "he took his sketchbook out. If he goes back to his studio and paints Melikhovo's broken fences and sagging porch, should I take offence? I wouldn't, because that's how it is."

"You conflated Lika with Sophia. She isn't like Sophia at all."

"There you're wrong. She's like her when she keeps company with her. Miss Mizanova is altogether too impressionable. Someone should watch out for her, or she'll get in with a bad crowd."

Then he too stood up and left the dining room. That he went without his coffee was the only sign he was bothered after all. When Masha brought it to his study a few minutes later, he seemed grateful to have his routine honoured.

ISAAC HAD CLAIMED THAT MASHA WAS THE ONLY PERSON Antosha would listen to. Though true, he often gave no immediate sign of having heard her. At school, Lika showed Masha his brief letter.

I was sad you left, Lika. Let's live peacefully. Jot me a few lines.

He had heeded Masha after all. This was as much of an apology as Lika's "humbled admirer" was constitutionally able to express.

Had he written Isaac too? Masha doubted it. Meanwhile, Lika and Antosha's flow of bantering letters recommenced. Was it a good thing? For Antosha, yes. But at school, Lika, no longer Jamais, now the more suggestive Cantaloupe, shared some of their teasing contents and her frustration, leaving Masha to wonder if Antosha realized the effect he had. Was he *trying* to keep her lovelorn? Was Lika's effect on him all that mattered? Perhaps there was nothing wrong with his heart. Perhaps he was simply a monstrous egoist, like Isaac.

Masha had little time for these games now, and less interest. She was the busy mistress of an estate, fully unthawed now. Their real work had begun. Along with the joy of it came an unexpected side effect: Father reverted to his serf roots. Out of the house all day, no longer underfoot or sharing his ludicrous pensées, he became for the first time in their lives a tolerable presence.

As for Masha, as well as the accounting, she took charge of the vegetable garden and the hens, Antosha the orchard and the flowers. He ran a free clinic too, and, after writing, would see patients, peasants who'd been gathering since dawn along the bench under his window, or squatting on the ground. Many had no shoes, or only bast ones. The whole length of the wall bore the stain of greasy heads and dirty heels.

Masha was sometimes called to help. Then she would have to don her white apron and hold his tray of instruments, while Antosha lanced, extracted, prodded and salved—oblivious to her disgust. Life as it was. Only rarely did he spare her. Once, a man stinking of tobacco came in plucking at his flies. Sores on his face. The French disease. Antosha dismissed her.

"Your kindness will bring the Kingdom of Heaven."

"May the Life-giving Virgin protect you, Doctor."

"For your goodness the Kingdom awaits."

This was his payment for work that would never end, a good word to a God he didn't believe in. For every patient he saw, three more waited. And his writing waited, as did his duties on the local sanitation council. He was cholera officer too, during the outbreak that summer. Come noon, an exhausted Antosha, ill himself, headed to his room to wash.

"Antonshevu," Mother would call. "When do you want lunch?"

"Soon. I'm going to write a letter first."

A half hour later, the family gathered in the dining room. In walked Antosha, looking rested, like he'd dosed himself with some rejuvenating tonic. Restored from writing Lika. Always that half-smile on his lips, like he'd just indulged in something ripe and sweet.

Two months later, Lika came again, en route to her aunt's estate, at the start of summer when Melikhovo's guests were few. Among the many still angry with Antosha over "The Grasshopper" was Isaac, meaning Antosha had indeed not written him. Isaac was sure not to follow Lika now.

Unfortunately, the blonde who Misha was courting, Klara, was visiting at that time too, butterflying her lashes in Antosha's direction. So another rivalry unfolded for their summer amusement, this time between two women. Apart from their hair, the visiting blondes were entirely different, Klara with brown eyes so far apart it wore you out to look from one to the other. Her mouth was wide too, as though she'd stretched it with an apple. Mainly Masha disliked Klara for the way she dragged the little brother around by his big ears, and how, every morning when Klara appeared for breakfast, she'd ask, "Any sign of the famous writer yet?" with Misha sitting right there at the table.

Together, Klara and Lika reminded Masha of cats, the one animal Antosha didn't love. Dogs were his favourite. "They are fine people," he always said. He even loved mice for their intelligent eyes and frugal ways. When he trapped one, he'd walk far into the woods and release it there. She'd expected two blondes at once would make him feel like a mouse himself, descended upon by rival felines.

She was wrong. Recently he'd bought a sprung carriage to make the trip to collect the post less painful. Off he raced each afternoon, a blonde on either side. If this was revenge on Lika for what she'd put him through at Bogimovo the previous summer, it was indistinguishable from his enjoyment.

During the day, the rising frenzy of Lika and Klara trying to out-laugh and out-mushroom-pick each other drove Masha to the solace of her garden. In the evening she joined the entertainment. Klara played the piano too, though her voice was a squeaking hinge compared to Lika's. The first night they put on an impromptu concert, which ended with Klara playing the Can-can and commanding Lika to dance.

"Not like that. Kick higher," she said of Lika's shy stepping. "You play, then. I'll show you how it's done."

She pranced a circle, flapping her skirt and flashing the lacy edging underneath. When she turned her back to the men and bowed, it seemed an undisguised excuse to show that she too was in jiggling possession of a pair of cantaloupes. During this orgiastic display, Father glowered briefly in the doorway. Mother looked bewildered, Lika embarrassed.

Antosha, face inscrutable, mock-whispered to the little brother, "How I love immoral women."

Misha's expression was as scrutable as Father's. *She's mine*, it said.

The next day Mother relayed Father's disapproval, and hers, obliging Masha to discourage another concert. She did it over coffee and rolls at breakfast.

Lika suggested they ask Antosha to read instead. "I'd love to hear 'The Kiss' in his own voice."

Misha had thankfully already left for the barn, for Klara replied, "I'd prefer the actual thing to a story about it."

Masha slapped her hand down on the table, setting their cups chattering in their saucers.

In response to her withering look, Klara said, "What?" as pertly as ever.

Later, Antosha refused Lika's request. "I can't think of a duller entertainment."

"Whist?" Masha said.

"There's one," Misha said. "Snore."

They settled on Post Office, Mother and Father joining them in the parlour. Masha was sentenced to be the postman. She passed around pencils and paper and delivered the anonymous messages.

God our Saviour loves you was the first of hers that she opened. Father, obviously.

Klara opened hers, shrieked, and pressed it to her breast. She refused to share it.

"'I love your stories. They are so filled with pathos, they make me weep,'" Antosha read out. "It must be for Misha." He slid it across.

"Very funny," Misha told him. "I suppose you're the author of this billet-doux. 'Meet me behind the outhouse at midnight.'"

Antosha admitted nothing. Instead he observed, "Cantaloupe wears a frown. Someone must have written her an unpleasant truth."

The frown became a wince. Then her silver eyes shifted briefly toward Klara's brown ones, widening now with feigned innocence.

MASHA BEGAN AN EXERCISE THAT SUMMER—PAINTING the house from the same angle, but in different light. If it went well, if she didn't get bored, she planned to continue through the seasons until she had produced a series. She chose a side view that included the fenced pasture for the way the horizontal rails, recently repaired, guided the eye—first across the foreground, then diagonally to their happy house. They'd never lived in one before.

To think that last summer she was running away! What a ninny. Where would she have ended up? With Aleksander's moody thumb pressing down on her back? In a basement room again, sharing the kitchen with strangers?

The second last day of her visit, Lika sought Masha out while she was painting. "Oh, Masha. How lovely. May I watch?"

Though Masha could have done without an audience, she appreciated the praise and so accepted Lika's nervous presence. It didn't take her long to speak.

"Do you remember that girl at the Diary School, Anya? I had her and then you had her?"

"The pretty psychopath?"

"Yes! Klara reminds me of her."

A cat fight, Masha thought, laying down the first wash of sky. Hisses and clawed swipes. She blotted the page here and there with a balled rag to form the clouds.

"She follows me everywhere in case I get Antosha alone. I only got away now because poor Misha insisted on sitting her down for a talk. You didn't write, 'Give up,' did you? In Post Office, I mean."

"No. I wrote that you'd look pretty holding a hoe."

"I'll help you tomorrow, Masha. I promise. Do you think Klara wrote it, or Antosha? Because, here's the thing. My father sent me two tickets to the Caucasus. To take a holiday with a friend."

Masha turned to look at her. "A friend?"

"Did *you* want to come?" Lika hastily asked.

She wasn't inviting Masha. "Thank you for your kind invitation, but I'm much too busy for a holiday. As is Antosha, if you're thinking of inviting him."

Lika blurted, "He's taken such a fancy to Klara. Or he pretends to. She's a great one for innuendo."

Klara with her lace-edged culottes. Her barefoot rush back to the dining room with her dress open at the back, past Antosha's room. She'd left something on the table, she claimed. Misha, of course, was completely smitten the way he'd never been, or allowed himself to be, with Lika. He liked Lika, liked being seen with her too, because she was beautiful and associated with Antosha. But there was something missing. Passion, Masha supposed. That shivery thing.

She turned away from Lika without comment and dipped her brush, diluting the red to get the right shade for the house. The shade on Lika's face.

Oh, Masha thought. A dull feeling settled on her, like after blurting out something stupid. Not passion. Passion was what women felt. This was lust. Her brothers were lusting after Klara. The realization came with that childhood image—the convict dog-catchers in Taganrog on the march with their cudgels and hooks.

Lika seemed to have read her mind. "I'd hoped there was more than *that*. He seemed above it. Because of the things he writes and all the good he does."

"Than what?" Masha kept her eyes on the picture.

"*That*," Lika said.

Masha muddied the water with the brush. Should she mention the houses in town that Antosha most likely visited every time he went? The actresses whose company he enjoyed. As an only child raised by women, would Lika even know about such things? How to put it so as not to disillusion her completely? *Men have physical needs that must be met.* Or maybe Lika *should* be disillusioned.

Before Masha could answer, Lika said, "I think I'm distracting you." She walked back to the house hugging herself.

THE NEXT TIME MASHA ATTEMPTED THE SCENE WAS dusk the next evening. She struggled more. The light changed from moment to moment. A ripening peach, a fevered cheek. What advice would her teacher give, he who had sat before a thousand twilights? *Look. Open your eyes.* She kept dropping colour onto the wet page while Isaac's long finger circled. *Where are you, Masha?*

Here I am. Finally!

She couldn't keep up, and before she knew it, darkness had nearly fallen, defeating her. She packed her brushes and paints, folded her stool and headed in, taking the same route as the viewer's eye, along the fence. All the lamps were lit inside the house. Lika was playing some sugary melody on the piano.

Then, out of the gloom, two light-coloured figures detached from the birch copse ahead. Masha heard, "Just ask your sister."

It wasn't Lika playing.

Masha should have signalled her approach, or walked the other way, but she was curious what Lika was saying about her. Neither of them noticed her frozen in place ten yards away.

"Really, I won't put you under any obligation. You said you love immoral women, so you won't be bored with me. I have stories too, you know."

What was the silly girl talking about? Masha could see them standing close, but couldn't make out their faces.

"Stories?" he asked.

"Yes. True ones," Lika said. "Are you coming with me?"

"Unlikely. I don't interfere with the lives of young ladies. It's a principle."

Masha almost snorted at this lie.

"Besides," he went on, "if your father's paying for these tickets, isn't he likely to come after me?"

Lika slapped Antosha's face. Masha's breath sucked back inside her and she nearly cried out.

"Will you come?" Lika asked again, and at his "no," she threw herself at him, pounding his chest, aiming for his head too, which he turned away protectively. Eventually she stopped. "Aren't you going to fight back? I assure you I'd prefer it to this endless stalemate. No? Then I'll have to thrash you till you agree." She lifted her arm as though to strike him again.

Antosha seized her wrist, causing her to shriek. "Now you've made me hurt you, when that's just what I've been trying not to do!"

He so rarely raised his voice. It alarmed Masha as much as the scuffle that preceded it. Then he reached for Lika, out of anger or to comfort her. They simply merged into one. All Masha saw of Lika were white hands travelling up and down her brother's back.

"Will you come?" Lika pulled away to ask.

As Masha walked on, shaken, unseen, she heard her brother lie a second time. He said he would.

How disturbing. Masha went into the house. To get to her room she had to walk through the parlour where Klara was still playing. Klara stopped and stretched her mouth like a frog tsarevna.

"Where did everyone go? I can't find Antosha anywhere."

"Where is Misha?" Masha asked.

This was too subtle a rejoinder. Klara shrugged. "Off somewhere sulking."

Masha went to her room and closed her door.

She blamed this invitation of Lika's on Klara prancing around the parlour and jiggling her rump. Antosha himself had said Lika was too impressionable. The mores of their set—the arty crowd, Bohemians—were to blame as well. This set that Masha had invited Lika into. She'd invited Lika, but she was herself only an adjunct to it, through her brothers, by choice. Neither of them prohibited her from joining in; rather her sense of self-protection did. But if Masha did join, she would be protected in any case—unlike Lika, who lacked not only brothers but, increasingly it seemed, the sense that her self was worth protecting.

THEY WERE GOING AWAY TO THE CAUCASUS TOGETHER. Lika told Masha this before she left Melikhovo the next morning.

"Tell no one."

She sounded triumphant but looked battle-weary. No need for Masha to disabuse her, she decided. Antosha was sure to do it.

For the rest of the summer, letters travelled back and forth between Melikhovo and Lika's aunt's estate in Tver. Antosha didn't share them, but Masha could guess their contents. Lika trying to firm up their scandalous plans, Antosha steadfastly non-committal. Had Masha been wrong not to tell Lika it wouldn't happen? This question now and then burbled up to disturb her present contentment, along with the uncomfortable feeling that she might be guilty of the same maddening reticence as Antosha.

Other women wrote Antosha too, of course: Vermicelli, and the Maly actress who liked pink ties and curled hair, Kleopatra. Others with unfamiliar names. And not a single case of cholera occurred in the twenty-five villages under Antosha's supervision. With the threat of the epidemic, their expected summer guests cancelled. Everyone was afraid of catching cholera on the train.

"Misha says I live in a flowerbed of beautiful women," Antosha told Masha one morning. "But this is the bed I prefer."

Just the two of them again. How she enjoyed those days alongside him in the garden. Physical work freed her mind. Past grievances dissolved. If someone proposed to Masha now, she'd refuse outright herself. She had her vegetable children. Into her palm she'd shaken seeds barely bigger than ones her own body wasted. Those she rinsed out with the rags, but these she sprinkled on the earth. And they grew! Hundreds of heads of cabbage, the cucumbers Misha filled his pockets with before he went out to the fields, and those terrifying artichokes. Onions, radishes, potatoes, potatoes, potatoes.

In the spring they'd lit bonfires in the orchard to protect the blossoming trees from frost. Apples, peaches, plums and fifty cherry trees that, though immature, all drooped with bounty now. Everyone clamoured for a share, Father for the fruit liqueur he enjoyed concocting, though wouldn't drink, Mother for cherry pie, the starlings to gorge themselves.

"So we should stuff our faces," Antosha told her, "or there'll be nothing left for us."

They filled their mouths. Juice dribbled down Masha's chin and bloodied her dress; she only laughed. Sister and brother, side by side, wagering who could spit the pits the farthest.

Antosha trounced her, then said, "It still feels odd."

"What?"

"To pick cherries and not get beaten for it."

What to offer after this but silence? Soon it became a companionable one. Masha gathered the buckets, carried them to the kitchen. When she returned, Antosha was back among his roses, secateurs in one hand, sucking on the pad of his thumb.

"What's wrong?" she asked.

She meant his thumb, but he answered differently. "I've just tallied my literary achievements thus far this summer. Thanks to cholera, almost nil. And I've thought about literature even less than I've written it. Quite happily."

"What have you been doing behind that closed door, then?"

He peered at the thumb. "I stare at the pile of pages that is Sakhalin Island and shudder."

"Are you still working on that?"

He gave her a bitter smile. "Punishment is perpetual."

This came too soon after his comment about the cherries. The morning's dewy pleasure evaporated.

"I did finish two stories. One tolerable, one bad. Thank God we have no rent. But all in all, sister, I have but one regret."

"Who?" Masha asked.

"Who?" He laughed. "What are you getting at?"

Since the mood was spoiled, why not say it? "I heard you were supposed to go to the Caucasus with someone."

"And let an epidemic sweep through the district? And leave all this work for you?"

He gestured around them. She'd been right to trust him. He had a perfectly reasonable excuse, a noble one. But had he used it?

"Did you tell her that, brother? That you couldn't go?"

"To her face? No. It's prosaic to bring up work when a young lady propositions you. And you should see her when she's disappointed. All the life drains right out of her. I can't stand it."

"How about in those letters you've been writing to her? Did you make it clear you weren't going to interfere?"

He looked at her strangely. Did he recognize his own words and guess she'd overheard them, or did he hear the two words she'd left unsaid?

This time.

"Sister, Lika is very special. I think you understand that. I wouldn't hurt her for anything. Don't you want to hear my regret?"

Masha wiped the sweat off her brow. "All right."

"It's that I still think about that damned play." He showed her his thumb. "A rose attacked me. See? It's nothing. Just a prick of the skin. But how it hurts."

3

I N AUGUST, OLGA WROTE. UNBEKNOWNST TO MASHA or Antosha, she'd been staying for months just eight miles away at a psychiatric hospital, working as an assistant.

Antosha urged Masha to go see her. "Bring her back if you can. I have no one here to quarrel with." Melikhovo was still empty of visitors.

"But she's an astronomer. What's she doing there? Why isn't she at the observatory?"

"I've just mentioned a possible reason," he fondly said.

Masha drove off the next day to find the hospital, worried for Olga and nervous about the place. Had she been dismissed from the observatory, or had she left of her own volition? She'd practically lived there. And what would the hospital be like? Masha pictured the Zoological Gardens with lunatics in place of animals.

Along with those concerns, there was another. After eight months, a letter had arrived in Smagin's unmistakable scrawl. *You are to me even now the most enchanting and incomparable woman . . .* Words that threatened to scratch open a mostly healed wound. Though the sprung carriage jostled her less than the one without springs, she was still rattled. Was she supposed to answer Smagin? *Thank you, but I cannot accept such forward compliments.* She wouldn't involve Antosha again. She'd deal with the man herself.

Meanwhile, a sweet-sour odour kept wafting off the driver as they drove along, inclining her to nausea. One of their farm hands sweating off last night's binge.

Formerly the hospital had been a manor house, red brick with a mansard roof and unusual embellishments: loinclothed Egyptian caryatids that stared stonily down from the facade, figures straight out of a delusion. Masha employed the knocker, but before anyone could answer, a young beardless man in a straw hat came around the outside corner of the building—a groundsman, she assumed.

"I'm here to see a friend who works here. Olga—"

He cut her off. "She's a patient."

"No."

"There's only one Olga. She helps him too. We all do."

The door opened on someone she presumed to be the doctor, a short, broad-chested man more formally dressed. He was as muscular as an acrobat, better proportioned for the circus than psychiatry, his eyes strikingly dark, like jet beads on a mourning necklace.

"A friend of Olga's," said the groundsman.

The doctor introduced himself as Vladimir. He ushered Masha inside.

"Olga eschews praise, so I'll give it to her friend. She's a great help to me, in particular her insights with regard to our female patients."

The empty hall amplified his quiet voice as they walked. If there had been shrieking madmen somewhere, Masha would have heard them. Everything looked clean. Some of her apprehension lifted.

"Any chance she could get away for a visit?"

"No one's under lock and key here."

Masha stopped. "You don't mean she *is* a patient?" Olga was the last person Masha would suspect of mental frailty. She could barely articulate her next question. "How did this happen?"

The doctor looked at her. "I can't disclose personal details.

She's responding well. She shouldn't see you upset, though. Take a moment."

Masha pressed her eyes to stop her tears. Olga's peculiarities demanded reinterpretation. Her slovenliness, for example. Masha had always assumed it was an admirable disregard of opinion. But was it actually a symptom? When she took her hands away, the doctor was holding out his handkerchief. She shook her head and gestured that she was ready.

Poor Olga. Her intelligence made her lonely, and loneliness made her prickly. Masha's artichoke friend.

They stopped before a closed door. Hairy knuckles rapped. Silence.

"Someone's here to see you, Olga," the doctor said.

Olga wasn't necessarily eager to answer. There simply wasn't far to go in what turned out to be a dim former linen cupboard. But at the sight of Masha, Olga's unguarded expectation vanished and made plain a fact—that she'd been hoping for someone else.

She introduced Masha to the doctor, who turned to her with more interest now.

"The writer's sister? What a delight. Please tell your brother he has many fans here. We often read his stories aloud in the evenings, thanks to Olga, who suggested this entertainment. Will you show her our grounds, Olga?"

Olga had sat down on the unmade cot and was staring at the floor, this woman who had perched on the windowsill at Bogimovo and crowned herself tsarevna. Her bun looked matted, like she didn't take her hair down when she slept.

"Take a walk," the doctor said.

Olga's bowed shoulders lifted, then fell again.

He smiled at Masha. "I'll leave you. Enjoy."

As soon as he was gone, Olga said, "He's dogged on the subject of exercise. Has us doing calisthenics before breakfast. Of course, the rest of us would prefer to lie in bed with the blankets over our heads. Sit, why don't you?"

The only other furniture that fit the dim room was a chair and a small desk piled with books. The tang of stale tobacco and unwashed body hung in the air. There was a curtain on the opposite wall, so logically a window. In three steps Masha reached it.

"Don't," Olga groaned. "I like it dark."

Astronomers do. They need darkness. Masha remembered visiting the observatory, the starred vault of its ceiling mysterious and holy. Olga some kind of priestess.

"I'll just let in some air." She raised the sash, then went back and sat on the chair. She'd brought gifts but waited to present them.

"Why are you here, Olechka? Did something happen at the observatory?"

Olga wriggled one finger into the ratty bun. "They made it impossible. They undermined my work. They stole it. They harassed me." Grievances expressed flatly, with none of her energizing invective. Masha had no doubt who "they" were. She remembered the hostile looks they'd received walking down the hallway, and how Olga had warded off their evil eyes by flicking ash off her cigarette. Now she was in a mental hospital to be cured of female brilliance.

"I'm working here now," Olga said.

She pointed at the books. She was mainly the doctor's secretary, but she'd read enough now that they discussed diagnoses too. Mostly they treated depression, hysteria and chronic onanism, though she suspected the latter was a fraud.

"Really, Olga?" Masha said prudishly.

Finally, a soupçon of disdain. "A man will go mad if he seeks pleasure on his own. What's his recourse? A prostitute. How convenient. And what are women to do? Never feel pleasure?"

"They get married," Masha said.

Olga gave her a devastating look. "As if that guarantees pleasure of any kind."

Masha thought of Smagin's letter then, a possible case in point. She waited for Olga to say that the doctor was an idiot and that she already knew twice as much as he did. That she didn't depressed Masha. It meant her cure was working.

She lifted her bag onto the desk and began to unload it. "I brought cherry preserves. And you can never have too many handkerchiefs, according to Mother."

"Nothing from Antosha?" Olga averted her eyes.

"He wants me to bring you back. It will be peaceful at Melikhovo. We have no visitors. Will you come?"

This time when Olga touched her head, she seemed to realize how frightful her hair was. She pulled out her pins and proceeded to rake her hair with her fingers. Masha hadn't seen it down since their Guerrier days. Olga had always been thin, but now she looked as emaciated as Vermicelli. After fashioning a bun barely more kempt than its predecessor, she stood and motioned for Masha to follow.

She had not answered the invitation.

On their way, some of the doors they passed were ajar or wide open. The doctor's, where he sat writing at his desk. In another room Masha glimpsed rows of cots, most neatly made, and an old woman standing at the window twisting her fingers into shapes against the light.

They stepped outside. To the left was a kitchen garden where

Olga said they grew their food. Several people were hoeing—patients, Olga confirmed. She pointed to a bench farther along a path where the lawn reverted to meadow. Beyond were woods. The clouds had amassed in earnest now. Flat-bottomed, they seemed heaped upon a plate.

No sooner had they reached the bench than Olga said, "I forgot my tobacco. Wait."

Masha watched her go back and procure a cigarette and a light from a man in the garden. He was the person Masha had met out front. She recognized the straw hat.

Olga returned at a slower pace. "There," she said, finally sitting beside Masha. "I exercised."

All this time Masha had been waiting for Olga to respond to her invitation. Should she be like the doctor and gently press? Or should she bully her like Olga had bullied her at Bogimovo? Or just drop it? Really, she felt so sorry for her.

Finally she said it plainly. "Will you come to Melikhovo?"

The cigarette tremored as Olga brought it to her lips. "I'm thinking about it. You asked why I came. I'll tell you." She brushed ash off her skirt. "Have you heard of invisible stars?"

"No."

"Dark stars. Newton's Law proves they exist, though no one has ever seen one."

"What are they?"

"Stars of sufficient mass and size to acquire an escape velocity greater than the speed of light. Gravity renders them invisible. Tonight, look up. Then you'll understand."

She was talking in riddles. Masha slumped helplessly. "But do you feel better here?"

"I feel useful. Look—"

She pointed at two women walking in the distance along the

edge of the trees, one with a basket. Both were studying the ground. Looking for mushrooms, Masha assumed. The breeze stirred the trees around them, creating undulating patterns in the foliage.

"The younger one is Katya. She dissociates. You wouldn't believe what was done to her." Olga spat out a thread of tobacco.

It was getting cooler, and Masha shivered. "Dissociation. Is that like psychic blindness?"

"Psychic blindness is a normal momentary phenomenon." She held her next drag inside her. It released with her words, and the breeze snatched it away. "Why didn't he come with you?"

"Antosha? He's working," Masha said.

"He should come here. See what it's like." She turned to Masha. "He could put it in a story."

A drop of moisture hit Masha's cheek from the *p* in Olga's "put." This sounded more like the old emphatic Olga. Or maybe it was rain. Masha held her palm out to the sky.

"I've been thinking about him a lot here. Differently now, as a psychiatrist might. He's a real case history. Just compare him to how Aleksander and Kolia turned out."

Masha withdrew her empty hand.

"Why were they ruined and not him?"

"Kolia's dead," Masha said. "Please don't speak ill of him."

"Where is Aleksander? You never mention him."

"In St. Petersburg. He's married. He has two boys. Let's change the subject. I didn't come here to have my family insulted."

Olga stopped, but her eyes stayed narrowed. It was the look Masha always thought of as "waiting to pounce," but the next thing she said was benign, so Masha relaxed again.

"And you love country life?"

"Yes! You should see my garden."

"Is Antosha still in love with Lika?"

"They're writing a lot of letters. I'm staying out of it."

Her brows sprang up with mock surprise. "Are you? You didn't use to. You used to bring us all around after lectures. Ekaterina—remember her? Sticking her bugs with pins? Dunia and Vermicelli. Me. Others too. There was that girl with a wine stain birthmark on her neck. What was her name? Your brothers argued about what country it was shaped like. "Atlas," they called her. There was something unsavoury about the whole situation. Dunia called your house Masha's Brothel."

It took a moment for Masha's shocked tongue to move. "This is your illness speaking, Olga. Tell me that it is."

Olga turned to Masha and did something she'd never done. She smiled, showing all her teeth, which were jumbled and nasty. Masha stood up and for a minute could only stare. Then she turned and walked rapidly away, arms swinging, trying not to cry. She took the path around the house. The hoeing man, probably one of the incurable masturbators, straightened and watched her pass. God knows what he was thinking. When she was sure she was out of Olga's sight, she broke into a stumbling run.

Olga wouldn't have caught up, except that Masha had to wake the slumbering driver. Then the rain started in earnest, and his shaking hands fumbled with the slippery carriage top. Olga hurried out with Masha's empty bag. When Masha reached down for it, Olga seized her arm and pulled her into a long, desperate embrace.

"I'm sorry. I didn't mean those words for you. I'm terribly unhappy. There's a note for Antosha in your bag."

As they drove off, Masha refused to look back. The unsheltered driver, rain running down his collar, cursed on her behalf. Masha's Brothel? They *asked* to come. They wanted to, Olga just as much as any of them.

Rain blew onto the seat. She lifted the bag into her lap. The smell of the driver reminded her of Kolia and turned her stomach. Olga was right about that. Kolia had been a drunk, and Aleksander was one still. Whenever they invited Aleksander, they prayed he wouldn't come. He hadn't for years, not since Father left the warehouse and came back to live with them again.

Then she was lost in those bad memories. The storeroom. The terrified birds twitching in her skirt. Their first year in Moscow, before Antosha joined them. Two cellar rooms, Father's screaming and his uselessness. Begging the bishop for a free place at the school. She'd prostrated herself before him, but he'd refused her. Antosha's arrival saved her.

She'd calmed enough to see the dripping hedgerows they were passing and feel the crackle of paper through the cloth under her hand. Without any compunction, she took out and unfolded Olga's note. She would tear it up if she had to.

Two agonized sentences:

I'll come, but I implore you to treat me, if not gently (that's not possible with you), then not too roughly. I have become impossibly sensitive.

By the time they reached Melikhovo, the horses were muddied to their flanks, but Olga's words had washed away Masha's anger.

AT DINNER EVERYONE GRILLED HER. ANTOSHA WAS amazed that the patients weren't locked up, that they were treated as free human beings.

"Even entertained," he said. "And so well."

"But why's Olechka taking a cure?" Misha asked.

"A cure for what?" Mother asked.

Father muttered something about her needing an exorcist.

"She's not like us, Mother," Antosha said. "She's a higher being soaring among the stars, free and independent."

"I assure you, brother," Masha said, "she has earthly feelings."

"Remember her at Bogimovo, putting Dr. Wagner in his place? She told him his shirt was an attempt at superior plumage." Antosha laughed.

"Olechka has a poor opinion of men," Mother said.

"Rightly so," he said.

"Ninety-nine out of a hundred have no brains," Masha added under her breath.

Antosha laughed again. He assumed, of course, that he was in the one percent. He was, but could there be a different organ that he lacked?

After dinner Masha took Olga's note to Antosha's study, but did not immediately hand it over. Its intimation of violence brought back the scene she'd witnessed the night Lika had slapped him. Was he really trying not to hurt them?

She spoke from the door. "Olga's still in love with you after all these years. I felt so terrible for her today."

His shoulders sank, and he placed the pen in the stand beside the rearing horse.

Masha said, "I introduced you to all my friends. I knew they'd fall in love. It made me feel important, to you and to them."

He looked up with a weary expression, removed the pince-nez and massaged the red mark that it left. A bizarre thought popped into her head then, that the terrible burden of all this passion weighed on him there—*on his nose*—where other men felt it in their hearts.

He answered as a doctor, a psychiatrist even. "When we idealize love, we assume those we love possess qualities that often just aren't there. It's a source of continual suffering."

"That's true," she said.

His brow pleated. "But is there really such a thing as love?"

"Of course!"

"I mean romantic love. Does it actually exist, or is it just physical attraction? Is it a psychosis? It often presents as such. Could we live without it, or would life be unbearably dull?" He put the pince-nez back on and looked out the window at the garden, that riot of colour, their south of France. "Do flowers feel it?"

It came to her then that she hadn't made herself more important, but the opposite. Had she thought they wouldn't like her for herself? Yes, she had. She was always shy at school because she'd had to beg for that free place and believed everybody knew and despised her for being poor. Worse than poor, from the peasantry. Serf stock, like the people in the huts they visited at Bogimovo, living in filth with the flies and their pathetic sweet wrappers pasted on the walls. She'd never shaken off the feeling, not even during her Guerrier courses, though Antosha had paid for them fully. By then she despised herself.

Some crude emotion welled up in Masha. She strode over and slammed the letter on the blotter, startling him. His surprise gave way to consternation, then to something else. His handsome features smoothed.

He was disappointed in her. Her outburst. Her incontinence. His disappointment pitted against her anger, but for once he was the first to turn away.

4

O LGA DIDN'T COME. HAD ANTOSHA EVEN ANSWERED her note? Masha was afraid to ask.

Late that summer, she set up her easel in the garden. She wanted to paint her cabbages, their heads grown to human size, dressed in their pretty green ruffs. After the first wash, she set the paper aside to drink the paint and tried to amuse herself with a cartoon portrait of a woman's shoulders, neck and hair, but a cabbage for a face. Masha thought of Olga again and the strange things she'd said about the stars. Then her accusations.

What would happen to Olga? What would happen to any of them? Masha's corset felt so tight. Why did she wear it? She got off the stool and stood, trying to take a full breath.

Father, at work on the other side of the garden, came along the path pushing the wheelbarrow. He noticed Masha, who had by then sunk to the ground. With a shout, he began running. Halfway, he lowered the barrow and stumbled on without it.

"Nothing," Masha told him from where she lay, her head in its predestined place in the row.

He bent over her, a hand on each knee, the white tendrils of his beard reaching down. She hadn't seen Father from below like this since she was a child. Filling his sadistic little eyes now—love and concern.

"I just felt dizzy," she told him. "I'm fine."

To prove it, she pushed herself up and with her dirty hand

brushed off her skirt, making it worse. Then she teetered into the house where Mother berated her for the condition of her just-laundered dress.

Antosha still hadn't budged from Melikhovo, not even to go to Moscow let alone the Caucasus with Lika. He was having an odourless earth closet installed and the windows double-glazed. There were cucumbers to pickle too, and potatoes and tulip bulbs to inter for resurrection in the spring.

So much to do. Work, work, work. They had to go on living.

When school resumed, Masha moved to another room in Moscow's Tverskoy district, larger so that Misha could stay when he came to town. (Antosha grumbled about this. He thought they could do without Misha now, that he should go back to the tax office.) Masha's first guest was Lika.

Forgoing tea, Lika walked around with the jam dish, eating straight from it while studying Masha's paintings.

"I like this one best." The pond at Melikhovo with the house behind it. She clattered her teeth against the spoon and smiled. "Remember you drew me, then tore it up?"

"Should we try again?" Masha asked. It would be easier to say what she planned to tell her, if she didn't have to hold Lika's gaze.

Lika settled at the table with her chin propped up in one hand.

"How was Tver and your aunt?" Masha asked.

"Boring. I almost died. I would have gone back to Moscow, except she wouldn't let me. 'Likusha! It's time to stop running around with these Bohemians!'"

Masha was outlining, working fast. "So she knew about your Caucasian holiday plans?"

"No! She would have murdered me, or Granny would have."

That Lika's plans had come to naught they both knew, so why not just bring it up?

"Couldn't you find another friend to go with?"

"No. Antosha tortured me all summer with his letters, pretending to be making up his mind."

Masha chose her tone as carefully as she would choose a colour, adding sympathy to firmness. "He had no intention of going."

Lika's eyes dropped momentarily. Under her lids, a barely perceptible undulation. She looked up again with a different expression. Philosophical, even stoic.

"Weren't there any men in Tver?" Masha asked.

"Ha. You sound like your brother. He wrote that I should find myself a soldier from the barracks near my aunt."

"Why don't you listen to him?"

Careful words again, the barbs removed. Masha went over the feathered lines so that she could look at the page instead of at Lika. She wanted to warn Lika, but not sound like she was speaking ill of Antosha.

"Because there are other women interested in Antosha. You realize that?"

"Klara, you mean?"

"And others. I wish you had a different nose. Or that you'd stop wiggling the one you have."

"I deserved what he did when I visited."

Masha glanced up. "What did he do?"

She was thinking of the scene she'd witnessed in the birch copse, but Lika, still holding herself in her pose, answered more generally.

"Encouraged my competition. Even so, I was disappointed that he liked Klara's sort. I was stupid not to realize that."

"From what I've observed—and remember that I grew up with five brothers—most men like any sort of woman who comes around. You don't know men."

"Actually, I do." Something caught in Lika's throat then, and she had to break her pose to cough.

"Tea?" Masha asked.

Lika declined with a wave, but Masha couldn't bear the sound of coughing. She left her sketch and went to pour a glass of water from the jug on the sideboard. It was a dry cough, shallow-sounding, not deep and moist like Antosha's. Nothing to be concerned about. It almost sounded false.

Lika wiped the tears off her face with one hand, then accepted the glass. After she drank, she took out her handkerchief and wiped her nose.

"There," she said with superfluous dabs and a smile. "I suppose I'm not fit to draw now."

Snorting at this false modesty, Masha resumed her place and Lika her pose. But something was different now. Partly it was Lika's expression. She was subdued. Sad. Her grey eyes looked straight ahead as though seeing nothing. Better just to get it over with. Masha set the pencil and book aside.

"Lika, Antosha loves you as my friend." She nearly cringed to hear herself speaking words so similar to ones Georgi had used on her. But hadn't they done her good? What if she was still mooning over Georgi? "He never stays long with any woman. Misha would. Don't you like Misha?"

Lika smiled, which was good. "Misha's a darling."

"Fall in love with him instead."

"How about I fall in love with . . ." She looked around. "This spoon." With two hands, she snatched it off the table and began kissing it all over. "Spoon! I can't live without you!"

Masha, stern schoolmistress, crossed her arms. Lika tossed the spoon back onto the table. The clink of it hitting the saucer sounded like *ouch*.

"Have you really never been in love, Masha?"

HADN'T SHE BEEN? SHE THOUGHT SHE'D LOVED GEORGI. What she'd felt for Lieutenant Egorov had been retroactive—*idealized*, as Antosha had put it. The actual blinking, bald, finger-crooking person who'd proposed—he'd vanished the moment he left the room. The fiasco with Isaac barely counted. Svoloch she'd loved. She loved Antosha.

Now another question begged to be asked. If those were her purest, most enduring feelings, had she ever been in love?

Mariushka's oft-muttered expression came to mind. "Better to marry than to burn." Was it love if there was no fire?

IN OCTOBER LIKA WROTE ANTOSHA A LETTER SO PRO-vocative that it would have burst into flames in any other man's hand.

> *I am burning my life. Come as soon as possible and help me burn it out. I am becoming the sort of woman you would not have to feel an obligation toward . . .*

Masha read it when she came to Melikhovo on the weekend. Had her warning had a contrary effect, then? Had Masha unwittingly blown on the embers of Lika's passion? And was she, Masha, incombustible?

Antosha wasn't there. He'd gone to visit Alexei Suvorin in St. Petersburg. For his friend and patron, he travelled that between-season road, its frozen ruts agonizing for a hemorrhoidal personage despite the carriage springs.

She dropped the letter on his desk where the bronze horse stamped his hoof in disapproval. The fact that Antosha had left it out proved he had no intention of participating in Lika's cremation. He probably wanted Masha to speak to Lika, which she already had. Should she try again?

She was not alarmed until the following weekend when she returned to Melikhovo and discovered that Antosha still wasn't back as planned.

"He stopped over in Moscow," Mother told her.

"In Moscow? Why?"

"It's snowing now. He wants to wait until he can travel by sledge. That road really makes poor Antonshevu suffer."

Mother shook her head—sympathetically, Masha thought. But then her bottom lip trembled, and she tearfully added, "He was in a terrible temper before he left. Every morning he said such spiteful things to me. Then instead of apologizing, he said, 'I'm the one who should cry, Mamasha. I have a bunch of grapes growing out my backside.'"

The snow would fall over the woods and fields. It would fall over the road and gradually, layer by layer, fill those painful ruts. And what would Antosha do in Moscow while he waited? Help Lika light those matches and build a pyre of her life? Maybe he'd left the letter for Masha to read so that she would know exactly what he was doing. To implicate her even further.

Masha didn't want to be implicated. Olga's suffering had changed her. Too late for Olga and the others, but not Lika.

She went out to the henhouse. The flock was hers, though she stopped short of naming hens that she would eventually meet on her plate, stripped of their feathery skirts in cinnamon and black. They seemed to know her, jerking and bobbing all around her as they pecked the grain out of her hand.

Afterward, Masha sat on a bale of hay and, hugging herself, listened to their clucking gossip. Misha came in wearing his ridiculous farmer's cap. His ears made the crown sit too high. He was surprised to find her there.

"Who are you hiding from? Mother?"

"No. I'm just thinking."

"Did you feed them?"

"Yes."

He turned to go, then stopped. "Thinking about what?"

"Lika. What does Antosha say about her?"

He frowned. "That she's the most incomparably beautiful creature you ever brought home."

Masha thought she might vomit and hugged herself harder. "What's he going to do about it?"

"Nothing. He's running around with some actress. Anyway, you needn't worry about her. Once he told me, 'Brother, you must be careful with girls like Lika.'"

"What did he mean?"

"I'm not sure. That she was so young, I think." He stamped his farmer's boots and went out.

By Sunday the snow was thick enough that Misha drove Masha to the station in the sledge. At school on Monday, after some subtle questioning, Masha determined that Lika had no knowledge that Antosha had even been in town.

Her relief made her link arms with her friend and say, "After school I'm taking you to Filipov's!"

—

THE FOLLOWING WEEKEND MASHA STAYED IN MOSCOW.
Antosha would be home, and she preferred to avoid the grim situation that Mother had tearfully described. The writer and his bunch
of grapes. Also, she was still concerned about Lika's incendiary letter, her private determination to turn herself into *the sort of woman
Antosha would not have to feel an obligation toward.* Masha wanted to
stay close to Lika, to chaperone her, as she should have been doing
all along.

They went shopping for dress material, which was infinitely
more amusing than being snapped at by a hemorrhoidal personage.
Lika bought a bag of gumdrops, screwed one into each eye socket,
and squinted to lock them in place. With one red protruding eyeball
and one green, she pretended to inspect the goods. A clerk rushed
over—the look on his face! They fell into each other, laughing.

Later, as they were leaving Muir and Mirrielees, a voice rang
out. "Masha! And is that *Lika?*"

Here was someone to protect Lika from: Klara, crossing the
street, smiling froggily.

"I just had my hair curled. Let's have tea before my hat flattens
it again."

Masha answered for them. "We already have."

"At least show me what you bought."

They stepped back inside the store, out of the cold. Klara cut
in front of Lika, causing Lika to tread accidentally on Klara's foot.
Klara retaliated with the toe of her boot, according to custom.

"There," Klara said, smirking. "Now we won't fight. We'll be
friends."

Masha showed Klara the fabric, a dark green wool, and was
rewarded with an indifferent nod. Lika offered her gumdrops.
Klara stuffed her whole hand in the bag, tearing it, and popped one
in her mouth.

"Sweet. Just like being carried away by two brothers at once. I've been wondering about you, Lika. I haven't seen you since the summer. I asked after you when I saw Antosha, but he had no news."

Lika glanced at Masha but directed her question to Klara. "Were you at Melikhovo?"

"No. I saw him here in Moscow a few weeks back. He was with Tania Shchepkina-Kupernik and her consort."

"Tania?" Lika asked. "Who was *she* with?"

"Lidia Iavorskaya. You know, the actress. Tongues are wagging about those two."

"What do you mean, 'consort'?" Masha asked.

Klara turned to her and, with her tongue, moved the gumdrop to the other side of her mouth. "You're a teacher. I think you know the meaning of the word."

Offended by Klara's tone, Masha said, "Well, goodbye," and pushed open Muir and Mirrielees' ornate door.

She and Lika headed for the tram in silence, Lika's troubled inward gaze causing her to walk an uneven line. Masha guessed that she was turning over in her mind what Klara had said. Antosha had come to Moscow and not told her. Heartlessly, he'd left her to burn.

Good, Masha thought.

A consort is a husband, wife or special companion. Or a habitual disapproved-of associate.

Why hadn't she just said "friend"?

By Christmas both Antosha's hemorrhoids and his irritability had shrunk by half. The whole family cheered up with him. Masha enjoyed the break from school and her self-assigned chaperoning.

Their relationship—Masha and Lika's—was a colt, delicately awkward. Lika had no idea that Masha had read her reckless letter, or that she, Masha, had vowed to thwart this recklessness. That Masha had singled Lika out to be her means of atonement on behalf of all her friends. But for now, Lika was safe in Moscow under Granny's watchful eye for the holiday. Reprieved, Masha finished a painting of Melikhovo in the snow, which everyone admired.

Smagin wrote again to wish her good health and a long life. He added in a barely legible postscript, *I'd like to meet you one more time before I die* . . . Was he ill or just gloomy? She decided not to reply.

One morning something happened to dampen the seasonal mood, a few minutes of friction reminiscent of so many in their youth, when Antosha seemed to belong more to his band of brothers than to Masha.

She entered the dining room to find Misha reading aloud a personal advertisement from the *Moscow Record*.

"'Wishing to marry, there being no suitable brides in our area. I invite girls desiring matrimony to send their terms. The bride must be no older than twenty-three, blond, good-looking, of medium height and of lively, cheerful character; no dowry required.'"

He lowered the paper and grinned across the room at Antosha, who was just then pouring his coffee to take back to his study. Masha recognized their pranking tone, the matching glint in their pince-nez. The nascent joke they would be unable to resist.

"Don't send that to her," she told Misha.

"To whom?" Misha asked, feigning ignorance.

"Well, send it to Klara if you want. But not to Lika."

Antosha said, "Klara will take the old man's offer."

Misha's ears turned to petals on either side of his head. "Listen, you two. I may as well tell you now. I plan to propose to Klara next time I see her."

"Wonderful," said the older brother on his way out the door. "Maybe then you'll move out."

Once they were alone, Masha told Misha, "Don't send it."

"Aren't you going to congratulate me?"

She muttered something assuaging to the poor ass. It was a foregone conclusion that Klara would refuse him. God help them if she didn't.

Masha forgot all about the advertisement until a few days later when she noticed the *Record* folded on the parlour table and chanced to open it. A mutilated page hung down.

Misha was out in the barn. She had to dress to go after him, though her rage would have kept her sufficiently warm. Passing the earth closet, she heard whistling inside, and banging both fists on the door, she accused him through it.

"I didn't!" the little brother roared back. In falsetto he added, "My tongue is not deceitful!"

She tramped around the house to Antosha's study and, bracketing her eyes from the outside glare, peered in at him. He was writing but noticed her immediately. As soon as her expression registered, he shrank down.

She stamped inside the house and threw open his door. "Are you completely heartless?"

What a face looked back!

"When did you post it?" Masha asked.

"Yesterday. I'll write to her, sister. Forgive me, but it was just too delicious not to send. She has a marvellous sense of humour. She'll laugh, I know it. I love to hear her laugh. It's better than church bells."

"You know nothing," Masha told him. "It astonishes me that you can write the things you do when you are completely incapable of understanding how other people feel."

"Am I?" He shrugged. "Tell me what to do. I'll do it at once."

Though Masha saw his real need was to placate her, not Lika, she told him, "Get on the train. Go explain yourself in person. Apologize. She's had enough letters from you."

Act Four

—

1893–1896

Masha: What is the point of love without hope,
of waiting whole years for something . . . one doesn't
know what. . . . But when I'm married there'll be no time
for love, new cares will drive out the old ones . . .

1

HOW STUPID. FARCICAL, IN FACT. HE RETURNED not the same day, but the next, and shut himself up in his office straightaway. Writing and tending to patients. Avoiding her.

Finally she burst in. Had he apologized for his cruel joke? Lika accepted, yes? Of course she would. Why did he tarry? Why had he stayed the night?

Antosha did something then he'd never done before, not with her at least. He placed his hands flat on the desk and leaned in. A more stable position from which to shout.

"What is it you want from me! What?"

For a moment Masha just stood there, stunned by his inexplicable anger and the vehement cant of his body. She opened her mouth. Nothing. She might have been trying to reply in a foreign language.

His fury soon fell away, leaving behind the rarest expression. It reminded her of when Lika had confronted him over "The Grasshopper." Then he'd evinced regret, but this had to be . . . remorse? Yet he wasn't offering it to her, his sister so hurt by his tone. His sister who had sent him to apologize, never thinking what form the apology would take.

Masha found her words. "You didn't . . ."

The taciturn author was at a loss.

Sickened, she gathered up her disgust and left.

After she'd finished crying, she lay on her bed picturing the scene as his former amanuensis. Her handsome brother, scented handkerchief pressed to his nose, climbing the cat-reeking stairs to Lika's flat. Granny answering his dutiful knock, the joy on her powdered face nothing compared to Lika's when she heard who was at the door. Innocent Lika tearing out her curling papers and hastily dressing. A carriage ride, more teasing banter, dinner at the Hermitage Hotel. The obsequious waiter hovering, his hand earnestly pressed to his white linen breast.

"'The stream was asleep. A soft flower, double-petalled on a tall stalk, touched my cheek—'"

Antosha cut him off. "Oysters, please."

With a bow, the fawner stepped away.

Masha heard Antosha's quiet, low-pitched voice, tender as those petals he wrote about. She smelled the sweet tinge on his breath. Not scent, but rot in his lungs.

"You do like oysters, Likusha?"

What Masha couldn't hear, though she strained so hard to, was "I'm sorry."

She should have known. Known that he would do the easier thing and take Lika upstairs to his room.

Masha's imaginings stopped there, just short of Antosha's capitulation and Lika's eager submission.

In the New Year, when school resumed, Lika seemed to be avoiding Masha too. The dark shadows around her silver eyes, rather than spoiling her looks, enhanced them—the gravitas of sleeplessness.

The first time they encountered each other in the hall after the break, Masha stiltedly asked how Lika's Christmas had been. Lika chirped some platitudes, then moved along without asking about Masha's, which would naturally include a mention of Antosha. Her reticence confirmed Masha's fears. Unseemly to discuss a lover with his sister. Dunia had been the exception.

In the past, Masha had thought of these as the boring periods in Antosha's affairs, after he lost interest and her friends withdrew in confusion, the shards of their hearts spilling out of their hands. Why had he so abruptly turned cold? They were unable to ask her. With no other subject of interest, poor Masha would be pelted with small talk for months. Then would come the inevitable confrontation, their faces rouged with anger. They were angry at *her*! Eventually, though, they accepted their dreams as bygone. Those who still wished Antosha in their lives reconciled with Masha.

This time, though, Masha felt that she was the one carrying the emotional burden, a soiled mound of it filling her arms, unwieldy and difficult to see beyond, as she stumbled toward the tubs. Instigator of the very thing she'd been trying to prevent, Masha accepted full responsibility for it. She felt as sorry for Lika as she'd felt for Olga that day at the hospital, though Lika would not end up like Olga, she was sure. Lika was beautiful and young, and soon this painful episode in her life would be thought of in the past tense too. But in the meantime, the present needed to be endured.

This intermission in their friendship left Masha bereft during those frigid months of winter. She longed to see the silly Lika who flapped her arms or snatched up a spoon and declared her love for it, not the subdued version ducking into her classroom to avoid talking to the sister of the man who'd bedded, then rejected, her.

Masha liked the Dairy School, so much so that she went

despite how irregularly they paid her. Morning assembly, the rows of girls obedient out of sleepiness. The smell and sound of chalk. Cows returning to the courtyard at the end of the day in a clattering finale. She took pleasure too in female competence and dedication to a purpose beyond the reach of men. Most fulfilling were the moments when understanding bloomed on a girl's face. Masha's pupils were also her flowers, and she carefully tended each of them, making sure none felt the way she had in school. She didn't even favour intelligence. The dimmer ones might later flourish just as well as those who could conjugate in French and recite the capitals of the world.

But now this painful awkwardness with Lika, coupled with Masha's regret, spoiled these quotidian gratifications, which in winter were all she had.

At Melikhovo, Antosha tried to make amends. Not long after he lost his temper, he called her to his study where a stack of pages waited on his desk. At first Masha thought he was giving her something to copy, hoping to wind their relationship back to an earlier, better time.

It was indeed an overture, but not the one she thought. The manuscript was Vermicelli's.

"Would you read it and tell me just how asinine it is?" he asked.

Masha took it. It was called *New Ways of Achieving Piano Technique*, and while some of these "new ways," such as hanging weights from the wrists, seemed like corporal punishment, how was unmusical Masha to judge their efficacy?

When Masha told him this, he said, "She's asked me to help her find a publisher. I just wondered how much of a laughingstock it will make me."

A few weeks later, Masha received an effusive letter from

Vermicelli about having her work accepted for publication in a performing arts journal. At last, a letter Masha could bring to *him*.

One glance and Antosha dismissed her thanks. It was nothing. Then he offered a rueful smile as though to say, *See? I'm not such a monster. Not only did I help her, I didn't even sleep with her.*

Yet a tight bud of resentment stayed furled inside her. An October rose that might never open. Masha felt it whenever she looked at him.

SPRING CAME SLOWLY, THEN ALL AT ONCE, AS IT DOES IN Moscow, as though to forestall mass suicide. Masha stepped outside the school and felt the urge to unbutton her coat. Snow mould and the tang of new leaves sharp in her nose.

Lika stepped out behind her. Seemingly as taken aback as Masha, she pealed a nervous laugh. But then their mutual discomfort thawed too, and there was only relief. When Lika first came to the Dairy School, they used to leave together like this.

"I thought I'd take a walk in Sokolniki Park," Masha said.

Lika heard the invitation in her voice.

Years before, Isaac had won a student prize for his painting of Sokolniki Park, a path edged by two ragged golden lines of fallen leaves, the sky a funnel above. Lika had never seen the painting or heard the story about it. Masha told her on the tram.

"Kolia complained to Isaac that the path was waiting for someone. Isaac left him alone with the picture. When he returned, Kolia had added a woman."

Lika was sitting beside Masha, self-conscious again as soon as Isaac's name came up.

"She was an afterthought," she said sadly.

"Have you seen him?" Masha asked.

"Isaac? Yes. He's well, or at least saner around me. He and Sophia are finally quits."

She gave Masha a tentative sidelong look that seemed to say, *Are we moving closer to our subject?*

Not on the tram, Masha thought, and Lika nodded as though she'd heard it.

For the rest of the ride, Lika filled Masha in on the Moscow gossip. With the little brother still rarely in town, Masha barely knew what was going on. Sophia's salon was now passé. Either "The Grasshopper" had tainted it, or Sophia and Isaac's breakup had.

"I suppose no one wants to be seen in a parody," Masha said.

Everyone went to the Hotel Louvre now, Lika told her. It was where Lidia Iavorskaya stayed.

Masha recognized the name. She was the Korsh Theatre actress famous for her flamboyant clothes and deep, rasping voice. Klara had mentioned her that day outside Muir and Mirrielees. Antosha associated with her, so said Klara, the papers and Misha. *He's running around with some actress.*

The tram swayed to a stop and emptied out. Everyone had the same idea, to run headlong with arms outstretched into spring. Hats tucked under their arms, gloves stuffed in pockets, Lika and Masha walked closer than they had been sitting, along May Alley, toward the centre of the park, their pace quicker than those who had disembarked with them, a joint effort to leave listening ears behind. They would sort it out where only the trees could hear them.

Lika spotted something on the ground and stooped to pick it up. A feather with white and black striping on the vane. She stuck it in her hair, then carried on without a word, though she looked pleased when Masha laughed.

Masha said, "I'm sure Antosha told you that I sent him to you. You've been avoiding me. I don't blame you for being angry."

On Lika's face—that familiar bloom of understanding. "Oh, Masha. I wish you'd spoken before! I'm not angry with you at all. I thought you were disappointed in *me*, or disgusted. I wasn't sure."

Masha stopped and faced Lika, not Kolia's black-clad afterthought, but a blonde in a pale grey coat with the white of her blouse showing where her collar was open, a splayed hand on her chest. The ridiculous feather. Her open, honest face.

"He didn't take advantage of me, Masha. I wanted to."

She was defending Antosha. Masha sighed and began to walk on, unabsolved.

"Maybe you did want to go with him. But when a man takes a woman to the Hermitage and buys her wine and oysters, when the woman is giddy with love and champagne. Well . . ."

She looked back. Lika was pinching a cluster of catkins off a hazel bush.

". . . the cards are stacked against the woman. She has to return the generosity in some way. This is particularly true if the man is older and successful and charming. Are you listening to me?"

Lika caught up carrying two sets of catkins. What was this crow game about? She wasn't serious at all. Masha felt the urge to shake her, but knew that if she did, it would end another way, with Masha sobbing on her shoulder and confessing, "How I missed you, how I missed you, how I missed you."

"He didn't take me to the Hermitage, Masha. We went to the Hotel Louvre. To Lidia's salon."

Masha was looking in Lika's face, but what she saw now was the scene she'd imagined after Antosha had shouted at her: the curling papers, the carriage ride, the obsequious waiter. But it all crumpled before her eyes.

"I'm not ruined, if that's what you're worried about." Carefully, Lika draped a catkin over Masha's right ear, another over the left. "That was no longer possible."

They tickled her neck, these silly catkin earrings. Masha touched them on both sides. *That was no longer possible?* What did she mean by that? This was Lika's trick. Masha recognized it now. To distract her after she'd said something troubling, like that time she'd had a coughing fit in Masha's room.

"So you slept with Isaac too?" she asked straight out.

Lika's mouth dropped open. At first it was hard to decipher the reason for her surprise. Masha sensed that her guess was both wrong and right. Right in that Lika had succumbed to Isaac, and wrong in that she hadn't actually been alluding to him just now.

Lika began to cry. Her ungloved hands lifted to catch her sob. Masha, taken aback, reached out and drew Lika close, so her own body absorbed her quaking. One of the catkin earrings fell to the ground.

"What is it, Lika? What happened?"

"Nothing I care to talk about," she managed to say as she came up for air. "I'm just happy we're friends again. You always think the best of me, Masha."

She didn't sound happy.

"I hope you'll invite me again to Melikhovo. I honestly bear Antosha no hard feelings."

MONTHS PASSED BEFORE MASHA DID INVITE HER. As soon as laughing with Lika had been added back into the pleasure of her workday, Masha hesitated to upset the delicate equilibrium of their reconciliation. Hesitated, too, to question her about what she'd said that day in Sokolniki Park. Behind her words lurked something that could not be politely—or safely—approached, not even with the utmost delicacy.

2

THEIR VEGETABLE KINGDOM WAS EVEN MORE resplendent that summer, their second at Melikhovo. And there were additions to their animal one—two dachshund puppies, a brother and sister, upon whom Antosha bestowed medicinal names, Bromine and Quinine.

The human news was mixed. Mother had three teeth pulled and consequently developed the habit of sucking her lip into the gap, which drove Masha around the bend. Misha finally returned to the tax department, but to the office in a nearby town, convenient to Melikhovo. He had indeed got himself engaged to Klara, to Masha's horror, but then was jilted so ignominiously that even Antosha, increasingly annoyed by his freeloading, felt sorry for him.

It happened like this: Klara was supposed to have spent Easter with them, but unexpectedly wrote to say she couldn't come. Weeks passed without a letter, until Misha, naturally concerned, took himself off to Moscow. He arrived to find her house packed with wedding guests.

"Who's getting married?" he stupidly asked.

Klara.

He hightailed it back to the station. For many glum weeks, he pored over her letters, showing them to the family, begging them to find hints of her treachery.

"It's in her handwriting," Antosha said. "Only a psychopath would scrawl like that."

The little brother couldn't be consoled, which didn't stop the elder from giving counsel. "Be like me, or our sister. Masha is one of those fine, rare women above matrimony."

When she heard that, Masha had to go over to the samovar and wash the bitter taste out of her mouth. How had he decided that? For days, she silently seethed over this comment.

No cholera this year. Natalia visited, but only stayed a week. Olga still hadn't come. Masha made do with Antosha's visitors, the ones not still offended over "The Grasshopper." Many held fast to their umbrage, but Antosha hardly lacked for friends. The house was full all the way to August, Mother fretting as usual about feeding and accommodating them.

Then one day, Masha found herself remembering what Antosha had said the first time she'd invited Lika to Melikhovo. "I knew something was missing from our paradise." Masha couldn't agree more. Lika had said she wanted to come. Would Antosha mind?

On her way to ask, she stopped herself. Why should she ask him? Lika would be her guest, not his. Masha wanted Lika for herself.

Lika readily accepted by post. *Yes, yes! Next weekend? Something to live for . . .*

A few days after that, the latest batch of hangers-on departed Melikhovo. Antosha, reading his letters after a quiet lunch, suddenly declared he was sick of company.

"Yet here's Alexei sending someone to see me."

He tossed the page down. Masha, clearing the table, checked how he was sitting in his chair. He'd been coughing at night too. Did the writing go badly because he felt unwell, or did he feel unwell when he couldn't write? After all these years, she still couldn't tell.

"Who?" she asked.

"Ignati Potapenko. A writer. Plays and novels. He's an impresario of sorts too. I met him years ago in Odessa, that summer I travelled with the Maly Theatre. The God of Boredom, we called him, though he's decent on the violin."

Mention of the Maly reminded Masha of its director, Aleksander Lensky, one of the ones still holding a Grasshopper grudge. Antosha must have thought of him too, for he ground out his cigarette and said he had to take a walk before returning to his desk.

"Otherwise bile may come out of my pen." He called to the dogs. "Bromine! Quinine!"

Masha followed him to the vestibule, where he put on his cap. "When's this boring man coming?"

"You watch. He'll ask for money. Suvorin warns me he will, yet he sends the beggar down." He broke off coughing and turned his back, answering her between the bouts of hacking. "I've no idea when."

"Because I invited Lika," Masha said when he'd recovered.

No comment. If he was uncomfortable with this news, he didn't show it, though Masha searched his face for an emotion. She wanted to say something. What? *Be kind.* In his present mood, it might backfire, so she held her tongue.

He opened the door, and in a frenzy of adoration, the dachshunds leapt against his trousers, receiving no rebuke for the dusty prints they left. With Antosha they didn't bark but emitted the strange warbles that to Masha sounded vaguely English. Brom was black; he killed Masha's fowl. Quinine, the bitch, was red. In both colour and shape, she reminded Masha of Svoloch, which deepened her resentment of them. Together they got into almost as much trouble as the mongoose, tunnelling in the garden, distributing shoes all over the house, grabbing patients by the trousers, defe-

cating on the paths. Their snarls sounded homicidal, yet Antosha
not only tolerated their behaviour, he loved them. They slept in his
room at night.

"Come, my short friends. Let's take a walk and forget the
annoyances of the world. We'll admire my sister's eggplants, so like
an aging actress's breasts."

He set off down the path past the bell on the post, the dachshunds criss-crossing in front of him, their funny ears flapping.

With the dogs out of the way, Masha headed for the henhouse
to feed her charges—twenty-nine hens and forty-seven chicks.
Down five birds, thanks to Brom.

At the station, Lika seemed ebullient and joyful,
as oblivious as ever when the stationmaster muscled aside the porter and carried her bag to the carriage himself. As soon as they
started driving, though, Masha noticed that her dimples appeared
too often and that she laughed in a higher register. By the smell of
her, she might have absent-mindedly applied scent more than once.

Lika was in the middle of a full-blown attack of hand-flapping
nerves. It was Masha's first inkling that she'd erred.

The second came when they got to Melikhovo and stepped
into the vestibule together. Lika's gaze, which had failed to settle
anywhere on the drive, now fixed itself on Antosha's closed door.
Impossible not to think of that other reunion, when he'd tilted her
face and washed it in colour, when she'd thrown her arms around
his neck and squawked. This time the door did not open, and Lika
just stood there, limp.

Antosha showed himself at dinner, of course, but his manner with Lika bordered on aloof. He didn't tease her. No Lika the

Beautiful, no Jamais, no Cantaloupe. When necessity forced him to speak to her, he addressed the negative space around her.

"Please excuse me," he said, before dessert was served. "I have a hideous amount of work." He offered the rest of them a half-portion of a smile and no particular one for Lika, who nonetheless forced her own smile until the deformity of her dimples showed.

Lika retired early, but probably slept as little as Masha, who tossed in bed in search of an appropriate object for her anger. It was as though Antosha's devastating neutrality were directed at *her*. She heard him through the adjoining wall murmuring to Brom and Quin and yearned to march in and strangle all three of them. But then he began coughing, and she wondered what she had expected from him. This was how he always acted post-affair, until he could be sure there would be no outbursts from the lady. Did she want him to start teasing Lika like before? Wasn't this better? And wasn't Masha just as cruel for inviting Lika? No. Lika had accepted. She'd wanted to come. She should have stayed away if she was going to sulk.

The next morning, Masha and Lika worked in near silence in the garden before the sun got too hot. Mother asked for peas, and Masha sent Lika to pick them. They sat together in the shade of the veranda, Masha roughly stripping the shells, the peas plinking irritably into the bottom of the bowl. All these feelings! They were always other people's. Would she never feel something for herself?

"I'm sorry," Lika finally moaned. "I'm tedious company."

Masha threw the empty pod into the basket at her feet. "You are. Why did you come, if it was going to hurt so much?"

"I didn't know it would. Maybe I should leave."

"Don't you dare go." Masha blurted it, surprising them both. The sparrows were quarrelling in the birch copse. She didn't want to be like them, but every time it was the same. Antosha made them cry. She wiped their tears.

"Don't be angry at him either, Masha. Everybody warned me he would be like this, but still I went."

"Who warned you?"

"You," Lika said. "Isaac and Sophia. That Kleopatra woman."

Masha frowned. "The actress?"

A queasiness settled on her. She didn't want to know the nature of the warning. She was his sister. It was unseemly. Yet she hadn't forgotten Olga's note to him, imploring him not to treat her roughly. Words like pins left behind in a new dress. Why had Olga never come? What had Antosha written back to her?

The sound of horses. A droshky appeared, its burly, bearded passenger leaning forward on the seat, talking to the driver, deep in some anecdote.

"Halloo!" he cried out when he noticed them. "Does the writer live here?"

Masha remembered then. She whispered to Lika, "That must be the God of Boredom. Antosha was expecting him."

She set her bowl at her feet and stood, just as Brom and Quin tore around the corner of the house. The visitor had been about to step down, but now he halted, one foot in the air, as the barking dogs advanced, on his face a mixture of understandable alarm and wonderment that such creatures could exist.

He pointed to the ravening dachshunds. To Masha, who was hastening to his rescue, he said, "What are they?"

"Stop it," she told the dogs. "Hush."

They wouldn't heed her, despite the ungentle prodding of her foot. By then Antosha had heard the commotion and come out. As he passed Lika on the veranda, she reached out and touched his sleeve. He glanced back the way he would if his jacket had snagged on a twig. Masha, feeling it as Lika must have, flinched.

Antosha gathered up the dogs, one under each arm, jiggling and scolding. "Where are your manners?"

The visitor, still standing in the droshky, addressed him from his higher vantage, hand pressed to his broad chest. "Ignati Potapenko. Excuse the pedestal. I would prostrate myself if I weren't afraid of your dogs."

His tone, so high-flown, could only be self-mocking. He'd found a way to make a fawning speech palatable.

He plucked a handkerchief from his pocket to swab his red face. "Do you remember me? We met in Odessa. I begged Alexei to make the introduction. Forgive me if I was too bold, but I lurked around Moscow for a week, until I learned you never came anymore."

"I remember. Welcome. This is my sister, Maria. Her friend Lika's there on the veranda. She's wearing a long face now, but wait until you see her smile. Bromine. Quinine." He lifted each dog as he named them. They licked their lips. "If you let them sniff you, they'll leave you be."

Ignati hesitated to extend his hand. "Will I get it back?"

Antosha laughed. The dogs did as he promised, sniffed the meaty, bearded stranger, then wriggled to be put down. Ignati picked a violin case off the droshky's seat, leapt to the ground and whirled around.

"What an Eden you live in!" As he walked off with Antosha, the driver cleared his throat.

"Ah, my good man. Apologies."

Ignati set the violin on the ground, so he could ransack his pockets. This was the sort of moment Antosha found excruciating, so he paid.

"No matter," he told Ignati as they continued toward the house. "You'll repay me, I'm sure." He shot a look at Masha. *I told you so.* But it pleased him when a guest took an interest in the garden. He said to Ignati, "I'll get my cap and show you around."

Ignati left his instrument on the veranda and, after bowing deeply to Lika, followed his host inside.

"Now Antosha won't be able to work," Masha said, sitting beside Lika again. "We'll all suffer for it."

She glanced at Lika, already suffering, and sighed.

Antosha and Ignati came back out by the side door, the one that led from the vestibule to the garden. Though Masha and Lika couldn't see them from where they sat shelling, they heard Ignati's booming voice. He exclaimed over the roses, then entreated Brom to release his trouser leg. Antosha told the dog to desist.

Then Ignati asked, "Who's that beautiful girl? What's her story?"

DURING LUNCH IGNATI MENTIONED THE POND, WHICH he'd noticed driving up. Could he have a swim before going back to Moscow?

"It's more of a fishing pond than a swimming one," Antosha told him.

"Do you fish?" Ignati asked as he helped himself to sour cabbage, the last uneaten dish on the table. He'd put away two servings of kasha with mushrooms, cold soup, beef pie and a third of the Olivier salad. In three bites he'd devoured a peach. Now Mother, sucking her lip into the toothless space, realized there was no stopping him.

"Blini," she said, and hurried out.

"I do fish," Antosha told Ignati. "You?"

"There are few things I like better."

Antosha pushed his chair out to cross his legs, folded his hands on his knees and regarded their guest, who didn't know him well enough to read his pose as mock-serious.

Ignati hadn't spoiled Antosha's mood. He'd improved it. For one, Ignati's presence made it less obvious that he was ignoring Lika. He could enjoy his lunch now. Except Ignati was more than a convenience. In his exuberance and indefatigability, he reminded Masha of Isaac—without the irritating egoism. Sudden friendships were rare with Antosha, who was not only reserved but guarded against sycophants. But he'd lost his spiritual brother just as he'd lost his actual one. There was an unfilled role in his life and, until now, no understudy.

"Here's a question for you, then, writer to writer," Antosha said. "Be honest. Which do you prefer, fishing or writing?"

"Fishing," Ignati replied. "I wouldn't write at all, except I need money. Only a confirmed masochist would."

All this time, Lika had been silently pecking at her food as she listened to their conversation. Now she said, "I can't believe that. It must be wonderful to be a famous writer and read all about yourself in the papers."

"Who? Me?" Ignati laughed loudly, showing teeth decorated with cabbage remnants. "I'm a slave. I can't ever stop. I was writing on the train. Third class, all that hubbub. Out the window I see a cloud shaped like . . . a piano. I can't just look at it. I have to write it down."

He turned back to Antosha. "If you'd allow me a dip in your pond, I would be made new, and my toil easier on the return trip."

Masha spelled it out. "It's a mud hole."

Mariushka limped in with a platter of blini. Ignati's narrow eyes widened. Father came after, with glasses and three small bottles of liqueur, a rare honour bestowed now because Ignati had mentioned that his father was a priest.

As she served, Mariushka watched Ignati's face. He kept nodding—one, two, three, four, five.

Antosha said, "Speaking as a doctor, I advise against swimming. For the sake of your digestive processes."

"Am I eating too much?" he asked Mariushka.

"'And the hungry soul—'"

Ignati finished for her. "'—he filleth with good.'"

Mariushka stepped back in awe; everyone else burst out laughing.

"Stay, why don't you?" Antosha said. "We'll fish tonight."

Masha glanced at Lika, who was playing with the corner of her napkin. Did the attention Antosha gave Ignati hurt her? Masha couldn't tell.

"Let's leave the writers to their gudgeon talk, Lika," she told her.

They both rose. Ignati's eyes followed Lika. Still hungry!

He called after them, "Are we losing both ladies at once? What agony!"

In her room, Masha gathered her stool and painting box, and they set out from the house toward a little view she had in mind. She made Lika carry the stool.

Was he handsome, this God of Boredom? The long narrow nose and narrow eyes softened his blockiness. His abundant beard was neatly trimmed. If his appearance was only satisfactory, the vigour he exuded and his obvious good humour made him attractive.

"What do you think of him?" Masha asked.

Lika shrugged.

"He keeps whipping out his little book and jotting notes. I wonder what he's saying about us."

They reached the place. A hedgerow with the rye fields beyond bleaching gold. Above, clouds wisped the blue. Masha opened the box in her lap and tilted the easel up.

Lika sank into the grass beside her. She was so quiet, Masha assumed that she'd fallen asleep, but next time she looked, she saw another paintable sight—Lika on her back, the green blades touching her cheek. Close by, a bee pivoted in a clover flower. Arms extended above her, tips of her forefingers and thumbs touching, she was looking at the sky through the shape she'd made.

Later, on their way back, as they neared the house, they heard splashing and incensed barking. Despite the quantity he'd eaten and the medical advice he'd received, there was no keeping Ignati out of the pond. As Ignati frolicked, Antosha stood by, hands in his pockets, shaking his head. The physical contrast between the men became obvious then; the spirited personage in their pond was healthy.

"I was wrong," Antosha told Masha as she and Lika came up beside him. "He's the God of Amusement."

They watched Ignati's hairy back rise from the murk. He burst into the air, whipped his head around. Water sprayed in a vortex that caught all three of them. Antosha and Masha stepped away. The dogs went wild.

Was it then or earlier, lying in the grass and gazing at that blue triangle her fingers made, that Lika decided to be amusing right back? She went over to the pond's edge, dipped her hand and splashed water back into Ignati's face. He returned fire. The dogs took Lika's side.

Smiling, Antosha cleaned the droplets off his pince-nez. "I don't care to get wet. I'll see you at the house." He turned and headed off, Brom and Quin racing to catch up.

"Ladies!" Ignati cried out. "Avert your eyes!" *Ladies*, he kept saying, but it was Lika to whom this playful god spoke. "I beg you. The merman wishes to climb onto dry land."

Ignati's clothes were hanging in a tree. Lika hooked the trousers on one finger and slung them over her shoulder. He roared out for her to leave them. Instead she marched over and threw them at him. Ignati managed to keep all but one leg out of the water.

She was acting like a headless chicken. While this was an improvement on the morose creature she'd been up until then, Masha didn't fully believe the transformation. Though the actors may be different, the lines don't change the second time you see a play. Neither does the ending.

Back at the house, Antosha had retired for his nap. Ignati, who had been directed to the rain barrel for a rinse, dried himself and settled in for a doze on the veranda, still muttering about his wet trouser leg. Inside, Masha laid out a hand of Patience while Lika softly played the piano. After twenty minutes, Ignati appeared in the doorway, filling the whole frame, chagrin on his face.

"Forgive me if this is rude, but I need to work."

"The dining table is free," Masha told him.

"This is embarrassing. Look." He drew a thick sheaf of folded pages from his pocket, word-darkened from margin to margin. "Would you have any paper?"

Masha went to get some. "You play exquisitely," she heard him telling Lika when she returned.

Hours later, Mariushka came to complain that she needed to set the table.

"Set it," Masha told her, and Mariushka did, working around the toiling author, who, she reported with even more awe, didn't once look up but continued streaming ink as though he were some kind of writing machine.

ANTOSHA HAD SCRIBBLED SIXTY KOPEKS' WORTH, HE claimed at dinner. "But you should see what this maniac produced. A page for my every line."

"For the money," the maniac said. "For the money."

Misha, home now from the tax office, quizzed Ignati on what he was paid for these lines, then bragged that he'd had a story accepted for publication.

"Which one?" Antosha said. "'The Man with the Big Arse'?"

"No, 'The Man Who Had a Brother with a Big Arse.'"

After the elders left the table for their geriatric pursuits, Ignati produced a box of cigars. Shortly the room, already filled with Ignati's booming laughter, filled with smoke.

"May I take a puff?" Lika asked.

Ignati let her, and she nearly coughed her heart onto the table. He rushed to pat her back. Misha pressed a glass of water into her hands. Meanwhile, the doctor sat at the head of the table and did nothing to save her.

"You've killed her, Potapenko," Misha said.

"I hope not. We've just met."

"I'm fine." Lika gulped the water.

When Ignati casually took out his notebook, Lika put Masha's comment into words. "You keep writing things down. Read it to us."

He only pretended to. "'Beautiful girl longs to be a singer. Career destroyed by cigars.'"

Everyone laughed, and Lika asked, "How did you know I want to be a singer?"

Ignati pointed to Antosha, who smiled inscrutably.

Something occurred to Masha. If Lika was acting, if she was trying to make Antosha jealous, she would fail. But if in the process she actually fell in love with Ignati, wouldn't that be the best outcome? The protective feeling she'd been harbouring for Lika lifted then, along with her dislike of Antosha's behaviour. Instead, a wave of gratitude rushed in for this big happy man who had succeeded in infecting them all.

Next Ignati asked Antosha what he was working on, a question Antosha always deflected. He surprised them now by answering.

"It's about an academic. A nobody who suffers from megalomania. It's boring, I'm afraid."

"Nothing you write is boring," Lika said.

He drew reflectively on the cigar. "I'd like to write a decent play."

"A play? What about a novel?" Ignati asked.

"With Tolstoy looking over my shoulder? No, thank you."

"I suppose Pushkin's ghost is stopping you from writing poetry. And yet the great playwright Ignati Potapenko doesn't scare you?"

"Who? That hack?" Antosha said, and Ignati roared.

They were purposely lingering, waiting for the fish to start biting. Antosha rose and went to the window, abandoning his cigar.

"Is a play without theatrical effects possible?"

"You do need drama," Ignati said.

"But must it always be so overwrought?"

"What do you mean?"

Antosha's back was still turned. "All that breast-beating and sinking to the knees."

"It's *de rigueur* at the Abramova Theatre," Misha said, scraping the ash off his cigar.

Antosha looked at Ignati over his shoulder. "Couldn't he love, say, comically? Or silently?"

"How will anyone know he's in love?" Lika asked.

Now he looked directly at her. "With subtler gestures."

Her face flushed with confusion. Masha, too, wondered what he meant. Was he hinting at something or joking again?

Then Misha barked out, "She thinks that some people are too subtle as it is."

Antosha smiled. "But you're right, dearest Lika."

She beamed to hear, finally, an endearment.

"The audience wouldn't understand. And if they did, they wouldn't like it. No, it's hopeless. No more tea, thank you, Masha. We're going out now."

"Where?" Misha asked. "Oh, fishing. Snore."

Ignati pushed himself up from the table with both hands, the cigar in his teeth. He paused to say to Lika, "Afterward, we'll hear you sing."

While they'd been talking, Masha had taken note of the sky's concentrating red. The window was open, and they could hear the frogs gathering in their nightly choir. She rose to light the lamps. Lika helped.

"Misha, go get Mother, and we'll play whist."

He'd finished his cigar and was cleaning under his nails with a knife. "Whist? Snore."

Then, from outside, Antosha called, "Masha! Mother! Come!"

They hurried out and around the house to where they met the awestruck fishermen. An enormous moon, ten times its normal size, crimson, was sinking into the pond and setting fire to the water. Ignati waved his rod in the air.

"Ladies and gentlemen, behold the celestial orb!"

Mother and Father appeared. "What's happening?" Mother cried. Father took one look and hurried back inside to pray.

"Get your paints," Antosha told Masha.

Impossible to capture such an event. Lika's white dress had changed colour, Masha's too, and the paper trunks of the birches—all washed in a rosy hue. The moon was the painter now.

"Why does it look like that?" Mother warbled. "What's happening? What does it mean?"

"Fear not, Mamasha," Antosha told her. "It's not the end. The world, so harsh and senseless, will go on. It's a magic trick called refraction."

"Like a mirage," Lika said.

"Exactly."

"Antosha," Mother began, hand on her heart.

"Yes, Mamasha, I feel it too. A poem."

Lika set off to walk around the pond. She looked spectral in the gathering dusk, her dress glowing against the darker backdrop of the trees. Antosha followed her with his eyes.

"This afternoon I had a dream. I just remembered it. There was a figure all in black." He pointed to Lika. "There's his negative."

An owl tremoloed in the distance. Then Ignati, watching Lika too, burst into "I Love You" from *The Queen of Spades*.

Only later did Masha get the chance to ask Antosha about the dream, after the unlucky fishermen returned, and they had all gathered in the parlour. Lika was at the piano, Ignati lifting his violin out of its case. The moon had shrunk to its habitual size by then, but the mystery remained, a feeling in the room.

"That thing you dreamed, brother. It made me shiver. Tell us more."

"There's nothing more boring than people's dreams," he said.

"No, tell it," Lika said.

A black-robed figure. Now he thought it was a monk. "Really, it's dull." He waved his modest hand and only finished at the insistence of the whole gathering. "It replicated itself. Moved like a skipping rock around the world. That's all."

Misha yawned. Ignati tuned his instrument. Masha pressed him. "But what did it mean?"

"It meant"—he leaned forward, kind eyes crinkling—"dinner was as yet undigested."

Everyone laughed, then Lika began to play. She chose "Angel Serenade," and Ignati, on the violin, joined his voice to hers.

It had to be as obvious to Antosha as to Masha what Lika was doing. Reminding him of his former jealousy and passion, of when he was free and generous with outward signs. Lika sang to Antosha while Ignati sang to her. He'd already fallen in love with her, had from the first sight of her glumly shelling peas on the veranda.

Antosha watched what was happening, but he was seeing something different. Masha recognized his look, the one that surely appeared on every writer's face when all the pieces of a story finally fall into place.

"Your voice is so beautiful," said the God of Love when the song ended. "You shouldn't be singing in parlours, but in concert halls."

The compliment made Lika lift hopeful eyes to Antosha, just then rising from his chair.

"Thank you, Lika. Everyone? Please, excuse me."

They watched him open the doors to his study and, with a parting nod, close them behind him.

"He's going to write," Misha told the room.

▬

AFTER THAT FATEFULLY TIMED VISIT, LIKA BEGAN
visiting Melikhovo with Ignati. For the rest of the summer, the
whole family looked forward to the lively concerts they put on—
except Masha.

Ignati was married. Lika had found out even before Masha and
already resigned herself.

"Antosha only ever needed me when the weather was bad or
he was bored," Lika told her, as though this excused her behaviour.
"I wrote and asked if he would even care if he never saw me again."

"What did he say?" Masha asked.

"He didn't reply."

So Lika accepted Ignati as her consolation prize. What a catastrophe. In the fall, she quit the Dairy School again. Ignati wanted
her to concentrate on her music. He thought she was good enough
to go on stage, not just in Russia. In Europe.

Then, for six months, Masha barely heard from Lika—until,
out of the blue, a letter came.

Take pity on me, Masha, and come to say goodbye forever to an
unfortunate woman like me. On Saturday evening, I'm leaving for
Paris . . .

The two sentences contradicted. If going to Paris to sing was
her new dream, why should Masha take pity on her? What was
unfortunate about it?

3

MASHA STOOD—ARMS OUT AT HER SIDES, crucified without a cross—while behind her, her dress-maker recounted her oft-told tale of marital affliction.

"I always knew when he was on the vodka because he'd start going through the cupboard. Taking out my dresses. The next place they'd hang would be the second-hand shop, where everybody'd recognize them."

Masha cringed as the picked seams released her. The dress, her dark green one, had been hanging in Mother's wardrobe by accident. Last weekend Masha rediscovered it with fond elation, like she was reuniting with a long-lost friend—until she put it on, and the friendship soured. Soured as hers with Lika had, once Lika had started consorting with Ignati.

"I ran away, but he found me. What a thrashing I—"

Masha's arms were leaden wings. She interrupted. "Why did you marry him?"

"Pardon? Oh, it was arranged. A berry not picked rots in the rain. That's how it is in the villages and how it will always be. The city's different. Life's better here."

More ripping. Masha could take a full breath again. "It's the same tedious life, but with trams."

"No one beats you. I'm happy here. So happy. Yet all the time I know he's coming for me, and I'll have to let him in."

She stepped in front of Masha with her little blade, three pins still jutting from her lips. Tight brown braids criss-crossed her pungent scalp. She lived and worked in this one room. All she had was her machine, a table and chair, and the icons to remind her of her duty to a brute. Yet she was happy. And Lika, who had no duty at all to Ignati, who had sounded so unhappy in her letter, why was she going? At least the dressmaker had religion as an excuse.

A thought escaped Masha. "Women are such idiots."

Startled eyes flicked up, fearful raisins pressed into the dough of the dressmaker's face.

"I was thinking of a friend, not you," Masha told her. "She's running off to join a married man."

"That's a sin." She finished, her smile disarmed of pins. "All done, Miss. Come back Wednesday."

After the fitting, Masha took the tram to Muir and Mirrielees for a few things she needed. Keeping busy, so she would be unable to bid the "unfortunate" Lika farewell. Normally Masha wouldn't even be in Moscow on the weekend, but Antosha had left for a month in Yalta to shake off his worrisome, worsening cough. It would be boring at Melikhovo without him. They'd been getting on well again since Lika took this ill-chosen course and Masha could blame everything on Ignati.

Winter was releasing its icy hold, yet the sidewalks were still slushless. She decided to walk back to her room. On Tverskaya Street, she side-stepped shoppers lingering before the windows. That week she had her pupils memorizing passages from *Eugene Onegin*. *The sleigh, more swift than steady / Bumps down Tverskaya Street already.* Something, something, *parks and pharmacies . . .*

Pharmacies. How romantic.

She could feel Lika's letter under her skin. Masha had really let Granny down. Then she thought, why am I responsible for Ignati?

Why didn't Lika's mother protect her, or her father go after the cad? Her father was probably busy with his own mistress. Antosha had his actresses. I'm *rotting*, Masha thought. She paused before one of the poetical pharmacies and considered going in for valerian drops.

Ahead was the Hotel Louvre, where the celebrities stayed. Just then two women stepped out—a mother and daughter, Masha guessed from their affectionate gestures and the difference in their height, the mother in a red ostentatiously feathered hat. The father stepped out after them, his hat still in his hand. After an effusive exchange of kisses, the three of them parted, the women heading briskly in Masha's direction.

Valerian drops? She was turning into a spinster hypochondriac. She walked quickly on, away from the thought.

Now the two women from the hotel were right in front of Masha. She'd been mistaken. Both were young. The taller in the show-offy hat Masha recognized from her pictures in the paper— none other than Lidia Iavorskaya. Of course. The Louvre was where she had her salon. The smaller, a brunette, was less pretty, but something about her attracted Masha more. A free manner, possibly a corsetless body too. Inquisitive eyes, close-set and brown, flicked over Masha in passing. She smiled. Masha had pupils like this, seldom the prettiest, who shone from the inside. It reminded her of Lika too, back when they'd first met. Was this the person Klara had called a *consort*? Upside Down? No, Topsy-Turvy.

The left-behind man was still on the steps. As he settled his hat on his head, Masha glimpsed a forehead made prominent by dark retreating curls.

"Isaac?"

"Masha!"

No ambivalence on his face, or caution in his turpentine embrace. He plunged down the steps and seized her. The last time they'd seen each other, he'd been crawling toward her on his knees. He'd run all over town saying he was going to challenge Antosha to a duel. Every human emotion roiled within him, except embarrassment.

The arms around her felt thin, bony even. He held her out and searched her face—for proof of her affection, or to know if she took Antosha's side in their ongoing dispute? Nearly two years had passed, and Isaac and Antosha still weren't speaking. She did take Antosha's side, of course, but how wonderful to see Isaac!

"What are you up to?" she asked.

Instead of answering, he linked her arm with his and led her away from the hotel, his much longer stride making her feel hurried, which was what gave the ruse away. She must have caught him in an assignation. With Lidia Iavorskaya or Topsy-Turvy?

"How's the painting?" he asked her.

"I'm still at it. I love it actually. It's the one thing I do for myself."

"Why don't you ever bring me something to look at?"

She noticed his pallor then, how it made his eyes seem blacker and more melancholy.

"You were my pupil," he chided. "All my pupils are close to my heart, you especially. Because of Kolia."

So Antosha didn't exist. Masha said, "I paint when I'm at Melikhovo, not in town."

"Come to my studio. Do you have time? It's not far. I want to show you a painting I've just finished." He threw an arm in the air to flag a passing a cab. "A storm settled on my canvas. These hands?" He raised them. "These eyes? They played no part. I want you to see it. Masha, convince me I really painted it. Tell me I'm a genius."

She laughed. "I can tell you that now, but I'll come anyway."

He gave her a skeletal smile as he helped her into the cab. Climbing up after her, his face showed strain. He told the driver the address, then said to Masha, "I haven't been well. Trouble with some part of my heart, I forget what. Starts with *a*."

"Aorta?"

"That's it. Unheard of in a man so young, the doctor says. But now I have a permanent residency permit. Maybe it will get better."

The previous summer, Jews had lost the right to live in Moscow. Isaac explained how he'd managed to come back. "Dr. K., with his police connections, got me a temporary permit."

"Dr. K. did?" Masha asked, astonished.

Isaac leaned in. "As a certain person wrote, 'That man is killing me with his magnanimity.'"

Smiling, Masha said, "If you can quote from 'The Grasshopper,' Isaac, surely you can forgive Antosha."

He spread his long arms. "I will. As soon as he apologizes."

There was little chance of that. Masha sighed. "Your painting's in his study at Melikhovo. The one that used to hang at the bottom of the stairs."

"I have no quarrel with his excellent taste. And I'm far from the only offended party. Lensky from the Maly? He and Antosha are finished."

"Why?"

"Your brother called him fat."

Masha couldn't suppress her scorn. "If there was a fat man in the story and Lensky saw himself in him, is that Antosha's fault?"

With no adequate reply, Isaac turned priggish, tugging out his handkerchief and wiping his nose to close the subject. "With regards to my permit, thank God for rich patrons. I'm fixed for life now. I smell coffee."

Masha patted her bag. "I've just come from Muir and Mirrielees."

"And what about Lika? You heard she's leaving? I saw her last night. She was twittering away—Paris and Potapenko! Paris and Potapenko!"

Masha turned fully in the seat to face Isaac. "Do you know Ignati?"

Of course he did. They all attended the same arty parties. Lidia Iavorskaya's parties. Isaac might be able to tell her what Ignati had arranged for Lika. Strangely, though, at Masha's question, he grew evasive about Ignati, though he'd mentioned him first. He brushed at one shoulder of his coat.

"I see him around."

"And?"

He faced her. "What?"

"What do you think of him?"

"I think he has two wives. Driver, it's the turquoise house on the right."

"Two?"

He turned back to Masha. "He divorced the first. It's why he's always broke and starting up these agenting schemes. He's got to pay for them both. Stop at the gate. Oh, he's great fun at a party. He makes the party, especially with Lika at the piano. Does he have these musical connections he claims? Will she become a famous singer? I doubt it. The Paris wife—number two—is calling him home, but he's not finished with Lika, so he's bringing her along."

Already pressed against the seat, Masha had nowhere further to recoil to. "What are you saying? His wife's in Paris? I thought they were separated."

"Naturally he'd tell you that," Isaac said.

"Does Lika know she's there?"

"I have no idea."

The carriage stopped. Isaac paid and climbed down.

Masha said, "Thank God she's not going on her own. Some other singer's going with her."

Isaac offered his arm to Masha, who needed it.

"Yes, she's going with that little opera singer, Varvara, isn't she? I see them together. Double the fun. It's all the rage." He opened a lacy iron gate in the wall and waved her in. "Yes, Lika ran from the bear to the wolf. Do you remember how I lost my head over her and wanted to shoot myself? I don't know why she didn't pick me. I'm by far the better man."

The grounds surrounding the mansion were still snow-crusted. Against it, the bare bark of the shrubbery looked red. Sparrows quadrilled along the path. That stupid, stupid girl, Masha thought, her approach sending the birds into the air. *Unfortunate* popped into her head again. Now she would have to go see Lika. She couldn't possibly know about the wife.

Masha barely looked at the grand house, had not even taken in Isaac's previous comment. Now he pointed out the closer wing, where on the second storey three large arched windows faced south.

"That's the studio. Damn it, I'm feeling it again, this thing that starts with an *a*." Pressing his heart, he stared up with what seemed a rapturous expression. "It's from the excitement. I can't wait for you to see it."

"Is it pain?" Masha asked.

"Yes!"

"Perhaps I should talk to—"

"The doctor whose name starts with an *A*? No thank you. There. It's passed. Just like that." With a laugh, he walked on. "Wait till you see it."

"Are you sure you're all right, Isaac?"

"Yes, yes."

They came to a set of French doors at the end of the wing. Isaac entered without knocking, causing a bell to sound. A liveried manservant appeared and bowed. Isaac raised a hand to him and in the same gesture directed Masha to a curved staircase. Isaac's patron was as rich as Alexei Suvorin. Even the carpets told her that.

They made their way to the studio, which was at the top of the stairs. Breathless from the climb, Isaac threw open the doors, revealing a high-ceilinged room with generous light.

"I don't even pay for it," he told her.

There were a half-dozen large paintings on easels around the room and more sketches pinned to the walls, yet she knew without asking which painting he wanted her to see. It swallowed her. A little church overlooking a lake, a clutch of restless trees behind it, tilted crosses in the cemetery. The prowed shapes of the bluff and lake pushed her forward to the layered drama of the sky. Isaac rarely painted figures, offered instead sky, land, water and the deeper meaning of their configurations. The only people here were dead. A painter didn't need people, not the way a writer did.

Standing there, smelling the paint, breathing in Isaac's work, she finally understood their conflict. To Isaac, Lika was a pretty, vivacious girl, one of many to threaten suicide over; to Antosha, she was a subject. Unmistakable traces of her turned up in story after story. And that night at Melikhovo, when Lika and Ignati played their duet, Antosha had left the room directly afterward and wrote "Angel Serenade" into "The Black Monk." He put in the red moon too. It was the strangest thing he'd ever written.

"I knew you'd see it," Isaac said.

She turned to him. "What do you see?"

"Me?" Surprised to have the question turned back on himself, he exploded with the answer. "I see my soul. The thing that fares so poorly here—" He waved long fingers, taking in the room, but meaning the world. "It lives fully there, only *there*. That's why I suffer. I hope you're suffering, Masha. Are you? Because the artist must. It's the only way."

She burst into tears without knowing why, except that when she looked at the painting again, the black mass of cloud became that rebuking flock that had terrified him at Melikhovo, and she— she was an empty church. Chaste and alone on the bluff staring out at the cold flat lake of her life.

Isaac pulled her to him. "Good! This is good! Cry." He rocked her. "I wanted to marry you once. Did I ever tell you that?"

Embarrassment caused her to press harder into him. "Yes."

"You were just a girl. How old are you now?"

She sniffed. "Thirty."

"Thirty! Thirty is a fine age. Women get better and better. You're plump now too."

He lifted her chin and kissed her. The scent on his beard was decidedly female. Masha's whole body flooded with heat. The dark cloud moved closer, and she heard those complicated twitterings. So hot in her coat, she let him undo the top button to get at her neck. *I am burning.* Should she take it off? *Come and help me to burn it out.* He kissed her collarbones, her eyes, and she felt her own avid response. But as his long fingers tugged at her next button, she took fright and pulled away.

"I was on my way to say goodbye to Lika."

He looked hopefully down at her. "You'll come back, though? My quarters are just below."

"What? Tonight?" she asked.

"Yes. Come tonight. Tomorrow I really have to leave town.

Give Lika my blessing. I'd like to kiss you again. May I? I think I'm falling in love again."

He was mad, of course, holding her face, tonguing her relentlessly. She'd mocked Lika for claiming transmutation, but now Masha pressed against his body to bring it on herself. Hardness pressed back. How she yearned for love. She'd been tying her laces so hard, cinching in her need.

When Isaac pulled back a second time, it seemed as though he'd drawn out a pin and was holding it between his teeth.

She wanted to tell Lika. Wanted to make light of Isaac's kisses to a friend, to jokingly confide, so she could sift through her feelings and know if she would go back. She climbed the cat-reeking stairs. She would go back. Why shouldn't she, too, hurl herself into disaster?

Lika answered and almost knocked Masha over in her embrace. Over her shoulder, Masha saw Granny coming down the hall, her wobbly face streaked where the powder had washed off.

"Who is it? Varvara?"

"Just ignore her," Lika whispered. She turned to face Granny bearing down on them. "It's Masha."

The old woman grabbed Masha's hand. "Please stop her. I've telegrammed her mother, but she can't come."

"Granny, I'm going away to sing. When we're settled, I'll send for you."

Ignoring Lika, Granny told Masha, "She's running off with that man. She's out all night with him. She doesn't get home till dawn."

"Granny, you're embarrassing me."

The old woman swung around and slapped Lika, and kept on

slapping while Lika raised her arms to protect herself from the whirl of hands.

"Pig!" Granny screamed, and Lika broke free and ran down the hall. "A pig will find mud anywhere! Even in Paris!"

Lika's door slammed. Granny turned to Masha, who was backing away in alarm. "How did this happen? How? Talk to her. Please."

She helped Masha out of her coat. She wasn't accusing. Perhaps she'd forgotten the favour she'd asked.

"I did everything to keep her safe. In Petersburg I slept in her room. Her mother was always having parties. Showing her off to guests. Some of them . . ." She trailed Masha to Lika's room. "I didn't like the way they looked at her. Please make her stay."

"I'll talk to her." Masha knocked. "It's me."

The door opened, and Lika pulled her inside, leaving poor Granny in the hall blotting her devastation on her sleeve. Clothes were spread all over, the trunk half-filled with sheet music. Lika sank down on the bed, hair in disarray from Granny's assault.

"She sent a telegram to Mama." She stared at the floor. "Mama will be happy. Paris is even farther than Moscow."

"I'm sure that's not true," Masha said. "She'll be worried."

Lika looked up, and for the first time Masha saw something ugly on her face, a bitter expression, like she was about to spit. Her mouth opened, as though she really would, but she was only drawing a breath, which she held inside for what seemed an unnaturally long time. She let it out all at once.

"Mama only cares if she wants the man for herself. Otherwise, they can do what they want, even to me." Then, smiling, she lifted a chemise off the bed and asked in a bright brittle tone, "Help me pack?"

Masha stayed by the door. Until Granny started slapping Lika, she'd been half distracted by thoughts of Isaac, sensations of Isaac. Now everything soured with Lika's comment, which was, in fact, a confession. A confession delivered through the years of their friendship, as one might drop crumbs to find a way out of the inescapable dark forest of childhood.

How obtuse Masha had been. Deliberately, she thought now. She remembered that day last spring in Sokolniki Park when Lika insisted that Antosha had not "ruined" her. *That was no longer possible.* Then she'd sobbed, not over Isaac. Masha had had nothing to say. *I have stories too, you know. True ones.*

Stories such as would make any woman cry.

Masha was a teacher. She loved her girls, was a girl once herself holding Mother's hand on the street and watching them beat the stray dogs. Mother's horrifying warning was the only protection she could offer.

Lika carried on chattering, engaging her hands to avoid Masha's eye, using the silken piles to distract Masha from what she'd said. "Can you believe I'm going to Paris? We start lessons right away." A timid glance.

Should she press for more? Lika had changed the subject. Wasn't that her right?

Masha finally settled on "Please don't go."

"I know you don't approve of Ignati."

"I just came from Isaac's studio. Lika? Ignati's wife's in Paris."

Lika, still folding, let out another puff of air, upward this time, ruffling her bangs. "Isaac doesn't like Ignati. But, Masha, I've finally fallen for someone else. Antosha's very fond of him. Did you know Ignati looked over his accounts and discovered Suvorin owed him a lot of money?" Two chemises went onto the pile. "It's such a relief to know where I stand with a man, even if it's second place. Ignati put his finger on it. He says Antosha has a way of making people open up without ever revealing himself. Why are you looking at me like that?"

Before Masha could reply, a creak sounded from the hall. "Granny, stop listening!" Lika called.

"Pig!" came through the door.

She turned back to Masha. "I'll stay away from the wife. What else can I do?"

No qualms at all. Yet it felt like just months ago that Masha was standing in the chest of drawers brushing the shoulders of an eighteen-year-old sculpted out of powdered sugar. How had this happened?

It happened because Masha had invited Lika.

"And when this married man and his wife toss you aside? What then? I'm asking as your friend. Because it seems to me—if I understand you properly—you've been hurt enough."

Lika brightened. "*Are* we still friends, Masha?"

"Yes! That's why I'm here." She came and sat beside Lika on the bed.

"Not on the dress."

Masha pulled it out from under her and tossed it in the trunk. "I feel to blame for this situation, Lika. I didn't realize . . ."

"What?" Lika asked.

"If I'd known your situation."

Lika shook her head. Too late for words. They were only syllables filling the air. How could they change the past? Lika leaned in then and embraced Masha; there was something childlike in how hard she clung, a desperation.

"Why would I blame you for anything?" Lika asked.

"You wrote that I should pity you."

Lika looked Masha in the eye. Hair unkempt, her cheeks so red they still seemed to be burning from Granny's slaps.

All she said was, "I hope you won't think too badly of me."

On her beautiful face, Masha read an unhappy ending.

WHEN SHE LEFT LIKA, MASHA PAUSED TO TOUCH HER mouth and discovered tenderness. Between her legs, something sang. Yet the smell of cat as she went down the stairs made her ill. The whole situation did. How could she go back to Isaac after that?

She longed to, though. She longed for it.

4

ONTHS PASSED BEFORE MASHA FOUND OUT about the parties at the Hotel Louvre. Antosha was barely home in all that time. After Yalta, he'd gone to St. Petersburg. Then there were briefer jaunts, if he wasn't coughing too badly. Yet the times he was home, they had some painful disagreements, upsetting to them both.

Lika's predicament was the cause of their discord. Letters postmarked from Paris piled up on his desk during his absences.

When he returned the first time, Masha asked for Lika's news, knowing it full well, since she'd been receiving unhappy letters of her own.

Irritated by her prying, Antosha handed them over. "Please read them, if you're so curious."

This one had come while Lika was en route.

I shall die soon. Darling, write for old time's sake, and don't forget that you gave me your word of honour to come and see me. Don't forget the woman you rejected . . .

Darling? Such an intimate tone. The second had come two weeks later, after she and Varvara settled in the house Ignati had found for them. It was full of foreign girls who wanted to be singers, which sounded to Masha awfully like a brothel.

I barely see Potapenko. Sometimes he comes for half an hour in the morning, presumably without his wife knowing. Every day she stages scenes and hysterics. He claims she has consumption. She's obviously faking it . . .

"Did you know his wife was in Paris?" Masha asked Antosha.

His lips compressed. "Certainly not."

"But you seem to have promised that you would visit Lika. I suppose it was a joke. What are you going to tell her this time?"

"Would you like to vet my reply before I send it?"

His cool tone offended her, so she said yes, simply because he expected no. An hour later, he called her back to his study and showed her his letter.

Lika, when you're a rich and famous singer, give me alms or marry and support me, so I can be idle. In the meantime, I'm obliged to stay home and write.

P.S. Potapenko should buy you a ticket back to Moscow. Tell him I said so.

"Hers are the typical complaints of a mistress," Antosha said.

He had a point, but Masha had to wonder if he might have written more sympathetically if he wasn't also writing for the sister he was annoyed at. She handed back his letter.

"And Ignati?"

"Do I have to show that to you too?"

"Please."

"Then wait a moment."

She went to the window and looked out at the garden, their

still snowy south of France. Soon spring would come, and they'd be working harmoniously again. Antosha was having a writing cottage built, Masha overseeing the project. She'd hired the carpenters. The lumber was already stacked in the yard.

"Done," he said.

She left the window to read what he'd written. A single sentence: *You are a pig.*

"Will that do?" he asked.

EASTER CAME AGAIN, BUT NOT LIKA.

> *I'm not coming home, Masha. I've been unwell and am taking a ghastly concoction on the doctor's orders. If I go anywhere, it will be Switzerland for a cure. Did I mention addressing my letters to Madame? This will help with the landlady . . .*

Masha's brothers, Ivan and Misha, converged on Melikhovo. (Misha had finally moved out after he was transferred to a town north of Moscow.) And as hadn't happened in many years, Aleksander came, bringing his two sons. Antosha saw their eldest brother whenever he went to St. Petersburg, but Masha hadn't for several years and so was surprised to see an ogre cross their threshold. Or had she just forgotten how tall and broad he was?

His boys disturbed her even more. Eight and ten, they displayed sadistic traits; Antosha caught them tormenting Brom. Something was off in their appearance. Both had small heads and thin upper lips, above which the skin was curiously smooth, features common in children of alcoholic mothers and bestial grandfathers, Antosha told her.

Aleksander lived to dispute. He drank too much, expressed his hatred of Father in disrespectful remarks and made outrageous demands of Antosha. Why couldn't he build a dacha at Melikhovo?

Because then his children would be sodomizing the dogs with sticks every summer. Antosha avoided spelling this out, which caused Aleksander to revenge himself with sarcasm. Several times he referred to Antosha as "a sick man," which upset Mother. Another time he said, "You and our sister have a false relationship. Don't you see it? Any kind word from you and she's all yours."

"Ha!" Antosha replied. "She's practically dictating my letters."

Masha brooded over Aleksander's comment. Mainly she was annoyed that from the outside, gratitude looked like weakness. When she was younger, or even a few years ago, he might have been speaking the truth, but not now; Masha managed Melikhovo, and on most matters Antosha deferred to her. Also, without her, he wouldn't have been able to travel as much. Aleksander, who saw her so rarely, couldn't be expected to see beyond her adolescent self. But it was also true that, lately, her gratitude conflicted with her sense of worth, a thing she treasured more knowing that Lika's had been stolen from her.

One night, Aleksander even had a go at Masha. He brought up her suitors. It upset her so much she forbade herself to think of the encounter. Accusations from so antagonistic a person didn't merit reflection.

But Olga's assessment of her elder brothers came to mind then—their contrasting temperaments and its cause, the miracle that Antosha had risen above the fate of the other two. And so she found herself on Antosha's side again.

The whole family under one roof proved too much for him. On Easter Day, as soon as it was polite to, Antosha escaped to

Moscow and stayed there until his three brothers had left. When he returned, it was only for a week, setting the pattern for the coming months—visits to friends, a Volga River cruise with Aleksei Suvorin. Masha kept busy in the garden.

Now when he was home, neither of them mentioned Lika.

Send me your news, Masha. It's medicine to me, better than creosote and cod liver oil . . .

WHEN ANTOSHA RETURNED TO MELIKHOVO THAT JULY, the writing cottage was finished. With its steeply pitched roof and gingerbread eaves, it would, he joked, attract fairy-tale visitors, lost children, heroic woodsmen, and witches disguised as beautiful women. Masha had it painted pale blue and white, the door red.

One afternoon she was returning on foot from the fields, arms swinging freely in the heat. Her secret pleasure that summer was going without the restrictions of a corset, feeling the sweat trickling down her back. She passed through the cooler orchard, where the swallows skimmed the ground around her feet. Nearing the cottage, she heard a familiar kettledrum laugh.

"Two desks will fit. We'll write together. You can finally start that play of yours."

"If I ever finish with Sakhalin Island."

Ignati? Relief washed over Masha. Lika was back, thank God.

"What takes you so long? I can't comprehend it," Ignati said as he and Antosha stepped out the red door together. The dachshunds burst out too. Ignati saw Masha standing there and waved in an exuberant arc. "Hello!"

"Is Lika with you?" she called back.

His "no" sounded so matter-of-fact that Masha assumed he meant Lika was in the house. She glanced over her shoulder, then back at Ignati, his grin still fixed in the middle of his beard. Antosha looked away.

"She's still in Paris," Ignati said. "Busy with lessons. I brought you a gift."

It took a moment for her to comprehend what he was saying. He'd taken Lika off to Paris, then left her there with his angry wife? And now he dared to turn up and greet Masha, Lika's friend, as though he'd done nothing wrong?

"May I have a word with you, Antosha?"

Antosha followed her along the path and into the house, coughing all the way. Mariushka was just bringing a tray of tea things from the kitchen. Antosha held the door, keeping the dogs out with his foot. In passing, the cook said, "Tea's served on the veranda."

He nodded. "Please let Ignati know. I'll join him in a moment."

As soon as they were closed up in his study, Masha cried out, "I knew this would happen! He's deserted her!"

Antosha coughed again. "Varvara's with her. Masha, he told me it was tough going with the wife. Lika had no sympathy for her. He was being pulled in both directions. He had no choice but to leave before they ripped him in half. You have no idea what that feels like."

No, she didn't. They looked at one another, Antosha through the pince-nez, and neither moved. How many times had she stood in this room as still and silent as this moment, holding the tray of boiled instruments, the hands of the clock scraping its own face? She'd watched him lance and staunch and stitch and had trained herself not to gag. This skill she put to use now.

A trapped fly battered itself against a pane, while outside, a bird sang. No, it was Ignati whistling as he passed the window, hands pocketed, his big chest thrust out. Masha let him move through her peripheral vision, but Antosha turned his head. Ignati noticed them and made an exaggerated gesture of surprise. Pinkie finger crooked, he mimed drinking tea. Antosha laughed.

Sheepishly, he turned back to her. "I'm sorry, sister, but he amuses me. I know he's a rake, but I'm so tired all the time. Dead tired. He has such energy. He makes me feel alive."

Just as Lika used to—before Masha stupidly sent him to apologize. Then he'd tossed her aside. No, he'd handed her over to Ignati. She remembered the moment now, Ignati ransacking his pockets for the fare while the droshky driver waited. *You'll repay me, I'm sure,* Antosha had told him.

While she thought of something to say, Masha let her gaze fall. Piled neatly on his desk were the hundreds of pages of *The Island of Sakhalin.* Until he'd mentioned it a few minutes ago, she'd almost forgotten the book. Forgotten his trip. Yet all this time— nearly four years—he'd been returning there on the page. No one ever came back from Sakhalin Island. Tears threatened, and she released him from her judgment yet again.

"In your stories," she said, "people are always dreaming of a better life. Like in 'The Black Monk.' Remember? The monk says that a great bright future awaits humankind. Do you believe that?"

"You have to give people *some* hope." He coughed. "I'll make him leave in the morning."

"Thank you. Please tell Mariushka I'll have dinner in my room."

That night Masha lay on her bed under Kolia's painting of Antosha. Young and handsome, he was turned three-quarters, long hair hanging over one eye. And right in the centre was a bare patch of canvas, as though someone had sliced off his ear and stuffed the hole with batting.

She wished she were deaf. Such a jolly meal they were having four rooms away. Later they conversed as they fished in the pond, words mingling with the evening vespers of the frogs.

"Fishing or writing?"

"Fishing."

"Fishing or vodka?"

"Fishing."

"Fishing or fucking?"

A long pause. "Fishing."

In the morning, Masha found Ignati's gift on the dining table, a set of English watercolours in a wooden box. She unlocked it with the key. The inside label was indecipherable. She'd forgotten all her English.

Compartments to hold the coloured tablets, a slot for brushes, a lidded jar and mixing trough. Two drawers for storing paper. She picked out a tablet. Ultramarine. The whole sky compressed into a wafer. She sniffed it, then touched it to her tongue. Though it nearly broke her heart, she shut the box in the china cabinet. If Lika came back in one piece, then she'd use it.

THAT MORNING, AS WELL AS THE PAINTS, THERE WAS A note from Antosha saying that he'd gone with Ignati to deliver *The Island of Sakhalin* to his publisher. It was a lie. A week later Misha came across the manuscript while searching Antosha's study for cigarettes.

"He quit smoking," said Masha, who was in the study doing the building accounts that night. "They made his cough worse. It's bad enough."

"And what? He threw them out? He could have donated them. So much for being a man of charity."

Misha opened the lower drawer of the desk, and there it was. When Masha expressed her surprise, he barked a harsh laugh.

"He wasn't in town to deliver any manuscript. He was running around with Potapenko. I saw them at the Hermitage. Now that the scandal's died down, it's safe for everyone to show their faces again."

Masha tried not to let the little brother see how much the lie stung. Why hadn't Antosha simply left? Or told the truth? Probably because she disapproved so much of Ignati. She was only mildly interested in Misha's gossip.

"Which scandal now? The papers are full of them."

He perched himself on the edge of the desk and looked down at her with an odd expression—a pitying one. "The papers wouldn't touch this one, sister. They wouldn't get past the censor. You don't know? Lika didn't tell you?"

Told her what? Lika wasn't giving Masha the full story of what was going on in Paris. But Masha, who had copied out so many lines, was practised at reading between them. A young woman, abandoned by her bored lover, falling into "poor health." It didn't take much to imagine the plot. Every train station book-rack carried numerous versions of it, both titillating and cautionary.

Misha went on. "I'm talking about the scandal in the Hotel Louvre and Hotel Madrid. Once the little girls were evicted, everyone scattered, Ignati to Paris, followed by Lika. Antosha to Yalta—"

Masha looked up. "He went for his cough."

"—Isaac to Europe."

The mention of Isaac brought heat to her face. Once she'd cooled, something else sank in. *The little girls*. They'd been talking about Antosha's Sakhalin Island manuscript, so she naturally thought of the child prostitutes. And then she thought of Lika, similarly handled. She settled the pen in the stand next to the postal scale and stared at it, unable to speak.

"Lidia Iavorskaya and Topsy-Turvy Tania," Misha said, and instantly she was subsumed in relief. Not *actual* children, then.

Misha was such a gossip. Here he sat, the little brother whom she'd bossed her whole life, ears sticking out, wearing a superior expression behind his pince-nez. Anything literary thrilled him, because, Masha liked to think, he had no talent. The truth was he did—he published his stories regularly—but compared to Antosha, he was a nonentity. How dispiriting would that be? She felt a swell of sympathy for him.

And then he spoiled it. "Oh, sister. It was *ooh-la-la.*"

Masha wouldn't countenance lewdness. "Leave."

But he wouldn't, not until he'd finished his malignant talk. It was the parties he wanted to tell her about. "Those two were hostesses."

Lidia and Tania. Masha pictured them walking away from Isaac on Tverskaya Street, Lidia with a crimson ostrich roosting on her head. Tania the bright little woman she'd mistaken for Lidia's daughter from a distance.

"Were you even invited to these parties?"

"I was. Topsy-Turvy invited me. Lika introduced us. I met Isaac there. He was a regular, but only if Antosha didn't show. Will those two ever make up?"

Lidia, he said, had been living in the Hotel Louvre, Tania in the shabbier Hotel Madrid. Tania was an actress too, but also a writer. The two hotels were connected through a corridor that everyone had dubbed the Pyrenees.

Tania was the one who had spilled the beans about "The Grasshopper." Masha remembered now.

"Do you know why they call her Topsy-Turvy?" He made a gesture, like he had upended a glass. "Inverted. A devotee of Sappho,
if you follow me. Dancing and refreshments in the Louvre and
various other entertainments available in the Madrid. Everyone
welcome. Anyone could join in. Do you follow? The continual
stream of merrymakers crossing the Pyrenees finally tipped off the
management. Anyway, the little girls ran off to Naples and apparently caused some scandal there."

He seemed to want to stun her, and he'd succeeded completely.
On the ledger before her, the numbers she'd been trying to add
made no sense.

Then he softened, as though he regretted his own salacious-
ness. "Actually, Tania's nice. I think Lidia's the debauched one. And
poor Lika. She really got in over her head. The night I went there,
she ended up crying on my shoulder about how she'd botched
everything. Potapenko's the worst sort of man. She should have
picked me. Why didn't she?"

"I suppose you went too," Masha said.

"Through the Pyrenees?" A hand on his chest, an incredulous
face. "Me? Sister, I'm no explorer. Besides, I only heard about it after
the fact." He frowned. "I just want to meet a nice girl and get married. Don't tell the big brother that."

So RISIBLY INNOCENT WAS MASHA, EVEN HER OWN
dreams mocked her. At the Dairy School her pupils, her *little girls*,
vanished. She had to go looking for them. She climbed the stairs,
opened the door on a smoke-filled room. A man fell flat on his
back. There can never be too much vodka, only not enough. And
dancing, naturally. Dancing and blindly running their hands over

each other's faces and bodies. *Double the fun.* In the middle of it all, the most beautiful bird flapped its wings and croaked. It was Lika.

Someone leaned close to ask why she wasn't singing.

"I don't know the words," Masha said, tearful and confused.

She woke remembering how she'd smelled and tasted a woman on Isaac. But was it Lidia *and* Tania both? All the while, she'd been falling straight into the storm. Thank God she hadn't gone back to see him.

But why did Antosha lie about delivering his manuscript? What other lies had he told? And how was she supposed to pretend that she didn't know these things when he came home?

As it turned out, she had time to practise keeping her face straight. Antosha went for an extended stay with Alexei Suvorin. Was it the scandal that kept him away, or her? Meanwhile, Lika's letters to him continued. The ones to Masha were a quarter as thick.

Exciting news! I'm going to Switzerland after all . . .

Autumn came, and Masha began teaching again, hurrying back and forth to Melikhovo to help with the harvest. Every weekend Father asked why she hadn't brought Lika with her.

"We haven't seen her for so long, God bless her."

"She's still abroad, Father. She's studying to be a singer."

Masha, too, could lie.

A FLUSH TOILET WAS INSTALLED AT MELIKHOVO IN early October, while Antosha was still away. Father refused to try it. There was something indulgent, and therefore sinful, in easing the discomforts of life; only by embracing suffering could they comprehend Christ's. Mother was more willing, but confessed she found it repulsive to move her bowels under the same roof where she ate. After four days, she was reaching for Hunyadi Janos's promised relief. Mariushka had been persuaded to pull the chain on the cistern, but the violent swirl of the water made her scream.

Finally, Antosha came home. Brom and Quin rushed to the vestibule where he was stepping out of his muddy galoshes. They cavorted around him, reciting Shakespearean sonnets. Antosha headed straight for the water closet, set down his suitcase and peered in at the new apparatus. With a smile and a nod to Masha in the hall, he stepped inside and closed the door.

The dogs sniffed the hotel labels on his suitcase, then settled dotingly in front of the door, heads cocked, waiting for their oft-absent master to re-emerge. Watching this lesson in devotion, Masha felt heavy not just in her heart but in her thickening body. The stolid weight of herself. She perspired more. A veil of sweetish odour covered her, similar to Antosha's cloying exhalations. The sweetness of rotting things.

Then an elephant sounded off in the lavatory. Quin let out a surprised bark like a higher-pitched fart. This was something they hadn't considered before the installation—the presence of a listening audience, private moments given a porcelain echo. How would Antosha adjust, this man who cherished his privacy to the point of secrecy?

She was still thinking of the parties in the Louvre and Madrid and his unimaginable participation. How he'd been the one to take Lika there.

Yes, there had been many improvements at Melikhovo of late, largely due to Antosha's increase in income. While away, he'd written to tell her how to spend it. The money was thanks to Ignati acting as his agent. Apparently Ignati's own exigencies made him an expert at squeezing out of publishers what was owed. Masha supposed she should be grateful, particularly for the toilet, but she couldn't be when her comfort had its source in such a reprehensible cad.

Meanwhile, Lika's letters to Masha were so giddily cheerful that Masha knew she must be feeling the inverse.

The mountain air makes you drunk. It's better than champagne. You should see the pretty brown cows with their necklaces of bells . . .

Masha pictured the cows clattering into the Dairy School courtyard, bulky with bovine destiny. Herself watching from the window with her unfortunate friend's head resting on her shoulder. Seven months after her flight from Moscow, Lika had left the swelter of Paris to spend the summer in Switzerland. The math was elementary.

Take pity on me.

5

MASHA'S UPSETTING ENCOUNTER WITH ALEK-
sander the previous Easter happened the night Masha
and Mother had tried to teach his boys to play whist.
Either too young or too stupid, they couldn't follow the rules at
all. The elder taunted the younger, who commenced wailing. This
brought Aleksander flying into the room to knock their heads
together, literally, and send them off to bed.

Mother, upset by his behaviour and, no doubt, the memories it
stirred, retired herself, leaving Masha alone with the ogre.

Like Antosha and Misha, Aleksander's eyes were weak, but
he favoured spectacles of tinted glass over a pince-nez. His long
beard and shorn head exaggerated the length of his face. Though
he could be jolly, his vileness while drinking overshadowed all his
better moods. Masha tried never to rile him, but that night his
rough behaviour disgusted her too much.

"You're a harsh father," she told him, collecting up the abandoned cards to lay out a game of Patience. "I would have thought
you'd have a gentler touch with your own children."

"And you know about raising children?"

"I'm a teacher."

He brought the bottle and two glasses over to the table.

"No, thank you," Masha said.

"Go on." He took a seat across from her. "Don't be such a bitch.
Have a drink."

She should have left the room too, but then ill conduct would triumph, so she stayed, keeping her eyes fixed on the cards.

He filled the glasses. "Why don't you have children?"

"I asked Father if I could, but he strangely insists on wedlock."

Aleksander laughed. "Then marry, why don't you? Why are you slaving here for Antosha?"

She glanced up. "Am I slaving?"

He lifted his glass in the air, waiting for her to follow suit. When she didn't, he drank down his own. "It looks like it."

"Did it occur to you that I love Melikhovo?" She gathered the cards and snapped them as she shuffled. "Besides, no one I particularly care about has proposed, not that it's any of your business. What's so amusing now?"

"Who would *dare* ask you? They're all terrified of falling out of favour with the famous writer."

He picked up her untouched glass and flung its contents at the back of his throat.

The younger boy appeared in the doorway. "Papa?" he quavered, which caused Aleksander to cough and spray the carpet. The child stiffened in terror, his naked legs stork-thin under his long shirt.

"Bed!" Aleksander roared.

"Bed is a good idea," Masha said, tossing down the cards before Aleksander noticed they were shaking.

"It's the truth," he told her departing back.

THE DAY AFTER ANTOSHA RETURNED TO CHRISTEN THE flush toilet, Tsar Aleksander III died. His father, Aleksander II, had been a reformer. He'd emancipated the serfs and was loved for it, yet that wasn't enough to turn radicals into friends. After his assassination, his son took the opposite approach, repealing many of the elder's reforms. So Aleksander III was mourned as tyrants are, insincerely. The schools closed for the three days of the charade. Masha had no reason to go back to Moscow.

During those three days, Antosha was called away several times to see patients. He complained bitterly, as usual, about driving on the bumpy autumn roads. "My heart's so badly jostled, I'm no longer capable of love."

Yet it seemed to Masha that these protestations over house calls were also insincere, that he actually wanted to go. She didn't know how to manage the conflicting feelings his evasion caused. If only she had separate compartments, one for her anger, red, one for her resentment, green, one for her sorrow, blue. One for her love too, for she yearned for their former closeness, not this nervous distance. What colour would it be? At the same time she knew her long face, an imitation of their brother Aleksander's, and her accusing silences, kept him at a distance.

One morning he reached out. In the dining room before his day's writing began, he told her, "Sister, our dear Father has no end of praise for how you managed things while I was gone. 'Glory to God, she puts any man to shame.' I suppose you didn't have any time to paint. All because I felt restless."

"We did rather feel like you were running away," Masha said.

"Not at all."

He turned his kind eyes on her, but she couldn't allow the matter of Lika to pass. Possibly Aleksander's comment was still festering inside her too.

"Perhaps it was your conscience you were running from."

He drew back with a look both querying and offended.

"It's quite obvious Lika's pregnant," Masha said.

No reaction now. Antosha poured out his coffee, lifted the cup, and took a sip.

Of course there was the other matter, the unspeakable one. Did he know what had happened to Lika, who was once "happy-seeming and preternaturally kind?" These words described her well and were the very ones he'd used to warn Misha off the youngest girls in the brothel.

"I didn't make her pregnant," Antosha said.

The utter reasonableness of his reply could only provoke. "You did nothing to stop it from happening!"

At the sound of Masha's raised voice, Mother appeared in the doorway.

"Good morning, Mamasha," Antosha told her, slipping out.

The next day the schools reopened, and Masha went back to town.

HOW LONELY AND FRIGHTENED LIKA MUST BE. MASHA imagined her moving her green-stoned ring to her marriage finger. Taking Antosha's picture from her bag to show the landlady. *P.S. This gift obliges me to nothing.*

Yes, ma'am. He's my husband. He'll be joining me soon.

That must have been the most painful thing of all.

Misha stopped in at the Moscow flat unexpectedly one night. When he asked the news from Melikhovo, Masha only shrugged. She was the one staying away now. She hadn't been home for two weeks.

"Well, I have some," he told her without his usual relish.

It turned out that he'd come specifically for this purpose. Not to gossip, but to comprehend, the way he had when Klara had betrayed him and he'd kept thrusting her letters at them. He paced the rug, filling the flat with the stink of his cigarette. Some cheap brand.

"I went to see an editor about a story. Guess who I ran into there. Ignati."

"Don't tell me," Masha said. "He needed money."

He turned in surprise. "So you know all about it?"

"No. It was a joke."

"Some joke. Ignati told me he'd just made a 'quick jaunt' to Switzerland."

In Lika's last letter to Masha, she'd finally sounded as desperate as she probably was. *I'd give ten years of my life to be sitting on the veranda at Melikhovo with you. I was a fool not to let you stop me from going away* . . . Masha wrote back but received no reply. By the probing way Misha was looking at her now, she knew he'd guessed Lika's condition.

"He goes there, then comes right back. I wonder why. And he drops a chummy hint about our big brother saving his hide." He sucked on the cigarette and made a face, as though his own smoke sickened him.

"Did she have it?" Masha asked.

"She must have."

"A boy or a girl?"

"Sister, he didn't even *mention* Lika, let alone the baby. He just said he got stuck, and Antosha sent him money to come back. 'Ha ha ha! What a fine friend!' and he shoves out his chest. Then he shakes my hand goodbye and goes off whistling some damned Ukrainiac song. That's brutal, don't you think? He's left Lika there all on her own with a newborn. What a monstrous cad! I'm disgusted that Antosha would help him like that. I suppose he feels he owes Ignati, but still. Is anyone helping Lika?"

"Has she written you?" Masha asked. "She didn't answer me. I'm afraid she's moved."

He shrugged. "I haven't heard from her at all."

"I'll go see Granny, then."

"That's it?" he asked. "You're not going to say anything to the big brother? Even after this, he can do no wrong?"

"I'm not going to take Ignati's word for anything."

Misha extinguished the cigarette in the tray and, without a word, left. Before the door slammed, it let in a chilling draft.

Masha went out straightaway; otherwise she wouldn't sleep. She took a cab to Arbat. There the old woman, powderless and dressed for bed, three times denied Lika through the space in the door.

"I don't know what you're talking about. No, I don't have her address. What child do you mean?"

Masha had been too frank. But as she turned to leave, Granny said in a bewildered mew, "A girl," then closed the door.

It was about eleven by then and snowing. The whole city smelled of it. The rooftops and naked branches of the trees, the boulevard benches all freshly layered, virginal in the streetlight. The first-snow feeling that Nature treated them to but once a year.

A girl. Masha needed to walk off the news.

Once a peasant woman surprised them by giving birth at Melikhovo. She was waiting in line for treatment when, abruptly, she struck off through the garden. Masha was tending to her cabbages, but the blatancy of the woman's trespass, the curious way she walked—half-lurch, half-waddle—drew her eye. She wasn't visibly pregnant. In that case, she would have been confined. When she got down on all fours behind the artichokes, Masha marched over to see what was going on.

Such animal straining. Masha ran for Antosha, pounding her fists on his window.

The snow was thick enough now to leave prints. Under her feet, it spoke in squeaks. She must have been walking for ages, seeing nothing. Psychic blindness. The Hermitage Hotel was just ahead, and, as she passed it, Masha glanced inside at the line of men at the bar talking and laughing in their world behind the glass. How she'd love to go in and warm herself with a drink. What would happen if she did? If she walked through the door and joined them in their row? She pictured pulling off her gloves, throwing them down and, while she waited to be served, watching the empty fingers slowly curl.

A baby girl like Evgenia.

More footprints here. Passersby flowed in both directions. There was a definite sense of merriment in the air. She couldn't remember how Evgenia died, just Mother bent over the cradle, Masha clinging to her while she rocked with silent grief.

Masha stopped in her tracks. Was it *her* fault? Had she dropped Evgenia or left her unattended? Mother never wanted to talk about her to Masha. Had she destroyed that life too?

Cabs lined the street, the drivers bundled on their boxes and, like their horses, occasionally shaking the snow off themselves. One spat, and at the sound of it, she lifted her head to see a whole row of students coming toward her, arms linked, singing some coarse song. She waited for them to break ranks and pass on either side, but instead they surrounded her, their multiple arms groping her through her coat. A mouth reeking of alcohol mashed painfully against hers.

"Get off me!" Masha shoved aside the one who'd kissed her. She got a few good kicks in too.

They lurched back, seemingly astonished by her resistance, except for the one rubbing his shin, who grimaced.

It was nothing to them. They'd probably mauled a half-dozen women on their way. Now they lumbered off toward Sobolev Lane, hooting laughter. Masha stood there shaking, not just with anger, but with the physical thrill of her defiance. It flooded her body, warmed her up.

Nearby a cabby drew up another bloodied wad of phlegm and expectorated on the white, white snow.

6

I KNOW THIS LETTER WILL APPEAR TO COME OUT OF *the blue after so long . . .*

Masha paused with the pen in hand. He'd probably think she was with child and needing rescuing.

You once wrote that you hoped to see me again before you died. I pray that your demise isn't forthcoming. In fact, I'm wondering if you would like to visit us, for I would very much like to see you again too . . .

She posted the letter on her way to Melikhovo.

Mother and Father expected her every weekend, were perplexed by her absence. Why even tell them she was coming home? She hired a sledge at the station. As she neared the house, Brom and Quin heard the harness bells and came out barking, leaping like rabbits through the new snow, just their heads showing. They were so funny. Why did she hate them so?

Their barking drew the famous writer from his desk. He stepped out on the veranda and watched her trudge along. When she smiled and waved, such relief showed on his face; his enveloping embrace when she reached him reiterated it.

Long ago she'd copied out his comical "Elements Most Often

Found in Novels, Short Stories, Etc." The last line read: "More often than not, no ending." This was his ideal—a dramatic scene averted, never to be mentioned again. Their life as it was.

He didn't notice she'd brought no bag.

"You're still wearing black," he said. "For the Tsar?"

"No. I'm in mourning for my life."

He roared with laughter.

After an effusive welcome from Mother and Father, they all sat down to lunch. Antosha pulled the bay leaf from Mariushka's cabbage soup, passed it between his lips, and placed it delicately on his saucer.

"I've been thinking, sister. Why don't you move into my study?"

A peace offering. "Where will you work?" she asked.

"I have the cottage now. All a writer needs is a chair on which to settle his tender backside and a place to lay his page. You'd make better use of the space."

"That's generous," Masha told him.

"Antonshevu gives us everything," Mother remarked as Mariushka ladled out her serving. "We owe so much to him."

"Our Saviour more," Father added.

"Mamasha, it's we who owe you," Antosha said. "You gave us the gift of life."

"This sweetness is better left for dessert, no?" Masha lifted her spoon and took a sip. "Please pass the salt."

Antosha laughed again, this time until he coughed.

After the meal, instead of napping, he joined Mother and Masha in the parlour. With Brom and Quin sitting expectantly at his feet, he offered a matinee performance of the dachshund skit. Every evening the dogs took turns placing their forepaws on his knees. Then Antosha would entertain everyone by dispensing advice, medical or spiritual, or simply passing along farmyard gossip.

This afternoon he told Quin, "Our dear sister has been staying away. Why, she won't say. I fear that she was cross with me. But Quinine, as a sister yourself, you know that without one, things go to rack and ruin, and quick." He patted Quin's sleek head; with each touch her eyes closed in bliss. "Masha is the heart of this household. After Mother. Mothers must always come first. Brom?"

Quin put her front paws back on the floor. Brom lifted his.

"Brom, I advise you to confess. You'll feel better getting it off your chest. How many hens did you kill? Three. What's that?" He leaned in, and Brom licked his ear. "A chicken is not a bird? What of it? You must confess."

Throughout the monologues, Mother wiped tears of hilarity off her face. Masha laughed too, in spite of herself.

Then Antosha yawned and said he had to lie down and think for a few minutes.

While Masha helped Mother stack the tea things on the tray, she turned the question over in her mind. Was she prepared for the answer?

"I need to ask you something, Mother."

She looked up, face as bland as a cow's.

"How did Evgenia die?"

Mother started, as she always did when this lost daughter was mentioned. Creases complicated her simple face while, slowly, her lip was drawn into the toothless space.

"She had a fever. We sent for the doctor, but it was useless." This she said dully, as a presentation of fact. But then the emotion came, tinged with accusation. "Why? Why do you ask me this now?"

"I just wondered. You never told me."

Mother set down the dishes. She crossed herself, then made the sign over Masha. In the doorway, she paused with one hand on the jamb, as though this short distance was too much. Her back stooped more than before. Masha lifting this painful burden off her conscience had reminded Mother of hers.

"Mamasha, I'm sorry," Masha called as Mother shuffled away.

Masha put away her regret for now. Drowsiness would have fully settled on Antosha. She went to his room and, ear to the door, heard the rumblings that confirmed sleep. Soundlessly, she stepped inside.

Hanging in the dim air, scent and pulmonary decay. She could just make him out curled on his side in the narrow iron bed, one hand in a boyish fist under his cheek. He was still in his jacket, the blanket pulled to his waist. Thirty-four years old, two years older than Kolia when he died, his breath moving in and out of him more laboriously year by year.

Across from the bed was the washstand with his fishing rod propped against it. On a nail above the ewer was the mirror in which Masha slowly emerged from the gloom. His devoted sister, amanuensis, supplier of women. Her furious face.

Perhaps she made a noise. Or had he sensed a vindictive energy, something catlike, a Mrs. Svoloch standing at the foot of his bed? He rolled onto his back and opened his eyes. Making out her shape, he started and sat up.

"Sister?" Felt around for the pince-nez in his breast pocket. "What's wrong?"

"Did you send money to Ignati, so he could leave Switzerland?"

Her eyes had fully adjusted. She saw the ivy on the wallpaper she'd helped hang. She saw his frown.

"I gave him money, but not for that."

"For what, then?"

"So he could hire Lika a wet nurse."

Of course. She shouldn't have believed Misha's third-hand version of events. "Well, he ran away and bragged to Misha that you funded his escape."

Antosha coughed. When he removed his hand, his mouth was set in anger. "Thank you for telling me. I'll speak to him." He stared at her. "Is there anything else?"

Briefly, she wavered, her fury tamped down once again by his reasonableness. She cast her eyes around the tidy room. The rug on the wall next to the bed keeping out the chill, Mother's curtains and the slit of light between them.

"Yes. Someone suggested to me that I might have got married if not for you."

"Who? Aleksander, I suppose. Oh, the ass." With a sigh, he swung his legs over the side of the bed, then sat squeezing the bridge of his nose, the blanket hooked on one foot.

"People—" Lika, she meant. Isaac too. "People have also suggested that you have no feelings."

Without looking at her, he said, "How am I supposed to answer that accusation? Do you have proof?"

"Svoloch."

He nodded. "Ah. Because I didn't want a wild animal tearing up the house, I have no feelings."

"You didn't cry at Kolia's funeral."

"Sister, I do my crying on the page." He said this so wearily, almost as a plea, that she nearly backed down again.

"I've had suitors. You drove them off."

"I've driven no one off."

"Not Lieutenant Egorov?"

"Who?" He squinted up at her, then remembered and twitched with irritation. "Egorov again? He's haunting me."

"You said it was too bad, after all, that you didn't let him marry me."

He turned his gaze on the washstand while his hands kneaded the fabric of his trousers, breath growing even more ragged.

"I said no such thing. Perhaps I expressed regret for selling a decent man short, but that doesn't mean I forbade him from marrying you."

"What happened, then? Or with Isaac or Aleksander Smagin? Did you turn them away or merely wither them with your disapproval? Are there others afraid to ask me because of you?"

"Others?" He pulled himself up straight and looked at her. "Who do you mean? And would you actually want to marry a man who places more value in his future brother-in-law's opinion than his future wife's?"

Masha altered her posture too, stiffened her back and lifted her chin, the pose in which she'd successfully calmed nearly a decade of excitable girls enough to educate them.

"Why didn't you ask my opinion? Can't I decide? Do you consider me at all? Am I even a person to you?"

"Pardon?"

She couldn't believe how she was speaking now. Her words poured out, expressing things she had not even realized she felt. "Because I sometimes feel that you see me as an author, not a brother. A none-too-imaginative author, actually. Am I that cliché, the burdensome unmarried sister? The spinster inclining now toward hysteria?"

He made a noise through his nose. She wondered if she'd gone too far. Was he insulted?

"I don't want to be a burden," she said.

He still wasn't looking at her. "Masha, I admire and respect you more than any woman." He pressed his heart. "Is that what you want to hear? More praise? Because if you feel taken for granted, I'll try to do better. I have many preoccupations, as you know."

"This is what I mean. You're speaking the words I want to hear. You add the appropriate gesture. But do you actually feel this?"

Something occurred to him then, and he looked up with a disbelieving expression. "Have you received a proposal, Masha?"

"Perhaps."

Now she saw it, what she was really seeking. A glimmer of true alarm behind the lenses.

"From whom?"

"Does it matter?" she asked mildly.

"Obviously it matters!" Exclaiming made him cough—four or five times—then he continued in his reasonable voice. "Masha? Say you married Egorov, or some other nonentity, for how effectively he ran his soup kitchen. What then? He'd still beat you when he felt like it and whore around the town, and, even worse, bore you half to death."

"You have a grim view of your sex."

"I admit it. I know my sex well. As for the other half of humankind? The impression I get from many women, including our own mother—I'm speaking medically now, as well as as your brother. For many women marriage is—"

He untangled himself from the blanket and tossed it on the bed as he stood, but with the first step stumbled on one of his shoes lying there. "Damn it. My leg's gone to sleep."

"For many women marriage is—?" Masha prompted.

"Nasty, painful and ugly." He meant the act for he looked away.

"Yet many seem to enjoy it," Masha told him. "Even in pairs."

Had she ever in their whole lives seen shock on that inscrutable face? For the first time, his lack of reply was not a conscious act, not due to reserve but to a complete failure of words.

"Anyway," she went on. "Can't the woman decide for herself? Because nasty, painful and ugly is what we get in any case."

He threw up his hands. "Go ahead."

"I'm going to marry Aleksander Smagin."

And now something truly astonishing happened: an utter abandonment of restraint. Contempt settled openly on his face and disfigured it.

"Smagin? That bumpkin? The King of Persia?"

"Yes," Masha told him. "You don't approve?"

"I don't!"

A knock came at the door. "Masha?"

It was Mother.

"Mamasha, we're discussing something," Antosha called. "Can it wait?"

"Of course. Yes."

Masha could hear her retreating steps. She paused to allow them, bolstering herself further with crossed arms. "What's wrong with Smagin, besides his handwriting?"

One finger raised, Antosha limped over and placed an ear to the door. Satisfied that Mother wasn't listening, he uncrossed Masha's arms and took her hands in his. Dropped them and instead cradled her face. The hands that wrote his stories, now holding her head. The kind downward-slanted eyes looking into hers.

"You're a thousand times more intelligent than Smagin."

"I'll marry Isaac, then. I like the way he kisses."

He let her go. She had to laugh. He was like one of those

Abramova Theatre hams, or a commedia dell'arte clown. Lips jutting, brow sinking in moral outrage. Next he would be pounding his frail chest and sinking to his knees.

"Have you been seeing Isaac?"

"Do you prefer him to Smagin? Because for me, either will do. I want a life."

"Isaac has the French disease."

This sobered her, but she managed not to show it. "In that case, it's Smagin, which is good since I've already written to him. He's coming next weekend to ask for my hand. I'll be here too, to give it. Is there anything you need from Muir and Mirrielees when I come back down?"

"Masha," Antosha said. "You have a life. It's here. With us."

"Well, write if you think of something. I'm going back now. I only came to give you this happy news."

As soon as she was on the train, Masha laid one arm along the window ledge and wept uncathartically. In her mind these futile tears simply mixed the colours into a muddied mess. All she really wanted from Antosha was what everyone else wanted from him. If he couldn't say the words, not even to her, perhaps she should have asked him to write them out.

On second thought, she'd read too many of his letters to expect comfort by those means.

She straightened and, blotting her eyes, forced herself to think of Smagin. Of Aleksander! In a few days he would nod goodbye to his icons, to his starched mother in the misaligned picture on the wall, to Kalina showing all her teeth, and step joyfully out of his crooked house.

"Xenia! Olga! Mikhail! Let's go!"

He wouldn't beat her. She was more likely to beat him.

And so she gave herself up to the idea, willingly, stood before her pupils all week feeling nostalgic for them already. Antosha had put his finger on the worst thing she'd have to suffer as a married woman. She would laugh out of boredom and then, for a little variety, burst into tears. Or perhaps she would, like Natalia, start a peasant school. She'd have a garden, and eventually human instead of vegetable children. Girls. The first she'd name Evgenia, the others after friends.

She would tell him the moustache chafed.

She would show him exactly how she wanted to be kissed.

BUT IN THE BACKGROUND OF THESE MUSINGS, AN unanswered question needled her: Why had Antosha lied about his manuscript? He could have said that he had appointments. Why even mention this book? She sensed it had something to do with the purpose of the place, which was suffering. The suffering of children. His own suffering as he journeyed there, the family's too. His other lies were rational; this one was not.

The night Misha had discovered the manuscript, she'd lifted out the stack of pages from the drawer—his longest work by far. She'd read random passages, footnotes, whole chapters. It was a scientific book, meticulously detailed, even the horrors. In the past, every letter he left out or put into her hand had contained a message. A message to her. For the first time, reading this, she couldn't understand him.

———

THE EVENING BEFORE SHE WAS TO MEET SMAGIN AT
Melikhovo, she tried on her dark green dress. Again! It was like forcing her hand into an unstretched glove. She pictured Smagin—
Aleksander—dropping to his knees to propose and her bursting
open at the seams as she accepted him.

Voices sounded in the hall. The key scraped, and Misha
stepped inside, surprised to see her there holding her dress closed
at her nape.

"I thought you went to Melikhovo." To whoever was in the hall,
"Masha's here."

The voice that replied was female. "Your sister? Lovely."

She ducked under Misha's arm like a slippery child. No taller
than a twelve-year-old, frizzy brown curls framing her face, Masha
recognized her at once from Tverskaya Street. Topsy-Turvy Tania.

Tania seemed oblivious to Masha's discomfort. She came right
over, smiling warmly, and pressed Masha's available hand. "I've
heard so much about you from your brothers."

"Nicer things from Antosha," Misha said, opening a cupboard.
"I left a bottle, Masha. Or did you drink it?"

"Anton worships you," Tania said.

She was such a curious creature, tilting her head, an animal
inquisitiveness in her expression. Masha detected no trace of
affectation. No self-consciousness either, let alone shame. Didn't
she know that Masha knew about the scandal? Wasn't she embarrassed?

"We're going to the theatre." Misha crossed the room with the
bottle in one hand and the pickle crock under the other arm. "I
would have invited you, but I thought you were at Melikhovo."

"I'm going in the morning."

"Please come with us," Tania said.

"Tania likes your paintings."

She'd been before. Was Misha using her room for assignations? For—it made her squirm to think it—orgies? Surely the landlady would have complained about excess traffic in the stairwell and peculiar noises.

"I do like your paintings," Tania said. "This one in particular." The one of Melikhovo in winter, she meant. A pink and red cake in the snow, the arched veranda where Antosha had stood watching her trudging approach the week before. "Watercolour is so difficult."

"Do you paint?" Masha asked, letting go of her dress to take the glass Misha held out.

"No, but I can tell. It seems like poetry. It's harder to write a really good poem than a story. The way the pink reflects on the snow in the shadow of the house. Because that's true, isn't it? Shadows aren't necessarily grey."

"Isaac taught her," Misha said.

"That explains it."

She said something next that Masha took at first to be preposterous. That she should apply to the College of Art. "They're taking women now." Then, "Your dress is undone. Turn around."

Masha obeyed, felt the fingers start up her back, fastening her, as the vodka warmed her from inside. Then they stopped.

"Were you getting ready for bed?"

Masha nodded. "I have an early train tomorrow."

"Misha. Drink up."

Tania tossed back her shot, cuffed Misha on the shoulder, then walked backwards to the door, smiling the whole way. "I've been waiting so long to meet you, Masha. I'm sure we'll see each other often now. I'll bring you a poem."

Not in the least embarrassed. She didn't give a damn what anyone thought.

Good for her.

Misha shook the brine off a pickle, tucked it in his pocket and crunched a second as they went out the door. He waved goodbye. They hadn't even taken off their coats.

As soon as they were gone, Masha peeled herself out of the dress and left it in a pile while she went to the window and peeked out the curtain. A moment later, they came out of the building and started down the street. There was nothing amorous between them, Masha could tell by the easy way they'd been, and still were, conversing. She couldn't hear them, but she saw Tania's dramatizing hands and the friendly distance they held between them as they walked. So small, yet so audacious. Was she real?

"I've been waiting to meet you too," Masha said.

No moon tonight. The stars stared down the night all on their own. The sky seemed sprayed with them, and those were only the ones she could see. The ones allowed to shine, or that allowed themselves to. She peered at the blackness and thought of Antosha's monk and his sparkling prophecy. What would her future as a wife be?

SHE SHOULDN'T HAVE DRUNK THE VODKA. INSTEAD OF helping her sleep, it kept her tossing in bed, fretting about the coming day and how she would have to face Smagin, face and accept him. He was a good man. Why did she feel that she was being punished?

Antosha's manuscript came to mind again. The passage about the flogging. He'd described it with such clinical precision. Every five blows the executioner had taken a little break to give his poor tired arm a half-minute's rest.

The prisoner's hair is stuck to his brow, his neck swollen; his body, still covered by weals from the previous lashes, has already turned crimson and dark blue; the skin splits from every blow.

The drawer in Antosha's desk had a lock. He often locked it because sometimes he left money there. But it was unlocked that night. He hadn't been hiding his manuscript. It was under the ledger, the ledger he knew she'd take out to do the accounts. It was she who was meant to find it, not the little brother.

Punishment is perpetual. You can never come back from that place. You're there forever. The children too. The children stay.

The storehouse door always creaked to announce her. Sulphur, cloves, tallow. Motes in the air. She would listen for his breathing and sometimes hear the scurry of mice. This was why Antosha loved mice. Before she came to him, they came first, while he lay, insentient, numbed, so still that they weren't afraid of him. Each beating Father gave thickened him, became protection from the next. Layer upon layer, redundant, for soon he learned to secret elsewhere the true and tender part of himself, his feelings too. Not in the bottle, like his brothers. In the inkwell. He did his crying on the page.

But first came the mice. The bright beads of their eyes, their curious glances as they went about their business reminded him that he was still alive and would one day grow up, and no one would beat him then.

And now there is a curious stretching-out of the neck, the sounds of retching. The prisoner doesn't utter a word, simply bellows and

wheezes; it seems as if, since the punishment began, a whole eter-
nity has passed, but the overseer is only calling "Forty-two! Forty-
three!" There is a long way to go to ninety.

And Masha would creep in, just as quietly. No need to speak.

SHE DIDN'T GO. SHE STAYED THE WHOLE WEEKEND IN
Moscow. Shortly, a letter from Smagin arrived saying that he'd travelled to Melikhovo with his honest heart full of hope.

Maria, it cost me great effort to refrain from having a scandalous
row. I hated you and would have crushed you if you'd dared show
up to face me. Only your brother's constant hospitable welcome
saved me.

7

WEEKS BEFORE THE PREMIERE, ANTOSHA went to St. Petersburg so he could attend rehearsals. So he could explain the play. *A comedy, three female parts, six male, four acts, a view of a lake, a lot of talk about literature, not much action, one hundred and eighty pounds of love.* Such a peculiar title. *The Seagull.*

He sent Masha her ticket and a note. Ignati had acted as the play's agent and would be there with his wife. *Tell Lika not to come . . .*

Masha arrived the day of the premiere, stepping blearily down from the all-night train, scanning the platform. There he was, her stern-faced brother, coughing as he paced. From his overcoat pocket, he took a square of paper, spat and repocketed it. Then he saw her and, unsmiling, raised one hand, more a gesture of resignation than a greeting.

Outside the station, the sky was a blue Masha always thought of as imperial. Antosha looked older in that brighter light, ashen and grim, an undertaker not a playwright.

"It's a déjà vu. Remember *The Wood Demon?* They don't know their parts. They understand nothing. The acting is horrible. Only the actress who plays Nina is any good."

He helped her into the waiting carriage. "You shouldn't have come."

"I wouldn't miss it, brother."

He climbed in beside her, nodded to the driver to start. "And of all the disasters? Miss Mizanova showed up yesterday."

"What?" Masha looked at him in surprise. "She told me she wasn't coming."

"She's staying at the Angleterre. We're going there now. Did you hear that, driver? To the Hotel Angleterre."

Before Lika ran off to Paris, she'd sworn to Masha that she and Antosha were still friends. Since her return, she'd been a frequent welcome visitor to Melikhovo, still Father's favourite and Antosha's too, it seemed. During these visits, the baby went unmentioned. Lika left her in Moscow with Granny, who was looking after her as joyfully as she had looked after Lika.

Antosha and Lika's rekindled affection accorded to his pattern: a long flirtation, a brief affair, his withdrawal. Dunia had been the one to spell out the latter for Masha. "He cannot tolerate extended intimacy. He reacts to it the way others react to pain." She then went on to describe in unseemly detail the physical retraction that accompanied the emotional one. It was the last time they spoke.

For others, such as Olga, the possibility of friendship remained (though they rarely saw her now, despite her proximity). But where Olga never stopped grasping at Antosha, Lika returned from Europe with someone she loved more. And so Antosha enjoyed her company most. Their friendship blossomed until it resembled nothing more than a long and settled marriage—teasing affection, loyalty, bickering and, Masha assumed, sexlessness.

Christina. Her name was never breathed in public. If Masha hadn't been an intimate, she might not have known the child existed. Masha first saw her at the Arbat flat, shortly after Lika returned, when the baby was nine months old and crawling, Lika chasing her around the parlour, shepherding her away from the samovar in case she tried to pull herself to a stand with the tablecloth. A determined little lamb with a nimbus of white curls. Intelligent too—quite aware that she was running her mother ragged. Her pink face shone with mischief, though some of the shine was her copious drool.

When Lika picked her up, Christina squirmed to be released, just like Svoloch when Masha had trapped him in an embrace. Twisting for freedom.

"You need more tea." Lika plunked the small damp personage into Masha's lap. Christina turned and, smiling, seized her by the nose. Her nails, though tiny, proved as sharp as claws.

"Ow!"

Nose scratched, hair pulled. Yet when Lika brought her refilled glass, Masha heard herself say, "Please. Let me hold her for just a minute."

She might never be a mother. Or, then again, she might. Who could tell the future? Tania had decisive views on the issue: never. Marriage: never. "Why, when you can have a lover instead?" Apparently there was an effective means now to avoid becoming a mother by your lover. It cost thirty-five kopeks at the pharmacy and resembled sausage casing.

Tania lived to scandalize, but such good she'd done everyone. Masha was painting in earnest, and when she was ready, she'd apply for the College of Art. Tania had also orchestrated Antosha and Isaac's reconciliation, dragging Isaac out to Melikhovo, where the two men embraced on the porch, then passed a happy weekend never mentioning their three-year quarrel. Antosha said that Tania was writing stories now and they were very good, which meant they were, for he was about as generous with literary praise as he was with apologies.

Masha bounced Christina and let her twist her nose again. Such a sweet, impish face. *Oh, my darling baby.*

Then Granny came into the room to collect Christina for her nap. Lika picked her up and gobbled at her neck.

"No one will ever touch you. No one will ever hurt you," she whispered before handing her off.

NOW IN THE HOTEL ANGLETERRE, LIKA STOOD BEHIND Antosha's chair, so he could lean into her as he confessed his dread. Every time he coughed, which he did continuously, the back of his head bumped against her body.

Lika stroked his hair. "This is why I couldn't do it. Go on stage, I mean. The nerves!" She made her funny flapping gesture, mocking herself now.

Antosha used the chair to push himself to his feet. "Excuse me. I'll be right back."

After he left, Masha repeated the warning she'd given Lika weeks before. "Ignati will be there." Lika hadn't heard from him since Christina's birth.

She shrugged. "Masha, don't blame him. I don't. I *thank* him. I have my little girl."

Then Antosha came back, but it was only to bid them farewell. "Ladies, I'm going to get my hair cut before the execution. I'll see you at the theatre. If not, I'll meet you back here."

"You're sitting with us, aren't you?" Masha asked.

"I have a seat." He smiled, then covered it to cough.

So it would be like *The Wood Demon*, when he never showed up in their box.

The image Masha would carry into the theatre that night was of the discovery she had made after Antosha parted from them.

In the hotel lavatory wastebasket, a half-dozen folded squares of paper with scarlet roses bleeding through. Blood to accompany the execution.

H<small>E'D BEEN RIGHT ABOUT HOW IT WOULD GO.</small>

The lights dimmed until the only illumination came from candles guiding the stragglers to their seats. Of these there were many. People continued conversing in the aisles, making no move at all to sit. Yet before the audience had fully settled, the velvet layers of curtain opened, revealing a second makeshift stage and a painted backdrop of a lake. From the first moment there was a sense of prematurity, of starting too soon. No one was remotely ready for what they were about to watch.

Something must have been going on backstage. Those actually watching grew restless, causing an infectious murmur of discontent to spread along the rows. Finally, a man and woman bolted onto the stage and, in uncertain tones, began.

He: "Why do you always wear black?"

She: "I'm in mourning for my life. I'm unhappy."

Shock shoved Masha back in her seat. It never really left, not until the curtain came down at the end, though foremost in her mind were those tidy paper squares folded around his roses.

Life as it was. Long conversations filled with non-sequiturs that seemed pointless until the pattern emerged—a comically long chain of unrequited passion. An audience fed on slapstick and farce couldn't stomach irony. There was hissing. People rose from their seats and left.

Their outrage only grew from act to act. It was as though the actors were in stocks, there to be pelted with jeers and insults. For one of Nina's entrances, a pair of arms emerged from behind the curtain to shove her onto the stage. Greasepaint couldn't conceal that she'd been crying, real emotion while the others delivered their lines by rote, as though they couldn't fathom the meaning of what they themselves were saying. All the while Masha watched her namesake fumble through feelings she'd thought were secrets. Was that worse than what Lika endured—the stilted re-enactment of her mistakes, her life described as *ruined*, a wounded girl flapping around the stage? Her life heckled. Lika stiffened again and again, but said nothing.

It ended, thank God, before a full-blown riot ensued. Masha couldn't bring herself to look at Lika. She gazed on the wreckage below—crumpled programs, cigarette stubs, smoke hanging over everything. Even then, the players and playwright crushed, snatches of vitriol reached them. "The fall of talent," someone shouted at the empty stage.

Antosha wasn't coming. Masha summoned the nerve to face Lika, now weeping quietly beside her.

I love him. I love him even more than before. A subject for a short story.

"Let's go," Lika murmured.

Outside in the cold, stars nailed down the sky. They drove to the hotel. Masha hoped that Antosha would be there. She couldn't be angry with him. Not yet. He'd been punished enough for now.

They checked the lobby. No Antosha, and no message at the desk.

Back in her room, Lika went to change and wash her face, while Masha stood at the window, even more agitated at the thought of Antosha wandering and coughing in the cold. Lika came back and lay on the bed like a figure on a tomb, swollen eyes closed, hands clasped on her chest. How hurt she must be. Nina, Lika. He had barely bothered to change her name. The ineffectual way he disguised Isaac came to mind. Blue eyes, blond hair. At least in Masha's case, should anyone think it was *her* mooning for the young writer Trepilov, she was protected by Maria, the most common name, Masha its common diminutive. But no one would mistake her because there was no outward resemblance except a sharp, sharp tongue. Which didn't move now. What to say?

Lika spoke first, just as Masha thought she must have fallen asleep. "How I miss my Christi. I can't bear to be away from her. Why do I go away? Granny's there, of course, but when I come back, we fight. We both want her for ourselves."

Why had she come? Masha had warned her, but about the wrong thing. Ignati had never showed. Or perhaps he'd hidden behind a pillar.

"I hated that Irina."

The aging actress in the play, she meant. Trepilov's mother, lover of the famous writer Trigorin, who seduces Nina.

Lika put on a mocking voice. "'Am I really so old and ugly? If you leave me for a single hour, I shall never survive it . . .'"

It was from the scene where Irina realizes that Trigorin has his sights on Nina. She wants to leave at once, to keep them apart. She fawns over him to get her way, *my wonderful magnificent man, my master . . . you're the best of all the modern writers, the only hope of Russia . . .* But before they leave, Trigorin sets up a rendezvous with Nina in Moscow.

"Irina knew he'd take up with Nina anyway. She was just asking not to hear about it. At least Nina loved him back. I hated him. Mother showed me off, made me play. I hated them all."

She opened her eyes and looked at Masha. Five-kopek pieces with tarnished edges, filled with tears. She was the most incomparably beautiful creature. *Spectacular.* It was why Masha had brought her home, why Antosha had fallen in love with her. Or so she'd thought.

Of course Antosha knew what had happened to her. He must have sensed it at once. The broken child in each of them pushing and pulling, then finally clasping hands.

"Poor Nina." Lika stared at the ceiling now. "How wonderful the play was, Masha. Wonderful and sad. Oh, your brother's a bastard. I'll tell him so myself. But poor, poor, Nina. I thought my heart would break. I don't know what I'd do if I lost my Christi."

Nina's baby dies. Christina was alive. He'd actually learned something from "The Grasshopper"—how to use another's life and yet make her feel lucky for it.

It was past midnight by then. Antosha wasn't coming. The only place he could be, aside from the icy bottom of the river, was at Alexei Suvorin's. Masha came and kissed Lika.

"Good night, dear friend," Lika said. "Thank you for everything."

THE SERVANTS MUST HAVE GONE TO BED, FOR ALEXEI opened the door to her himself, alarming with his white beard and black Satanic brows.

Smiling as though nothing was the matter, he said, "He turned up a half hour ago, but won't see anyone. Except, perhaps, you."

Alexei led her through the chandeliered entry hall, down the rose-carpeted corridor. Paintings flashed past her eye. She could hear the birds rustling in their gilt prison on the landing.

He knocked on Antosha's door but didn't wait for a reply. From the darkness, Antosha spoke.

"I beg you, don't turn on the light."

Aleksei did. Masha squinted. Electric lights were so cruel.

There was Antosha lying with his face to the wall, the blanket over his head for good measure.

"Your sister's here."

Masha went to him and bent over his shrouded form. "Where have you been, brother?"

He answered from under the blanket. "Walking the streets. Sitting on benches. I've decided. If I live another seven hundred years instead of seven? I won't write another play."

"Congratulations," Masha said.

"Nonsense," Alexei said. "It was the acting. Awful sets too. A few tweaks and it will be perfect. I made some notes."

Antosha coughed for a spell, then his hand emerged and felt around blindly for Masha's. She made it available; he squeezed hard.

"You're not angry?" he asked.

"No."

"I can't bear it when you're angry with me."

She was sure of it then. All those secrets her namesake had spilled? Her yearnings for love? They weren't mockery or betrayal. He understood and loved her most.

"Go to bed, sister. I'm taking the early train tomorrow. When you come to Melikhovo, bring Lika with you."

LIKA CAME AND STAYED THREE DAYS, HELPING TO NURSE the wounded playwright through what he claimed was "influenza." Whether she gave him the promised dose of her anger, Masha didn't ask. She doubted it. It would hardly have affected him anyway once the news arrived: The second flight of *The Seagull* had been met with rapturous applause.

Masha and Lika returned to Moscow together, Masha to work and Lika to Christina.

Three weeks later, Christina was turning two. Lika invited Masha to celebrate. A party of four: Christina, Lika, Granny, Masha. Masha brought a honey cake from Melikhovo, a book with twenty sweet chapters stuck together with icing. She didn't tell Mother who it was for.

But on the day of the party, a note came saying that Christina was unwell. *The doctor says her chest is full of phlegm. She's wheezing terribly. We'll postpone.*

Then no word for four days, so Masha went around to the Arbat flat. Strangely, the stairwell smelled more strongly of incense than of cat. She found the door ajar.

The priest had just left, Granny told her, sitting all alone in the cold parlour in her crow garb. There was no expression in her voice, just the unadorned words.

"Poor Lika. What an angel she has lost."

First came that familiar twice-lived feeling when she recognized scenes she'd read or even copied out. Usually an urgency would gather around these moments no matter how quotidian and fill her with the sense that her life did have meaning. That it was real, or at least worth noting. Sometimes tears sprang to her eyes.

But now her eyes felt as dry as the unlit samovar on the table. As though she'd wept so many tears in the theatre for the imaginary child that there were none left for the real one.

Granny said, as though reciting, "May the Lord console my Lika and lead her toward a good and sensible life. Will you help her?"

"Yes." Masha gestured down the hall.

"Don't. She wants to be alone with her."

The cake was already five days old by then and stale, yet when Masha got back to her room, she didn't throw it out. A story that would never be read, only seen. She left it on the sideboard and watched as, day by day, the mould crept over it. The bugs came too, from their winter crevices and, at night, mice.

Finally Masha took out her paints.

She cried then, for Lika too, who was left with nothing now. Soon Masha had to set down her brush so she might sob into her hands, the way she had in the theatre. The actress who played Nina had been so good. Bravely fighting back the jeers, she'd captured Lika perfectly, all in white—even her face, streaked with grease paint. Already she was growing famous for this role, for single-handedly keeping the play alive.

Masha saw it then—the mirage. One image of Lika producing another, the second producing a third, endlessly transmitted on stages around the world. The monk had claimed that a great bright future awaited humankind.

She'd asked her brother, "Do you believe that?"

"You have to give people *some* hope."

Here it was. Years from now—even a hundred years, Masha was sure—Lika would be there, as radiant as ever, flapping her thin arms.

Author's Note

THIS NOVEL IS A WORK OF IMAGINATION BASED on fact. Passages from actual letters appear in dialogue. Quoted letters have been paraphrased, rephrased and occasionally redirected to other recipients, and events rearranged or condensed. Much is omitted in the service of the narrative and much imagined, particularly Lika's backstory. Many details and lines are borrowed from Chekhov's stories and plays, for which I clasp the author's warm and generous hand in gratitude.

Thanks are also owed to the Canada Council for the Arts, the Access Copyright Foundation, the BC Arts Council, Bruce Sweeney, Patrick Crean and Jackie Kaiser. I'm grateful to Rimma Garn for applying her Russian sensibility to the manuscript.

Marina Endicott, Shaena Lambert, Kathy Page and Barbara Lambert, without your insight and encouragement, these pages would be empty.